Volcano Verdict

Volcano Verdict

Jonathan Miller

COOL
T I T L E S

Published by
Cool Titles
439 North Canon, Suite 200
Beverly Hills, CA 90210
www.cooltitles.com

The Library of Congress Cataloging-in-Publication Data Applied For

Jonathan Miller—
Volcano Verdict

p.   cm
ISBN 10: 09673920-98
ISBN 13: 978-09673920-97
1. Mystery   2. American Southwest   3. Legal Thriller   I. Title
2006

1 3 5 7 9 10 8 6 4 2

Cover design, and book editing and design by
Lisa Wysocky, White Horse Enterprises, Inc.

For interviews or information regarding special discounts for
bulk purchases, please contact us at njohnson@jrllp.com

Cool Titles and Jonathan Miller
proudly support the Ingram Cancer Center

Also by Jonathan Miller:
Rattlesnake Lawyer
Crater County
Amarillo in August

DEDICATION

The author dedicates this book to Ned Miller.

ACKNOWLEDGEMENTS

Please read the acknowledgements online at:
www.rattlesnakelawyer.com

ACT I: LASER GEISHA PINK

Prologue:
Alleged Incident

THE EARTH RUMBLED BENEATH her feet.

"What the hell do I do now?" Jen Song asked herself. She had a bad case of Adult-onset Attention Deficit Disorder in the best of times, and sharing the top of a volcano with a dead body and an evil giantess made it even worse.

Jen's mind quickly raced to the worst-case scenario. After seventy thousand years of dormancy, this hundred-foot lump on Albuquerque's west side, more a rocky nipple than a mountain, would sneak one quickie eruption during tonight's fireworks. No one would hear the rumbling amidst the explosions; all eyes would turn to the sky, rather than the lava rushing toward the city below. Who cared about a few more dead bodies in a river of fire?

Jen's white tank top showed one of the Laser Geishas, a character on a hip late-night cartoon. Laser Geisha Pink, almost a dead ringer for Jen, was a teenager dressed like a sexy superhero. Jen now desperately wished she had superhero powers to fly away from the very dead Edward Hobbs and the very alive Sandrina Santos, who joined her at the summit.

Was Hobbs dead when she got there? Had Sandrina called her?

Had she called Sandrina? Had she slept with the fat man lying there when he'd been alive? God, she hoped not, but she had slept with worse.

What the hell had just happened?

Several white flashes of light came at once; they glistened off Jen's diamond nose stud. Her eyes darted from the fireworks show by the Sandia Crest to the show by the airport. On a clear night like tonight, she saw fireworks in Albuquerque, Rio Rancho, and even the show way up in Los Alamos that was supposedly designed by nuclear scientists.

She looked around the caldera—the crater on the top of the volcano. It was flat, maybe forty feet wide, and filled with broken beer bottles and cigarette butts that were nestled in the volcanic rocks. People had partied up here for years—sex, drugs and even rock and roll—but the ground had never shaken like this before.

"Earth to Jenita!" Sandrina shouted at her, her Brazilian accent slurred by alcohol and God knows what else. "I thought you Chinese girls were smart!"

"I'm Korean, damn it!" Jen said in her soft, child-like voice. Jen wanted to say something more, but she was intimidated by Sandrina's towering silhouette. With her long blond hair, Sandrina looked like a female professional wrestler—a bad, bad girl—especially when she smiled her evil, toothy smile.

Sandrina pointed down at Hobbs, not quite grasping that he was dead. "Your mom is a nurse. Maybe she can save him."

Jen stared at the body lying on a down comforter, and propped up by a few pillows. Hobbs's bottle of pills with their mysterious Spanish labels had spilled, and they orbited Hobbs's limp hand like an asteroid belt.

Attorney Edward Hobbs was her boss, or had been. After his arrest last week he was about to be disbarred: he had transported illegal Mexican prescription drugs into America with intent to distribute, a second-degree felony.

Hobbs had bonded out soon after the arrest. The price of freedom: a million-dollar surety bond. He knew his days were numbered and he might as well go out with a bang, bang, bang, in all senses of the word. He had literally died with a smile on his face, and, of course, those red strangle marks around his neck.

Jen's mind was totally blank about how those marks got there. Another flash, another boom, and Jen lost her balance. So much for her years of *tae kwon do*. Upon landing, Jen cut her hand on the sharp edge of a dark volcanic rock. Drops of type O blood fell on the dirt. When she rose, the blood dripped on Hobbs's neck. She certainly didn't want to make things worse by wiping the blood off.

"Jenita, what the hell are you thinking?" Sandrina asked, her voice barely audible over the constant beat of the explosions.

Sandrina looked as if she wanted to kill her right there. Even an inebriated Sandrina could tear her limb from limb, as Jen's limited martial arts training hadn't progressed much past the basics.

Jen's eyes darted from the body, to the fireworks, then to the lights of the city to the east. As revelers celebrated America's birthday, a few campfires and truck headlights shone down on the desert below, part of Albuquerque's "Open Space," the area in the city that hadn't yet been gobbled up by development. This was the perfect place to watch fireworks—unless, of course, you were dead. . . .

"I've got to call someone," Jen said. "I'm totally freaking out. I don't know what we're supposed to do."

Who could she call? She probably should call her mother, Chan Wol Song, but the poor woman was disappointed enough in her as it was. Jen swore under her breath, repeating a string of insults that she had heard all her life from her mom. No, Nurse Song would not be happy to hear from her. This was far worse than driving drunk in ninth grade. This would even be worse than spending the night with the football player during senior prom.

After a fierce internal debate, she dialed another local number. It took her four attempts to get the digits right. In addition to having ADHD (Attention Deficit Hyperactivity Disorder), Jen was dyslexic.

"Well?" the voice on the other end asked.

"It's bad. Real bad. Hobbs is like totally dead!"

"Don't say anything over the phone," the voice said. "For God's sake, don't say anything over the phone!"

"Duh!" she shouted, sounding like a five year old. "I didn't do it! I don't think—"

"I don't care," the voice said.

Didn't care that Hobbs was dead? Didn't care who killed him? She awaited more wisdom from the voice. It didn't come.

"What the hell should we do?"

"Hang on. Let me make a call."

The phone went dead. It felt as if the principal was calling her mother, or worse, her father. Jen knew her mother would find out what was happening one way or another.

There was a brilliant bouquet of fire over their heads, the grand finale. The view was to die for. Literally. Sandrina couldn't take it any more. "You're on your own!" she shouted to Jen. "I can't wait!"

Sandrina walked to the edge of the caldera and looked out onto the desert shining in moon- and firelight in the Open Space below. In the flickering light, it looked more like outer space than Open Space. Sandrina lost her balance, tripped over some loose rocks, and fell into the darkness.

A few of the big black volcanic rocks followed her down. Just a little landslide. Well, as much land as could slide down a rocky hundred-foot hill. Was Sandrina dead? Unless there had been a last-minute redemption in the landslide, the volcano would render its verdict. Sandrina would definitely go straight to hell.

So would she. Jen's mind catalogued all her sins. She hadn't even made it past the fourth grade when she lost count. She looked at the open pill bottles that lay by Hobbs. Too bad the labels were in Spanish, she sure wanted a handful of something. Anything. She couldn't remember what she had already taken, if anything. Then she heard a faint slew of swearing in a distinctive, slurred Portuguese. Sandrina was still alive. Was that a good thing?

Down below, people came over from one of the nearby campfires. Sandrina verbally taunted the people with whup-ass right out of wrestlemania.

"I'm calling the cops on you, you crazy bitch," a reveler shouted. Jen felt safer up here with the dead body. Hobbs looked peaceful, at least. Peace sure would be nice right now, and Jen held way too many pills in her hand. She brought them closer to her mouth.

Total darkness. Total silence. The fireworks were over, but Jen couldn't get the rumbling sound out of her head. The body rolled . . . or did it?

"No. It's nothing," she said to herself. "The body didn't move at all. I'm just imagining it. I am a stupid idiot!"

God she hated herself; always had.

She'd take the pills if the volcano didn't finish off the job. She'd give the phone—give life—ten more minutes, max.

A police car hurried up the winding Paseo del Volcan Road through the Open Space. Cops came quickly on the Fourth, must be one of those yearly "super-blitzes." Somebody better tell her what to do, fast. Her eyes followed the red and blue lights illuminating the desert scrub and rocks. Could the cops see her? Suddenly the phone rang and Jen jumped up. If she had been closer to the edge she might have fallen off.

"I heard from him," the voice said.

"Him? The 'Him?' "

"The 'Him,'" the voice said. Hobbs's death would make the front page of the *Albuquerque Journal*, possibly even above the fold. Jen should have known this would go all the way to the top.

"He said everything will be taken care of," the voice said coldly. "Don't say anything to the police, of course. He told me to set you up with a lawyer named Luna Cruz who can help you through this."

"Luna Cruz . . . isn't she—"

Jen didn't finish her sentence. There was a pause, along with an absolute silence down below. The cops must be talking to Sandrina, but too far away for her to hear. Jen felt the pull of gravity harder than any time in her life; then more rumbling. If the volcano really blew, it would be at this exact moment. She put the pills down. She wouldn't need them, after all.

Jen braced herself, and wondered how high into the air she'd fly, and whether she'd die from the fire or from the fall.

But nothing happened, the rumbling stopped and the gravity released. The police car picked up Sandrina, then turned and raced away from the Open Space. The super-blitz had to blitz to somewhere else.

"I don't know why the hell he wants this Luna Cruz," the voice in the phone said. "But she's all you got right now."

Chapter One
Aggravated Burglary Under $250

"WHAT THE HELL DO I do now?" Luna Cruz asked herself.

Luna surveyed the old Crater County Medical Clinic, a two-story building with fake adobe and genuine round, wooden ceiling beams known as vigas. The clinic was a cheap knock-off of the ancient Taos Pueblo, but while the pueblo had survived for hundreds of years, the clinic had barely lasted thirty. The landlord, Crater County, had voted to dissolve itself. The clinic would be demolished tomorrow. It had been closed for years, waiting for county funding, but now that there was no county, the state was able to condemn the property for a toxic landfill. That figured. Crater had always been a dump.

"Crater County, it's not a real crater, it's a state of mind," she repeated the old joke. Now it wasn't even that. Since the clinic closed, everyone in Crater had to drive twenty miles down I-40 to the nearest hospital. Or, they could die.

In the shadows of the setting sun, Luna barely made out the small NO TRESPASSING sign and padlocked doors. It was late in the afternoon, if she wanted to trespass, she'd have to trespass in a hurry. Luna was on her way out of town as well. Once the district attorney, she had just been cast out of the Crater.

The local paper helped with her demise by claiming she had used a county fax line to enter triathlons and had labeled her the "Triathlete Cheat."

"She's a total bitch," a typical redneck voter told Channel 8 News, which had neglected to bleep the profanity. The county's other eight-hundred residents had almost unanimously voted against her. She hadn't lost to an actual opponent, just to the budget. Channel 8 figured it would cost each taxpayer the price of one six-pack of domestic beer to keep the D.A.'s office open.

"I lost to a damn six-pack of Bud," she said out loud to no one in particular. She'd hoped she could beat a Heineken, at least.

All felonies in the county would now be prosecuted by the State Attorney General's Office. The new Attorney General was Diana Crater, whose family had founded the county. Diana still had property here and could have voted absentee.

"Did you vote me out too, Diana?" Luna asked out loud. Only a handful of people had actually voted to keep her. There was only one "Don't Recall" vote, maybe two, that she didn't know by name. Luna hoped Diana was that vote.

Luna just wanted out of here. At dawn, she'd made a trip to her new apartment in Albuquerque. This was the return trip, and she felt like Indiana Jones on a treasure hunt. Her late mother was the morning's adventure. Luna had already ransacked her old home—the home she called the Mothership. Now it was her late father's turn. The Crater County Medical Clinic was either his temple of doom, or his Camelot.

She went around the back, but couldn't budge the door. The first floor windows were boarded up, apparently to discourage transients. Luna saw a second floor window, broken from the inside. There was an old pine tree nearby that had defeated all but the most acrobatic of trespassers. If she could make it up the tree, it was an easy swing inside.

Luna smiled. She was in tree-climbing clothes—her University of Colorado sweatshirt (Go Buffs!) and black spandex biking shorts, originally intended for a last afternoon bike ride around her former jurisdiction. Looked like breaking and entering would be the workout for the day. She still expected to feel a small silver cross swing against her chest, but she had lost it a few months ago. The cross was a memento of her first murder case; she had often touched it to remind herself of the victim. In some ways, she was glad to be free of the memory.

Luna shimmied up the pine tree. At thirty-three, her body did not quite have the flexibility of her college triathlon days, but her lean muscles still worked fine. She quickly reached the top.

Emergency lights flashed, sirens blared. . . .

Instinctively, she froze against the big tree, hoping to look like just another dead, wooden branch. Dead wood, that sure felt appropriate.

She didn't know the new sheriff's deputies from the next county over. It wouldn't do her much good if she did. As a private citizen, she'd spend the next forty-eight hours in jail in the next county before arraignment, just like everyone else. The convicts from her tenure here as district attorney certainly would *not* be glad to see her. Hopefully, Diana would just give her a deferred sentence, if she were convicted.

The lights passed, and headed toward the Crosswinds Truck Stop. I'm not public enemy number one anymore, Luna thought. She frowned, and stared at the window for a moment. This would be her last official act in Crater County, one way or another.

It was a bit of a reach and the drop was just enough to be dangerous, but Luna forced herself to jump through the window. She shattered the remaining glass in the window and nearly broke through the rickety floor. The acrobatics made a small cut on her right hand.

Luna's type O blood dripped onto the boards. She had now left a DNA trace. Shit. Her blood was an improvement on the dirty floor; at least it was fresh. The boards held several mysterious stains, a number of used hypodermics, and a few dead rats.

Absent-mindedly, she tried to turn on the light, but of course there was no power. Worse, she left another bloodstain as evidence. The shadows made Luna feel as if she was in a black and white movie, but she sure wasn't bleeding ketchup. She finally found a dirty package on the counter that contained a gauze bandage. At least the bandage was clean.

Luna stared at an open bottle of pills sitting on the counter. She didn't know their contents—anti-anxiety, anti-depression, anti-psychotic or maybe just anti-gas? She picked up the pills in her bandaged hand. This whole nightmare could be over with a single swallow. . . .

Just at that moment, the late afternoon sunlight hit a jagged shard of glass on a window at precisely the right angle. A rainbow shimmered on the floor by her feet as the sunlight refracted down from above. How perfect. She'd literally be at the end of the rainbow. Luna fiddled with the pills, and stared at the vibrating rainbow as it slowly glided along the floor.

No, this was her dad's place, and all she had left of him. She couldn't do it here, just couldn't. Somehow, he would know. She didn't know about people rolling in their graves, but his grave was barely a mile from here. He would do somersaults in that silver coffin, especially after all that had happened. Besides, she hadn't yet found her goal for the evening. After that, who knows?

The rainbow on the floor disappeared as the sun set beneath the window. She put the pill bottle down and went down the stairs. They creaked a bit under her weight. The stairway was pitch black, and when she got to the door at the bottom, it was shut.

For a moment, Luna felt trapped. "*Welcome to the Hotel Crater County*," she sang to the tune of the Eagle's "Hotel California." She had always regretted pursuing athletics instead of singing, but it was way too late for that regret right now. "*You can check out anytime you want, but you can never leave.*" Luna's lower body strength easily kicked open the door, and she entered the clinic's cramped waiting room.

Headlights from a car on the nearby road illuminated the side of the room, and she saw the end of her quest, her holy grail for the day. Her eyes lit up at the photographs of the clinic's grand opening thirty years ago. The glass fronting all the frames was broken, of course, but the pictures had survived. Even in this light she recognized her father, looking quite dapper in the clothes of the day. He had the biggest brown eyes. Everyone always told her that she had her father's eyes. She never forgot those eyes. Shit, she looked at them every morning when she looked into the mirror.

Her mom stood next to her father, her arms around him very tightly. Her mom had her back arched, as if shielding her husband from the very pretty Asian nurse standing beside them. The pretty Asian nurse stood with an Asian man, her husband. Luna had never bothered to learn his name.

And there she was, the cutest little three-year-old ever. It had been her birthday and that had made it such a special day. Her father had said, "Luna my love, this clinic is your birthday present."

Luna didn't recognize most of the other people in the photograph—a probable mix of nurses and bigwigs from the state medical board. She did recognize the governor, who shook her dad's hand with mucho gusto.

"I see dead people," she said as she looked at the picture. Her father had died in a car crash when she was eight, just a few years after that picture had been taken. Her mother had died several years ago at the hands of a deranged killer. Luna didn't know or care about the governor. If the dead could vote, there were at least two more votes she could have counted on.

Finally, it was time to complete her quest. She saw it in the corner—the picture of her dad posing to take her temperature as her mother held her hand. The colors had faded to resemble a Civil War photo.

Luna had promised herself she wouldn't cry, but she broke down when she saw that photo. Damn, she missed him. She quickly regained her composure and surveyed the rest of the wall, mostly pictures of her father with staff—the pretty nurse and the three tattooed male techs who looked as if they were right out of prison. One tech, Jonah Ruiz, had been convicted of attempted criminal sexual penetration of a minor, and was hopefully in the joint for life. She had been that minor, and thankfully, he had pled out before trial. God, she hated that man. Even now. She sure didn't need that picture for her collection.

Headlights from behind the clinic flashed on and off. Probably just kids necking. She sighed. Putting these pictures up on her walls at her new apartment tonight wasn't much of a reason to live . . . was it enough?

The first few pictures hung on rusty nails, but iron bolts secured the "temperature picture." She pulled as hard as she could, then finally, her years of swimming defeated the dry wall. The rusty bolts popped out, grazing her arm. More type O blood on the floor.

Suddenly Luna heard the back door open. Someone had a key; that couldn't be good. Luna hid behind a desk as she saw a flashlight go around the lobby.

"Luna?" a female voice cut through the darkness.

Someone knew her name. That couldn't be good either. Luna could wait it out, but she figured she could take most women, especially in the dark, so she might as well take this head on.

"I'm over here," she said. "Who is it?"

"It's me," the voice said.

Apparently not everyone in the group picture was dead after all.

Chapter Two
Aiding and Abetting

"It's good to see you again Luna," the woman said. She'd been in the southwest for thirty years, but still had the slightest trace of a Korean accent combined with a touch of New Mexican Spanish lilt. "It's been a long time. It's me, Chan Wol . . . Nurse Song."

Luna checked the staff picture to positively identify Song as the pretty nurse, "Nurse Song." Luna was the only person who called her that because it sounded so much more appropriate than Nurse Chan Wol. Chan Wol meant "healing moon" in Korean, which was appropriate for a nurse. The nurse often sang sweet Korean lullabies to Luna when the little girl came to the clinic. Nurse Song would be in her fifties now, and still wore faded, pastel-pink nurse's scrubs, perhaps the same ones she wore in the clinic. She hadn't aged a day, but she looked pained. Maybe she wanted Luna to represent her on her divorce or something.

Luna had seen Nurse Song briefly at her mom's funeral three years ago, but that was the only time in the past twenty-five years.

"What are you doing here?" Luna asked.

"I figured I could catch you here tonight," Nurse Song replied. "I knew you'd come for your father's things. The locks were never changed. I . . . I heard you'd be practicing in Albuquerque. I tried to call the D.A.'s office here. It gave your cell number, but the number didn't work."

Luna had never liked giving the public access to her cell phone, but as district attorney, it was part of the job description.

"Crater is like the Bermuda Triangle for service," Luna said. Actually, her phone had been cut off for money owed once the county stopped paying for it. Hopefully her check had gone through, and she'd have service by tomorrow.

Luna felt a wave of nostalgia when she saw Nurse Song. The nurse had been her surrogate mother all those summers when her dad was alive and her mom worked on a novel she'd never finish. Luna would come to the clinic, but her dad was busy healing lepers, giving sight to the blind, raising the dead, and what not. Nurse Song kept her from bothering the great man while he worked his miracles.

Nurse Song picked up the "temperature" picture. "I remember the day of this picture," she said. "You were so excited. Your parents had this pretend argument. Your mom said 'Luna my love, you're going to be a lawyer.' Your dad said 'Are you sure, Luna, my love? You're gonna be a doctor. Are you sure you want to be a lawyer?' He always asked you 'Are you sure?' "

"Are you sure?" Luna could hear her father saying those words right now. She wasn't sure about anything anymore.

Nurse Song continued. "And you kept singing that you were Luna and you were sure you were going to be the first lawyer on the moon after you won the Olympics in everything."

Luna never made it to the Olympics; she had choked big time in the trials, and actually limped into the stadium rather than ran. As for being the first lawyer on the moon, that was simply a child's fantasy. "Could you give me a hand with these pictures?" Luna asked.

Nurse Song hesitated, she'd been by the book all her life and taking pictures was tantamount to theft. Recently, both the county and state had made it clear to the general public that the entire building and everything in it was state property and not to be bothered. But then she smiled, grabbed the rest of photographs and the two of them started toward the back door. "I guess this makes me an accessory."

"Don't worry, I can represent you," Luna said, than instantly regretted it. What was she getting into?

They walked out to the parking lot. "I borrowed my husband's car," Nurse Song said, pointing to a Hyundai. Luna made out a figure in Nurse Song's car. The figure lit a cigarette.

"It's about my daughter," Nurse Song said, indicating the figure. "She's in major trouble in Albuquerque and you were highly recommended as someone who could help."

Luna wondered who could possibly have recommended her, after all that had happened. As they loaded the pictures into the trunk of Luna's blue Saturn, she tried to turn off her thoughts. Luna had inherited the car from her last boyfriend, a lawyer named Marlow. Luna had to slam the trunk shut a few times before it clicked. With the click, she heard the glass in a photo frame crack.

"Open a window, Jen!" Nurse Song yelled, then pantomimed the motion when the figure ignored her. After another moment, the figure reluctantly complied. Smoke wafted out of the car like a vent straight from hell.

"Why do you need to see me?" Luna asked.

Nurse Song took a deep breath. This was hard for her. She pointed at the figure in the smoky car, with obvious distaste. "My daughter, Jen."

"Jen?"

"Her name is Chan Wol, after me, but it was anglicized to Jen, because that's the way she said it as a baby," Nurse Song said with some real regret. "She was a legal secretary." Nurse Song said that with even more regret, as if Jen should have been a Supreme Court Justice by now.

"Her boss, a lawyer, just got arrested for smuggling pills in from Mexico. He bonded out, then died on one of the dormant volcanoes outside of Albuquerque, watching the fireworks on the Fourth. Jen's blood was found at the scene. She admitted she was there, but says she didn't kill him. She's in bad trouble.

"Jen told me her friend, Sandrina, called and that Jen's boss was dead when Jen got there. Either Sandrina killed him, or he overdosed on the pills. They say it's an 'open count of murder.' "

An open count of murder. That could be anything from involuntary manslaughter (eighteen months), to murder one (life in prison), to gulp, the death penalty.

"My daughter is innocent," Nurse Song added, as if trying to convince herself.

Innocent clients were worse than guilty ones; you actually had to fight for them. "That's good, I guess," Luna said. "So why do you want me?"

"She's got to turn herself in tomorrow, first thing in the morning. She needs a lawyer. We want you."

Luna didn't like the sound of "First Thing in the Morning," especially this late in the day. Jen exited the car and walked toward them. She wore an outfit that could only be described as Gothic Lolita, a pseudo school-girl look in black. Jen was too old for the look, which younger girls in Asia and copycats in Los Angeles had long since dropped. Luna noticed Jen had a swivel in her walk; Jen was used to having boys, and men, look at her from behind.

Up close, in the rays of the sunset, Jen looked mid-twenties, and almost, but not quite, like her mother. The "not-quite" made all the difference in the world. Her mom was Korean, but Jen looked far more tropical—deep tan, dark sun-bleached hair, and big brown eyes. She had a little diamond nose stud, which filtered a tiny, shimmering rainbow from the sunset. Even standing still, Jen was in constant motion, vibrating with energy. Luna found a Hawaiian metaphor: Jen was a Mauna Kea, a volcano about to blow.

"So will you save me?" Jen asked. Her accent was California beach girl, and slightly spacey, as if she could be an intern in a Santa Fe "mixed media" gallery rather than a Seoul "office lady." There was desperation in her voice. The way her eyes darted all around—something just wasn't right with the girl.

Luna's self-preservation instincts told her to run like hell, but she didn't have anything else going on at the moment. Luna walked over to the girl and shook her hand. "My name is Luna Cruz," she said. "I'm a lawyer."

Jen's grip was damp—a guilty grip, Luna thought to herself.

Jen stared at her strangely, as if recognizing her from a past life. *Déjà vu* can be a bitch sometimes. "I know who you are."

Did I prosecute this girl for something, Luna asked herself? The numerous faces from past trials all blended together over time, but I would have remembered a girl like this. Most likely, Jen was the girlfriend of some loser she had put away. Who was the killer right after the Jeremy Jones case? No, Jen was probably the girlfriend of the guy after that one, Mayhem Moreno, right?

"If you don't want me to be your lawyer, I understand," Luna said. "I've got better things to do."

Luna hoped they didn't catch her in the lie. "You can always get a public defender."

"I want a real lawyer," said Jen.

"I don't know how real I am," Luna replied.

"And besides, I'm like innocent," Jen said. "I didn't get there until he was already dead. Sandrina probably fucked him to death."

Luna tried to back out nicely. "Are you sure you want me? This would be my first criminal case on the defense side since the University of Colorado Law School where I did legal aid clinic."

Luna didn't mention that she got a "C" in the legal aid clinic.

Nurse Song touched Luna on the shoulder. It was a warm touch that brought back good memories. "I've got a feeling that you will fight for my daughter. Besides, you're almost like family."

Luna had to take this case. Representing Jen Song, accused of an open count of murderer, wasn't a real good reason for her to keep on living, but it would have to do for now.

"Remember, I'm innocent!" Jen said, almost as if trying to convince herself.

Luna said nothing. She didn't know who was in worse shape right now, Jen or herself.

Chapter Three
"Ain't Saying Shit" Clause

LUNA AWOKE IN A cold sweat before dawn. Her muscles still ached from the trip back from Crater. Like Jen, Luna wasn't as young as she pretended to be. Maybe she should have swiped some of those pills after all; they had to be good for something.

Despite the dust and the piles of boxes, her new Albuquerque apartment was almost fit for human habitation. Hopefully her rent check and deposit would clear by a dollar or two.

Luna had already nailed the "temperature picture" over her bed—the first thing she'd see every morning, and the last thing she'd see at night. There was a small crack where the glass had broken, but the picture would remind her that somebody had once actually loved her. Luna put in enough nails for the picture to survive an earthquake, or at least the rumbling of the big trucks on the freeway.

She lived in Sky Village Apartments, adjacent to the constant humming of interstates 25 and 40. Traffic on I-40, the mutant stepchild of the old Route 66, ran all the way from the Atlantic Ocean to Barstow, California, on the edge of the desert. The highway then met with I-15, then I-10 and went out to the Pacific. I-25 was the old Pan American Highway, running from Alaska to *Tierra del Fuego*.

There was a stately Catholic cemetery on the west side of the apartment's parking lot, on the other side of an adobe fence. I-40 actually ran right through the cemetery. Luna felt trapped between the quick and the dead.

The phone rang. Thank God. Her check for the phone bill had cleared!

It was Nurse Song. "They're going to be here in thirty minutes." So much for a morning run. "I can be there in twenty."

The Song family lived in the Southeast Heights section of Albuquerque, near the state fairgrounds. This was the city's Asian immigrant ghetto, primarily Vietnamese, although there was a healthy mix of Koreans and Chinese. The small adobe houses with their smaller dirt yards filled with saber yuccas felt like a mix between a Mexico City *barrio* and the Mekong Delta. The Vietnamese and nearby Hispanic gangs battled over an area called the War Zone. Someone had recently nick-named it the Mexican Mekong.

Luna didn't know if there were any Korean gangs in the mix. She didn't think so. Many Koreans in Albuquerque were scientists at Sandia Labs. Others ran restaurants specializing in everything except Korean cuisine. As a rule, they were very law-abiding.

On the way, Luna passed several tiny Vietnamese restaurants on Louisiana Boulevard and a surprisingly big and modern Asian supermarket, famous for its Albuquerque Octopus—which was Octopus flavored New Mexico green chile. The market, in its orange and green earth-tone stucco, was by far the nicest thing in the Mekong.

The Songs had a modest adobe home near Louisiana Boulevard and Zuni Street. Zuni Street had the unfortunate nickname of "Crack Alley," after both the human and the pharmaceutical varieties. The Songs had gravel in their yard instead of grass. Many of the other homes in the Mexican Mekong lacked grass as well. Xeriscaping was the city's hip public relations term for discouraging water-hogging grass and plants. Xeriscaping looked great in the rich areas of town, but not in the Mekong where the lawns just looked dead. The Song's xeriscape also had a saber yucca that appeared as if it had already lost a few duels.

Inside, the house was decorated with modest Asian art. There was a sheathed sword, fit for a midget Samurai, hanging on the wall. The sword actually looked more valuable than the house. Luna couldn't help but notice that there wasn't one family picture on the wall. Not one.

Mr. Song, a small, wiry man dressed in a blue shirt with a vaguely familiar logo, headed for work as Luna arrived. He did not make eye contact. Nurse Song, still in her faded pink nursing scrubs, ushered Luna into the cramped living room.

Luna figured now was the time to bring up a retainer agreement, but Nurse Song had already hustled into the kitchen to take care of a whistling teapot.

Today, Jen stuck with the Gothic Lolita look, but her ripped black plaid skirt was maybe an inch longer. Jen could raise the dead with her shirt unbuttoned one button too many, which revealed a black bra. Her nose stud looked even bigger and shinier in the daylight.

Jen sulked as she sat on an ancient couch with a gigantic Hispanic man who wore a buzz cut. He wore a red University of New Mexico Lobo Wolfpack Pride t-shirt, and filled it out like a linebacker. Growing up, he must have had steroids stuffed in his stocking every Christmas. Luna couldn't help but wonder if Edward Hobbs had had any pills for this man in his sleigh full of goodies.

"Calm down, Jen," he said, exasperated. "It's all been taken care of."

He got up when Luna approached and nearly hit his head on a hanging lamp. "I'm Adam Marin," he said in a deep voice. "I'm Jen's boyfriend. . . . I'm also a cop."

He pronounced his last name Marine, with the accent on the last syllable, and the name certainly fit. He had a marine's million-mile stare.

Marin reminded Luna of her first true love, the late Nico Duran, who also was a cop. She wanted Jen to break it off immediately, as Jen looked more afraid of him, than in love.

Marin headed toward a back door. "It's not a good idea for me to be here, if you know what I mean." He handed Luna a card, which read, ALBUQUERQUE POLICE DEPARTMENT (APD) VICE SQUAD, then headed out the back door to Crack Alley.

Jen relaxed when he left, as if she was happy he was gone. Luna almost sat down on the couch next to Jen, but decided against it. Luna sat in the chair on the other side of the room, almost as if she was Jen's psychologist. In a way, she was.

"Just don't say anything," Luna said. "They can use it against you."

"Duh," Jen said.

Nurse Song puttered away in the kitchen, making her family's meals for the entire week. Luna knew she should ask about a retainer, but she had no idea what to say. What did the murder of a lawyer go for these days?

Before Luna could come up with a sum, she heard a sharp knock on the door. Both Jen and Luna jumped up, and emitted the same gasp of surprise. They stared at each other and couldn't help but laugh. If they had both actually said the same words at the same time, Luna would have said "Jinx," an old game from her childhood.

"I'll answer the door," Luna said. Two big cops waited outside. Cop One, whose nameplate said OÑATE, was the boss. Cop Two was just along for the ride. Luna knew from her New Mexico history class that Oñate was the name of the Spanish explorer who had chopped off the feet of the Acoma Indians during colonial days. This Oñate was probably a descendant, although he looked like he had some tribal blood in him as well.

"Jen Song?" Oñate asked. Jen swiveled over to the door. Luna noticed that the girl wore five-inch pumps, which made the swivel difficult to maintain. Oñate stared at Jen's painted toenails, as if sizing up a trophy for his wall.

"You're under arrest for the murder of Edward Hobbs," Oñate stated. "You have the right to. . . ."

He kept talking as Cop Two, the dumb one, handcuffed Jen. Cop Two looked at Luna. "Who the hell are you?"

"I'm her lawyer," Luna said. "I guess."

Luna knew she should project confidence, but since the recall election, confidence was hard to find.

Luckily, Luna had her gray plastic "Bar Card" with her, proving her legal identity. She'd had it laminated, but the lamination had already started to fray.

Oñate stared at the frayed card, checking for an expiration date. "Does she wish to make a statement at this time?"

Luna quoted her old friend Marlow. "She'll take the fifth amendment, the 'ain't saying shit' clause."

Oñate let Luna ride with Jen in the back of the squad car. There was fresh blood on the seats. Trying to provide the moment with a bit of levity, Luna said "Out, out damn spot," when some smudged on her outfit.

"Lady Big Mac, right?" Jen added.

"Lady MacBeth," Luna said.

"Duh," said Jen. "Don't you know when I'm kidding?"

"Not yet," Luna replied.

Oñate glanced around from the driver's seat for a very long moment. "You're that D.A. out in Crater County, right?" he asked.

"I was," Luna said.

They passed under a billboard for Attorney Paul Dellagio that read, I SUE DRUNK DRIVERS! It showed a ten-foot head with a huge mustache looking at a gigantic black vehicle running over a little girl's tricycle.

"*The only name you need to know . . . Dial LLL-AGIO!*" Luna couldn't help but hum the jingle from the radio ads that even made it all the way out to Crater. "*LLL-AGIO!*"

Luna then looked at the arrest warrant. It told her nothing, of course, just that Jen was wanted for the open murder of Edward Hobbs. There were a few more felony counts of trafficking controlled substances under 30-31-20 of the New Mexico Revised Statutes. Trafficking was a team sport, so she already knew the final count, conspiracy.

There could have been Federal charges, in light of crossing state and national boundaries, but it was just in State court for now. That was good, wasn't it? No notice of intent to go for the death penalty. Yet.

They eased on to I-40 and suddenly the cop car zoomed to eighty miles an hour. Jen's sarcasm left her once they got on the freeway. The cops were obviously in a hurry to take her to their final destination. Jen looked even younger and weaker in the car, and she leaned against Luna for warmth.

Luna expected Oñate to stay on I-40 and go all seventeen miles to the Westside jail. Instead, he exited on Sixth Street, and headed south toward the nine stories of sleek marble whiteness that was Albuquerque's Metropolitan Court.

"You're really lucky, Jen," Cop Two said with a smile. "Who did you have to blow to get this kind of treatment?"

Jen didn't blush, and looked genuinely hurt. "I'm not a whore, okay?"

"Officer, I can have your badge for that," Luna said sternly. She didn't know if she really could, but it sounded tough in front of the client, and the cops.

They came to a side entrance on Slate Street that took them underneath Metro Court. The marble wall was indeed like a clean white slate. A private guard in a blue windbreaker opened a gate for them.

They all got out of the car in the underground parking lot, which was barely illuminated by flickering florescent lights. Guards dragged a large blond woman out of the darkness toward a brown bus labeled METROPOLITAN DETENTION CENTER.

"Sandrina. . . ." Jen said with a frown.

Sandrina stopped before getting on the bus, which made the guards stop with her. Sandrina turned to face Jen. She had bruises all over her body, as if an angry mob had stoned her for adultery, yet one look from Sandrina would have scared off any mob.

"I'm going to fuck you up so bad Jenita," Sandrina yelled, her voice slurred, as if she'd downed a few shots with her fellow inmates in the holding cell. "Can't wait to see you in the Bitch Unit tonight!"

Luna took a moment to place the accent—Brazilian. She'd lost a race to a Brazilian woman once, who like Sandrina, was an Amazon from the Amazon. Sandrina kept swearing at Jen in Portuguese until her guards slammed the police car door behind her.

"Not even, Sandrina," Jen yelled back when Sandrina was safely out of the underground lot. "I'm bonding out right now."

Right now? With murder and trafficking, the bond would be a bitch all right. Jen wasn't going anywhere for a while.

Oñate hustled Jen into an elevator, and the doors closed in front of Luna.

Luna sat still in the darkness. The florescent lights flickered. Now what?

"No one allowed down here," a guard yelled. He pointed toward the exit to the outside world.

Luna was about to protest that she was a lawyer, but figured that wouldn't do any good. So Luna had to exit, then re-enter through Metro Court's main entrance on the bustle of Fourth Street. The entrance to Metro Court was a white dome that looked vaguely like the Jefferson Memorial in Washington.

Luna felt a bit like a tourist until she got to the metal detector on the inside. Luckily there was an "Officers of the Court" line," and Luna just had to show her Bar Card to get through. She wasn't used to big city security. The metal detectors were set to the maximum—Luna thought she'd beep for using irony.

She took the up elevator and wandered around before she found the right room on the other side of the dome, Room 960, a small courtroom packed with the latest in electronic equipment. For the less fortunate souls stuck seventeen miles away at Metropolitan Detention Center (MDC), judges did the arraignments by video. After Luna arrived, but before she could even catch her breath, a deep voice called Chan Wol Song, a.k.a. Jen Song. The guards hustled the shackled Jen up to the podium.

Jen looked at Luna. "Are you coming?"

Luna hurried to the podium. She couldn't make out the judge who sat behind a huge computer terminal with a thin flat screen.

"Luna Cruz for Jen Song," she said

"Did you say Luna Cruz for the sun?" the deep voice asked incredulously.

Luna spoke more clearly and distinctly. "Luna Cruz for Jen Song." Luna had her game face on, just as she did at the start of a race. "We waive a formal reading of the charges." She then added something she'd seen experienced private lawyers do when they were stuck out in Crater, and unsure if they wanted to come back. "I'm standing in for the purpose of arraignment only."

With those magic words, she could still back out before this case made it to District Court.

"So noted," said the invisible judge. "How does your client plead?"

"The defendant enters a plea of not guilty," Luna said, sounding like a real lawyer.

Real lawyer or not, the judge had already made up his mind and had a hundred more cases to go that morning. "Considering the gravity of the charges, bond will be the sum of one million dollars bond, cash or surety."

The invisible judge rattled off some conditions of release, stating flatly that Jen could only leave the house with her mother.

"My mother works all the time," Jen blurted out like a bratty five-year-old. "So does my dad."

"Is there any other party willing to be a third party surety?" the invisible judge asked, still not looking out from behind the monitor.

Jen looked at Luna longingly. This girl was desperate all right. What the hell, Luna thought, this was all just for show anyway.

"I'll be her third party surety your honor," Luna said. "I'll be personally responsible for her, *if* she can post the million dollars bond."

"So ordered," the invisible judge said, as he hit some keys on his keyboard. The guards ushered Jen out the back door.

Well, that was relatively painless, Luna thought, and I scored a point with Jen. Luna deftly maneuvered past the video equipment as the next defendant, a five-time felony drunk driver, hit the screen.

Not knowing where to go, Luna took the escalators down to the dome section of the courthouse. This was the nicest courthouse she'd ever been in. Even people paying their traffic fines at the customer service desk look like they could be in line at Disneyland

Nurse Song joined her in the lobby. It had only been a few minutes, but she looked years older. She was shorter than Luna remembered. Nurse Song forced a smile when she saw Luna's face. Luna still loved that smile.

A well-dressed man with earrings approached them. Luna stared at the crucified hula girl tattooed on his bulging arm. Was that indicative of Jen's fate?

"Ms. Song, could you sign here?" he asked.

Nurse Song signed the documents. Before Luna could say anything, a tattooed hand flashed a pen in her face.

"Ms. Cruz, I'm John Barcelona, the bondsman. Could you sign the third party surety forms here?"

She looked at the bondsman. "Huh?"

Barcelona laughed. "When she gets out she'll be under house arrest, with her mom or in your custody."

Jen was actually posting bond?

Nurse Song and Barcelona hurried to the customer service window, ahead of others in the line.

Moments later, an electronic door clicked open and Jen walked out into the lobby dome. Luna felt shock, as if Jefferson himself had stood up inside his own memorial and asked her for some snuff. The dim lighting of the dome tried to dampen Jen's voluptuous beauty, but failed utterly. Cop One undid her handcuffs; he was more surprised than she was.

Jen quickly ran out, if you could call her fast swiveling gait a run, then hugged her mother as if she'd been inside for five years, rather than five minutes. Luna noticed that Nurse Song's return hug was nowhere near as strong.

Luna looked down at the "Order of Release." One million dollars bond, just as the judge had said. Nurse Song had to have given at least $100,000 in cash to the bondsman. Wow. . . .

Jen looked at Luna. "Thank you," she said.

Luna ignored her, and faced Nurse Song. "I saw your house. Where did you get that kind of money?"

"I got it from someone from back home," she said. "Family sticks together."

If the money was from Korea, it was probably clean. The bondsman would now be on the hook for the million. Actually, as a third party custodian, so would she. Luna shook her head. She already had a bad feeling about what lurked outside the door.

They walked outside, through the bulky metal gates, into the vast concrete courtyard with its scrap-iron statue of the scales of justice. A mass of cameras waited, as if Jefferson had now come out to do a news conference. Everyone who was anyone with a camera stood in the huge group of people. Luna felt invisible next to her client: the moon next to the sun. Every camera pointed at Jen's cleavage, encased in the black bra.

"Who are you?" one reporter yelled. He was a young Hispanic man with a metallic tie and metallic hair who looked all of fifteen. Was he covering the story for a kid's network?

Jen elbowed her. "You're on!"

"I'm Luna Cruz, Jen's lawyer."

"With an 'S?'" the boy asked.

"With a 'Z,'" Luna replied. She tried to reclaim her roots at that moment. "The Spanish spelling."

Luna took a deep breath. She felt as if she was back in the stadium, utterly exposed during her big choke at the Olympic triathlon trials. She stared at Jen and that glistening nose stud. She really didn't know what to say. She didn't want to box herself in too early. Jen clung closer to Luna, as if they were already trapped in their own box together. Luna couldn't help but push her client away. Don't hug me and don't cry Luna wanted to say.

"Just be cool," Luna whispered to her as Jen fidgeted. Was the girl on speed or something?

"I *am* cool," Jen whispered back. "How about you?"

Luna looked back at the cameras. "I've just been retained," she said at last. "Ummm . . . no comment. . . ."

The cameras got a few more clips of the two of them for B-roll. Luna knew that they'd run the clip of her pushing her slutty Gothic Lolita client away a million times before this was over. Shit.

Nurse Song grabbed them both and ushered them into an old yellow station wagon that was illegally parked on a side street. The cameras followed the station wagon as it drove east down the six wide lanes of Lomas Boulevard.

Inside the car's ancient, but immaculate, interior, Luna couldn't help but think that the money should have been spent on a new car rather than bail, but she said nothing. Luna finally felt like the first lawyer on the moon.

Chapter Four
Land of Entrapment

THAT NIGHT, LUNA ADJUSTED her ancient TV to catch a stray signal from Channel 8, the "Land of Enchantment's Most Enchanting Station," as she checked her e-mail. She had always joked that New Mexico was the Land of Entrapment, but that wasn't funny anymore now that she was a defense lawyer entrapped here. Anyway, cable TV was a luxury, but her Internet was a necessity.

Unfortunately, every thirty seconds her computer got a pop-up ad that read VIRUS DETECTED! RUN BVG RESIDENT SHIELD FOR WINDOWS. She remembered that one of her defendants, Mayhem Moreno, had done his first round of mayhem because he'd been enraged by a constantly repeating pop-up ad. She felt like doing the same.

But before Luna could smash her computer, the TV turned to the lead story. "Legal secretary Jen Song stands accused of killing her boss, attorney Ed Hobbs, on Albuquerque's west side," the "teenaged" reporter stated. The camera added all of a year; he looked sixteen now. When did news anchors start looking like high school kids? When Luna had her thirty-third birthday, that's when.

"Song is represented by attorney Luna Cruz who recently lost her job as Crater County District Attorney after voters soundly rejected—"

Luna hit the mute button.

Next they showed footage of Ed Hobbs's beautiful home in the

High Desert subdivision, the last house before the granite over-thrust of the Sandia Mountains kicked in. Hobbs had definitely done well for himself. Here the xeriscaping actually looked elegant, a higher form of desert indeed. His home reeked "drug baron," but had the slightest restraint, as if dealing prescription drugs weren't quite as baronial as cocaine.

The camera then dissolved to a picture of the crime scene, a close-up on a human-sized indentation in the black volcanic dirt. The wind had been reluctant to blow it away.

The teenager stood next to a photo of the late Mr. Hobbs. Luna gasped. She realized she had met him once at a D.A. convention a few years ago. The guy came across as a D.A. lifer who always wore an American flag on his lapel with a red, white and blue striped tie.

"Jen, please tell me you didn't sleep with this guy," she said out loud.

Hobbs had left the D.A.'s office for the "dark side," of criminal defense, then fallen into the black hole of drug smuggling.

The final picture was Jen's mug shot. Jen had actually tried to look sultry in the photo, as if flirting with the cameraman. At least you couldn't really see the diamond stud.

Luna turned the TV off, and turned back to her computer. She hoped her e-mail inbox was full, with real e-mail actually outnumbering the spam. Luna had recently joined an Internet dating service. When her on-line profile said she lived in Crater, she didn't get a single response. At first she was "Film Geek with a Killer Bod," but that got all kinds of weird responses. She thought one response might be from Director Quentin Tarantino, but she couldn't tell for sure.

"Crater Countess" didn't do much either. When she went with "Triple Threat 33," and a photo of her in a tight triathlete outfit, her mailbox had exploded with seemingly high quality men, and a few curious women. Her late mother would have thought she was some kind of *whore d'oeuvre*, trying to find a mate in this way, but these were different times. She worried about her biological clock.

Unfortunately, once she opened her e-mails, she found that all the letters were disguised spam. They said, "responding to your ad," but were really inducements to save money on drugs to improve her love life. If only the perfect man came in a bottle with a five dollar co-pay. Where were all these drugs coming from now that Hobbs had gone?

Her phone rang, a demanding ring with an exclamation point. It was Jen, of course, needing to talk. Her mom and dad both worked brutal hours, and Marin, the almost-Marine, wasn't much of a listener either.

"Am I allowed to go out?" Jen asked.

"You can't do anything," Luna replied. Why couldn't the girl stay in custody where she wouldn't be a danger to self or others? "I can get you back in jail if you want."

"Whatever." Jen said. "But if I call you, you pretty much have to take my call no matter what, right?"

"I'm your lawyer, not your friend, Jen," Luna said in her most impersonal prosecutor voice. "I only have to talk to you about your legal issues, not your personal life."

That hurt. "You're pretty much all I've got right now," Jen said. "My sort-of boyfriend doesn't want to talk to me now that I'm officially a criminal. That, and like twenty million other reasons. . . ."

She wanted to go on as if Luna was in her sorority or something.

"I don't get it, Jen," Luna interrupted. "There are a lot of lawyers in town. You guys obviously have money from somewhere. Why did your mom want me?"

"Because she's crazy about you—she even clips out stories about you. A few years ago when you had that big case, she watched every day. You're like the daughter she never had."

Luna felt for the girl in spite of herself. "You can call me if it's an emergency on personal issues. Is this an emergency?"

The phone went dead.

There was a beep from her computer. Maybe the perfect man had just e-mailed her? Unfortunately it was that damn BVG

Resident Shield for Windows again, offering yet another "last chance to sign up." She sure empathized with Mayhem Moreno. It sucked when spam was your only social life.

That Saturday Luna went to Coronado Center, the largest mall in New Mexico. She felt like Coronado must have when he camped out here in 1540—lost, hot and a little scared. He'd been looking for the Seven Golden Cities of Cibola, but her seven cities were people—maybe a former D.A. from her days at Metro, a refugee from Crater, or perhaps someone she took the bar exam with and borrowed a number two pencil from. She hoped she'd see a lawyer who remembered her from somewhere and offer her a dream job. Who knows, perhaps she'd see the man of her dreams sitting in the vibrating massage chairs at an upscale gift shop.

The vibrating chair was not as good as the real thing. Luna still felt tense when the pimpled clerk finally asked if she wanted to purchase one for "only two thousand dollars if you buy today."

Luna milled around Hot Dog on a Stick in the crowded food court, waited behind some jabbering junior high gang girls, then reluctantly bought a corn dog and coke, the cheapest protein in town.

She wandered through the cavernous mall like a lost spelunker. None of the moving stalactites in football t-shirts, or stalagmites in pink tank tops, noticed her presence. She then wandered through Macy's. Everyone looked like someone she had known, but they all looked right through her, as if she was invisible.

My God, more people walked the lingerie department in Macy's than the entire population of Crater County. The value of push-up bras alone was probably greater here than Crater's gross domestic product. Luna wanted to put an announcement on the Macy's intercom, "Does anyone out there know Luna Cruz? Anybody? Please come to the Lancôme counter." Surrounded by forty thousand people, she had never felt so lonely in her entire life.

On her way out to the parking lot, she actually did run into someone she knew—Heidi Hawk, an obese Navajo woman wearing factory-second turquoise, who was also a refugee from Crater. Heidi had been gone for over a year, so she had missed the vote, but Luna liked to think that Heidi would have given her the benefit of the doubt. Heidi was with a few friends who were equally as massive.

"Hey," said Heidi.

"Hey," said Luna.

"Call me at District Court sometime," Heidi said. "I'm a clerk at Grand Jury."

That was it; the best Heidi would do for Luna. Heidi left abruptly with her posse and didn't ask Luna to join them.

Luna had no memory of what she did for the rest of the day. When she was finally ready for bed, she looked at the temperature picture and cried herself to sleep.

Chapter Five
Death to Bambi!

"WE'LL MEET FIRST THING tomorrow," Luna told Jen over the phone Sunday morning. It was nine o'clock. Jen had already called twice to ask whether friends could still visit her. "I think I still have friends," she said.

"I'm your only friend right now," Luna said, instantly regretting it. "Don't talk to anyone! We'll talk Monday morning."

Luna almost hung up, then saw the stack of bills on her table. "Bring a retainer check with you."

"How much?" Jen asked.

Luna had no idea. "Surprise me."

Luna reluctantly brought her cell phone with her when she put her bike on the Number 99 bus to the East Mountains. She wanted to attack the Sandia Crest from the east, a long route through the pines. It would be hard to be depressed at high altitude.

She started pedaling in the rustic little village of Tijeras, where Old Route 14 emerged from the freeway. Route 14 cut through a forest with trees taller than herself, a welcome change from the desert.

She giggled at what one of her Internet correspondents had called himself. "Arnold was the Austrian Oak," he wrote. "But I'm a Jewish Juniper."

Luna eventually ascended into Oak country after passing a few Jewish Junipers near the freeway, or were they aspens? She could not really tell trees apart. She'd failed biology a few times, both in high school and college. She noticed the homes here were wooden as well—more A-frames than adobe on the relentless incline through Cedar Crest, Sandia Park and the other small, funky villages.

Normally on bike rides she'd let the lactic acid in her legs act as a natural high, but something was different today. She tensed as black Escalade SUV passed her with some regularity. The Escalades were big and shiny. How many Escalades could there be out here?

Several miles later she made a left onto Rural Route 536, the turn off to the crest road at the little hamlet of San Antonito. One building actually looked like a Little Alamo, except it sold cheaper souvenirs. Her phone rang; it was Jen again. She pulled off the road.

"Luna, I'm scared," Jen said. "I just got a phone call from some weird guy. I don't have caller ID and he said I was like totally, totally dead. Where are you? Can you come over?"

"Jen, it's a Sunday. I'm biking to the top of the Sandia Crest. I'll see you tomorrow. Call Adam Marin. He's a cop, right?"

"I guess so," she said. "Do I have to call him? Can't I just call you?"

Something definitely had happened. But it was Sunday and Jen was not her problem. Not yet. A lawyer had once said: the presumption of innocence was green. Jen hadn't yet given her the green.

"I'll talk to you tomorrow," Luna said.

"You really should be nicer to me," replied Jen as she hung up.

Luna's bike almost started up the hill by itself, eager to get into the mountains. Luna had biked past a few cabins when a black Escalade passed so closely it nearly ran her off the road. It definitely was the same one. There was no license plate, not even a temporary tag on the side. Probably just local rednecks, she thought, but the Escalade was far too nice for local rednecks.

Suddenly, Luna shivered. Had Jen just threatened her on the phone? The spam incident with Mayhem Moreno had planted his name in her mind like a bad radio jingle. He even had "MAY" tattooed on one cheek, and "HEM" tattooed on the other. Luna remembered that, according to witnesses, Mayhem began his rampage after his computer had been disconnected during a three-way "webcam chat" with his girlfriend, who was in the room, and someone from parts unknown. Enraged, he and his girlfriend tore up the town, shouting "Computers suck!" The girlfriend, an Asian woman, was never located. Could she have been Jen? Jen wouldn't sic Mayhem Moreno on her own lawyer, would she? But then, how well did she know Jen? A girl who could post a million dollar bond couldn't be all good.

No, Jen had sounded more bratty than brazen.

"Innocent until proven guilty, beyond a reasonable doubt," Luna chanted as she headed uphill, trying to convince herself,

That soon became "IUPGBARD," a chant to herself as she pedaled past a sign announcing the start of the Cibola National Forest. She glanced downhill when she got to the next turn. She'd probably hit eight thousand feet already.

Luna was naturally paranoid, but that didn't mean people weren't out to get her. It wasn't just the altitude making her heart race right now. Since her father hadn't come home that day so long ago, Luna had always feared something bad lay around every bend. When her mother had been murdered, that only confirmed her thoughts. She passed a few more trailheads and didn't see the Escalade anywhere. So far, so good.

After a few more miles she passed the base lodge of Sandia Peak Ski Area. Its elevation was close to nine thousand feet. After a few more miles of jagged switchbacks in the pines, she was at 10,678 feet, the summit of the Sandia Crest. The crest was more a twenty-mile long ridge than a mountain, but 10,678 feet of altitude was nothing to sneeze at, especially in such thin air.

"I still got it," she said to herself.

Luna got off her bike and looked down at the greenish sprawl of Albuquerque way down below to the west. Even from up here the trees looked sickly in the summer drought. She traced the long straight boulevards of the town. There's her apartment, right where the two interstates hit. She then found the Mexican Mekong—Louisiana Boulevard and Zuni Rd, a.k.a. Crack Alley—a few miles to the southeast. The area was a brown splotch, decidedly less green than the rest of the city. That's where Jen is, she thought to herself. Luna instantly felt guilty.

Oh what the hell. She dialed Jen's number. No answer. No machine after twenty rings. She must really be pissed, Luna thought.

The wind picked up. This high above sea level, Luna could kiss the jet stream. It was twenty degrees colder up here, and far more humid from the lush mountain foliage. She felt cold sweat on her body.

On the other side of the parking lot she saw another damn black Escalade. Just hikers, she told herself. They're probably going to hike over to the Summit House for a cappuccino.

What kind of truck had hit her dad? She didn't remember. But she did remember where she'd seen a vehicle similar to the Escalade. It was on Dellagio's billboard, running over the little girl's tricycle. No need to tempt fate. She got back on her bike and headed down the road, where she picked up speed. Thank you, gravity. The wind was in her ears, but she definitely heard something behind her. It was the black Escalade.

The switchbacks came way too fast; she couldn't look behind her. "IUPG," she said to herself. "BARD."

Luna sensed the Escalade gaining on her and pedaled even harder; gravity wasn't enough. She had a better turn ratio then her pursuer, so she gained distance on the turns, but the Escalade easily made up the ground with each straightaway. Luna felt like the little girl on the tricycle must have. She almost didn't make the next turn, and spun out on the dirt for a moment before getting back on the road.

Was Mayhem Moreno driving? She couldn't see through the black windows. Just to be safe, she pedaled harder, despite cramp-

ing in her legs. Another turn came way too fast. She braked slightly, and hugged the center line of the road.

Honk!

A second Escalade almost collided with her before she swerved
onto the gravel. It was dark navy, as if the driver had decided that
navy was the new black. The navy Escalade roared past her.

Finally, she saw a trailhead parking lot further down the road.
She'd turn into the safe, forested harbor and wait this one out.

"IUPG," she said to herself. She was just being paranoid, but
damn it she had a right to be paranoid with Jen as her client.
"BARD."

She got to the edge of the road; then heard the sound of gravel.
The navy Escalade had turned around. No need to wait for it. She
couldn't get her dad's totaled car out of her head. The bastard who
did it had driven away, too. For a moment, she pictured Jen driving
the Escalade.

Luna hurried up the dirt trail, her bike struggling to stay in the
uneven ruts. She glanced back, and saw both the navy and black
Escalades in the parking lot. Both vehicles opened their doors, but
through the trees, she couldn't make out the figures that exited the
vehicles.

She hurried deeper into the aspens. The sign at the trailhead
announced the start of the "Old Man's Loop Trail." Shit. This trail
would take her right back where she started. The people in the
Escalades could just stay and wait her out, and then . . . well, who
knows what they would do.

Bang! Bang! Bang!

Luna heard three gunshots, but she couldn't tell from what
direction. People weren't supposed to hunt up here, were they? Then
she remembered TV reports about an influx of deer in the east
mountains, and how that influx had caused havoc in the villages
below. Many usually upright citizens now sported bumper stickers
reading DEATH TO BAMBI!

She heard a fourth shot echo off the granite rocks, then heard more rustling down below. Either someone was pursuing her, or a hunter mistook her for one of those pesky deer. Death to Bambi, indeed. She had better get moving.

Off the trail to her left, Luna saw a streambed offering some cover. She hurried through the brush, and down to the streambed. The streambed wasn't totally dry; mud and rocks splashed up as she rode her bike. A few hundred yards later, she made it back onto the road, a short distance below the trailhead parking lot. At first she wanted to flag someone down for help, but her paranoia increased. Every vehicle had a gun rack.

Before the armed car came around the bend, Luna quickly found another trailhead and rode her bike cross-country through the pine forest. She almost ran into a deer drinking from a stream. The deer had Jen's scared eyes.

"Are you trying to kill me, Jen?" Luna asked the deer.

The deer shook her head. "I'm innocent," the deer said with her eyes, then quickly ran away.

After another shot, she heard the deer go down. Luna hoped the shot came from hunters, but perhaps it was from one of the people in the Escalades. She couldn't be sure. Damn it!

Luna stopped her bike for a moment and looked at her right leg. She was bleeding slightly. Where did that come from? More rustling in the distance. She couldn't tell whether it was wild animals or wild people.

Luna had taken the Number 99 bus at Tijeras. All she had to do was make it there and take it back. Good old Number 99.

"But that's just what they expect me to do," she muttered.

No one would expect her to bike twenty miles back to her home, so of course she did just that. After a few more miles of forest she found a back road that paralleled the old highway. It took her five hours, and several thousand calories of effort, but she finally made it back to the electronic gate at Sky Village.

Maybe she had just been paranoid after all. It could have been hunters up there, gunning for Bambi. But she had been a D.A. for years; she knew criminals were capable of anything. She wanted to ask the guard at the complex whether anyone had dropped by looking for her, but the guard was nowhere to be found. Luna didn't have her gate card with her, so she sneaked into her own complex, riding behind another car.

If she could do it, a black Escalade gunship could definitely sneak in, too. . . .

When Luna opened her apartment door, she saw the place had been ransacked. She had another moment of panic—maybe Mayhem Moreno had already been here—until she realized that things were exactly how she'd left them. Any mayhem here was her own doing. Perhaps her mind had been playing tricks on her the entire time.

After wiping off her blood in the sink, she called Jen.

Jen picked up immediately.

Luna got to the point. "Jen, did you send someone after me?"

"Luna, I don't think you understand," she said. "I told you that I think someone is coming after me. So whoever's coming after me is probably coming after you."

"And who's that?"

"I don't want to say yet."

The phone went dead.

Chapter Six
The Presumption of Innocence is Green

THE BUILDING THAT HOUSED the State Bar of New Mexico didn't have an official name yet. Luna had first visited here the week after she was admitted to the bar for the "Bridge the Gap" Continuing Legal Education (CLE) that was required of all attorneys. Luna had delusions of grandeur, hoping that someday the building might be named after her. Luna now laughed as she pulled into the parking lot. She still hadn't bridged the gap.

The building was north of downtown, off I-25—the shiny glass and brick complex collectively known as the Journal Center. Luna had sworn off biking in the Albuquerque traffic, especially in this heat, so she had reluctantly driven.

With its modern architecture, the Journal Center resembled the high-tech buildings located in Silicon Valley. Most of the staff here favored blue jeans and shirts and had the tired, bloodshot eyes of workaholics. A sign on the door read PARDON OUR CASUAL APPEARANCE TODAY. The sign had been there during Luna's entire tenure as a lawyer.

Jen and Nurse Song, who was still in nursing scrubs, were waiting outside when she arrived. According to the Conditions of Release, Jen could indeed leave her home with her mother, or with Luna. Still, seeing Jen on the outs was disconcerting. Criminals should only be seen in court or in jail.

"We're wearing the same outfit," Jen said.

Luna had worn her favorite arraignment outfit, a dark gray conservative suit. Jen wore a similar gray outfit, but her skirt was a few inches shorter, her blouse unbuttoned one button further down. Jen also filled out her suit much better than Luna ever could.

"It looks better on you," Luna couldn't help but say.

"It feels way tight," Jen said, giving her a hug. "You look great, too. I wish I had your legs. You're taller than I am. I just look tall because of the high heels. My fuck-me pumps."

This was too much information—especially during a hug. Luna tried to play "hugologist," and analyzed the contact. The hug was warm and tight enough—"I'm really glad to see you," even a trace of "I know I really need you," but there was still an element of "I'm holding back."

"There's a problem," Nurse Song said when they walked into the building. "The receptionist said you didn't reserve a room for us," Nurse Song frowned. "She had never heard of you either."

Alarmed, Luna turned and saw a new receptionist. The usual woman was friendly, but this chick had an icy stare. She was a hip young woman with black eye-liner who looked too cool to be hanging with a bunch of lawyers. She looked like she belonged in a Hollywood nightclub that required a secret password to enter.

"I really need a room to meet with my client," Luna said.

No response.

"Meet with my client" apparently wasn't the secret password. Neither was "It's an emergency."

Luna pleaded to no avail. The young woman wouldn't budge. Every room was booked for the morning's Continuing Legal Education (CLE) program. Each time the outside door opened, more pinstriped lawyers dumped into the atrium. If a terrorist wanted to take out the state's legal community, this would be ground zero.

Luna recognized many of the faces from her job quest when she started her career. Mr. Gordon, a tall man in a dark suit had rejected her for a part-time job because she "seemed more interested in running marathons than in practicing law." The city attorney didn't think she had an adequate legal writing sample to qualify her to prosecute parking tickets. Ms. Little, who was actually quite big, had never gotten back to her. Not even after five years.

Not a single lawyer came over to shake her hand. Not one. Why do all the lawyers hate me, Luna thought?

Other than some hippies from Harvard, the New Mexico legal community was inbred. She'd met some of these people in high school, back when they did "Youth and Government" and debate team. Luna had come from a small town they had never heard of, so the Albuquerque kids viewed her as a pathetic hick. Telling them she had money in Crater, that her dad had been the greatest doctor in the world, didn't help. She'd then gone away for college and law school, which the UNM law grads took as an insult, especially since the University of Colorado wasn't that much better than UNM. Then, when she'd failed to make the Olympics, the legal community treated her as if defeat was her comeuppance.

Luna scanned the room. No one made eye contact. It had taken her years to gain some measure of their respect, especially when she had made it to district attorney, but after the recall election—a nearly unanimous recall election—she was back to square one. No, it was worse, her square was off the board. A murmur came from the crowd. "She's the one," someone said out loud.

The receptionist whispered into the phone. "Should I call security? I don't even know if she's a lawyer."

Luckily, Luna saw a picnic table outside, on the other side of the giant glass windows. Luna pointed outside, at a bench, and the receptionist nodded. The outside world was beyond the bar center's jurisdiction.

The trio skirted around a throng of lawyers to reach the outside. The view was of a concrete drainage ditch, then past overly green corporate grass, and onto the ten stories of the faux Mayan step-pyramid of a gigantic hotel. There was a smidgen of shade from a few very young trees.

Luna looked at Nurse Song when they sat down at the picnic table. "I need a retainer before I can do anything. It's got to be a cashier's check."

Luna hoped that the Songs would mutter something about tough times and needing an installment plan. Luna would just say no; the presumption of innocence, after all, was green. Please God, *don't* let them have the money.

Nurse Song smiled, and handed Luna a pink gym bag. "Would one hundred thousand in cash be enough to get us going?"

Luna's heart stopped as she opened the bag. Inside, she saw stacks of hundred dollar bills. Lawyers on the West Coast could charge millions, but one hundred thousand was way, way above the going rate in Albuquerque. Luna would have to go to the bank and open a lawyer's trust account to ensure the funds were used only for Jen's defense and not for Luna's personal use.

Nurse Song closed the bag. "I can always go to one of the lawyers here if you don't want to help us."

Nurse Song glanced at the horde on the other side of the glass, where dozens of lawyers stared at them. Well, they stared at Jen, but the pink gym bag with the hint of green had caught their attention. Ninety-nine percent of them wouldn't touch a criminal case like this with a twenty-foot pole, but that still left one, maybe two.

Luna took another breath. "Where did you get the money?"

"From Jen's family."

"Is any of the money mixed in with anything illegal?"

Nurse Song was firm. "Not that I know of."

There were the Chinese Triads, and the Japanese Yakuza, but Luna had never heard of any Korean mobs. If the money was from Korea, it was probably clean. Luna took the gym bag. She didn't have corporate stationary yet, so she sheepishly wrote out a receipt on a yellow pad. But hey, she was officially worth more than a six-pack of Budweiser, way more even, than a case.

Jen took one of her old retainer agreements from Hobbs's office, "We'll make this a real agreement."

"Like I'm a real lawyer?"

"Well, I'm not a real criminal," said Jen. "So we're even, I guess."

Jen signed the agreement, then looked at Luna. Luna looked over the retainer agreement. It looked pretty boilerplate, and Hobbs probably used the same one as everyone else. She stared at it intently, but couldn't find anything unusual. She knew she was missing something, but couldn't figure out what. But after more hesitation and another glance, Luna signed.

"Maybe we should have signed it in blood," Jen commented.

"Is there anyplace we can go in private?" Luna said in reply.

Nurse Song didn't smile. "I suppose we can go to my house, but it's a mess."

Luna laughed. Nurse Song didn't know what the word mess meant. She was always immaculate and her workspace at Luna's dad's office had always been sterile, in all senses of the word. The only contamination in her life, apparently, was Jen.

"I'll have to meet you there." Luna picked up the bag. "I have to stop at the bank."

Luna walked back though the lobby carrying the pink gym bag. The other lawyers gave her wide berth, as if she was radioactive.

"Do you know what the hell you're getting into?" It was Georgia Viti, head of the disciplinary board, here doing her annual stern lecture on legal ethics.

"I have no clue what I'm getting into," Luna said, avoiding eye contact. "But I've already taken the money, so I guess it's too late."

At her bank's classy main branch downtown, Luna felt guilty from the get-go. There was a western landscape on the wall that was reminiscent of Crater, but Luna was a long way from home. The teller was a red-haired woman who, in her black outfit and big silver cross, looked like an Irish nun. The teller-nun called a branch supervisor, and Luna immediately recognized Raymond Rossi from Crater. They'd closed the branch there, and he'd managed to get this assignment. Rossi had left Crater before the vote, and Luna didn't really know which way he would have gone. Since he'd been Luna's banker and knew how quickly Luna had gone through her father's inheritance, and then her mother's—not to mention the district attorney's office's limited budget—the vote would probably have been an emphatic "no."

Rossi told Luna that she would have to sign all sorts of papers and that the transaction would be reported to the IRS and to New Mexico Taxation and Revenue. "Let's hope things go better for you here in Albuquerque," he said. "For both our sakes."

Luna now wished she'd just left the money under a pillow, but she had to play by the rules. She didn't want a repeat of the recall election, where critics accused her of having a slush fund. She had not actually embezzled any money, but her record-keeping was not the best, so she couldn't prove that she hadn't flown to the Caribbean, as some anonymous person had suggested.

"Jen, Jen, Jen," Luna said. "You better be clean."

Chapter Seven
Target Letter

AFTER AN UNBEARABLE HOUR, Luna closed Jen's bedroom door behind Nurse Song. In the living room, Nurse Song had brought out the family album and rambled on about her daughter being "too smart to be a legal secretary," and, "too smart to be twenty-five and still taking introductory-level courses for an associate's degree."

Luna couldn't help but remember her own mother describing her faults to strangers, how she was running instead of studying. It was her father who had always bragged about her, and she'd missed that after he died. Jen's father apparently didn't brag much about her; he was so quiet he probably didn't say anything about her at all. Luna empathized with Jen's discomfort.

"She treats me like a kid," Jen said, glancing at the closed door. "I hate her sometimes. Everyone treats me like a kid."

Jen had spent a quarter-century on this earth, but she had the room of a teenager. There were only two family pictures, a big one with her mom, and a small one of an adorable three-year-old Jen in a white *han-bok,* (pronounced hon-boak), the traditional Korean costume, bowing to her dad. Luna thought of the picture of her with her own father, but Mr. Song didn't look especially happy to be in the same frame as Jen.

"I hate my dad," Jen said as Luna stared at the poster.

"I loved mine," Luna said awkwardly as she scanned the rest of the room. Everything was pink, and posters of the last decade's teen idols were still on the walls. Jen even had a few immaculate dolls, some in Asian motif, some inexplicably in Navajo dress. Some dolls had missing heads. Luna absent-mindedly picked up one that had a Native American outfit. Was it Sacagawea, or Pocahontas?

"I think I was Navajo in another life," Jen said. "Mom told me about the Indians out in Crater County. I always thought they were so cool, so romantic."

Luna tried to make conversation. "I did a term paper in high school on Sacagawea. She's my idol."

"She's my favorite too," Jen said, pointing at a pretty doll that still had a pretty head. "This is my Sacagawea doll. She always knew where she was going."

They both smiled. Neither woman knew where she was going right now. Luna then checked out a wall of photos showing Jen performing *tae kwon do.*

"I probably used to know twenty ways to kill you," Jen said with a slight giggle. "But I forgot them."

Without warning, Jen suddenly wrapped her arm around Luna in a choke hold.

"Jen, I can't breathe!" Luna gasped. After an instant, a very long instant, Jen let her go.

"I didn't forget everything, I guess." Jen said with a giggle.

Luna was pissed. "Don't ever do that again!"

"Don't you know when I'm kidding?"

"Not yet."

"I'm sorry," said Jen. "I hope you don't mind if I change out of my suit if it's just you and me."

Luna tightened. Is the girl going to take her clothes off? This was way too weird, especially with those decapitated dolls.

Jen didn't wait for an answer. She grabbed a pile of clothes from her dresser. She then hurried to the bathroom and closed the door.

Luna felt uneasy in the room alone. She glanced at pictures of old boyfriends on Jen's walls. They were an endless parade of tattooed losers, but no Mayhem Moreno, thank God. In college, guys who had a thing for Korean women were called *han-bok* hard-ons. She swore she had prosecuted one *han-bok* hard-on on the wall for trafficking cocaine. She'd have to look him up when she picked up the files. Maybe Jen had shown up for the guy's court or something and that was why Luna felt she knew Jen from somewhere.

She then saw Jen's cell phone on the mantle; she couldn't resist checking the last few numbers dialed. Sure enough, she found her own number from Saturday, then another number, then her own again. Jen had called her, then someone else, then called her again.

"IUPG," Luna said to herself, "BARD." The number after hers was instantly recognizable. "LLL-AGIO."

"The only name you need to know," Luna sang softly.

The toilet flushed and Luna jumped.

Moments later Jen returned, now in sweats and no make-up. Without all the eye shadow, Jen looked much younger. She took a piece of paper off her desk. "I got this."

Luna looked down at a "target letter," informing Jen that she was the target of a Second Judicial District Grand Jury. "So I guess this is for real," Jen said.

Luna got right to the point. "How did you meet the victim, Ed Hobbs?"

"I started at the community college and he taught the legal writing class. I had the highest grade in the class so he hired me a couple days a week."

Time to spring the trap. "How long were you two having an affair?"

"You've been waiting to ask that one, haven't you?" Jen was no dummy; she looked Luna directly in the eye. "Never. I never slept with him. I mean he wanted to, but I was like, not even."

One thing was sure; Jen was a lousy poker player. Her eyebrows arched up and down, her lips pursed, her face became red, even the nose stud seemed to sparkle more. Luna felt she could read her like a book. Or maybe that's what she wants me to think. . . .

"Are you sure?" Luna asked, sounding like her dad.

Jen sat up. "Yes, I'm sure."

"Let's start with the conspiracy count."

Jen laughed. "Out of the frying pan, into the fire."

"Did you know Hobbs dealt in illegal prescription drugs?"

"He told me he had cancer. I called a lot of people and set up appointments with doctors, pharmacists—legit people. They always worked at hospitals. I also called a lot of lawyers, but that wasn't weird, 'cuz he was a lawyer and all. Let me show you something."

Jen pulled a scrapbook from under her bed. It was color-coded with shiny labels for each part of her life. Jen apparently had some organizational skills when she put her mind to it. Under the red heading of "Hobbs," Luna found Article H-One, an investigative report from the local paper, published after Hobbs had been arrested, but before he died.

According to the article, Hobbs once really did have cancer, large-cell lymphoma to be precise, but had been in remission for several years. He had made contacts at various hospitals and soon transported cheaper Mexican prescription drugs to them. A lot of the drugs were also sold on the streets, often to people whose prescriptions had expired or whose benefits had run out.

"Would you be willing to name names?" Luna asked.

"Do I have to?" Jen replied incredulously, as if Luna had asked her to cut one of her ears off.

Luna had played this game as a prosecutor a million times. Go after the small fish to get the big fish. Still, Jen looked like she was scared shitless of the big fish. Jen fiddled with one of her decapitated dolls, an action figure of a soldier who could pass for Marin.

"You will have to give up someone if you want to walk away from this," Luna said.

Jen said nothing for a moment. "I don't know. Luna, I'm afraid of these people. You should be, too."

Luna let it go. Marlow had once said that defendants "don't spill their guts on the first date." Luna took one more look at Jen; the girl wouldn't give it up, time to move on. "Just tell me what happened on July fourth."

"I got a call from Sandrina about eight-thirty. She said Hobbs had gone into some kind of shock from like drugs or sex or something kinky. She told me to meet her at the volcano. That's where they were. It's a good place for drugs or sex, I guess."

"Why would she call you?"

"Because my mom is a nurse; she figured I'd know what to do."

"Why didn't she call 911?"

"Sandrina isn't the type to call 911. She probably has some warrants or something. She's a total freak."

"So what happened when you got there?"

"I went over and Hobbs was already like totally dead. I think Sandrina did that auto-erotic thing and strangled him. Or maybe he just overdosed."

The auto-erotic thing—strangling someone during sex. Ouch! The lab results hadn't come back yet. Cause of death was still unknown. Jen could be telling the truth.

"So what did you do?"

"I freaked out, then I went home. Sandrina got arrested and she said I did it. She's lying."

Luna knew enough about criminal defense not to push too hard, too soon. This was still the first date after all. Luna didn't know if she wanted to know the answer to the next question, but she had to make some kind of a move. "How did your blood get on the body?"

"I tripped and fell and I guess I like bled on him after he was dead. They took a DNA sample from inside my cheek when I was at Metro. But don't worry. I told you I didn't fuck him. Not that night. Not ever. Not even!"

Jen was so insistent, she could be telling the truth, but something wasn't right. Time to go for it again. "Did you know about the drug conspiracy?"

"I had no idea what was going on until I read about it in the papers," Jen said.

"Have you ever done drugs?"

"Yeah. I did when I was kid. I had a problem when I was seventeen, but I never got busted or anything. I don't even drink any more. I had a DWI when I was a kid, but it got dropped. I had this really good lawyer, the one who writes novels and all. He like totally got me off. He didn't even charge me. I think he has 'yellow fever,' you know, like an Asian fetish or something."

"How about prescription drugs?"

"I had a bad reaction to Prozac and Zanax. I was really hyper as a kid, so they put me on Ritalin, but it didn't work—made me sleepy." Jen smiled again, as if to prove attention deficit. "I've got ADHD—ADD with the hyperactivity, a two for one bonus. How much longer are you going to play lawyer on me?"

"I'm not playing," Luna said. Luna tried to think of other questions, or better yet, change the subject. "Do you do martial arts?"

"Kinda," Jen said. She pointed at one wall. The ribbons on the wall got smaller as Jen got older, the last picture of Jen in her martial arts outfit showed a black eye and a dejected look. Jen had natural abilities all right, but absolutely no focus.

Jen turned the radio on to the Top 40 station. Her attention was rapidly deficitting.

"Jen!"

Jen reluctantly turned it off. Luna knew she didn't have much more time.

"Anything else?" Jen asked. "My favorite soap's coming on." Luna almost lost her temper until Jen smiled. "I'm just playing you."

Luna then noticed a section of the scrapbook marked "Luna." There were copies of articles of her big wins, like the Jeremy Jones case, as well as the recall election.

"I wanted to know who my lawyer was," Jen said.

Luna was soon lost in thought as she read her own press: the good, the bad and the last few pages of ugly. Had she really been such a great lawyer way back when? Had she really fucked up her own life so badly since?

"Earth to Luna," Jen said. "Are we done? Could you help me with my legal writing paper? You being a lawyer and all? It's my last class for summer session and if I don't get it done, I'll like totally fail the whole semester."

"Ummm . . . let's talk more about the case," Luna said.

"I don't have anything more to say. The paper's due tomorrow and other than my mom, you're like the only smart person I know."

Luna shrugged. No one had called her smart in a while. Helping Jen with her paper seemed like quid pro quo. Luna had once helped an old boyfriend, a bartender, with his paper on Greek mythology, pounding away on her laptop on top of a barstool. She had felt like a slut then, and she felt like one now.

Jen's paper was on the long-term economic effect of smoking bans in public places. Jen had great writing style, and turned a phrase or two, but she tended to repeat herself, and sometimes had weird transitions. She also used the words "like," "totally," and of course, "totally like," in her sentences.

"It's got to be ten pages," Jen protested when she saw the result. Luna feared that Jen was going to use one of her *kung fu* moves on her again.

"Well you've got to give your opinion," Luna said, warily. "Are you for smoking bans or not?"

"I'm trying to quit," she said. "But it's hard. Since I can't smoke in bars, I quit but I'm totally jonesing for a cigarette like all the time."

"Then write down your own opinion and you've got a paper."

Jen wrote down a few paragraphs. Luna read them over, caught a few typos, and added a final sentence about smoke and fire.

Jen read over the paper. "You can like read my mind," she said.

"Huh?"

"You're all writing it the way I was thinking," Jen said. "Except you like totally clean it up. I knew you were smart."

Luna couldn't help but smile. "I guess so."

Jen stared at her intently, as if daring Luna to penetrate her forehead and go all the way into the cerebellum. "Do you believe me when I said I didn't do it?" Jen asked.

Luna didn't know what to believe. But she did know something, it was very important to Jen that Luna believed in her.

"Sure. I believe you," Luna lied.

That night Luna's phone rang. At first she thought it was Jen again, but the caller ID read UNLISTED GOVERNMENT NUMBER.

That definitely couldn't be good.

"Hello?" Luna said.

"Is this Luna Cruz?" The voice was the deepest she had ever heard, like that of an evil robot.

"Yes, who is this?"

"Ms. Cruz, are you the attorney representing Jen Song?" No, the voice was real. Luna could detect just the slightest hint of a New York accent, something a robot most certainly would not have. He sounded as if Darth Vader had joined a South Bronx street gang.

"Depends on who's calling," Luna said, trying to muster up some courage. She couldn't make out the name in the depths of the baritone, she did make out that he was with the U.S. Attorney's Office. "What was the name?"

"Jorge Washington," he said gruffly. "Like the father of our country, if he was Dominican. I cannot tell a lie, the cherry tree and all that."

"How can I help you, Mr. Washington?"

Because of his voice, Luna couldn't help but think of him as Darth Vader. Luna knew the minute she head that voice that a quick plea was out of the question.

"Quite frankly, there is nothing we need at this time," Vader said. "We'll wait for the grand jury to indict your client. Then we'll get back to you."

That, like totally, didn't sound good. . . .

Chapter Eight
Dual Diagnosis Day

THE UNIVERSITY OF NEW Mexico Hospital Mental Health Center was on the edge of a quiet residential neighborhood, near the law school. The squat adobe houses of the neighborhood contained underpaid college professors and Marxist graduate students. The health center, a two-story brick building, looked out of place amidst the adobes—as if it couldn't decide whether it was a prison or a school-house. The mentally ill residents smoking furiously outside the building under the watchful eye of armed security guards sure did not look like graduate students. Well, most of them didn't.

"Do we really have to do this?" Jen asked as they entered the clinic. "I'm not crazy. Well, not all crazy."

"I've got to check out everything," Luna said. "Maybe we'll find out something useful. Insanity might help at sentencing."

"Sentencing? So you're already saying I'm guilty?"

Shit. Jen didn't miss much when she actually paid attention.

"I've got to keep all options open," Luna replied. "Dr. Romero can help us do that."

Dr. Romero had moved to Albuquerque after her stint at the Las Vegas State Hospital in Las Vegas, New Mexico. Las Vegas, New Mexico was "Vegas for poor people." She'd gone to Crater for Luna's own incident—"possible suicidal ideation," after Luna swam naked in a lake in the middle of the night. The two had bonded, as much as a doctor could bond with a patient. Luna often called Dr. Romero as an expert witness in trials because, with her patented "Reality Therapy," the doctor had little sympathy for the mentally ill, even Luna.

Jen's wardrobe for the day avoided reality. She wore a t-shirt, this one of the entire Laser Geisha Team—a team of superhero girls in robotic ninja outfits of pink, blue and green. The small t-shirt and loose khaki shorts left plenty of room for her slightly soft belly and a golden belly button ring.

Luna had also worn khaki, a khaki pants suit with a blue top. She looked more like a law student than a lawyer.

"I'm Laser Geisha Pink," Jen said, noticing that Luna stared at Geisha shirt. "You can be Laser Geisha Blue, she's the leader. It even goes with the color you're wearing."

Luna sensed another chance to bond with her client at a stressful moment. Luna's old boyfriend Marlow, the defense lawyer, would make a list of his clients' favorite things and incorporate them into his daily life as a way of empathizing with them, so he could "get it up" for his clients. Luna wouldn't go that far of course, but pretending to like the Laser Geishas would be a half-assed attempt to reach out to Jen.

Luna had actually watched the Geishas once in law school, pulling an all-nighter before her Civil Procedure final. The show was Japanese, allegedly for children, but adults had picked it up for the cheesy over-dubbing that often referenced American pop culture. Laser Geisha Pink had once asked to be called Laser Geisha Purple for example, in a speech that could have been stolen from the movie *Reservoir Dogs*.

"I want to be Laser Geisha Pink," said Luna, aping the speech she had heard from the TV show. "Pink is cooler than Blue. Pink can fly and I don't think Blue can do much of anything."

"No you don't want to be Pink; she's the crazy one. A total slut."

"But she's got the coolest laser shooting out of her eyes, right? What does Blue do again?"

"Blue just complains all the time about the Axis of Overlords, because they're men, and she can't get laid. She's the old hag. She can barely fly without Pink holding her hand. Just like you."

Thanks a lot," said Luna. "Isn't there another one, Laser Geisha Green?"

"She's the new one, they added her last season when the ratings started to slump. Nobody really knows about her."

The mental health unit was the mental health dumping grounds of last resort for the entire county, and this last resort had a wild mix of vacationers, as if it were spring break in hell. A few pierced and tattooed college kids waited anxiously, trying to recover from the "F" in calculus with a little therapy and a lot of pharmaceuticals. A few unemployed professionals looked embarrassed to be getting help for their depression, and hid their faces in old magazines like *Model Railroader*. Many of the other patients came right out of jail or the shelter. Staff dressed more casually than the patients, and it was hard to tell the doctor from the doctored.

Worse, Luna shuddered when she heard a guard mention that today was "god damn dual diagnosis day." Apparently god damn dual diagnosis day was the dumping ground for patients with multiple issues.

It was dim inside the building. Luna didn't know whether this was because it was supposed to be soothing, or because the unit didn't have enough money to pay for adequate lighting.

When she came to greet them, Dr. Romero stood out from the others in the faint light. She was very tall and looked like a surgeon general in her black suit and militaristic jewelry. She walked over to Luna, and gave her the lightest hug in history. "I had to juggle twenty schizophrenic meth addicts to see you, are you okay?"

"I'm fine," Luna said, slightly embarrassed by the doctor's concern for her mental health. "It's for my client."

Dr. Romero shrugged, and ushered Jen into her office while Luna waited in one of the waiting rooms. This particular waiting room was messy, and looked like a fraternity living room with opened newspapers and spilled coke cans. A TV played a game show at high volume, making the patients even more anxious. Suddenly Luna heard a commotion down the hall that was even louder than the TV.

"Charlemagne, how many times have we told you that you're not allowed to be here anymore?"

Charlemagne, who indeed was dressed like the ancient French emperor, was dragged out the front door by two big guards. Luna shuddered, and hoped she didn't go crazy while she waited.

Luna looked around and played "guess the dual diagnosis." Charlemagne was obviously a heroin addict, probably in for methadone, but could also be schizophrenic with sordid sex offenses thrown in. He had SLUT tattooed on the back of his neck, which didn't seem all that appropriate for an emperor. A pretty brunette chattered about a Republican conspiracy to a young man with a UNM Law School sweatshirt, who looked dazed from bad experiences with the Socratic method. Luna didn't even attempt a guess at their problems, they didn't seem that different from herself.

One aging gang-banger sat alone, staring at the game show on TV. He wore an Oakland Raiders cap and football jersey. He practically had "anger management" written all over him, in addition to some kind of substance abuse.

A grizzled alcoholic stumbled into the seat next to her. Luna thought of the unknown driver in the fateful crash that had taken out her dad. They never got the guy; this could be him. . . .

This man's eyes were totally yellow. Did he have any blood in his alcohol stream, or were those veins all Jack Daniels by now?

"Did you kill my dad?" she couldn't help but ask.

The man nodded. Then kept nodding to an invisible audience. Luna moved a seat down in case his delusions were contagious. She remembered her first exposure to the mentally ill when she took a criminal law clinic class in law school. She represented a young boy who was on Thorazine. She was so green she had thought Thorazine was a thyroid medication, as opposed to an anti-psychotic.

"Try not to go crazy in front of the court," she'd said to him.

"I can't make a promise that I can't keep," he'd replied.

Sure enough, his medication wore off halfway through his sentencing and it had taken five guards to stop his lunge for the judge.

The game show went to commercial, and Mr. Raider got up and came over to her. "I can get you cheap-ass drugs."

Cheap-ass drugs, in particular, cheap-ass anti-depressants, sure sounded good right now, but Luna certainly didn't trust Mr. Raider. "Go away," she said, waving her hand as if shooing a fly.

He vanished in a flash. Luna wondered if he had been a hallucination, but she soon saw him on the other side of the room talking to the law student. The two of them did a handshake deal for something to make the sting of the Socratic method go away, at least for the moment.

Luna "did the math," as Jen would say. If the law student had gone to someone like Mr. Raider for his pills for the entire year—after his prescriptions had run out for the month—even at a "cheap ass" price, that was some serious change. Worth killing for. . . .

A nurse shouted out "Cruz?"

Luna snapped to attention. She then realized that Cruz was also the name of Mr. Raider, and he got up to accompany the nurse. She sure hoped she wasn't related to an asshole like that.

 Suddenly, a nerdy boy with glasses entered with his mother. She wore a shirt with a Wal-Mart logo. They sat down next to Luna. Luna pretended to watch TV, but couldn't help but listen to the boy.

"I just said people were going to die at school," he said in a pre-puberty voice. "I didn't say that I was going to kill them."

Luna felt for the boy. She once wanted to take out her old high school. But she was over that, right? Maybe not. Might as well, get a "check-up from the neck-up" as a camp counselor had once said. She definitely had not recovered from the recall election and getting voted out of office by the entire town. Hell, she had not recovered from her childhood. Luna didn't really have any income right now, so she supposed she could qualify for the clinic's indigent services.

She went to the intake counter to fill out the paperwork. On the worksheet, she checked depression, agitation, and loss of sexual function. Hopefully, the last one she could cure through the Internet, despite the libido dampening effect of the BVG Resident Shield for Windows.

"I don't have any insurance right now," she said to the intake clerk, a dour woman. The intake clerk looked weary, as if she had this conversation about ten times an hour.

"How are you employed?" the intake clerk asked, not even looking up from her screen.

"I'm a lawyer," Luna said.

"I thought all lawyers were rich." The clerk looked up from her screen at Luna and her nice clothes. There was real anger and resentment on her face. Luna knew she'd lost another vote. "Honey," the clerk said, "just go to your million dollar an hour shrink, and complain that your mommy and daddy don't love you."

Luna wanted to say that her mommy and daddy were dead, but she said nothing, and slinked back to her chair. The boy and his mother looked even more anxious.

"In a minute," the mother said. "In a minute."

A guard hit the mute button on the TV. It was now way too quiet in the waiting room. Luna almost wished he'd turn it back on.

"What are you in for?" the nerdy boy asked her when his mother went up to check on the cause of their wait.

"I don't know," Luna said, shutting her eyes and hoping he would disappear.

"Did you kill somebody or something?" he asked hopefully.

"Not yet."

After another hour, Dr. Romero returned with an exhausted Jen. Even Laser Geisha Pink had faded on the shirt.

"Let's talk outside," Dr. Romero said to Luna.

"Wait inside," Luna said to Jen. "And don't go crazy on me here."

She half-expected Jen to say "I can't make a promise I can't keep," but Jen looked spent, as if she'd poured her guts out to the doctor and the doctor had given her a strong dose of reality, as opposed to a nice hug or a magic pill. The three Laser Geishas needed to re-charge as well.

Luna and Dr. Romero walked to a stone bench in front of the clinic. "She's sane all right," the doctor said.

There went one defense, Luna thought.

"She's oriented to time and place. Some occasional memory losses. Some pretty serious anger issues toward her family, especially toward her father and men in general."

"Enough anger to kill someone?"

"What do you want me to say?" Dr. Romero smiled. She had made those diagnoses all the time while at the Las Vegas State Hospital. She always erred on the side of guilt, because if one of her clients went on to kill, she could always say, "I told you so."

Luna looked at her. "I guess I have to go with the truth."

"I can't say anything with medical certainty," Dr. Romero said.

Luna noticed Jen in the corner. It was hard to read her emotions right now. "Does she like me?"

"I didn't ask," the doctor said. "Does it matter?"

Luna said nothing. Did it really matter? Jen was a client, not a friend. "Anything else?"

"ADHD, one of the worst cases I've ever seen. But she said she already told you that."

"Is she a pathological liar, anything like that?"

"No. She's very lonely. And completely honest. Almost too honest, like she's got a shot of Sodium Pentothol in her all the time. She always says what she thinks, even if it's socially inappropriate. She's very intelligent, but probably has a host of learning disabilities. She also has a narcissistic personality. In layman's terms, she thinks the whole world revolves around her."

As if to prove the point, Jen wandered outside, and stood a polite distance away from them. "Almost done?" Jen shouted.

"In a minute, Jen," Luna said. "So any advice, doctor?" Luna had tried to become friends with Dr. Romero, but the doctor always kept a professional barrier between them. To her, Luna would always be a patient.

Dr. Romero remained stiff. "My medical diagnosis is to plead her quickly. Whatever you do, don't put her on the stand. You never know what that girl is going to do."

"Is she dangerous?"

"I just said that you never know what that girl is going to do." Dr. Romero took a measure of pity on Jen. "You can come over and join us, Jen."

When Jen hurried over, Luna noticed that she'd lost her swivel.

"Here's a prescription for you," Dr. Romero said. "You can have it filled at UNM Pharmacy, but it's a madhouse over there."

A madhouse? Luna thought they were already in a madhouse.

Dr. Romero smiled. "I'll come with you to hold your hand if you like." She gestured to Jen. "Every once in awhile, I actually like a patient of mine. I think my schizophrenics will keep for twenty minutes."

Luna looked at the new crop of patients going in the door. Maybe it was triple diagnosis day now. Luna looked over at Jen, then at the Dr. Romero. "I think we'd both like it if you held our hands."

UNM Pharmacy was less than a mile from Luna's apartment at Sky Village. It was located on the corner of a barren stretch of University Boulevard and a small street called Camino de Salud, the street of health. Luna had never noticed it before, even though Camino de Salud had its own light to accommodate all the traffic. The entrance was in the back of a large warehouse that blended into the desert. The front of the warehouse could have housed weapons of mass destruction, for all anyone knew. The building's cinder blocks were painted a stucco color, but the gray of the cinder blocks had fought its way through the paint. The turquoise paint on the railings had also faded.

Inside the building, people waited impatiently for a magic pill to cure whatever ailed them. A wider range of people were here than in the mental health center, and there were more who were elderly. Most looked non-descript, but at the far left counter they saw a beautiful Native American woman in line. The woman looked exactly like Jen's doll.

"Sacagawea," both Luna and Jen said at the same time.

"Jinx," Jen said. "That's what you say when both of us say the same thing at the same time."

Luna smiled. "I know about 'jinx.'"

Then they heard Sacagawea talk, and they realized she was a man, in line for prescription hormones.

The sign on the wall for drop off read NOW SERVING 72. Announcements were made in both English and Spanish in a robotic voice that was irritating in both languages. There was a small plastic dispenser, the kind you'd see at a busy ice cream store. A small piece of paper read NUMBER 999.

Luna sighed. Nine hundred twenty-seven people to go.

The line would not move quickly. Every customer argued about something when they finally reached the counter. One wanted a bigger supply, another didn't want to pay their co-pay, the doctor screwed up the prescription. The techs looked glazed, as if they were on drugs themselves, although speed certainly wasn't one of them.

Luna did more math: a few hours to drop off the prescription at the desk, another few to get Jen's prescription filled. Luna didn't want to spend any more time here than necessary, and Jen grew more agitated by the minute. Strangely, Luna felt protective of Jen, and put her hand on the girl's shoulder. Her touch calmed Jen down.

"Thank you, Luna," Jen said.

"You're welcome."

Fortunately, Dr. Romero went to the far left counter and politely pushed aside the trans-gendered person. She murmured to the
tech, flashed a badge, then returned. "It'll take about five minutes."

Sacagawea shouted. "Who the hell is she? I was here first!"

Dr. Romero ignored her, and returned to Luna. Sacagawea shot
them a withering glare. Jen leaned closer to Luna, hiding behind her
back.

"Are those drug dealers?" Luna asked, pointing at some unsa-
vory characters lurking in the back.

"Some are runners for lawyers, trying to find accident victims.
Some are runners for doctors. And well . . . some really are drug
dealers."

Sacagawea now shouted at the tech. "What do you mean I have
to pay?" She mentioned the name of a particular county health plan
that provided for indigents.

"Not anymore," said the tech. "You're off that plan. You need to
go back to the main office on University Boulevard and file a protest."

"Protest this, bitch!" Sacagawea said, grabbing her crotch.

"Some people's benefits run out," Dr. Romero said by way of
explanation. "Then they are ripe for something else."

Sacagawea walked away utterly dejected. On cue, a gang kid
intercepted her before she got to the door. "I can get you what you
need," he said. "Cheap. Let's go outside."

Dr. Romero laughed for a moment. "I will deny saying this, but
that young man is pretty good."

Luna was curious, but Dr. Romero didn't elaborate.

Jen finally got her prescription. "This place gives me the creeps,"
she said.

As they left, Luna gave Jen a reassuring touch on the shoulder.
She didn't know why she did it; but Jen looked as if she needed . . .
something.

Chapter Nine
Legal Lap Dance

LUNA AND JEN SAID nothing as they drove up Coal Boulevard, which became Zuni street, a.k.a. Crack Alley, just west of Jen's house.

"That's where I went to high school," Jen said, pointing at a crumbling Highland High. "Go Hornets! I was a JV cheerleader. Never made it to varsity . . . in anything."

"Varsity isn't all it's cracked up to be," Luna said. "Sometimes it's much worse—making varsity and then losing it."

"You should be more proud of yourself, Luna," Jen said at last. "I don't think you know all that you have going for you."

"What?"

"I don't think you like yourself much," Jen said. "There's a lot about you to like. I think you're totally cool. I'm not kidding."

Luna said nothing, but was genuinely touched by Jen's statement. It was one thing to be called smart by Jen, but being called "cool" was a real compliment. "I can tell when you're not kidding."

"You're sort of the person I wanted to be when I was little. Like a role model."

Luna realized it had been a long time since she'd been a role model for anyone. She was surprised at how good it felt.

"Thanks, Jen. I'm glad I'm somebody's role model."

Jen smiled. "We're almost like friends."

"Almost."

She dropped Jen off at her home in the Mexican Mekong and Jen gave her a hug before she left, a best friend hug. Dr. Romero was right; Jen was indeed a very lonely person. Then again, she herself wasn't doing much better.

Luna let the hug linger. She needed human contact too, a psychic towel to wipe off the slime of the morning. Luna felt she wanted to join the Laser Geishas on the t-shirt, even if she had to settle for being Laser Geisha Blue, the raggedy old bitch who could barely fly. Super powers sure would be nice on a day like today.

"You really need to get an office," Jen said, "so I have a place to hang out."

"I'll get right on it."

"So can we hang out sometimes? And not, like, just talk about law. Girl stuff. You're all I've got right now."

Luna didn't have any one else to hang out with and not just talk about law. "We'll see," Luna said.

Maybe Marlow's method of bonding with his clients was a good thing. She had once asked him why he would ever bond with a client, why he ever wanted to be friends with an accused killer.

"Even accused killers listen to their friends," he had said. "If someone tells them to plead instead of taking some stupid-ass case to trial, they're more like to listen if they think you're a friend."

Jen pointed to her t-shirt. "These are my only friends. *Laser Geisha Pink!*" She said it in bad Japanese-English, almost like a record played too fast.

Luna hoped Marlow was right. "*Laser Geisha Blue!*" Luna said, imitating the voice.

Luna spent the rest of the morning looking at office space. She saw a nice place, a converted adobe house, right on Fifth Street, just behind Metro Court. She looked around the beehive of activity; these were the power lawyers meeting with paying clients. She could do well here.

The landlord was a sixty-something Hispanic man dressed in the latest golf clothes. He'd just returned after acing the back nine at Tanoan County Club. Luna saw what her father could have become had he lived—a small town man turned real estate tycoon in his retirement. This man had long, flowing gray hair and a beard, which made him look a bit like a Mexican Zeus.

Mr. Baca was someone you just called "Mister" and didn't ask for a first name. As she looked through the office, she took a call from Jen. Jen asked whether she should testify in front of the Grand Jury, "to tell my side of the story."

"Never, ever testify in front of a grand jury!" Luna shouted into the phone. "Once you tell your story, you're stuck with it. Jen, right now you're all over the place, you go up on the stand they will rip you to shreds."

That shut Jen up pretty good. "I don't want to be ripped to shreds."

"Don't call me, I'll call you," Luna said and hung up.

Mr. Baca smiled. "Are you a TV producer or something?" Luna must have sounded like she was a Hollywood player. Luna's khaki and blue outfit wasn't nice enough for her to be pegged as an actress, but she could pass for someone behind the scenes.

"No, I'm a lawyer."

Mr. Baca smiled. Lawyers were good tenants. He then gave her a quote and had her fill out a credit application. Luna was in a good mood as she filled in most of the blanks, but soon grew anxious as he called in the information.

"It will only take a few minutes," Mr. Baca said, smiling at her. It was a fatherly smile. "You'd be perfect."

His phone rang moments later. Mr. Baca frowned after listening to the caller.

"I'm sorry, but your credit was denied," he said. "I thought all lawyers were rich."

God, everybody keeps saying that. Luna got up, embarrassed. "Not yet."

"Now I remember how I know you," he said, frowning even deeper. "I saw you on TV."

"I'm handling a big murder case."

"No, that wasn't it," Mr. Baca said. "You were that D.A. out in Crater County. The one who got voted out. Everyone hated you . . . I mean *every*one. . . ."

Luna left in a huff. No, Mr. Baca didn't remind her of her father after all.

Luna toured a few more places, and the results were similar—either she couldn't afford it, her credit was denied, or someone just didn't want her due to the scandal. She checked her mail, too. The last of the law firms and state agency applications had all come back negative. It was official; no one in New Mexico liked her.

For lunch, Luna had the Olympian Salad at a Greek dive downtown, hoping the ground feta cheese contained steroids to pump up her mood. Her only companion was the *Albuquerque Journal.* When her phone rang, she checked the number on her caller ID. It was a number new to her; maybe it was a potential client.

Initially she thought the call came from a mechanical voice, but it was a real person. The bank had frozen the hundred-thousand-dollar deposit in her trust account, pending an internal investigation. She'd have access to a thousand dollars tops, until it was all cleared up.

With her savings, she could just keep her apartment for another few months. Shit! Mr. Mechanical stated that after the completion of the investigation, they could, possibly, release the funds. "It depends on the results of our internal investigation. That's standard policy with large deposits like this."

"Standard policy?"

"It's our standard policy when you don't have an established track record."

The phone went dead.

How do you establish a track record? Shit. Jen could plead to murder, but she couldn't plead to any drug conspiracy. Luna knew if the money was tainted she couldn't open a trust account, and without a trust account she couldn't be a private attorney. Not that anyone else wanted her these days.

Luna frowned when she got the lunch bill. She still wasn't used to downtown Albuquerque prices, relative to what lunch had cost at the Rustler Inn back home in Crater. Money was a top worry, and if she couldn't be a lawyer, she'd have to find something else to do. Luna grimaced as she envisioned saying "recall election" as the reason for leaving her last position when she'd fill out a job application. There was always retail, but Luna doubted she'd last a half-shift at Wal-Mart without gagging. The reaction of the intake clerk at the mental health unit made it clear that when it came to getting a regular job in Albuquerque, having a law degree was like having leprosy. Hell, having a law degree wasn't even good for getting a law job if you didn't come from Albuquerque and hadn't slept with everybody in town.

Luna knew her mother and father would roll over in their graves if she did anything sleazy. One sleazy law student friend had been a stripper in Denver at a place called Shotgun Willie's. No, while Luna still had the body for stripping, she had some self-respect. She was a lawyer for the duration. But Luna couldn't help thinking back to what her friend, the stripper law student had said. "Law is just one big lap dance." Luna wasn't sure what the girl had meant, until now.

Luna desperately wanted to feel like a lawyer right now, even if it was just pretend. There had to be some legal work she could do before the end of the day here in downtown Albuquerque, but what? Was there anyone she could see to do a lawyerly thing? She didn't need a desk, didn't need a staff. She was a lean, mean self-sufficient legal machine!

"*LLL-AGIO*" she hummed. "*The only name you need to know.*"

• • • • •

Dellagio's office was right down the street, on the western edge of downtown, in a neighborhood called Barrio Wells Park. It was right under another Dellagio billboard. My god, the man's head was the size of the entire second floor, the mustache itself the size of a wolverine.

The office was a compound of renovated Victorian houses, like the downtown of a rustic village in Vermont. The oldest, grandest house in the complex had belonged to a famed evil railroad magnate during the last century. In the driveway, she saw a black Escalade identical to the one that followed her on the crest. This guy didn't just chase ambulances; maybe he caused the accidents himself.

Luna took a deep breath and headed inside. The immaculate waiting room held some of the same people from the pharmacy and the clinic, although they had dressed up slightly for their lawyer. Dellagio didn't just do car accidents; some clients had medical or dental malpractice claims. They all looked in serious pain, and many were in wheelchairs or on crutches.

"I bet all these people need their drugs, too," she said to herself. She looked around and saw Mr. Raider huddled in a corner chatting up a man in a cast.

Luna went to a receptionist, a detached curator in this, the museum of misfortune. The receptionist was a pale Anglo woman, strikingly beautiful with dark hair. Dellagio spent his money on the highest quality of everything, except his clients of course.

"May I help you?" the receptionist asked briskly in a British BBC accent, practically perfect in every way. Her nametag read VICTORIA, and she could pass for a Victoria's Secret model, except for her height. She was beyond fit. Luna couldn't see an ounce of body fat on her.

Who said you couldn't be too rich or too thin? Luna was actually intimidated by Victoria's . . . vitality.

Victoria gave her a smile and scanned Luna's body, giving it a mental MRI as Luna wondered if the chick was checking her out.

"Is Mr. Dellagio in?" Luna asked.

"He's abroad right now," Victoria replied, compensating for her height with condescension. "Overseas. Would he know what this is concerning?"

"I think he would," Luna said. "I'm Luna Cruz. I'm representing Jen Song."

Victoria stared at her. "*The* Luna Cruz?"

Luna froze. Oh shit, not again.

"You're a runner, right?" Victoria asked.

"Triathlons actually."

"I'm Victoria Scarborough. I had a scholarship to run for UNM," she said, ashamed that she hadn't said Oxford. "We ran against each other a few times in college."

Luna couldn't remember who won in their races. At least Victoria hadn't been there for Luna's debacle at the Olympic trials. Victoria was a pure runner, while Luna also biked and swam competitively. Luna had more bulk now, and it was all muscle, right?

"I still got it," Luna kidded herself.

"I still train," Victoria said. "Do you?"

The sheer English iciness Victoria put into the words "do" and "you" indicated that she doubted Luna's fitness.

"A little," Luna said.

"I do personal training and sports massage on the side," Victoria said. "I'm also training in acupuncture. I can help you get back in shape. Let me know if you're up for a run sometime. You can bike if you want, if you still have a problem keeping up."

Luna frowned. Maybe she didn't still "got it" after all.

Chapter Ten
The Fake Phone Call Trick

LUNA DID A NICE long afternoon run around nearby University Golf Course, the Albuquerque running scene's answer to New York's Central Park. Luna pushed hard, passed joggers at will, and didn't smile at anyone.

Luna showered, then settled in at Sky Village for the evening and puttered around on the Internet. She had been on a *guy-atus* for too long, so she shifted to the personals on a dating site. There was a public defender in Aguilar. Nope, no starving lawyers. One "attorney/author" e-mailed her. She didn't write him back; she wanted someone who knew what he wanted to do with his life. Finally, one caught her eye: "Seeking Sacagawea."

"I'm looking for a woman who can guide me through the frontiers of life—athletic, dark haired, well-traveled, and well-educated," the ad read. "I'm a lawyer, 27, 6'5". . . ."

She looked at the picture. The words, "tall, dark, and handsome" didn't come close to capturing his essence. He was a little young, but so what?

Luna responded instantly, sending a picture of herself in a bathing suit from Las Cruces's Burn Lake Triathlon meet. She signed it "Sacagawea."

Luna anxiously waited for his response. Ever since she'd been voted out of office, she'd been embarrassed to call her best friend,

Diana. Consequently, she had no one to confide in. She couldn't call her mother, and certainly couldn't call Sacagawea herself.

"No one in New Mexico likes me, remember?" she asked out loud.

Well almost no one. She thought about dialing Jen to tell her about the e-mail, but she resisted the temptation. The girl was a client, not a friend, despite what Marlow said. Instead, she sat on her phone.

Minutes later, she got a reply to her email. The man could write in complete sentences, and even used metaphors. That was a start. He liked her picture. He asked about her cases. He signed it "Seek."

She e-mailed Seek back immediately. The man must have magic powers, because that damn BVG Resident Shield pop-up stopped popping up on her computer screen. They soon shifted into instant messaging. He had a Spanish surname, but she didn't bother to remember it. From now on, he would just be Seek.

Seek was from Tucson, which Luna had always thought of as a slightly nicer version of Albuquerque. He was half-Hispanic, half-Swedish—an enticing combo. He had gone to Cornell to do the high jump, long jump, and triple jump (all the cool jumps) before being injured.

"I've got a good heart," he said in his letter. "But a bad knee."

"I've got a knee fetish," she had typed back. "Sorry."

She worried whether he'd take the bait. "Seriously?" he instant messaged back.

"Of course not," she said. "However, my mom had bad knees, so knees are an issue with me."

They communicated by IM for four hours straight. He had gone to the University of Colorado Law School, her alma mater, but arrived just after she had left. He had many of the same teachers, but had done considerably better than she had. Good for him. They had lived in Boulder at the same time, ran the same trails, and eaten at the same restaurants. She was sure she'd seen him in the Pearl Street Mall once, his arms around a girl as beautiful as he was.

Thankfully, he didn't go to her disaster at the Triathlon Olympic pre-trial, which had been held in Boulder that year.

His family had set him up with their law practice—he got referrals from his sister who was a D.A.—and he did well for himself.

"I still practice my jumping when I hurry from courtroom to courtroom," he e-mailed. "I'm one pulled hamstring away from contempt of court."

Luna knew that wasn't funny, but laughed anyway. His charm came through even over the Internet. And still no pop-up ads!

The only sore spot was when he asked Luna about her own family. She just said both her mom and dad were dead and she didn't want to talk about it.

They agreed to meet the next night for dinner. She knew she acted too eager, but she had long passed the time for playing games. Tick tock, tick tock, after all. . . .

Luna wanted to place a collect call to her mother and father in the afterlife, and let them know that this could be the one. She couldn't call her parents, but she definitely had to call someone. Anyone. She felt a mysterious force inside her, almost a compulsion, a craving for human contact. Did she really know only one person in the entire world? Yes, she did. Just one.

Luna had made a small step of bonding with Jen over the Laser Geishas, perhaps she could bond further over something they truly had in common. Men.

She reluctantly dialed the phone. Jen picked up before the end of the first ring.

"Jen, I met a guy. I just had to tell someone."

Jen was flattered. "I guess you like me now."

Luna said nothing, this was more about "need," than "like." She wanted to go on about her impressions, but stopped herself. "I'll let you know how it goes."

"Good luck." Jen sounded sincere. "I'm rooting for you."

Luna smiled. It was good to have someone rooting for her for a change.

• • • • •

The next afternoon Luna read a pamphlet, "How to Defend Your First Criminal Case" at the law library. Just when she was finished, she realized it was aimed at people doing their own cases without a lawyer. Luna smiled. Maybe she wasn't really a lawyer.

Closing the pamphlet, Luna looked out at University Golf Course. She sure wanted to be running instead of studying. Jen called, of course, and Luna had to hustle out to the lobby to avoid the angry stares of the neurotic law students. Jen had a million questions, but Luna didn't have any answers. Yet. Still, Luna enjoyed feeling needed by someone.

"Are you excited about your date tonight?" Jen asked.

"Yeah, but you don't know with guys from the Internet," Luna said.

"I can do the fake phone call trick," Jen said. "I'll call you like five minutes into the date and if the guy's like a total loser nerd you can pretend like I'm having an emergency so you can bail out."

Luna laughed. She wasn't going to have an accused murderer play the "fake call trick." The last person who had done that for her was her old friend Diana Crater. Still, Luna was nervous about getting back into the dating scene. Maybe Jen's plan was right.

"Call me at exactly five after seven," Luna said.

Luna figured she might as well play lawyer, so while still in the lobby, she tried the D.A.'s office, but a secretary told her that Jen's files wouldn't be ready until after arraignment.

Luna took her long awaited run around the golf course in the afternoon, but it was mostly empty due to the wind. The solitude made her feel even lonelier.

That night Luna waited nervously at Ragin' Shrimp, a small New Orleans-style restaurant, just off Central Avenue, the famous old Route 66, in what was wistfully called the Nob Hill Neighborhood.

Even at its adobe and neon funkiest, Albuquerque could never pass for San Francisco, but the town's heart was in the right place. Ragin' Shrimp was the perfect first date. The prices were reasonable, the atmosphere mellow, and the food just sophisticated enough to pretend you were somewhere else.

Luna didn't want to bike it, nor drive, so went for the extravagance of a cab, a rarity in Albuquerque. Hopefully Seek would drive her home. Or to his place. . . .

Luna had felt her mother guide her in her clothing choices. It was still hot, so she could bare a midriff and wear black, of course. Her pierced belly button, a youthful indiscretion, had finally healed. She did have a push-up bra and went with her jeans a little loose, hanging as low as a woman over thirty would dare. She was almost as bad as Jen. What was the word for her, an over thirty woman trying to dress like a teenager. "Teenile?"

"Don't be a total tramp," her mother would have said. "If he's smart, he's got some imagination. Let him use it."

Seek was already there when she arrived. He looked even better, and at six-foot-five, even taller than his picture. He was still in a suit and tie from a day in court. His tie had a rattlesnake pattern. It fluttered in a draft and was an Armani, probably worth more than her entire wardrobe.

"Your picture doesn't do you justice," he said. "And I know about justice."

He hugged her. A good solid hug, not too forward, but definitely impressed with what he saw in her. She could learn to like this whole Internet dating thing. They sat down for dinner in a nice secluded corner. Luna awaited the phone trick, but almost hoped that Jen forgot to call. Seek was that good. Jen called her exactly at five minutes after the hour. At least the girl was dependable on some things.

"Are you okay?" Jen whispered into the phone.

"Perfect," she said.

"What does he look like?"

Luna looked at Seek. For some reason she wanted to impress Jen, show her that she was a player. "Do you mind if I take your picture? I want to show it to someone."

"Go for it," Seek replied.

Luna clicked a picture on her phone, and e-mailed it to Jen.

"He is *so hot*," Jen replied. She sent her own picture back to Luna. "Show it to him."

"Hey Jen, I thought you had this cop boyfriend."

"Not anymore," Jen said. "It's like ambiguous."

"Why didn't you tell me?"

"Remember when I said it was an emergency, but you didn't want to talk to me since it wasn't a legal emergency?"

"Are you talking to a client?" Seek interrupted, peeved.

"Just a friend," Luna said sheepishly. She showed him Jen's picture on the phone.

"She's hot," Seek said, then asked. "Isn't she that murderer?"

"She's also kinda like a friend," Luna said, putting emphasis on the word "kinda."

Seek's own phone rang before he could answer. He handed Luna her phone back. Seek excused himself to take his call. He frowned as he talked to whoever it was.

"So what do I do?" Luna asked. She instantly regretted that she was asking her own client for advice.

"Don't act too needy," Jen said. "You get that way sometimes. But don't be a total slut either. That's how I get into trouble."

Seek returned and Luna hung up. Luna ordered Cajun shrimp pasta, extra hot. He went with the curry, extra hot. They shared each other's pasta and soon got into a debate over Cajun versus curry. The only awkward spot came when the six-year age gap hit Luna over the head. Seek danced at clubs she had never heard of, and to bands that meant nothing to her. He was way too hip for her, way too hip for Albuquerque. Not necessarily a bad thing.

Luna discussed the case with him in general terms. He knew his way around courthouses and gave her some good advice about dealing with certain judges and prosecutors. His family had set him up with his own practice a year ago, but he was hardly spoiled. In fact, the man was smart as a whip.

"I work my ass off," he said.

"I've still got mine," she said.

"I see that." He smiled and looked at her with an admiration that was just short of lust. No, she hadn't lost it after all.

Luna had never believed in love in first sight. Until now. It had been years since Marlow had gone and she was ready. Really ready. Dinner over, she grabbed some mints to get the Cajun taste out of her mouth.

Seek offered to take her home. So far, so good. He drove a black Lexus convertible, and the inside smelled great—sugar, spice, and everything nice. She felt at home with him, although it bothered her that he was in junior high when she was in college. But those worries subsided when they arrived at the gate. For the moment.

"Do you want to come in?" she asked, expecting a kiss.

"I've got a lot of work tomorrow," he replied, stiffening.

Luna tried to read the moment. Was he gay? Was he married? About to be shipped off to the Army? Something was definitely up. Disappointed, she got out by the gate, then walked to her apartment. Outside her door, she suddenly felt very alone. She was having a post-date panic attack. She knew she had to call Jen. It was not about bonding with a client anymore, she genuinely had to hear a female voice that she could confide in.

But should she show vulnerability in front of a client? It was one thing to show that she was dating a big-time lawyer, but should she let Jen know the date hadn't gone totally as planned? She decided against calling Jen. Instead, she went inside and turned on the TV. In all her agitation, Luna had trouble falling asleep.

As she finally drifted off, she wished she had called Jen. After all, Jen was the only one rooting for her these days.

Chapter Eleven
Criminal Sexual Imagination

THE NEXT MORNING, LUNA called Adam Marin, Jen's boyfriend, or whatever he was, to set up an interview.

"I could drop by your office after five," he said.

She hated to meet anyone in her cramped apartment and explain the lack of office space. Time to put herself in her client's five-inch fuck-me pumps. "Can I just meet you at the crime scene?"

"I could get into a lot of trouble for this," he said. "I'm in enough shit as it is."

"I can get a subpoena, but let's keep it friendly. For Jen's sake."

"All right. I'll meet you there at five-thirty."

She wondered if she should have mentioned Jen. The way he said "all right" indicated that all was not right.

Anxious about meeting Marin, Luna took her usual drug. Exercise. As an athlete at CU she'd received a lifetime membership at the Midtown Athletic Club's "sister club" in Boulder. So, she had a place to swim outside during the hot August day. Midtown was, however, was packed with mothers and all their brats.

After finishing her swim, Luna sat next to a young mother who was rubbing sunscreen on two adorable kids. Maybe it wouldn't be so bad to rub sunscreen on her own kids someday.

"Tick tock, tick tock," her mother's voice said.

Luna went back to the locker room, and looked down at her body as she got into the shower. Because of her constant swimming, her breasts had defied gravity for another year.

"Not going to happen Mom," Luna replied. "I'm not ruining this body, this belly, or these legs just for your posthumous enjoyment."

Luna drove her Saturn out to the volcano's parking lot on the west mesa. It was four o'clock; plenty of time before sunset. The Balloon Fiesta came in the fall, and a few balloonists tried a late afternoon ascent as a warm up. One of them nearly landed on the volcano's top. Was that a rumble she heard? The volcanoes had been dormant for seventy thousand years, but definitely felt restless tonight. The balloonist ascended another hundred yards above the summit, just in case.

Seek had said something about seeing clients all afternoon who were in jail at the MDC. MDC wasn't that far from here. She had an idea. . . .

"Want to see the crime scene?" she asked him on the phone. "I think the volcanoes will erupt tonight. You have to get over here!"

"I like a good eruption."

"Who doesn't? Are you coming?"

A few minutes later, Seek's black Lexus coupe headed up the Paseo del Volcan. Luna liked men with nice cars.

She got in the plush leather seat, and they talked for a while. She wanted to tell him her deep dark secrets, but she was reluctant. She had been so alone in Crater since Marlow had left. Now that she finally had a man, she didn't know what to do with him. She just stared at him and smiled. Luna feared she would get arrested for criminal sexual imagination. But before imagination could turn to reality, lights flashed in the mirror and a police car pulled up behind them.

"We got a call, sorry I'm late. Been waiting long?" Adam Marin asked in a gruff voice as he got out of the car.

Luna looked at Marin, and knew she didn't entirely trust this middle linebacker of a man.

"You mind staying with me for a bit?" she asked Seek.

Seek stared at Marin as if he was wondering if he could take him in a fight. "So did you make sergeant yet?" Seek asked him.

"Fuck you," said Marin. "Those fuckers. That charge was bullshit, but because of that, I'm still stuck."

Seek smiled. "Hey, I just represented the girl on her DWI. I was not the one who sued you for harassing her."

Marin didn't smile, muttered "bitch," and then something else under his breath.

Seek gave him a glance, then answered Luna's question. "Yes, I'll stay with you."

They didn't have much sunlight left. It was an easy five-minute hike on a flat desert trail to the base of the volcano, then a short scramble over black volcanic rocks to the top. No one else was around.

Luna took a moment to take in the view, and tried to imagine fireworks in all directions. What did she call it again, criminal sexual imagination? This would be a great place to screw . . . and a great place to die.

"She did it," Marin said, getting her out of her reverie.

"What are you talking about?"

Marin pointed at the indentation in the ground. It was still there. "Her DNA is all over a dead drug dealer. Do the math."

Marin's voice created a mental picture in Luna's head. A naked Hobbs lay in front of her, his face blue. It was not a pretty picture.

Luna looked at Marin. "Why are you telling me this? I thought you liked her."

Marin said nothing. "I don't know. She talks to you more than she talks to me! She hasn't called me in weeks; too busy. You guys going steady or something?"

He sounded jealous. Luna thought of her old boyfriend, Nico, the cop. Cops must learn "advanced jealousy" as one of their required courses at the academy.

"She's so messed up," Marin said. "She'll do anything. She was in so deep."

"She knew about the drugs that Hobbs was dealing as part of his practice?"

"Of course she knew about the drugs. She would have been an idiot not to, and Jen's no idiot."

Luna shook her head. If it came to believing Jen or Marin, she'd stick with Jen. She went with the Sandrina scenario. "What about Sandrina?" she asked after a moment.

"I'm betting that Hobbs took them both up there at the same time. More bang-bang for his buck."

"She's not a whore," Luna said. More bang-bang for his buck. Luna didn't like the way Marin talked about Jen.

Seek looked at the indentation on the ground, visualizing the bang, bang. He then shared a laugh with Marin, a guy kind of thing.

"You guys shouldn't laugh," Luna said. "This is serious."

"Sorry," Seek said.

"The lab work will prove I'm right," Marin said.

"We'll see," said Luna.

Suddenly Seek's phone rang. "I've got to take this," he said.

He listened, then frowned as he hung up. "One of my client's offices was just raided by the Feds. I've gotta hold his hand. Will you be okay?"

Luna looked over at the indentation in the rocky dirt. There was so much she didn't know about the case. "I want to stay a little longer," she said.

Seek gave her a quick hug, but no kiss. What did that mean? He scrambled down the rocks, hurried to the parking lot, then drove off, dust trailing behind.

Now that she was alone with Marin, she went back to the indentation in the dirt. There was still some dried blood visible. When would the lab come back with the results, so she'd know what was going on? The sun set quicker than she expected; she didn't have much time left up here.

As she stared at the dirt, Luna suddenly felt a heavy hand on her left shoulder.

"Are you alive in there?" Marin asked. "It's like you're in your own little world."

"I just don't see Jen killing anyone," Luna said.

"You underestimate her," he said. "I sure did." The linebacker then put his big right hand on her right shoulder from behind, as if grabbing a running back to save a touchdown.

Luna's instinct for self-preservation kicked in. She was alone with a very big man, and that very big man now had his very big hands on her.

"Could you please take your hands off me," she asked, her voice sounding nervous. "I'm not really comfortable."

Instead, Marin tightened the pressure. She had thought Jen had beheaded the dolls in her room. She now knew he was the real be-header.

"You remind me of her," he said, bringing his hands closer to her neck. It was time for some unnecessary roughness.

He brought his body closer to her from behind. She knew there was no way she could fight him off, but she would sure try.

"My car's down there," she said nervously. "People know I'm here. I'm wearing a wire. I've got a knife. My boyfriend can be back in a minute."

Marin laughed. Seek was already miles down the Paseo. Marin wasn't strangling her yet, but he was inches away from her neck. She felt his pelvis grind the slightest bit against her body.

"Jen likes it hard, you know." He laughed again. "Actually, it doesn't matter what *she* likes, does it now?"

Luna brought her foot down as hard as she could on his foot.

Nothing. The man's entire body was hard. The steroids must have gone all the way down to his toes.

He laughed again and Luna felt her heart beat, or was that the sound of rumbling down below?

Then abruptly, Marin released her. "Just playing with you, that's all. Don't you know when I'm kidding?"

That's what Jen always said. Luna apparently didn't read people very well these days. "I can have your badge for that," she said.

"I checked your reputation, Ms. Crater County. Right now with your credibility, a good defense attorney can tear you a new asshole up on the stand."

He laughed as if that was funny. "A good defense attorney."

Luna nearly caused a rock slide as she ran all the way back to her car.

Chapter Twelve
True Bill

IT WAS GRAND JURY day, time to call Heidi Hawk at District Court. Luna had known Heidi since high school in Crater. Since the town's mines had closed, the great Crater exodus was one way down I-40 to Albuquerque. Heidi had left before the recall election, before things got too crazy.

She's probably one of the handful of people from Crater who wouldn't have voted me out, Luna thought, but then again from Heidi's coldness to her in the mall, she couldn't be sure.

Luna couldn't get inside the grand jury room of course, only prosecutors, witnesses and grand jurors could. Still, Heidi could give her the play-by-play from just outside the door. The prospect of an overly anxious Jen calling every five minutes about the indictment was unbearable. Luna also didn't want to wait with Jen in her bedroom with the decapitated dolls. And Luna's own apartment was too messy, even for Jen.

The New Mexico State Bar building was definitely out. They had scheduled another CLE, this time for prosecutors. Jen had suggested Starbucks, but Jen and double espressos sounded like a deadly combination.

Luna liked the solitude of the Sandia Crest, but Jen had a better idea and suggested the Bosque, the groves of cottonwood trees that ran the entire length of the Rio Grande in Albuquerque. The

Bosque was a giant state park, maybe twenty miles long. The forest—a quarter mile wide on each bank—included the only trees in Albuquerque not planted by man.

Luna felt a moment of anxiety. She had recovered from last night's near assault from Marin, but she would be relatively safe with Jen, right? She hated to say it, but Jen was indeed her "kinda like" friend. When she picked Jen up, Luna didn't know what to make of her kinda like friend's latest tight t-shirt, a picture of a young, crimson, demon woman, complete with forked tail over the caption RED HOT MAMA!

Luna parked at one of the entrances to the park, at the end of Candelaria Boulevard in the semi-rural North Valley neighborhood of Albuquerque. People had ranches out here, and it smelled like it. The Rio made the atmosphere as humid as the desert could get. Unfortunately, recent arson fires had devastated much of the park; it looked like a moonscape with scattered greenery. The park was technically closed, because fire danger was still so high. Despite the risk, the park's only security was a length of tangled, yellow crime scene tape.

Heidi called just as Jen and Luna ducked under the tape. "The first case of the morning came back early. They're starting yours in ten minutes. The D.A. is Roberta—"

Luna didn't catch the last name. Didn't Seek have a sister who was a D.A.? "Who are they calling as first witness?"

"Officer Juan Oñate, the arresting officer."

That was Cop Number One, the smart one.

"Thanks," Luna said. "Call me when you know something."

After walking through a grove of tree stumps that had been battered by fire, Jen took her to a long stretch of cottonwoods that had miraculously missed the devastation. The old-growth trees were thick here, and it felt much cooler in the shade.

They both heard people nearby, so Luna felt safe. "Let's stop here," she said, pointing to a fairly open space within earshot of the others.

In a clearing by the water, two teenagers made out, clothes bare-ly on. Out beyond a tree, two other teenagers tempted fate by smok-ing the world's largest joint. Luna knew one toke in Jen's lungs meant lock-up for the duration. Jen coughed ominously.

"Let's go," Luna said, "away from the smoke."

"Whatever," Jen said. "Smoking is not going to kill you. You seem all paranoid today."

"I have a right to be paranoid. I'm alone with an accused killer."

"You're my lawyer. I'm not going to kill you."

One of the stoners overheard them. "Yo, if she tries to kill you, just yell!"

Luna frowned. "Dude," Luna said, trying to sound hip, "there's a fire hazard here, you shouldn't smoke. Anything."

The boy put out his joint after one final toke, a real doozy. Despite the rescue offer, Luna knew she couldn't count on him for safety. Jen pointed to a path through the last remaining grove. "This way."

They hiked on a twisting dirt trail along the Rio until they reached a large, flat rock near a fallen tree that was leaning out over the water. Luna could imagine the Sandias and the Isletas, the clos-est tribes to Albuquerque, climbing out on the thick limb, dipping their feet in the river and forgetting about the evil white man.

"I used to come here during my wild days," Jen said.

"How wild?"

She pointed to a spot by the river. "I lost my virginity right over there."

"Way too much information," Luna said, but she was curious anyway. "You mean on that tree sticking out over the river?" Luna asked.

Jen nodded.

Luna tried to imagine the contortions involved. It would be hard not to get your back wet, but she supposed that was part of the fun.

"Well, not exactly the first time," Jen said. "Technically the third." She giggled. Jen had taken off her shoes and dangled her feet in the water. Luna half expected her to skinny dip, but Jen kept her sweats on.

Luna couldn't stand the sultry Rio air. She went barefoot and stripped to her sports bra. She found a big rock closer to the Rio and dangled just the tips of her toes. The water of the Rio was dirty, of course, but back in Crater she swam in much worse.

Jen looked relatively relaxed hanging three feet over the river on the edge of a sturdy branch. Luna relaxed too. They said nothing for a moment.

Luna felt like falling asleep right there, but she had some residual anxiety from last night's near assault. "How are things between you and Adam Marin?" Luna asked.

Jen fidgeted and the tree branch shook slightly.

"Why?"

"We talked last night. He nearly attacked me."

"He can be like that," she said. "He stopped though, didn't do anything, right?"

"Yeah, but it scared the hell out of me."

"He can be like that," Jen said again, as if that was explanation enough. Her eyes darted to follow a school of silvery minnows. The fish quickly swam downstream, and Jen's eyes kept pace.

"We wrestled a lot," Jen said after the fish finally left her line of sight. "He usually won."

"He said that you did it." Luna looked at Jen, searching for a reaction.

"He's just saying that. He's all full of shit. He's all jealous. I think we're pretty much history."

"History? Are you seeing someone else?"

Jen laughed at the absurdity of it, and splashed water on Luna. "Yeah . . . you!"

"This is serious, Jen."

The phone rang. Heidi again. "They're calling Officer Carson." That must be Cop Number Two, the dumb one.

"Just text message me," Luna said before hanging up.

"When will we find out the verdict?" Jen asked.

"We'll see. . . ." God, she sounded like her mother when she said that.

Carson was relatively quick. Next came the forensic experts.

The two women sat and talked about everything except the case. Luna was just following Marlow's advice, right?

Jen didn't stop talking. Maybe she had shot up on truth serum for breakfast. School was good. Adam was bad. Things were tough with her mom, even before this. She didn't talk with her dad. Jen had taken piano lessons of course, plus violin lessons, guitar lessons, even oboe lessons, and had dropped them all after a few weeks. So much for the myth of the overachieving Asian music prodigy.

Jen asked Luna a few questions, but Luna was still reluctant to share. She tried staying curt: she missed Crater County, missed being a big deal as D.A., but was glad to be back in civilization. Her first boyfriend, Nico the cop, was dead. Her last boyfriend, Marlow, had gone to Hollywood.

"I can tell you're really lonely," Jen said. "You miss your old boyfriend. You miss your mom."

Luna said nothing. There were times when Jen was capable of focus. This was one of them.

"I bet you miss your dad even more," she said. "I can tell you have good memories."

Luna stared at the muddy current as it inched past the sandy shore. Why the hell was she out here with an accused killer here in the middle of a dark forest and a river that could float her body all the way to Mexico—or at least to the Elephant Butte reservoir? And why was she having a good time doing so?

The answer to both was obvious. She had no one else to hang with in the entire world, and she now liked Jen. It wasn't about Marlow's "fake bonding" any more. Jen had crossed from "almost a friend" to a true friend. There definitely was something beyond lawyer-client. She just couldn't put her finger on it. There was also something about Jen that Luna had to know, something she already suspected. "Jen, can I ask you something that isn't about the case?"

"Sure," Jen said. "Anything."

"Did something bad happen to you when you were little?"

Jen nodded. She knew exactly what Luna meant. She came back on land and sat next to Luna—leaned next to her. "One of my camp counselors, a white guy. A couple of times. I didn't say anything to anyone at the time. I was too freaked." She didn't have to say anything more to Luna. "How about you?"

Luna took a breath. This was about telling something that she'd kept buried for a long time. This was real. Jen had shared with her; she had to share with Jen. "This guy who worked for my dad—Jonah Ruiz, a pharmacy tech. He tried to follow me around and hug me, that sort of thing. He even came into the bathroom while I was there, tried to . . . I was like seven."

"What happened?" Jen put her arm around Luna. Luna leaned closer to Jen.

"My dad found him in the bathroom with me, right as he was about to . . . before anything really happened. My dad beat the shit out of him and sent his ass to prison. God, I loved my dad!"

They sat still for a moment. Luna hadn't told anyone that in a long, long time. She sure needed someone to rescue her from the Ruizes of the world these days. "Let's talk about something else," Luna said.

"Well, I can tell you really like this new guy," Jen said, trying to be helpful. "He sounds great."

"I sure hope so."

They sat for another moment, a strange silence, comfortable, yet awkward at the same time.

Thankfully the phone beeped, and another text message ran across her phone. "Sandrina just testified. They're not calling Dellagio. They're done, sending it to the grand jury to deliberate."

Neither woman said another word. The water flowed past, but neither moved a muscle. They waited silently for fifteen minutes, and watched the branches flow down the Rio. A few fish tried to be birds, but failed. Finally the text came again, way too soon. "True Bill."

"Is that like *Kill Bill?* Who's Bill?" Jen asked.

"It means you've been officially indicted. It means that the fun is about to start."

Luna expected the phone to ring one more time. The U.S .Attorney with the Darth Vader voice owed her a call. She held the phone in her hand, waiting for it to vibrate, but nothing.

"What are you waiting for?" Jen asked.

"I don't know yet."

Luna dropped Jen off at her house. Neither parent was there, but Luna didn't want to go inside.

"One more thing," Jen said as she took off her seat belt. "I'm pregnant."

Chapter Thirteen
Double Helix

IT WAS TIME TO play lawyer again. Luna kept bugging the district attorney's office for the rest of the case documents, especially the forensics.

"All circuits are busy," the voice said over and over and over again.

Luna kept trying. This time she only lasted thirty seconds before disconnection. She finally remembered her old extension, 123, and dialed. A woman answered.

"I'm sorry, I was trying to reach the violent crimes division," Luna said. "Who has the discovery on the Jen Song case?"

The woman reluctantly connected her to another secretary. Unfortunately, Luna had to leave a message. Finally at three forty-five, she got a return call.

"There's a lot of discovery files," the secretary warned her in a high-pitched voice, with a strange emphasis on the word lot. "You do know there's a charge for copies, don't you?"

The high-voiced secretary then quoted an exorbitant price per page. Luna didn't have the money, so she reluctantly volunteered to go to the district attorney's office in person to decide which pages she absolutely had to pay for.

The Second Judicial District Attorney's bland four-story office building sat on the same corner as the Metro and District courts, but faced their backs, as if the cooler courthouse buildings had shunned it. Over a hundred lawyers nestled within the four stories of the building, segregated into various teams with various team leaders. Back when she was a D.A. in Crater, it was just her, and by the end it wasn't even that.

Luna had lasted here in the Metro division for a few months right out of law school, and had been fired for her "lack of focus," a polite way of saying she missed too much work for her Olympic training. They had still not forgiven her.

Inside, Luna was stopped by a receptionist named Beverly. Beverly was a dead ringer for Jennifer Lopez, and she should have been on a stage rather than behind a crumbling wooden desk covered with murder files. Luna showed her battered bar card, but Beverly would not let Luna inside without a case number. Luna couldn't remember it off hand, so she called Jen to get her date of birth so Beverly could look up the case and give her clearance.

"Are you planning a surprise party for me, Luna?" Jen asked. "It's this Monday." She then gave the year. Luna wrote it down and gave it to Beverly.

Beverly reluctantly looked up the file number. Everything checked out. She gave Luna a white badge, then smiled. "Good luck."

Luna passed through a metal detector then made her way to the elevators. When the elevator door opened, a platoon of people dressed in black suits came out, guarding someone in the middle. Had the President come to town?

Behind her she heard a deputy yell, "Mr. Dellagio, my sister got in an accident. She needs your help!"

She heard a voice from within the platoon call back to the deputy, singing in a whiny Chicago accent. "*The only name you need to know . . . LLL-AGIO.*"

The platoon exited the building.

"Why was Dellagio here?" Criminal lawyers came to the building all the time, but a big-time civil lawyer like Dellagio was a rare sight.

The only reason he would be here would be as a suspect in a case. He must have had the platoon with him to show that he was hardly the usual suspect they saw around here.

Luna finally got to the east side of the fourth floor, an open space bounded by cubicles for officer interviews. In each cubicle, a lawyer pounded a cop about "gaze nystagimus" in yet another DWI case. It had only been a few months since her last DWI case, but it still took Luna a few moments to remember that gaze nystagimus was something that cops looked for in a driver's eyes that indicated drunkenness. Defense attorneys always objected to it, but judges always let it in.

Danika, the secretary for the Violent Crimes Division, was a Halle Berry look-alike with an infectious laugh. She nearly crumbled under the weight of the overstuffed box in her arms.

"And this is just the first one," she said with a smile. She then hurried back with a second box.

"Those will be a good start," Luna said.

"We haven't organized them yet," Danika replied. "You can come back another time to see the rest."

"I'm fine," Luna said. As she took the box to a cubicle, she saw Adam Marin get up from another cubicle, done with his interview on a politician's solicitation charge. Marin gave her an intimidating glance, then smiled, but didn't say a word. He headed out the door, mumbling something to himself.

Luna heard the word "bitch" under his breath. She didn't know whether he was referring to her, Jen, or both.

Luna scanned the big boxes. She had an idea that the DNA reports might prove whether Jen had actually slept with Hobbs or not. If so, she'd have some idea whether her client was telling the truth.

Luna opened the first box, dug in quickly, but couldn't find the DNA reports near the top. She did find the arrest warrant for Ed Hobbs, and that would be helpful. Hobbs had been picked up one hundred miles north of the border, near the strangely named town of Truth or Consequences (T or C), New Mexico. T or C had the final border patrol checkpoint on the interstate to snare people who had dropped their guard and thought they were already home free.

Dogs had alerted on Hobbs at the checkpoint. The guards had opened the boxes in the back and found a cornucopia of prescription drugs. The street value was in the hundreds of thousands, and unless Hobbs had the worst case of sexual dysfunction, cancer, AIDS, shoulder pain and diarrhea in history, they most definitely were not for personal use. The drugs came from "origin unknown," but "Mexico is the most likely suspect" according to the report.

"Mexico is the most likely suspect?" Luna laughed. That really narrowed it down.

A few inches into the box, still no DNA, but there were a few police reports from interviews the cops had conducted. She hoped to find a name like "Mayhem Moreno," or someone else from Crater. She wanted to know if she had seen Jen before. No Mayhem to be found. She didn't see any other familiar names either.

Luna dug deeper, all the way to the bottom, and found a sworn affidavit from Sandrina Santos. She tried to decipher Sandrina's handwritten statement, but it was illegible. One box down, and Luna didn't know much more than when she started.

Luna started on the next pile from the box, the officer reports. The copies were illegible; she couldn't make out anything.

Luna had long since abandoned a semblance of a plan. She emptied the contents of both boxes on the table and looked at things randomly. She found a letter from the phone company saying that due to computer foul-ups at the service provider, there were no records for Jen, Hobbs, Dellagio or Sandrina for July fourth. Luna did not know whether that was a good thing or not.

Luna found one folder labeled TOXICOLOGY REPORT. Hobbs definitely had drugs in his system. He also showed evidence of strangulation. Luna hoped that the next page of the report would give a definitive answer, but she couldn't find the page with the diagnosis she wanted.

Luna frowned. She had once been this disorganized too, and she'd been voted out of office for it. Where the hell were the DNA reports?

Luna finally found them on the floor. She took a deep breath as she figured that the whole case came down to DNA.

The first page listed the various swabs taken from Jen and Sandrina. Sandrina was most definitely there—her DNA was listed as a mix of Germanic and South American Hispanic. Perfect match. Even better, it showed proof that she'd been the one who had sexual intercourse with Hobbs. Jen might have been there, might have killed him even, but at least she hadn't fucked him. Hooray!

Jen's DNA report indicated a match to the blood found on the body. Luna frowned. On the next page, the report listed Jen's results as an Asiatic, Southwestern Hispanic mix.

Mix?

Jen might look Hawaiian, but both her parents were Korean, right? There should be no mix. Either the experts had made a mistake and the evidence could be discounted, or someone besides Jen was there with Sandrina.

Luna savored the moment. One simple "motion to dismiss" and the $100,000 would be hers. She imagined a shiny new mountain bike, a shiny new wardrobe, and a shiny new boyfriend . . . not necessarily in that order. Thank you Watson and Crick for inventing DNA! Luna remembered her high school biology textbook with its double helix, the famed DNA sequence on the cover. She had defaced the double helix with all kinds of girlish graffiti.

Then it hit her like a ton of bricks. Luna tried to dial her phone, but it was dead—she had forgotten to charge the battery. She tried to put the phone down on the table, but it fell on the floor. The floor must have been incredibly hard, as her phone broke. Luna picked up the pieces, but the phone was still dead. She now knew who she had to talk to. She drove like crazy and nearly took out an ambulance on the way.

• • • • •

Today, Nurse Song was the reception nurse for the emergency room at UNM Hospital, the main public hospital for Albuquerque. Luna's father had done his residency here, right out of medical school. Luna herself had been born here.

"*You can check out any time you want, but you can never leave,*" Luna sang out loud as she found Nurse Song's station. Luna shoved the DNA document into Nurse Song's face. "Jen is my half-sister, isn't she?"

Jen would have one hell of a surprise party.

Act II: LASER GEISHA BLUE

Chapter Fourteen
Late Motion to Withdraw

LUNA AND NURSE SONG stood just outside the hospital door. Nurse Song smoked a cigarette, her first in twenty years, she claimed. "Your father and I had an affair," she said at last.

"How could you?"

"Because of you, Luna. I saw how beautiful you were as a little girl, and I wanted a child like you. My husband couldn't have babies."

She paused for a long moment, emotions warring inside of her. "Once I got pregnant, I moved here before anyone knew, and gave birth to Jen. A few months later I heard about your father. . . ."

She stopped, choked up with emotion. Dr. Cruz's death must have devastated her as well.

"Did he know?" Luna asked. "My father?"

"I never told him, but he knows . . . I mean he knew. I gave my notice and left Crater fairly quickly. My husband figured it out of course, but somehow we stayed together. I was taught not to get divorced. So was he."

"And Jen?"

"I haven't told her," Nurse Song said. "She doesn't suspect anything. She's not very bright sometimes."

Luna wondered if Nurse Song and her daughter talked at all.

Nurse Song blew some more smoke. Luna coughed; she had no tolerance for smoke whatsoever.

"So that's why you really hired me. Because of my father?"

"I hired you because I heard you were good." She didn't say that with much conviction.

"I have an ethical obligation to withdraw," Luna said. "I don't know if I can be objective about this case."

"Do what you have to do," Nurse Song said. "But I want you to stay. I guess."

Hardly a vote of confidence. Luna sighed. "I don't think you understand. You're not my client. Jen is. I have to do what she wants me to do."

Luna didn't want to get back in the car just yet. She hurried to a pay phone.

"Jen, I got the DNA results and I talked to your Mom to confirm it." Luna waited a bit, gathered up the courage. "You know that I am your half-sister."

She had expected shock.

"Duh. . . ."

"You knew?" Luna asked. "Your mother swears she never told you."

"I knew from the moment I saw you. I mean, look at my dad. My Korean dad. He looks nothing like me. It's so obvious. I'm not as stupid as you think I am—not as stupid as my mom thinks I am."

"I don't think you're stupid." Luna said. Time for a lie. "Your mom doesn't think you're stupid either."

There was a long beat. Jen stayed silent.

"I can withdraw," Luna said cautiously. "I don't know if I can do this being related to you. There might be a conflict of interest."

"Why would you withdraw?" Jen sounded hurt. "I totally want you to be my lawyer. I want you to be my sister too, and my friend. I need all the help I can get. Why would there be a conflict? You're on my side, right?"

Luna was stumped. She sure needed a sister right now, even a half-sister would do. "Other then objectivity, I can't really think of a reason."

"Neither can I," said Jen. "We're pleading not guilty, at arraignment on Monday, aren't we?"

"Of course."

That afternoon Luna took a long swim at Midtown to avoid the dry heat of the desert. After seventy laps or so, she got out and sunned herself. She didn't worry about skin cancer. With her father's dark pigment, the sun would just bounce off harmlessly, right? She looked around at the mothers and the world's largest pregnant women who hid themselves in the shade.

She called Seek from the outdoor phone by the pool. "Want to go on a real hot date tomorrow?" she asked. "My client's getting arraigned. We can call it . . . a trial date."

"I wouldn't miss it for the world," he said. "I guess you could say that I'm 'courting' you."

Some water from the pool splashed as a kid did a belly flop. She almost yelled at the kid, but stopped.

"Aren't you worried I might fall for your client?" Seek asked.

Luna said nothing. She actually was jealous of Jen, deep down. "Remember, she killed the last man in her life. He went out with a bang."

"I like dangerous women," he said. "Like you."

"Thank you," she said.

They hung up and Luna looked at the pool and stared at the kids. She wondered briefly what any children of Seek and hers would look like. With the Cruz bloodline, brains, and endurance, and Seek's height and power, the results would be awesome.

All right, Jen was crazy, and she was crazy too, but Seek seemed pretty sane. He would make up for the defects in the Cruz genes.

Another baby cried. She hated that sound. No, she didn't really want to be a mother after all, but as she saw the boy dog paddle in the pool she had a great feeling . . . she would soon be an aunt!

It was perfect, absolutely perfect. The Cruz bloodline would continue after all. Her dad's family traced a line back to Cervantes in Spain, and also back to Montezuma of the Aztecs. Her dad had been the one good thing in her life. His bloodline deserved to continue. Sure, that asshole Marin would contribute a line or two of code, but her dad's inherent goodness should counteract the recessive asshole gene.

Luna smiled. She wouldn't have to ruin her body, or have a child to care for, but she would have all the benefits. She'd help the child avoid the mistakes she had made, and be a better aunt than her mother had been a mother.

She then realized that if Jen went away for life—and that was a distinct possibility—she'd have to be the mother after all.

Chapter Fifteen
Zoo Docket

SINCE THE JUDGE FOR Jen's case always held his District Court docket call on Monday afternoons, Luna spent the morning with Jen at a big department store in Coronado Center. Luna had found a tear in her best arraignment outfit, so she needed a new one. She also wanted to have some control over what Jen wore. The Gothic Lolita look would certainly be a negative factor in any pre-sentence report. Docket call would be Jen's birthday party, so a new arraignment outfit would have to be her present.

The store was empty; most people had real jobs this time of the day. Luna felt guilty to have so much freedom, not a good emotion before an arraignment. They found a helpful sales clerk at the cosmetics counter, an exotic dark-haired beauty named Thelma.

"I want a face that says 'not guilty,'" Luna said. "For both of us."

"I'm not a magician," Thelma said with a smile. "You might have to spend some real money on some product."

Luna rarely wore much make-up. Still, she could appreciate Thelma's genius with blush and concealer. Luna soon looked like a young reporter about to get her own anchor slot.

Thelma also did up Jen. Thank god she'd taken out her nose stud. Thelma worked her magic, and the results were equally spectacular. "I guess she's just naturally prettier than I am," Luna sighed.

Thelma tried to sell some overpriced product, but Luna politely refused. "We're going to spend all our money on clothes today."

Thelma reluctantly had a passing clerk take them to women's suits. Jen wanted something slutty, of course, and Luna wanted something conservative. They finally found a suit that was a good compromise—gray, but showing a lot of leg.

"I saw it first," Luna said. "And I'm the big sister."

Jen shrugged and found something similar, but in a darker shade.

"Will that be cash or store charge?" the clerk asked. "Today only, you can save 25 percent if you open a store credit card account with us."

"I'll open an account." Luna said as she smiled at Jen. "Happy birthday." She then gave her information. The clerk called it in, and repeated the numbers a few times.

As they waited, Luna had a panic attack. God must be telling her something.

The clerk hung up the phone, a frown on her immaculately made-up face. "I'm sorry," she said, "but you've been denied by the credit department."

"Can I co-sign for her?" Jen asked helpfully.

"Do you two live together?"

"Kinda," Jen said. "She's my sister."

The clerk had a dubious look on her face, but after squinting a bit, she did see the resemblance. "I'm half-Japanese," she said. "I can tell these things."

Luna was sure this had to be some kind of violation of ethical canons, but damn it, she did want the new outfit. Jen was approved and the two sisters now had a joint account. Blood was thicker than water, but credit cards were thicker than blood.

That afternoon, Luna clashed with the metal detector in the Second Judicial District Courthouse. First it was her jewelry, then her watch, then her shoes. The large sheriff's deputy nearly made her undress before uncovering aluminum gum wrappers in a pocket. Jen breezed right through, although the deputy sheriff looked as if he wanted to frisk her body cavities.

Nurse Song had to miss this one, saying that she'd missed way too much work already on Jen's account. Perhaps it was for the best.

The Second Judicial District Courthouse was a bubble about to burst—it had a gigantic atrium and wide walkways, but the small courtrooms were filled to the brim with benches and people. In the hallway on the fourth floor, they passed a bald lawyer in a bad suit mad-dogging a younger lawyer. "I'm going to blow you out of the water," the older guy said.

The younger lawyer smiled, "I like a good blow job." His attention quickly turned to Luna. "Good luck," he said. She recognized him vaguely. Was he one of the guys who'd sent her a picture over the Internet? Was he the one who had made the Jewish Juniper joke?

Jen stared at the guy. "That was my lawyer for my DWI, the one with 'yellow fever.' "

The two women hurried to the ceremonial courtroom on the fourth floor. She had hoped she would be the only one on for the day, but unfortunately, it was "Zoo Docket." Luna thought the lawyers were kidding, but every judge in the district officially had a Zoo Docket once a month. There were nearly a hundred criminals listed and all would get their daily feeding of justice by the end of the day. Zoo Docket wasn't completely like a real zoo, because here there were no cages, and the tranquilizer guns had real bullets.

The media formed their own monkey house in the rear of the courtroom. Luna recognized the teenaged reporter, and a few others from national news. Dead druggie lawyers were big news.

"No comment," Luna said to each monkey in turn as she entered the courtroom.

Luna could have waived arraignment of course, but she didn't want to risk jeopardizing Jen's conditions of release without having a chance to talk before a judge. Besides, without new B-roll, the media would endlessly replay that same little shove from the booking.

Another young lawyer, a public defender, held a stack of files and shouted names into the gallery. "Daniel Salazar? Raul Lopez? Mike Gallegos?" he shouted. "You're on my calendar for the day."

No answer.

"OJ Simpson?" the young lawyer went on. "Martha Stewart? Michael Jackson? Fatty Arbuckle? Galileo? Socrates? Jesus Christ?"

A titter came from the crowd, but nothing from the other lawyers. Apparently the lawyer did this every Zoo.

The courtroom belonged to Judge Kurtz. Kurtz had been in a wheelchair all his life, and helped make the place disabled-friendly. Luna knew she wouldn't catch a break with Kurtz on her first case in Albuquerque.

Who was the Zoo clerk, Luna wondered? Luna didn't want to show ignorance in front of her client, so she made Jen sit in the row in the furthest back corner on the right side, all the way against the wall, away from the media monkey house.

Luna checked out the jury box up front, where the incarcerated defendants sat. It did indeed smell like a zoo on a humid day before cleaning. She recognized a few unfriendly faces from her days as a D.A. in Crater, including the infamous Mayhem Moreno.

"Bitch," Mayhem muttered under his breath. Apparently his eighteen-month sentence in the Crater County Detention Center, a.k.a. the Discount Prison, hadn't taught him a lesson. Luna remembered why she hated Mayhem. He had tried to buy a plea by saying he could destroy a mythical group of people called the Mondragon cartel, but of course clammed up at the last minute. "Those guys are all loco," he had said.

Luna had thrown the book at him. Now Luna feared that he would throw the book back, but luckily he was in shackles. Mayhem glared at her.

The Oakland Raiders guy from the pharmacy, Cruz, sat next to Mayhem in the jury box. He now wore orange like the rest of them, apparently he had been picked up for his various illegal actions. That guy did get around, but he looked naked without his black cap. Was he dealing on the inside now? Luna glanced at the docket. "Raider" had just two counts of possession of a controlled substance, not even trafficking. He'd probably get a reasonable bond and be out by the end of the afternoon.

Luna then continued her quest for the right person to check in with. The probation officer shook his head, and said nothing. The pre-trial services director, (who made it a distinct point to say he was "not with the probation department,") waved her away immediately. After chatting up the drug court supervisor and the petite woman who turned out to be the bailiff, Luna finally asked a paralegal intern who pointed out the correct table.

She checked in with the Zoo clerk, a polite woman who wore safari-style khakis. Jen was thirty-fourth on the docket, with Sandrina Santos right before her at thirty-third.

As Luna turned away from the Zoo Clerk, she saw Seek in the back. His suit was dark charcoal, and looked great with his dark hair. Seek sat next to Jen, and the crowds forced them almost on each other's laps. Seek stared at Jen. She hadn't yet started to show, but she was beyond voluptuous, and had that womanly glow. Jen was talking with Seek, and by the way she touched his shoulder, it looked more like flirting than a legal discussion. Pregnant with one man's baby and flirting with another. Jen touched his shoulder again. The girl sure had ADHD when it came to men.

Judge Kurtz called court to order while Luna was still in the front. The entire zoo hushed up immediately, as if the wrong word meant getting fed to the lions. Luna slinked across the wide courtroom floor to the back, and Kurtz gave her a dirty look. The judge pointedly said nothing until Luna had taken a seat. The judge then raced through the first thirty cases or so in little more than an hour, less like a zoo and more like a horse race.

The poor public defender was evidently covering for his entire office during a flu epidemic. "I'm Meryl Streep today," he said after standing in for lawyers named Lopez, Shattuck, Eisenberg and Park. "I'm going to play everyone in the office."

He finally got to play himself, his own case in which he represented Mr. Raider. The judge apparently wasn't pleased with the public defender's performance and actually raised Mr. Raider's bond.

The judge then called State vs. Sandrina Santos.

Sandrina just had to make an entrance. A guard brought her in through a side door. Even in handcuffs and leg shackles she made a fashion statement. Her jumpsuit was red, and when her blond hair, locked in long pony-tail, swung, Luna read what was printed on the back of her jumpsuit: HIGH RISK INMATE.

Sandrina strutted, as if she was looking for a pole to swing around. Luna could see that men wanted to stuff dollar bills into the big gap in the front of the red jumpsuit. They all thought that going out with a bang, bang, bang with Sandrina Santos on the fourth of the July sure sounded like a good way to go.

The judge caught his breath. "Button your shirt all the way up!" he said to Sandrina. "That's not what you said the last time," Sandrina said under her breath, before complying.

"Your honor, Shuba Assed for Ms. Santos," a woman in a head-scarf said as she hurried to the podium.

"One million dollars, cash or surety," Judge Kurtz said, not letting anyone say anything. "In light of your record before this court, Ms. Santos, you've been a very bad girl."

"That's what they pay me for your honor," Sandrina said. She then whispered something to Assed. Assed looked pained, but then faced the judge. "Your honor, it is my obligation as a zealous advocate to tell you that Ms. Santos wishes a brief furlough to visit her dying mother in Rio de Janeiro."

The judge laughed. ""I don't care if she posts a ten million dollar bond—she can't visit her mother anywhere, dead or alive."

Shit. This guy really meant business, and if an unbuttoned

Sandrina Santos couldn't sway him, absolutely nothing could.

As Sandrina was walked out, she stared at Jen and made a gesture with her mouth, something either sexual or cannibalistic. Cannibal cunnilingus? Jen wilted in her seat.

"Chan Wol Song a.k.a. Jen Song," the judge said next. Luna and Jen had to cross back over an entire row, including Seek, to get to the middle aisle. Did Jen just give him a quick lap dance as she passed over him? Seek sure had a smile on his face.

Mayhem muttered something under his breath to Mr. Oakland Raider as Luna went up to the podium.

Luna didn't get the name of the pregnant prosecutor who joined them, and she felt very self-conscious. Seek was behind them and could compare the two of them side by side. Jen glanced back at Seek, and smiled. The cameras rolled. Luna came alive in the spotlight. If only she could stay in this light forever.

Jen looked up at her with respect. "Do what you got to do," she whispered. They were a team again . . . for the moment at least.

Luna said her magic words. The judge quickly went through the rest of the ritual.

"Conditions of release?" he asked, very much aware of the cameras rolling.

The pregnant prosecutor hesitated and Luna seized the moment. "Your honor, my client has no criminal record. She has already posted a large bond. I can assure you that she has kept in constant contact with me . . . almost too much constant contact."

The judge nodded. "What does the State have to say?"

The pregnant prosecutor said nothing. She looked back at someone for guidance. Jen clutched Luna's hand. "Will I have to go to jail until this is over?" she whispered.

The judge nodded at a big deputy, who moved toward Jen. Mayhem muttered again to Mr. Raider. Jen squeezed even tighter.

The pregnant prosecutor must have received a signal. "Your honor, we have no objection to her remaining out of custody on bond pending trial."

The judge looked shocked. "Are you sure?" He sounded like Luna's dad when he said that.

"Yes, your honor."

"Definitely no objection on our part, your honor!" Luna nearly shouted.

"Very well," he said. "Ms. Song will remain under house arrest and will only be allowed to leave the premises in the company of her mother or her attorney. However, there is one thing I must make very clear to you."

Jen wilted under his stare.

"You are under house arrest which makes you officially a resident of the Metropolitan Detention Center. If you leave your premises alone, if you leave the state of New Mexico, if you even leave Bernalillo County, unless it's official court business, and most definitely if you leave the United States, it will be considered 'escape from jail,' an entirely new felony. The further you go, the worse the degree, especially if you cross state or Federal borders. It will most definitely be a factor in sentencing *when* you are convicted."

The Judge faced Luna. "And Ms. Cruz, as her third party custodian, *you* are responsible for this young lady's whereabouts. I can send you to jail on contempt if she violates. Are you sure you want to take that responsibility?"

There's that dreaded "are you sure?" question again, Luna thought. Luna looked at her sister. Blood was thicker than contempt, right? "Yes, I'm sure," Luna said. But was she?

The cameras kept rolling after Judge Kurtz gave a trial date in six months. Painfully aware of the red lights, Luna escorted Jen out of the courtroom. Luna shut the double doors behind them, and breathed relief that she had escaped the zoo and made it to safety. Jen nearly collapsed in her arms.

"That's your birthday present," Luna said. "Freedom."

Out in the hallway, Seek hurried to talk to them. He really did look like he was about to take off into the air as he ran.

Which of us is he coming to see? Luna noticed that Jen strutted just the tiniest bit. So Luna strutted as well.

Seek made it to within breathing distance. Suddenly a large African American man in a black suit and black tie came over to them, blocking his way. Luna's first impression was that he was a hit man out of an old noir movie. Another man wore a gray suit with a red and blue striped tie that just shouted "Fed." Luna figured out who they were immediately.

"I'm Jorge Washington of the U.S. Attorney's Office," the man said in that amazing voice of his. It was much louder and deeper in person than over the phone. "And this is Agent Griego with the F.B.I."

Luna felt Jen stiffen as Jen leaned in closer to her, nearly hiding behind her. It wasn't quite a hug, but Jen used Luna as an eclipse from the two big men.

Luna looked at Washington. He was in his early forties but had a *gravitas* about him, like he was indeed the father of his country.

"Would you both come with me?" With that voice, he was Darth Vader again.

"Do we have a choice?" Luna asked.

Vader didn't answer. He really did have some kind of magnetic power. They found themselves following him as Seek was left behind in Vader's dust.

Chapter Sixteen
OCDTEF

VADER USHERED THEM DOWN a back stairway, out a side door, and guided them to the U.S. Attorneys Office in a twenty-two story building, the tallest building in New Mexico. The apex was a reddish pyramid that fit nicely in the desert landscape.

He then took them into his office in the northeast corner of the building. The sign on his wall said he was in charge of OCDTEF, which Luna figured meant something like Organized Crime, Drug Trafficking and God knows what else. Inside, the office featured a magnificent view of the downtown area and the Sandia Mountains. When Luna sat down, she looked down at a beautiful Persian rug. "Spoils of war," Vader said with a smile. The Middle Eastern and South American artifacts spread throughout the room apparently came from conquered drug dealers or terrorists. Vader did not go through an explanation of each of his trophies, although he clearly wanted to.

Vader poured coffee. "From Afghanistan," he said. "A Tora Bora blend."

"My mom used to make that for my dad," Luna commented politely.

Jen sipped hers, and it perked her up like a shot of adrenaline. Her eyes followed the traffic below in each direction. Luna put her hand on her shoulder; the touch once again calmed Jen down.

"Anything said here can be used against her, right?" Luna asked.

"Quite frankly, no," Vader said, genuinely surprised by Luna's question. "This would be considered a settlement negotiation and those aren't admissible, of course."

Luna began calculating the grades that a guy like Vader had needed to land a job like this. U.S. Attorneys were the best of the best. She'd been rejected, naturally. Luna looked at Vader's diplomas—one from Notre Dame, the other from a New York City law school she had never heard of. Vader had played football at Notre Dame, and still had the build and stature of a running quarterback.

Luna took a glance at Agent Griego and tried to size him up. Luna knew that F.B.I. agents, even the dumb ones like Griego, had photographic memories. She had failed the entrance exam for the F.B.I. because of it. Well . . . that and the polygraph. Griego looked as if he could pass a polygraph with a gun pointed at his head, but he'd have trouble spelling the word without getting someone to prompt him the "poly."

"Why are we here?" Luna asked. "Her case is in State court."

"We can take over jurisdiction on the trafficking, as it may have crossed state and national borders," Vader said.

"Even the murder could be considered part of a drug conspiracy," Griego piped in. His voice sounded like a mongoose next to Vader the lion.

Vader breathed deep, and sucked the air out of the room with his next statement. "Accomplice to a drug conspiracy murder would make your client eligible for the death penalty."

Jen couldn't help but mutter "I didn't murder anyone" loud enough for everyone in the room to hear. Jen was beyond nervous now, and looked as if she needed to throw up. Actually, she ran to an open trash can in the corner of the room and did so. She let it all out, right there in the office. A few chunks spilled onto Vader's nice Persian rug, and formed their own little patterns. Spoils of war indeed.

• • • • •

"Are you all right?" Luna asked as she helped Jen to the bathroom down the hall.

Jen threw up a few more times while Luna held Jen's hair back, and patted her on the back.

"Morning sickness or stress?" Luna asked.

It took several minutes before Jen could answer. "Both. . . ."

They sat there for a few moments, holding hands. Luna wiped the gunk off Jen's face and saw real fear in Jen's eyes. It was more than that; perhaps for the first time Jen was genuinely afraid for her baby. Luna was, too. She might not get to be an aunt after all.

There was a knock on the door. "Are you ready?" Vader asked.

Luna looked at Jen who had a resigned look. "I guess so.

Back inside the office, Vader must have cleaned the mess by magic. He certainly could make things disappear.

"Let me guess," Luna said when they returned. "She's a nobody and you need her to make your case against a somebody."

"That somebody is Paul Dellagio, the lawyer," Vader smiled. His white teeth contrasted nicely with his dark skin.

"So what is really going on?" Luna played dumb, not too hard in a situation like this. "Talk to me as if I'm a six-year-old and don't know anything." She stole the line from the movie, *Philadelphia*, but meant every word.

Vader smiled again. He had seen *Philadelphia* too, and fancied Denzel Washington playing him in a movie. "For nearly thirty-five years, Dellagio has run an operation dealing with illegal prescription pills. He's based here in Albuquerque because it's a natural crossroads."

Luna stared out the window. She could see I-25 to the east, the "Oxycontin Expressway," and could make out the famed "Big I" intersection of I-25 with I-40, "The Vicodin Viaduct" off to the north.

"So? If an old lady can get pain pills for half-price by getting them from Mexico, why should the Feds care?"

"This is so much bigger than that," Vader replied. "It's not just the little old lady with a bad back. These guys deal with people at their most desperate and vulnerable, and get them hooked. You have no idea how far this goes. And, there's no regulation whatsoever. You think you're buying a liver pill and instead get a laxative."

Luna thought about Sacagawea at the pharmacy. Suppose she got a bad batch of hormones. Who could she sue?

"Why would a lawyer deal drugs?" Luna asked. "The guy makes a fortune on personal injury cases."

"He spends over a million dollars a year on ads," Vader said, shaking his head. "And that's in New Mexico alone. He also advertises in Arizona and Texas. It takes money to make money and where do you think the money comes from?"

Luna didn't answer. She couldn't even afford a two-inch ad in the Crater County phone book, which was called the "yellow page," even though it was only half a page. In the massive Albuquerque phone book, Dellagio took out several two-page spreads and had his name on the back cover, as well as the spine of the white and yellow books. He even had a pink-post it note attached to the front cover.

Vader showed them a piece of paper outlining a network—a tree with Dellagio at one root. "Dellagio's network is unique as he uses medical and legal people to do his distribution."

Luna thought for a second. "Lawyers and doctors—no one ever checks their bags or briefcases if they go to jails."

Vader pointed to another branch. "Personal injury lawyers like Dellagio refer their patients to certain doctors. These doctors offer the patients 'discounts' on special new pills that are highly addictive."

He then pointed out branches for hospitals, therapists, athletes, and entertainment companies. They weren't filled in completely.

Luna looked at Jen. Jen was hardly one of the "smart people" who get involved in things like this. She had been playing way over her head.

"I didn't know any of that," Jen piped in. "I just delivered envelopes."

Luna thought Jen knew better. "Jen, there are grown-ups here," she said, then instantly regretted it. Jen looked nauseous again. Luna grabbed the trash can and moved it toward her.

"Are you okay?" she asked.

Jen's face went through all the colors of the spectrum as she stared at the trash can. Vader looked at her anxiously. If one more molecule of puke made it to the carpet, he might lock her up for good.

Jen gallantly recovered. Her face settled on a shade of deathly pale. "Don't mind me," she said.

"What about the Internet?" Luna asked, desperately trying not to mind Jen.

"Oh, they're tied into that," Griego said in that taunting mongoose voice. "But the big drug companies began suing the Internet providers. No one actually orders through the Internet any more. Too much oversight. Even one Viagra pill in the mail sets up Federal charges of mail fraud."

"It's still pretty low-tech," said Vader. "A lot of the dirty work is done by hand. They can't use the mail as much since the Post Office began cracking down. Most of the deals are done face to face."

Luna thought back to the pharmacy. That was true. She looked up the diagram, and traced the tree trunk all the way back to the root. There was another box next to Dellagio, but it had been crossed out. "Who's in that big box?"

Vader frowned. "No one anymore, as far as we know. We heard some chatter that Dellagio's original partner died years ago, but we never knew exactly who he was. Dellagio moved here from Chicago and hooked up with some locals. There's also an organization called the Mondragon cartel in Mexico that might have a connection. My predecessor almost moved on them, but it all fell apart."

Luna remembered hearing about the Mondragon cartel from Mayhem. Vader wasn't telling everything. Luna tried instead to read Griego's face. She might as well try to read a stone.

"You've been after this guy for longer than I've been alive and you still have nothing?" Luna asked.

"Dellagio is smart," Vader said as if she'd hurt him. "This isn't some stupid mob. These are people with high SAT scores."

"We're calling it the Mensa Mafia," Griego said with a laugh. "But they ain't all that smart. A lot of them tend to disappear. It may be shiny happy pills, but drug dealers are still drug dealers."

Luna nodded. "Do you think Dellagio killed Hobbs?"

"We still like Jen for that," Griego mongoosed in, "as she was at the scene and her blood is all over the body."

"I didn't kill him," Jen said. "I didn't even fuck him, okay?"

Luna ignored her, and turned to look at Vader. "What do you want from us?"

Vader shook his head. "That depends on you. Quite frankly, let's just say that Hobbs's dying was not a good thing, especially after he was busted and before he could testify. We need names. Your client met with some people. You help us make the conspiracy case against Dellagio, her State murder case and all the conspiracy charges go out the window."

Griego tried to get back in the spotlight. "Then there's that Mexican cartel . . . if you can bring them down."

Luna forced a laugh. "We'll stick with Dellagio. I don't really think we're going to infiltrate the Mexican Mafia. Or what did you call it, the Mensa Mafia? That neither. My SAT scores are too low."

Vader smiled back, his first real smile of the day. "I agree. Just get us Dellagio. Get us something that puts him away."

Luna looked at Jen. Her attention was already back out the window; this time her eyes were following the clouds.

"We're still in the preliminary stages," Vader said. "Keep in mind that we will also be talking to Ms. Santos as well. But I'm sure something will stay on the table for a little while."

"Let me talk to my client," Luna said after a moment. "I like it when things are on the table."

Vader winked at her. Was he flirting, Luna wondered? She winked back, and actually didn't mind the attention. Maybe she was becoming more like her sister—ADHD when it came to men.

• • • • •

Luna took Jen outside to the concrete sculpture fountain at Civic Plaza. Luna thought the sculpture looked like an abstract assembly of her father's clinic, one block piled on top of another in a kind of MC Escher sort of way.

"Needless to say," Luna said with a half-smile. "I think we should help them out. You're guilty of something."

"I didn't kill Hobbs," Jen said. "You're too much like my mom. Can't you tell when I'm *not* kidding?"

Luna was about to say "not yet," but she took a good look at Jen. She could tell.

Jen played with the water in the fountain with her hands, and then wiped her face.

"What about Dellagio?" Luna asked.

"I don't know." Jen's eyes now followed the water as it dribbled off one concrete cube and on to another.

Luna shook her head as realization dawned. "It's his baby, isn't it?"

Jen nodded. The girl's ADHD sure came into play when it came to men.

Chapter Seventeen
Aggravated Assault

WHEN SHE WOKE UP Tuesday morning, Luna knew it was time for what attorneys call the "Come to Jesus" speech. She had to confront Jen and find out what really happened the night of the murder. She did not want to confront Dellagio until she knew what the hell was going on. She had to know for her own sake. Not just as a lawyer, but also as a sister.

The interview in Jen's room had been the first date. The other talks had been one long second date. Luna considered this the magical "third date," the time to score. She knew the secret to penetrating Jen's defenses, coffee, and lots of it. Caffeine was truth serum to someone with ADHD.

Luna walked outside her apartment that morning on the little dirt jogging track that circled the complex. It was now October, and the Balloon Fiesta had begun in earnest. Six hundred balloons floated above her head, taking over the entire sky. One balloon looked like a cow jumping over the moon, one looked like an alien monster complete with ears, one even looked like a hundred-foot Laser Geisha Pink, but that one was rapidly deflating. From beneath, Luna felt she was under a living, breathing entity—one of those creatures out of *Star Trek*. She heard the fiery blast of a balloon's heater. As it floated directly above her, a balloonist waved down at her before wafting back up to the heavens. Albuquerque wasn't all bad.

Luna had to call Jen from a pay phone. Her phone service provider told her she was a bad credit risk. Jen, the accused murderer, had perfect credit, of course.

The last of the morning's balloons landed, and the chase crews had finished stuffing the once mighty balloons into little duffel bags by the time Luna picked Jen up. Jen was dressed casually in a University of Colorado sweatshirt. Luna quickly realized it was her own sweatshirt from college. Jen must have taken it out of the car.

"Is it cool for me to keep this?" Jen asked.

"It's cool," Luna lied.

Luna took her to the Flying Star restaurant on Central and Carlisle near UNM in the Nob Hill neighborhood. Even though a few more funky shops had opened in the past few weeks, it still didn't look anything like San Francisco.

The Flying Star was an Albuquerque institution, if something so counterculture could really become established. Luna had come here a lot during her brief stint as a lawyer in Metro court. It was an eclectic mix of college kids and professors, gays and lesbians, chic students and slumming yuppies trying out the sinful éclairs over bottomless cups of decaf with sweet n' low. Today there were even a few balloonists, their sponsors' names on their t-shirts, bragging about their near misses with power lines and their own experiences in the ballooning equivalent of the "mile-high club."

Luna had done the "Flying Star after-movie coffee" almost every weekend when she was a metro D.A. She'd broken up with guys, seen old boyfriends with other women, and once had an entire tumultuous relationship with a co-worker—lusty beginning, ambiguous middle and nasty break-up—over the course of three cups of cappuccino.

Jen barely sipped her latte as they sat down. "Drink up," Luna said. Luna waited until Jen had taken a good gulp.

"Why did you sleep with Dellagio?" Luna asked. Dellagio was over sixty years old and Jen was twenty-five. Luna shuddered. "You were attracted to him?"

"He was totally nice to me," Jen said. "But he was kinda gross. I don't know why I slept with him."

Jen was far too casual. Luna didn't know why she did what she did next. Emotions just welled up inside her, like . . . well, like a volcano. She nearly slapped Jen's cheeks, stopping just microns from Jen's face. "You stupid little bitch!"

There was a stunned silence. Even a "near slap" that justifiably put fear in another could be considered assault in the eyes of New Mexico law.

My God, Luna thought. I just assaulted an accused murderer who knows *kung fu*!

A rugged looking balloonist and his dowdy wife stared at them in horror. There was a red mark on Jen's left cheek, as if Luna had really slapped her. Jen started bawling.

"Why'd you do that?" he asked. "I should call the police."

Jen said nothing as she wiped away her tears. She shook her head at the balloonist. "It's all right."

Luna tried to understand why she had assaulted Jen. Then it came to her in a flash. She wasn't slapping her client; she was slapping her sister. The girl had slept with a sixty-year-old drug kingpin. She deserved to be slapped.

They stared at each other. Jen waited for an apology, but Luna wasn't about to apologize. "I'll get you some more coffee," was all that Luna would muster.

"You do that," said Jen, holding back tears.

"Are you okay?" the balloonist asked Jen.

"I'm fine," she said. "My sister can be a total bitch sometimes."

When she returned, Luna looked at the balloonist. "Do you mind?"

The balloonist shook his head, and hurried away to plan another ascent. Life was so much simpler up in the clouds. Why did he have to land in a place like this?

Luna knew she had to keep going. "Did Hobbs ask you to sleep with Dellagio?"

Jen flinched, as if expecting another slap. "He didn't say any-thing about it," Jen said at last. "I figured it would help. I only did it once. He liked Viagra. He just didn't like using protection."

Luna shook her head. She wanted to slap Dellagio as well. The guy was sixty, not seventeen, and sleeping with twenty-five-year-old Jen approached statutory rape in Luna's eyes. "What was the rela-tionship between the two of them—Hobbs and Dellagio?"

"They didn't call each other very often," she said, "but when they did, they talked like they knew the phone was tapped. Like I said, I had to deliver files between the two."

"Let me guess, they were always marked attorney-client privi-leged."

Jen nodded. "Some were also listed as confidential medical files. I swear I never opened them. I don't know if they contained money or anything. That's it. I swear."

Jen took another sip of coffee. There was still some foam left from her latte and it made a mustache over her mouth. Jen licked some of the foam seductively. "So, how are you and Seek?"

Luna didn't like the connotation coming from Jen, especially with white foam still on her pouting lips. Luna said nothing, but wiped Jen's face for her. I clean up after this girl a lot, Luna thought.

"Thank you," Jen said. Jen refilled her drink with more coffee and chugged it down. Jen's blood stream was probably the color of *café au lait* by now, and the caffeine had given her the shakes.

Luna wanted to go in for the kill. "Before you went to the vol-cano the night of the murder, you were with Dellagio, right?"

"I went to Dellagio to tell him I missed my period. He was a total asshole about it. That's when I got the call from Sandrina, about Hobbs overdosing. Dellagio told me I should just leave."

"Did he threaten you?"

Jen shook her head. "He didn't have to. I was already afraid of him."

As Luna looked at her Jen said nothing, but cringed as if Dellagio had threatened her with far more than a slap. "I still am."

Luna knew that Dellagio would not rush to give Jen an alibi. She didn't know if she wanted to open Pandora's box with a paternity suit either. She remembered what Vader had said, witnesses in this case had a habit of disappearing. Time to change the subject.

"Did anyone see you there?" Luna asked.

"His secretary was arriving just as I left," Jen said. "That bitchy English one."

Luna smiled. That was Victoria Scarborough, the bony runner, if memory served. If Luna could find Victoria, Jen could achieve alibi, at least a partial one. But she would have to firm it up. Victoria was a bitch and wouldn't verify anything. Then again, Victoria had issued a challenge. Maybe it was time for that afternoon run.

"Can you give me something on Dellagio that we could use?" Luna asked. "Anything?"

Jen shook her head. Maybe she really loved Dellagio after all. It was obvious that Jen was someone who loved to be loved, *needed* to be loved. Guess that addiction ran in the Cruz genes. Jen's mother barely tolerated her, her father not at all. Even her boyfriend hated her. Dellagio had probably said a kind word to her and that was all it took. Jen had bit into him hook, line and sinker.

"I don't know," Jen said. "I just don't know."

"Jen, your life is on the line here."

Jen said nothing.

Luna looked down at Jen's belly. "Maybe two lives are on the line here."

"Let me think," Jen said. "Talk to Victoria. Then maybe you can go after Dellagio."

Jen had finished her last cup of coffee and didn't want any more. She was now too wound up to talk. Luna knew they were done for the day.

· · · · ·

Tonight's televised "Man in the Street Survey" was actually done at the Balloon Fiesta where throngs had gathered for the evening's

"Special Shapes Balloon Glow." Instead of asking which was their favorite balloon, the reporter asked, "Do you think accused murderers, especially murderers in gruesome sex cases, should be allowed out on the street?"

They then cut to a picture of Jen at arraignment, before cutting back to the fiesta.

One old redneck nearly spit into the camera. "I think we should just take 'em up in a balloon and drop 'em."

Luna gasped. Hopefully this guy wouldn't be on the jury, but Luna knew one thing for sure. With Jen admitting to delivering files, this case should never go to trial. Guys like that would convict Jen in a heartbeat.

Chapter Eighteen
Hot Pursuit

LUNA AVOIDED JEN WEDNESDAY morning, and instead hung out in the library, reading law review articles and trying to teach herself to be a defense lawyer. She grabbed a quick lunch at one of the high-class burger joints near Central and Fourth downtown. Out the window she could see arrows showing mile distances from here to Timbuktu. She laughed. Albuquerque was a crossroads all right.

It must have been a "take your staff to lunch day." The tables were completely filled with lawyers and their legal secretaries. Some even had their families along with them. Diners at most tables drank ice tea, while others started the weekend early and downed pitchers of light beer. Luna suddenly felt very lonely. She had no staff, unless she counted Jen.

Luna ordered a Portobello mushroom burger, and tried to formulate a plan. She needed to get Victoria to provide Jen with an alibi before she could confront Dellagio. After scarfing down her meal, Luna called Victoria at Dellagio's office. Victoria answered the phone like an English ambassador, but her tone turned positively cockney when Luna identified herself.

"I don't have to talk to you," Victoria said.

"As a matter of fact, you do," Luna said. "Or you will. I can subpoena your anorexic little ass, you know."

Victoria laughed. "I'd like that."

What did she mean by that?

"We can't talk here," Victoria said. "Maybe we can meet for that run we've been talking about. That is if you're up for it."

"Let's do it this afternoon at five," said Luna.

"You're on," Victoria replied. "A 'bollocks-on' run, okay?"

Luna had no idea what a "bollocks-on run" was, but she could not back out now. "Bollocks-on, it is."

After hanging up, she suddenly grew nervous. The prospect of a run against Victoria, at what she thought was a bollocks-on pace, aggravated her entire body. She hadn't felt this nervous since choking at the Olympic trials. Her legs stiffened, her heart rate increased, even the Portobello mushroom in her stomach decided to rebel. Luna quickly realized why she was so uneasy. In the last few weeks, she'd faced constant disappointment. She always bragged that she was a better runner than anyone else in the state. She might lose that claim as well.

That afternoon, Luna waited in her car outside Dellagio's compound for Victoria. She reminded herself that she was doing this for Jen, not herself. Victoria came through the door at four fifty-five, dressed in workout clothes—black spandex shorts and a black sports bra. The woman obviously had fake boobs, which almost looked ridiculous on her skinny frame. Almost, but not quite.

It was late October, and the weather was a warm Indian summer; the trees were still orange.

Victoria stretched a few times; achieving positions that Luna could barely imagine. Luna got out of her car and did a few stiff stretches of her own. Victoria smirked as if she had already found Luna wanting.

"Ready or not," Victoria said as if holding the gun for the Oxford-Cambridge row-off.

"Ready."

Victoria nodded, and headed south at a good clip down Eighth

Street. Luna quickly fell behind. Victoria had a good lead as she passed through the broken bottles on the nasty edge of downtown, and made it to the leafy Country Club area by the Rio. There was lots of shade here with the orange leaves, and it was pretty flat, except that the pavement was quite uneven for such a tranquil old neighborhood. Luna hadn't warmed up, but this bony bitch was not going to beat her. It wasn't about getting an alibi witness for Jen anymore. As the cliché went, this run was personal.

Victoria had now made it to the banks of the Rio. She found a trail into a southern section of the Bosque that was crowded with fishermen fishing in the man-made ponds. This area was just south of the new Tingley Lakes Park and had avoided most of the fires. The trail was a few yards from the river and zigzagged between dense woods, sandy banks and high weeds. Hikers and transients had carved out a veritable flow chart of rough trails, and Victoria knew the trails inside and out. Luna had to speed up, or she'd lose Victoria forever in the miles-long maze.

Luna sprinted into the Bosque, ducked under a low-lying branch, then jumped over a stump. She felt like she was inside a video game, but a scratch from a branch, right over her eye, made it all too real. After veering left, she saw footprints down the other trail. She stopped suddenly, nearly pulling a hamstring, backed up, and then headed in that direction.

Victoria twisted through the trees up ahead like a cruise missile. Luna tried to speed up, but tripped over a fallen tree.

Face first in the dirt, she wiped her face and felt a tiny trickle of blood mixed with mud. That did it. She picked herself up, really sprinting now, through the leaves Luna could see her quarry ahead.

Victoria now ran along the Rio, low to the ground so she didn't have to duck as much. Luna tried to catch up. It was an obstacle course now—holes in the ground, cans, broken glass, live and dead branches at all heights. At this fast pace, the video game kicked into the bonus round where risks and rewards were doubled. Luna cramped up, the jostling going right to her stomach.

Up ahead, Luna could see the aptly named Bridge Boulevard as its four lanes ascended the Rio. There was a cab waiting on the side of the road, right by the bridge. Had Victoria called a cab so she could leave Luna in the muck?

Parts of the trail had actually fallen into the river through erosion. Luna had to jump over a gap in the banks, and landed deep in some mud. She landed wrong on her left foot, and it really hurt. If the river didn't get her, the quicksand would.

She ran hard and splashed through more puddles, but she'd finally caught Victoria. They ran a few hundred yards at a blistering pace until Victoria finally slowed, gasping for breath. Victoria tried one last burst of energy, pulled away, then slowed when Luna kept pace and started to pass at the next open glade.

"I'm passing your ass," Luna said. "You can't stay with me, bitch!"

"All right," Victoria said between gasps, nearly collapsing. "You win."

Victoria stopped for breath, sat on a log. Triumphant, Luna returned to join her. Then Luna's Portobello burger decided to rebel. She bent over and threw up for nearly a minute. Luna felt her very soul had come out into the Rio Grande and was floating halfway down to the Gulf.

Damn it, I'm as bad as Jen.

When she looked up, Victoria was gone. Up ahead, the cab drove off with Victoria in it.

Luna retched again. She wiped, then looked down and noticed a business card by her feet. "Body by Victoria, personal trainer. Masseuse. DOM candidate."

There was a phone number. Her stomach felt better, but what did DOM stand for, dominatrix?

Chapter Nineteen
Touch and Concern

LUNA CALLED THE NUMBER. A spacy-sounding woman set up an appointment with Victoria for later that night. Luna didn't entirely trust Victoria, but the massage studio was part of the "Sacred Yucca Holistic Healing Center and Spa" and that sounded as legit as holistic healing could sound. The spa was located a few blocks from Ragin' Shrimp. She could smell the Cajun sauces a block away.

On arrival, Luna saw an acupuncture sign and realized DOM meant Doctor of Oriental Medicine. Luna's skin crawled. Ouch!

She knocked on the teak door. Victoria opened the door to reveal an empty lobby, and ushered Luna into a blank room, the massage studio. "I'll be right back," she said.

Luna debated undressing all the way and decided she had nothing to lose by doing so. The walls did not go all the way to the ceiling, so she could always yell if Victoria tried anything funny. Unfortunately, there was no one else here.

Luna was proud of her body, so she took off her outer clothes, then her bra and finally her panties and slipped under the sheet face-first. Victoria knocked. She didn't wait for an answer, just came in and closed the door behind her. She lowered the lights and put on soft music. The music sounded as if it came from a remote mountain region—maybe Nepal, maybe Peru, perhaps a jam session between musicians from both.

The music was also sensual. Too sensual. Did Victoria have ulterior motives? Luna had often felt like a "chick magnet" when she competed against female triathletes.

"I'll open up the back a wee bit," Victoria said. "Watch out, they can be a bit pokey."

Luna expected to feel Victoria's hands, but it was acupuncture needles that penetrated her skin. It felt pokey all right, but surprisingly good.

Victoria poked a few more times then touched her lower back. The back had opened up all right.

"How does that feel?" Victoria asked in her British accent. She sounded like Mary Poppins on ecstasy pills. The Inca-Sherpa re-mix music also cast a calming spell.

Luna was relaxed, but tightened when she looked up and realized the name on the DOM diploma on the wall was not Victoria's.

"Great," Luna replied. "Do you have a license to do this?"

"Soon," Victoria said. "I'm just working at Dellagio's so he can set me up."

Luna didn't like the words "set" and "up," especially here alone with Victoria and her needles. "Why couldn't you talk to me on the river? Were you being watched?"

"I'm watched here," Victoria said. "I'm watched everywhere. I wanted to see how badly you want me."

As a witness? As a woman? Luna said nothing.

Victoria told her to relax, and put a needle in Luna's feet. She then moved up a few inches. "Where does it hurt?" she asked.

"Everywhere. . . ." Luna replied. Victoria dug deeper into Luna's calves with her hands. Damn, that felt good.

"You just wanted to see me naked," Luna said.

Victoria said nothing; moved her hands to the back of her thighs. Luna drifted into semi-consciousness, fighting to stay awake.

"I'd like to ask you some things," Luna finally said.

"Ask away," she said, after another poke. "I can't guarantee that I will answer away."

"Could you be my client's alibi?" Luna asked.

"Yes and no," Victoria said.

"What do you mean?"

"If you want me to say that your client was with Dellagio on the east side the night of the murder and that Hobbs was probably dead when she got to the volcano to kill him, sure, I can say that."

Luna smiled. Warmth surged though all the muscles of her body. What were they called? Trigger points?

"Thank you," she cooed.

"Don't thank me yet," Victoria said. She removed the needles from Luna's back. "Now turn over."

Victoria held up the sheet and Luna turned over. Face-up, Luna felt very exposed, even with the thin sheet over her. Were her nipples erect? Victoria now took another needle and put it right in the middle of Luna's forehead. "Don't squirm," she said.

Luna tried not to squirm, but failed.

"I don't like your client," Victoria said. "I think she was bad for Dellagio. Bad for everyone."

"How so?"

"She was just bad, or as she would say 'like totally bad.' "

Luna intuitively tensed. "Did she know about a conspiracy?"

Victoria pressed harder. "If you want me to tell you that I never saw your client demonstrate any knowledge that she was transporting documents and/or money as part of an illegal conspiracy, I can tell you that as well."

That news made Luna feel much better, or was it Victoria's hands inching closer to her inner thighs? Luna couldn't help but think back to her one lesbian experience back in high school, with her old friend Diana Crater, the state's current attorney general.

Suddenly, Luna felt Victoria's fingers come down hard on a pressure point on her neck. Luna tensed. Her mind raced, was there still a needle in her forehead? Had it been drugged?

She suddenly flashed back to her experience with Adam Marin. Why do I keep going to dangerous places alone? Do I have a death wish? The answer came to her in a flash. I keep going alone because I've never had anyone else. Even Sacagawea had Lewis, and sometimes Clark. Perhaps I do this to punish myself. That's what Dr. Romero would say with her reality therapy. Bad things happen because you want them to happen.

Luna kept her body tensed, as if in anticipation of something terrible happening at Victoria's hands. Yet nothing happened. What was Victoria up to?

"Just relax," Victoria said at last. The pressure point on the neck was finally released. The feeling was better than sex. When she put her hands on Luna's shoulders, they were moist with more oil. "Jesus, you are the most sensitive person I've ever worked on. What's got into you? I won't kill you here."

Luna noticed that Victoria's tone opened the possibility of death after the session. Luna didn't know what to think.

"So will you testify?" Luna finally asked.

A long pause. Victoria got up from the table. Was she leaving? Wait . . . don't leave!

"They have a quaint saying here in New Mexico," Victoria said as she reached for something in the cabinet. Luna tensed, wondering what it was. "That saying is 'not even.' I'm not stupid. Well, not that stupid. I know you want to get Dellagio. He is my boss after all. But there are some rather nasty chaps that are *his* bosses."

She returned with more massage oil, then rolled Luna on her side and put pressure on a knot on Luna's lower back. Is she torturing me? No. Somehow, the knot in her back magically released.

"However, I appreciate your efforts on your client's behalf," she continued. "Give me a subpoena and I'll see that he gets it when he gets back. You can interview him next week."

Luna felt a moment of triumph. Victoria hit another pressure point, Luna howled in pain. "Just don't get your hopes up. He's much smarter than you are . . . which isn't saying much."

Victoria then took the needle out of Luna's head.

Chapter Twenty
Beyond the Scope of Direct Examination

LUNA DRAFTED A SUBPOENA to Dellagio to set up a deposition. Well actually, she had Jen e-mail a form since she had forgotten the format. She then called Victoria to set a date, and Victoria told her to do it immediately, tomorrow if possible, before he left the country. "He goes to Mexico for the Day of the Dead," she said without further explanation.

After Luna hung up, she panicked. Her printer needed toner, so she had to print the subpoena at the Song's from Jen's old printer.

"Are you sure you should do this?" Jen asked as the page printed out. "Don't you think this will just make him madder?"

"I don't think we have a choice," Luna answered. "And besides, I think he's pretty mad already. Anything in particular I should ask him?"

"The night of the murder he called someone and then got back to me. Whoever he talked to was the one who told me to hire you to be my lawyer. I want to know who *he* called."

Luna could see that Jen was terrified of Dellagio, and even more terrified of whomever he called.

"Anything else?"

"Yeah. Why hasn't he called me? He's like totally abandoned me here. Everybody has abandoned me . . . except you."

Jen stared at Luna with big eyes.

"Don't worry about me," Luna said. "I am not about to abandon you."

"No matter what?"

"No matter what."

Luna wondered whether she was telling the truth.

It was almost Halloween, and inside Dellagio's office lobby on Thursday afternoon there were a few pumpkin decorations on the wall. Luna tensed when she saw the court reporter already waiting. The court reporter's meter had already begun ticking on Luna's dime. Victoria, dressed immaculately in black, politely apologized that Dellagio was on his way as she ushered Luna and the court reporter down a red-carpeted hallway.

Victoria opened two oak doors, and took them inside Dellagio's office. This must have been the inner sanctum of the original owner, the railroad magnate. Other than some high-tech equipment, the room didn't look as if it had changed much since tycoon days.

After sitting in a plush chair, Luna checked out the diplomas on the walls. Dellagio had gone to Northwestern as an undergrad and for law school. Luna clenched her fist. She had been wait-listed at Northwestern, her father's alma mater. She hated anyone who went there, just because.

Luna noticed that the name on the diploma read "Bellizzi." "Did he change his name?" she asked.

"You're actually the first person who has noticed that." Victoria said, with some admiration. "There was a lawsuit by the Dellagio Casino, but he won."

The court reporter smiled at Luna. "You understand that I get paid for my time, regardless of whether he comes or not."

Luna understood all right. "Just bill me."

The three sat in total silence for another ten minutes staring at the empty corridor. Suddenly she saw a swarm of people on the red carpet, but didn't see Dellagio. She heard a steady rumble of sounds, people saying "thank you" and "congratulations" to no one in particular.

Was Dellagio invisible?

The oaken doors of the inner sanctum suddenly closed and Dellagio appeared as if by magic. She could see why she hadn't been able to make him out in the crowd. He was much smaller than she had imagined, about five-foot-four. He also looked much younger than his sixty years. His black suit, with a black shirt and no tie, completed the "Hollywood power player" look. Upon closer inspection, the man had had major plastic surgery done, and despite a mustache, he looked almost feminine. Luna thought he wouldn't look out of place in Jen's doll collection. Maybe that was the attraction.

Yet Luna saw something very hard in his steely green eyes. He gave the impression of a dangerous toy, a miniature action figure possessed by evil demons. At any moment, the hideous demon would emerge from the tiny shell of a man.

"Luna Cruz," he said, masking a strong south-side Chicago accent with a western drawl. "Now I remember how I know you. You applied to my office back when you were in law school at Colorado State. No, University of Colorado, right? A most interesting resume with the running and all. Sorry I never got back to you."

She had applied seven years ago. She was surprised he still remembered.

Dellagio laughed. He held up his index finger as if it was a magic wand, "If I could turn back time, maybe I would have hired you."

Luna forced a smile.

"Are we ready to go?" the court reporter asked.

"I keep forgetting that this is being preserved for posterity," he said glancing at the court reporter. "I'd better not say too much."

He nodded at the court reporter, who tidied up her machine, ready to begin.

"Do you mind if my assistant stays?" he asked, nodding toward Victoria. "She's my right hand man."

Victoria looked like she wanted to make a clever addendum to the "right hand man" comment, perhaps a joke about her left hand as well, but she thought better of it.

"She can stay," Luna said, "We've met."

Victoria frowned at Luna's words. She set up some recording equipment of her own.

"I'm ready if you are," the court reporter said, glancing at her watch.

Luna looked over at Dellagio. "I'm ready," he said. "For anything."

The court reporter nodded, and swore Dellagio in. Luna began with a few preliminaries then hit the big questions. "What was your involvement with Jen Song?"

"Sexually or professionally?"

"Both. Okay . . . sexually?"

"I had sex with her once. Apparently once was enough."

"What about professionally?"

Dellagio paused. "Since this involves a criminal conspiracy, I'm going to take the fifth upon the advice of my attorney." He pointed to the mirror. "The ain't saying shit clause."

Luna stiffened. Had she gone too far? She was in his haunted mansion after all. He may look like a little toy, but at that instant, he looked as if he was about to transform into something else. Did his green eyes show the slightest tinge of red?

Dellagio stared at Luna and undressed her with his eyes. Luna nearly barfed. Despite his almost girlish appearance, after the thousands of dollars of plastic surgery, this guy was old enough to be her father. He was almost old enough to be Jen's grandfather.

Despite his charm, Luna grew angry. There had to be some way to break this man. She took a deep breath and asked a few more questions to which Dellagio gave brief, non-committal answers. It was time to hit the money questions.

"Why did Jen come to see you the night of the murder?"

"She delivered some court documents."

"What kind of documents?"

"Attorney-client privileged documents. Ones that can't be released without a court order."

"Did she say anything unusual to you?"

"She informed me that she was pregnant. Is that unusual enough for you?"

"Did she say anything else?"

"I can't recall."

"Did she get a phone call while she was with you?"

"Yes."

"Who was it from?"

"She didn't say."

"What time was the call?"

"I don't remember."

"What was her demeanor as she took that call?"

"I can't read Jen," he said. "I don't even try. Don't delude your-self to think that you can either."

What the hell did that mean?

Luna had nothing. Yet. "What time did Jen leave that night?" Luna asked.

"I don't recall," he said. He then added, "Right as Victoria was arriving."

That jibed with what Victoria had said. Time of death was still uncertain. Jen would have to have sped all the way over to the vol-canoes, and arrived just as Sandrina had her quickie with Hobbs. After Sandrina was done, Jen would kill him. Possible, but unlikely.

"I know Jen called you from the crime scene," Luna said.

"If you say so," he said.

"What did she say to you?"

"She told me Hobbs was dead. She did not say whether she had killed him."

Luna smiled. "What did you tell her?"

"I advised her not to talk over the phone. Then I advised her to hire a lawyer. You."

"Why did you tell her to hire me?"

"Because you're good, aren't you?"

Luna frowned. "I had just been re-called by over ninety percent of the electorate, why would anyone in their right mind hire me?"

"Are you saying I'm mentally ill for recommending you? You seem competent to me. Is there something else I should know?"

Luna frowned. She was in a no-win situation. Time to move on. "She said you called someone else. Who was it? I could subpoena your phone records, you know."

Luna expected Dellagio to plead the fifth, but instead he got up, walked over to the court reporter's station and pulled the plug.

"I think it's time for you to take a smoke break," he said to the reporter.

"I don't smoke," she said.

He pulled out a pack of fine Cuban cigars from his desk. "I think it's time for you to start. Give them to your husband. If he doesn't smoke, it would be time for him to start as well. I'm suing tobacco companies these days."

The court reporter took the hint, got up and went out the door. He nodded at Victoria and she touched a button. A bookcase suddenly opened to reveal a blank room with a table and three chairs. Luna had thought she had made it to the inner sanctum. Apparently there was a sanctum more inner than this. The haunted mansion, indeed. . . .

"Why don't we finish up the deposition in this room?" Dellagio said.

"If you don't mind," said Victoria, coming closer, "do you have a cell phone with a camera?" Victoria asked.

"Not anymore," Luna said as Victoria actually frisked her.

"She's clean," Victoria announced.

Dellagio was already in the blank room, the "innermost sanctum," and looked at peace.

"Is this a panic room?" Luna asked.

"Do you see me panicking?"

He certainly wasn't. Victoria remained outside, and clicked a button after Luna entered. The bookcase closed behind them. Luna took a deep breath.

The panic room had a constant hum, to drown out any electronic surveillance, she supposed. Dellagio pressed a button, and a flat screen TV appeared showing a tropical seascape. At least the rhythm of the crashing waves made the hum bearable.

"It gets claustrophobic in here without windows," he said.

Luna tried to remain calm. "He can't kill me in his office," she told herself. "At least not during a deposition."

She stared at the seascape as if a giant whale would jump to her rescue. The rhythm of the waves somehow cleared her mind. If she brought in Dellagio, Jen would be free. If she brought in someone higher on the food chain, she might get Jen and herself witness protection, and a real window out to the tropics.

"I know you've met with the U.S. Attorney," he said at last. "The entire F.B.I. doesn't need to hear what I'm about to say to you."

"They know I'm here," Luna lied. She thought about the incident with Adam Marin on top of the volcano, but she could take all five-feet-four of Dellagio in a fair fight. She forced herself to be tough. This is for you, Jen.

Luna acted tough. "So who did you call that night?"

"My doctor," he laughed slightly. "Jen gives me a headache sometimes."

"I know what you mean." Luna didn't know how else to respond. She stared at the seascape. Palm trees swayed in the wind, but if there was ventilation in here, she sure couldn't feel anything. The other walls closed in.

"Are you sure?" she asked.

"I'm sure I really did call my doctor," he waved his magic wand finger again. "I know the Feds want me. I might have someone for them. And you can help me get that person."

"Me?"

Dellagio said nothing for a moment. He looked like he was playing a chess game in his head. "This whole thing revolves around you. I'll know more after I go down to Mexico during the Day of the Dead for a meeting."

"The Day of the Dead?"

"Someone's idea of a sick joke."

"Who?"

Dellagio smiled. "My co-defendants."

Luna had a vision of Mexican mobsters sitting around a round-table while outside the peasants paraded around with skulls or whatever they did on the Day of the Dead. A sick joke indeed.

"Can you give me names?"

"Not if I want to live."

"Why did you have people follow me in the mountains?" she asked. "Were those your co-defendants as well?"

"Luna, you are so paranoid," he said. "They thought you were meeting with someone. They drove around looking for other cars, then you disappeared. They thought you were in danger."

"From who?"

Dellagio smiled. "The cops. The F.B.I. Maybe someone else."

"Why did they shoot at me?"

"My guys didn't shoot at you," he said.

"Your guys? Were there someone else's guys up there?"

"I don't know," he said. "There's a lot going on right now."

"What do you mean?"

Dellagio looked like he wanted to tell her something, but instead he scanned the ocean as if there were sharks out there, listening in. Even in his fortress of solitude, he was still afraid of something.

"Luna, perhaps we can work together." He smiled. "Who knows, maybe all of this can be yours."

"I think it would take a lot more than a blank room with a TV set," Luna replied. "I'm not for sale."

Dellagio suddenly turned serious, and stared at her intently. "Everyone is for sale. What would it take?"

Luna shook her head. "You should have hired me when I was

right out of law school. Right now you can't afford me."

Luna stared at the sea. She smirked, maybe there was something that would buy her, but it sure wasn't in this office. "It definitely would not be money."

They sat in silence. The waves on the screen began coming faster. Luna thought she heard a tsunami heading in, but realized that the ventilation had finally kicked on. She shivered in the cold breeze.

"Jen's having your baby," Luna said, changing the subject. "Why haven't you called her?"

Dellagio stared at the seascape. "I've never had a child before. I always said I'd rather pay seventy-five cents for a condom than seventy-five grand for a kid's college education."

"I don't get it."

"Jen knows my number. You know my number. Hell, everybody knows my number. I'm here for her . . . really. . . ."

"You really should call her," Luna said. "The ball is in your court."

"Too many balls are in my court. Once this is all settled, I'll take care of her. I promise." He looked at Luna. "You've got to believe me."

"I do," Luna lied for the umteenth time since the case began.

Dellagio closed his eyes for a second. This was not a man who let himself be vulnerable very often.

"It's gotten way too complicated," he said, breaking himself from the reverie. "You don't know the half of it."

Dr. Romero had said that, too. What the hell was the other half?

There was a tear in Dellagio's eye, but he quickly caught it. "Let me do some thinking," he said, lifting the wand finger one more time. His moment of weakness was over. "Perhaps we can still be on the same side."

The same side? How could they possibly be on the same side?

Dellagio held up that finger again, and suddenly anything seemed possible. "I will get back to you soon," he said. "Give my best to Jen. Let her know that I will support her, all she's got to do is call me from a safe phone."

"I think she wants you to call her," Luna said. "Jen wants you to take the first step."

"It's too late for first steps," he said.

"So what's going to happen next?" she asked. She wasn't sure if she was asking Dellagio, herself or God.

"That depends on you," Dellagio said. "I promise I'll call you back a lot sooner than when you sent your resume." He pressed a button on the wall and the bookcase opened.

Chapter Twenty-One
The Long Arm of the Law

THAT EVENING, LUNA HAD dinner with Jen and Nurse Song. Luna found she liked the spicy Korean *bulgogi*. It almost felt like a family dinner.

"Will Dellagio help me?" Jen asked in the middle of dinner.

"Not yet," Luna said. "He hinted that he wanted to buy me off."

"But you're not for sale, right?" Jen asked.

"Not even," Luna replied.

"So what do you next?"

"I keep playing lawyer."

Friday afternoon Luna played lawyer with Oñate, the investigating cop, at the combined sheriff and police station downtown. There had been several attempts to merge Albuquerque with the surrounding Bernalillo County, but skeptical voters worried that their taxes would go up and repeatedly voted "no." The two law enforcement branches, APD and BCSO had an uneasy truce and shared the same downtown station. It was an ugly building, half old and industrial, half new and post-modern. Luna wasn't sure which was the sheriff's side and which side belonged to the police.

Luna entered the building and a female security guard asked for ID. The guard then gave her a white "visitor" tag and a map, and pointed to Oñate's office on the map. After a few wrong turns, Luna finally found him on the second floor. He wasn't happy to see her, and didn't get up from his cluttered desk.

Oñate took her to an interview room with a blank wall and two chairs. He'd probably done four interviews with lawyers already today and looked bored before Luna even began. He didn't improve during the interview, and read through his report in a monotone. Luna played devil's advocate, and practiced the cross she had learned from the textbooks in the law library. "You didn't see the incident. You don't know for a fact that he died from a drug overdose or strangulation. The blood does not necessarily mean that Jen killed him. . . ."

"Whatever," he smiled to each of her questions. She asked more, but he had nothing more to offer. He then made her sign a form indicating that she had completed an interview. "I get overtime for this," he said with another smile.

"You sure don't deserve it," she snorted.

As Luna headed out the door, she noticed that Oñate's desk was near Adam Marin's. Marin's workspace was filled with New Mexico Lobo football paraphernalia. One even was a poster that said, WHO'S AFRAID OF THE BIG BAD WOLF? with a poster of Louie Lobo, the mascot character who wore a wolf suit.

Luna went with a hunch. She had a million things to ask, but she summed it up in one question. "Is Adam Marin dirty?"

Oñate frowned, and invoked the police code of silence. Perhaps he was afraid of the big bad wolf. "That's an ongoing internal affairs investigation that I can't comment on. He's still working here, that's all I can say. Even if he was dirty, I wouldn't say anything to you without a court order."

Luna thought back to her relationship with the late Nico, who was also a dirty cop. Damn, she hated dirty cops.

As she was leaving, she found a new receptionist at the front of the building, a male intern. "Are you sure you gave your ID to me?" he asked in a squeaky voice.

Luna grew more and more impatient as the new receptionist kept fumbling. She wanted to slap the pip-squeak when Adam Marin came by. Marin gave her a dirty look.

"Let's go mountain climbing again," he said with a smirk. "I know a good route up the volcano."

Luna couldn't let that pass on a shitty day like today, not from a dirty cop. She glared at him. What could she say that would really hurt this asshole? She remembered when Seek had asked him whether he'd made sergeant yet.

No that wasn't enough. "How does it feel that Jen's having someone else's baby?" she asked at last.

It worked. Marin grimaced as if she'd punched him in the groin, and Luna savored his impotent look of frustration. Marin then muttered something under his breath.

"What's that, *Sergeant?*" Luna asked, pouring salt in the wounds.

Marin mumbled something else as he scurried down the corridor. Luna swore she him say, "I'm going to fuck that bitch up."

She wanted to report it to someone, but the intern pretended he hadn't heard.

Chapter Twenty-Two
Trick or Treat

JEN WANTED TO MEET Luna for dinner on Saturday for Halloween, but Luna turned her down. She finally had another date with Seek. Luna felt guilty abandoning her sister, but Jen was a big girl, she'd be fine on her own. Seek suggested that Luna meet him at PF Chang's off north I-25, a gigantic chain Chinese restaurant near other gigantic chain restaurants. Everything was bigger in this part of town, even the people. Most of the patrons looked as if their only exercise was walking across the huge parking lot.

Seek smiled at Luna. "We're the best looking people here."

Even though there was a long wait for a table, Seek said some magic words to the hostess, who immediately guided them to a prime spot.

The restaurant was good, but now that Luna had had real home-cooked Asian food, it paled in comparison. Every waiter and cook was Anglo with a funky haircut.

Luna was offended. "Remember when Asian restaurants had Asian people working in them?"

"So how's Jen?" Seek asked, as if that was his answer.

"Jen is Jen," Luna said. "Why do you ask?"

"I've never met anyone like her before," he said.

Luna wanted to hit him right there, especially as her mind flashed back to Jen licking the creamy latte foam off her mouth.

Seek read her expression and quickly switched gears. "I've never met anyone like you before either," he said. They soon talked about running and had a spirited debate about whether it was better to run short and fast or long and slow. Short and fast won by a nose.

He nearly screwed up again. "I hope I'm still in great shape like you when I'm your age."

Luna actually raised her hand for a slap, but stopped it inches from Seek's face.

"I meant that as a compliment," he said. "You have pretty much the ultimate body."

Luna smiled.

"I'm almost intimidated by you," he said.

Luna blushed, "By me?" she smiled. "Trust me, there's nothing intimidating about me at all."

"Luna, I don't think you see what everyone else sees. You're beautiful, you're strong, you're smart. You define yourself as Jen's lawyer, because it's so important that you win that case. I'm impressed by how hard you're trying for her, but it doesn't matter. You've got to see yourself as your own person. And your own person is amazing."

Every once in awhile, Seek said the perfect thing.

They went to his house in the rocky foothills on the extreme east side in a neighborhood called Sandia Heights. High above the city, they had a sunset view of the volcanoes twenty miles to the west. One look at Seek and she felt safe—totally safe. The earth wasn't going to shake unless he wanted it to shake. Luna tried not to do the math and figure out how much this adobe compound was worth. Either Seek was an amazing young attorney or he had parents who loved him a whole bunch.

She smiled. Probably both.

They drank a nice aperitif on his wooden patio just as the lights of Albuquerque came up below. There was a special Halloween weekend Balloon Glow at Balloon Fiesta Park off the freeway. The park was miles away and a thousand feet lower in altitude, but it seemed very close in the crisp, desert air. They saw the lights of the tethered balloons flash in sequence to form patterns.

They kissed after the third glow sequence and waltzed into Seek's bedroom. It had exposed adobe bricks and beautiful Native artwork that would put a country girl like Sacagawea in the mood. He lit some scented candles, then turned off the lights. Down below, the blinking lights of the glowing balloons were like strobe lights against the adobe bricks.

They slowly undressed each other. "Wow," Seek said. "You're so beautiful. Even more than I thought."

"Wow, right back at you," Luna said.

They embraced. Seek kissed her and she felt limp from the sheer power of him next to her.

Yet Luna felt uneasy, she knew something was wrong . . . somewhere. . . .

There was no glow over the Mekong. The balloons might as well be on another continent. This wasn't the type of neighborhood where kids went trick or treating either, so Jen should have been surprised when someone knocked on her door.

Jen didn't remember Adam Marin saying anything. After the knock she had opened the door just a crack, but he'd pushed it open so hard she fell over. Jen stayed on the floor, cowering from the kicks and punches. She tried to remember her martial arts training, but it was long gone. She tried to rise up, but Marin threw her back down again, slamming her head. She got up, but soon flew through the air, hitting the wall point blank.

Somehow, she grabbed the phone, but Marin easily grabbed it from her hands and threw it down, breaking it in shards. He threw her again.

Did her head go all the way through the wood? She could still see through the blood. Splinters smashed through her skull. She writhed in pain. Each splinter sparked a different memory.

Marin had done this before. Then she saw another boyfriend from her past, then another. Was that her Korean father beating her, or her real father? No, she had never met her real father and no splinter in her brain would ever bring him back to her, right?

She couldn't see Marin any more, there was just this strange faceless man pounding her head against the wall.

"Luna . . . Luna," she called into an imaginary phone.

"That bitch is going to get hers," the man said. "If you call the cops I'll kill you. Remember they'll believe me, not you!"

She rallied her body one last time. She pushed Marin weakly away, but then she stumbled. Blood now caked her eyes.

Marin let her fall into a bloody heap, and slammed the door behind her. The splinters went deeper and deeper into her brain as more memories raced around her head. Jen sank further into the darkness. She wanted to cry out but into the darkness, but her voice was gone.

Chapter Twenty-Three
Pain and Suffering

NURSE SONG GREETED LUNA at the UNM hospital emergency waiting room. She worked here, but she acted as nervous as if she'd never been here before. "She's still in the ER," Nurse Song said, real worry in her voice. Suddenly the lines on her face grew deeper. Nurse Song often hid her emotions, but her mask had crumbled. "They don't know if she'll make it."

The two of them sat there in uncomfortable plastic chairs, holding hands. Nurse Song prayed in Korean. Mr. Song was nowhere to be found.

"I do love my daughter," she said apropos of nothing. Her accent was thicker, as if the last twenty-five years hadn't happened. "You believe me, don't you?"

"I'm sure you do," Luna lied.

They hugged each other tight. Luna felt she was somehow responsible for Jen's plight. Well, she *was* responsible. If only she hadn't told that asshole, Marin, that Jen was pregnant. Luna looked around the crowded waiting room; this was excitement on a Halloween night in Albuquerque. The room was filled with anxious families waiting to hear the news about Loco Jimmy and his GSW. GSW was the police code for gun shot wound.

Luna remembered that prosecutors in Albuquerque used to have a punk band called GSW. That didn't sound so funny in this waiting room. This was just a DV with possible GBH, domestic violence with great bodily harm. Initials made the brutality sound so routine.

Luna cried as well. Jen was her only blood relative. She felt terrible for slapping her. She shouldn't have blown her off to have sex with Seek. Telling Adam about Jen's pregnancy had nearly signed her sister's death warrant. That made Luna hurt even more.

"Did she tell you she was pregnant?" Luna asked.

Nurse Song shook her head. "I supposed I shouldn't be shocked."

"That she was pregnant, or that she didn't tell you?"

"Both. Was it Adam?"

"It was Dellagio."

They sat still for a few more moments. Nurse Song finally grew impatient, and hurried to the reception nurse, a pretty Latina who guarded the reception desk like an MP in Iraq. "Anything on my daughter, Katrina?" she asked. "We've been waiting for hours."

Nurse Song pleaded with Katrina, using only her eyes. Katrina sighed, reluctantly made a phone call, then turned to Nurse Song. "They're doing all they can."

Nurse Song looked at Katrina. "I need to go back there."

Katrina was firm. "Chan Wol, you know the rules! There's nothing you can do. It's out of your hands. It's out of my hands. Go sit down there with your—"

Katrina was about to say "family," but she stopped when she saw the obviously Hispanic Luna. "Go sit with your friend."

Nurse Song went back to Luna. They tried to watch a television show on a crappy old TV that was bolted to the ceiling. A demented woman across the room laughed hysterically at a home shopping show selling jade heart pendants for $19.95. "Get your heart now!" the incredibly perky spokeswoman said.

Luna turned her attention back to Nurse Song. Luna held the nurse's hand and leaned against her shoulder, just as she had when she was little. Nurse Song used to sing a lullaby to her in Korean, and she now sang the same lullaby here in the waiting room. It still had its magic power. The demented woman fell asleep, and even the TV grew quiet. Luna drifted in and out of sleep. She heard the many intercom messages, footsteps tracking back and forth, and the screams of family members reacting to the bad news about Loco Jimmy's GSW. Through it all, Nurse Song kept singing, softly.

Luna shuddered when the sun rose. It was November first, the day of the dead. Finally, a few minutes after dawn, a female doctor entered. "Is anyone here from the Song family?"

The Song family? Luna laughed at the thought. She roused Nurse Song and they approached the doctor. Dr. Pang was a petite Asian woman, who looked younger than Jen. Why couldn't Jen be like this woman, she and Nurse Song thought simultaneously.

It's going to be bad news, Luna thought to herself. It has to be.

"Jen will be okay?" Nurse Song asked. "Right?"

"She'll be fine," Dr. Pang said. "She has a concussion of course. But there's no brain injury."

"There's a relief," Nurse Song said way too loudly.

"We'll have to keep her a few days, maybe longer," Dr. Pang said.

"And the baby?" Luna asked.

Dr. Pang finally smiled. "Babies. Plural. Twins. A boy and a girl. We did a sonogram. Her pregnancy is still viable."

"Can we see her?" Nurse Song asked.

"Normally I'd say no. She's still very weak. I know you work here, but I don't know if I can make an exception."

Nurse Song looked at her. "Dr. Pang, please. It's my daughter."

Dr. Pang felt for her. "I suppose it's okay. She's in a semi-private room. She's just waking up."

Luna and Nurse Song saw a comatose body wrapped in bandages as they entered. Nurse Song nearly fainted until she realized that the body was Jen's roommate. On the other side of the curtain they saw Jen, a black eye and bandaged, but otherwise healthy. She smiled. Both of them gave her a hug. Jen was too dazed to hug back.

"What happened?" Luna asked.

"Adam Marin came by," she said in a halting voice. "He didn't say anything, just pushed me down for no reason. We struggled, then he pushed me down even harder. I slammed my head into the door. I don't remember what happened after that. I was unconscious and woke up here."

Luna felt so guilty for taunting Marin about the baby. "I'm so sorry, Jen," she said. "I'm so sorry. It's my fault, all my fault. I told him about the baby. About Dellagio. I didn't know."

Jen nodded. "He would have figured it out anyway. We haven't had sex in months. I mean, I'm not having sex with two guys at the same time. What is it . . . serial biography?"

"Serial monogamy," her mom said, but Jen smiled, then stopped quickly. It hurt too much to smile.

Luna still felt guilty. She wanted to make sure this never happened again. No one was going to beat up her sister. She went to the phone by Jen's bed, and began dialing.

"What are you doing?" Jen asked after the first digit.

"I'm calling the police."

Jen grabbed the phone. "No. It will only make things worse. He said if I called the police he'd kill me. He's a cop! They'll like totally believe him over me."

"I'm your lawyer. We're doing what I say. No one's going to kill you. Not when I'm here."

Jen tried to protest, and Nurse Song touched Luna's arm. "Are you sure this won't cause more trouble?"

Luna looked at both of them. "Even if she doesn't call the police, assholes like Marin will keep trying to kill her anyway! That's been the story all her life."

Jen shuddered with that prospect. Luna knew she had to cheer her sister up. She remembered an old joke of her father's.

"You know you're having twins," Luna said. "A boy and a girl."

Jen said nothing. She was still pissed.

"I want you to name the girl, Denise," Luna said.

Jen shrugged. "Why Denise?"

"Because I want to name the boy, 'De-nephew.'"

Silence, then both Jen and Nurse Song laughed. Even a bad joke sounded funny after all of this.

"How about just Denny?" Jen smiled in spite of herself. She motioned for Luna to give her a hug. Luna complied. Luna didn't have to be a hugologist to figure this one out.

"Thank you," Jen said.

"You're welcome."

"I love you, Luna," Jen said, wiping a tear out of her eye.

Luna didn't say anything. She didn't know what to say to that.

Later that morning, Luna finally convinced Jen to let her call the police. She then sat with Jen until the officer came. Unfortunately, it was Officer Oñate. He made Jen go through the details again, kept prodding her for the inevitable inconsistencies. Jen wanted to dissolve into her IV tube, so Luna sat and held her hand.

Oñate was still in conquistador mode. "Why is Adam so mad at you?"

"She doesn't have to answer that." Luna growled. It really did feel like Jen was the one on trial here.

"I don't know if I want to go through with this," Jen said at one point. Oñate wrote that down and smiled.

Luna looked at the officer. "Look at her face. She nearly died; nearly lost her baby. Her babies. The asshole should be behind bars!"

Oñate shook his head. "We get these calls every day. Most of the time, the women don't even show up for court."

"She'll show up," Luna said.

"Don't forget your client is accused of murder."

"Accused does not mean guilty, and people who are accused can be beaten, too."

Chapter Twenty-Four
Pattern of Behavior

ONCE DR. PANG RELAXED the visitor hour rules, Luna sat at Jen's bedside for the next seventy-two hours. Nurse Song dropped in and out. Luna asked Nurse Song to write out the lyrics of the Korean lullaby on a piece of paper, and she tried to sing it to Jen in battered Korean. Jen pretended to enjoy it.

Jen and Luna talked about everything except the case. Instead, the sisters caught up on their missing twenty-five years. They talked about their first kiss, first sex, first everything. Luna let Jen ramble for the first few sessions, but soon found herself confiding in Jen. The only time they didn't talk was when one or the other was asleep.

Eventually they talked about Jen's relationship with Adam Marin. It had started peaceably enough a few years back, and he had never hit her before. Well, never hard, she said. Well, never that hard, she finally admitted. The beatings grew worse after he failed to make sergeant, due to a bogus charge of brutality on a DWI stop of a drunk-driving female. The charge may have been crap, but Marin had been more than brutal with Jen.

"You're a very pretty girl, Jen." Luna said. "You could do so much better."

"You really think so?" she asked. "You really think I'm pretty?"

"You're gorgeous. But I really think you need to get a restraining order against this asshole. You also need to put his butt in jail."

"I don't know." Jen said. "I don't want to go to court if I don't have to. I'm really scared, Luna. I'm really, really scared."

They fought about it for over an hour—whether to file domestic violence charges in addition to the criminal case. Jen didn't want to do anything, didn't want to rock anyone's boat.

"This is like totally bullshit!" Luna said after Jen still refused to budge. Luna stormed off in a huff. When did she start saying "like totally?"

Luna drove to the Second Judicial District Courthouse to get the ball rolling. She would force her sister do the right thing. The domestic violence clerk's office was on the second floor, and Luna ran up the curved stairs and down the hall to the left to the reception area. The reception area was bland enough to pass for a doctor's office.

"Are you the petitioner?" the clerk asked, just like an admitting nurse. She was an African American woman with beautiful green eyes. Her name was Synthia, and she looked like a rhythm and blues singer, built for comfort—not for speed. Synthia saw more domestic violence cases in a day than Luna had prosecuted in her entire career. She had no tolerance for bullshit.

"No. I'm not the victim," Luna said. "I'm her attorney. The petitioner is in the hospital. Her name is Jen Song."

Synthia nodded. "I know the name."

That didn't sound good.

Synthia showed Luna a thin file of Jen's prior cases. Luna knew that Jen had been here before and filed reports, but had never realized that the restraining orders failed because Jen had never actually testified in court. Adam Marin was not the worst respondent, nor the first. There'd been several guys on the Jen Song DV docket, guys going back to her late teens. With all the reports, Jen wasn't the girl who cried wolf; she cried wolf pack.

Luna's heart sank. "Oh Jen. . . ." Why couldn't she have known her sister earlier? The girl was a magnet for assholes.

Synthia handed her one more file. "You also need to see this one. She had one against the guy she killed. But it got dropped."

Luna read the name. Ed Hobbs. The late Ed Hobbs?

Synthia explained. "Jen Song filed it, then DNS (did not show) when it came time for the hearing."

Luna reviewed the files. Two weeks before he was murdered, Jen filed on Hobbs alleging that he had assaulted her. There were no medical reports attached, but there was an affidavit signed by Sandrina Santos, who arrived just as Hobbs had attacked her. Unfortunately, the day of the hearing, one week before Hobbs's ill-fated trip, Jen had failed to come to court and the case was dropped.

"Do you still want to file?" Synthia asked. "I'll do whatever you want."

"Let me think about it." She had Synthia make a copy of Sandrina's statement and Luna sat in the waiting room to read it over again.

Once she saw Sandrina's notarized signature on the bottom, Luna suddenly realized she had to way to save Jen. God, it almost seemed too easy. It would be pushing the envelope of course, but she had no choice. The whole case could be wrapped up this after-noon!

Luna remembered an Arab woman was representing Sandrina. A woman named Assed. Luna borrowed Synthia's bar directory as well as her phone.

Assed picked up her own call on the first ring. "Yes," she said in a no-nonsense voice.

"I'm Luna Cruz," she said into the phone. "I'm representing Jen Song and I have questions for Sandrina Santos about signing an affidavit in a domestic violence case between Jen Song and Ed Hobbs. Could I talk to your client?"

"She's going to take the fifth," Assed said. "You know the rules."

"Duh," Luna said. When did she start saying "duh?" Time to plant her trap. "I'm not going to ask anything about the current case, just the *prior* domestic violence between Hobbs and Jen."

There was a long beat on the other end. "I heard what happened to you out in Crater, Luna, and I think you got a raw deal. I'll let you talk to her, but you can only talk to her about the old affidavit."

"Thank you," Luna replied. "That's all I'll ask her about." What else could she say?

"I'm just doing this because you're a women, mind you," Assed said. "We've got to stick together. I'm going to meet with her this afternoon anyway. You can tag along. Meet me at the MBU at one-thirty."

"MBU?"

"Maximum Bitch Unit," Assed said matter-of-factly. "It's the unit at the Metropolitan Detention Center for girls who don't play well with others."

Chapter Twenty-Five
Maximum Bitch Unit

MDC, THE METROPOLITAN DETENTION Center, sat seventeen miles out of town on the deserted west mesa, high above Albuquerque. The MDC was even further west than the volcanoes. After taking the Paseo del Volcan exit off I-40 and following an I-40 frontage road west for a few more miles, Luna feared she was lost, until she reached a few crappy cardboard signs pointing south. Some of the signs had bullet holes in them and Luna wondered whether *banditos* lay in wait in the sagebrush.

A tumbleweed broad-sided her car, and pieces of weed sprayed like shrapnel. She nearly drove off the road dodging the next one, and almost ran into a billboard in the process. Talk about irony, the billboard was another LLL-AGIO sign, all the way out here. Luna smiled, the man knew about reaching a captive audience.

As she finally parked in the dusty MDC lot, Luna felt uneasy to see the volcanoes to the east for a change, their peaks rising in front of the Sandia Crest. She felt totally exposed out here, and not just because there wasn't another dwelling for miles. If Albuquerque was her own personal crater, she now stood on the crater's jagged edge.

The MDC looked like the Pentagon in cinder block. Luna now truly understood how lucky Jen was to be outside. If Jen were convicted, her appeal would work its way up the courts while enduring several years inside a facility like this. If Jen were found guilty, she'd spend the rest of her life in someplace much worse.

The MDC was co-ed, but Luna doubted they had a spring dance between the guys in Cellblock F and the girls in the Maximum Bitch Unit.

Luna waited in her car, which took several additional hits from tumbleweeds and their flying shrapnel. Assed finally pulled up along side her in the parking lot. They exited their vehicles, and shook hands; it was probably the loosest handshake in history.

Assed then looked at her in horror. "You better change, or they won't let you in."

Luna wore slacks, a short sleeve shirt, and opened toed sandals. If she could have found her lost silver cross, she would almost pass for a nun in a warm climate.

"Seriously," Assed continued. "You can't show arms or toes inside the jail. They say for safety reasons, but I think it's because it drives the inmates wild or something. It's their rule, not mine."

Luna grimaced. Assed was serious. The woman probably didn't know how to joke. Luna had never thought her toes would drive anyone wild, but she put on a pair of sneakers and a rumpled jacket that she had planned to have dry-cleaned. Luna then followed the other attorney into the surprisingly nice MDC lobby.

The receptionist had bleached blond hair, which contrasted nicely with her blue uniform. Receptionist at a jail sounded like the worst job in the world, but the woman handled it with military efficiency. Security was tight, of course, like Purgatory Airport with connecting flights to hell and heaven. Luna looked at the other people who were waiting to go inside the jail: the inmates' relatives. Some were scarier than the inmates. Luna beeped at the metal detector. Gum wrappers again. An obese guard of indeterminate gender practically strip-searched her in front of the inmates' families, then took the gum and threw it in a box labeled contraband.

"I wasn't going to stick it under the desk," Luna joked.

The obese guard of indeterminate gender didn't laugh.

Luna and Assed walked down the world's longest hallway, which had a nice white, brown and black tile pattern, but as Luna stared down at the pattern, it started to jumble together, like one of those abstract cubist paintings.

They kept walking and made a turn to the west. The MDC really did seem as large the Pentagon. Head down, Luna nearly bumped into a man walking a straight line on the white tiles, as if they were a balance beam. He held a sign that read D-12. D-12 walked gingerly on the white tiles, as if he thought each black tile was a deep abyss. Luna and Assed reluctantly went around him.

Near the end of the hall they turned left, then clicked through a series of doors. Unfortunately, they had to wait in the sally port, a small area the size of a gas station rest room for nearly five minutes. Through the bulletproof glass, Luna could see the Maximum Bitch Unit—sixty women in orange, staring at her from three sides. The women looked onto a common area from two stories worth of cells, which were themselves behind a wire mesh fence. Luna felt claustrophobic; it was hard to breathe. Finally the sally port door clicked open and she was in the bitch unit.

"You're that bitch from Crater!" one muscular Native American woman—Sacagawea on steroids—shouted at Luna from inside her cell. "I voted your sorry ass out."

Luna tensed. She was very glad now that her arms and toes were covered, as was her sorry ass. She then noticed a petite Asian woman finishing a table meeting with her attorney, and an even more petite translator, whose badge read Bee Tran. Luna recognized the attorney from Zoo Docket. He looked public defender casual: jeans, purple work shirt and Nike sneakers. Apparently he had forgotten to tell Bee Tran about the arms and toes rule, as the poor women wore an oversize men's jacket and dress shoes.

"Thanks, Thuc Doan Le," the attorney said. "See you next week."

"*Cam on Thuc Doan Le,*" said Bee Tran as she headed for the door. Luna heard the poor woman clomp in the size-twelve dress shoes. The translator was not happy. "Remind me about the dress code next time," she said to the lawyer.

Thuc Doan Le said nothing more to either of them. She picked up a broom and started sweeping the floor in the center of the pod. It was hard to tell if that was her job, or if it was how she passed time in jail. She looked like a freeze-dried version of Jen, and probably weighed less than eighty pounds on a frame well under five-feet. The woman had elaborate gang tattoos—dragons, tigers, and Chinese characters wrapped tightly around her arms.

"What kind of record does Sandrina have?" Luna asked, still staring at Thuc Doan Le.

"Prostitution. Perjury. Trafficking. A boatload of resisting and public affrays. The girl likes a good public affray."

A public affray was when two people had a fight in a public place and caused a danger to those around them. "Who doesn't?"

"Just don't get on her bad side." Assed ensconced herself in her files. The seriousness of the warning was clear.

Luna looked around the Bitch Unit, and tried to get a sense of the inmates staring at her from behind the cell windows. She thought she had beaten her claustrophobia, but it had returned with a vengeance. She counted the cinder block bricks, reminding herself that they really didn't want to crush her. I'm going crazy after only ten minutes, Luna thought, and I'm the sane one in the family. I'm Laser Geisha Blue, the old hag. Good old Laser Geisha Pink, the crazy one, wouldn't last until the afternoon shift change.

After Luna counted the number of cells for a second time, Sandrina, still in high-risk red, arrived. They must have brought her over from some hidden, even more secure cell somewhere in the unit. Sandrina entered the unit accompanied by a petite guard who looked like a ballerina, graceful despite her ugly navy-blue uniform. After releasing Sandrina, the blue ballerina pirouetted away.

Sandrina was the maximum bitch in the Maximum Bitch Unit. She'd been segregated from the other inmates, more for their protection than hers. Sandrina sat down with a clump, nearly collapsing the hard plastic chair with the force of her tailbone. Even seated, she towered over Luna.

"What's *she* doing here?" Sandrina asked in her voluptuous Brazilian accent. It sounded musical, like there was a *Carnivale* band backing her up. "She's that bitch's lawyer."

Assed tried to calm her down. "She just wants to ask a few questions about your affidavit in Jen Song's restraining order against Hobbs. She could subpoena you, and I wanted to save us the trouble."

Assed's tone calmed Sandrina a bit, but only a bit.

Luna tried to gain confidence in the lull. She hadn't been afraid of another woman since grade school, but Sandrina was every schoolyard bully rolled into one. Luna fiddled with her purse, just to make sure that Sandrina didn't steal her lunch money.

"Did you prepare the affidavit?"

"No. Jen did. We went to a copy place and used a computer there. I just signed it, in front of one of the bitches there who was one of them notary whatevers."

Luna handed Sandrina the affidavit. "Here's the affidavit. So tell me again what really happened in his office that day."

"I was dropping by the office—"

"Why were you going to the office?"

"I was picking up something. Or maybe dropping something off."

"What were you dropping or picking up?"

Sandrina just smiled. She wasn't stupid. Well, not that stupid. Assed look relieved.

"So then what happened?" Luna asked.

"I heard something in Hobbs's office. It sounded like a fight, so I hurried in and opened the door. Hobbs was like on top of Jen. He was saying 'If you fuck this all up, I'll kill you.' He stopped when I was there. After things calmed down and Jen and I met up, she wrote the affidavit, and asked me to sign it. So I did."

"Were you telling the truth in the affidavit?"

"Sure."

"And Jen never went to court?"

"She never went to court," Sandrina said, "because she was scared shitless of Hobbs."

Perfect. Luna now thought she had laid her trap. "So if she was scared shitless of Hobbs, it doesn't make sense that she would go with him to the top of the volcano."

"So?"

"So I think you lied to police. It's more likely that you killed him."

Assed looked at Luna. "You broke our deal. You weren't going to ask her about the murder."

Luna smiled. "I didn't ask her about the murder. I'm just asking if it made sense that Jen would go up there in light of the paper she filed."

Assed looked at Sandrina. "Don't say anything."

Sandrina returned the stare. "I'll talk if I want to talk, bitch."

Luna smiled. At least Jen had never called her a bitch. She had that going for her.

Without another word, Assed handed Sandrina a Xeroxed paper form. Luna caught the gist of it from a sideways glance. The paper said Assed had advised her client not to talk, but her client wanted to talk anyway. Sandrina initialed it, and handed it back to Assed, who put in a date and time next to the initials. Apparently they did this on a regular basis.

Luna held her breath. Would it really be that easy? Would Sandrina finally admit that she had killed Hobbs after all? It sure looked that way. Assed was washing her hands of Sandrina as it was.

The whole unit grew silent in their cells behind the mesh. Even Thuc Doan Le stopped sweeping.

Sandrina smiled at last. "If you think I'm gonna say I killed him, you're wrong. Jen did. *She* strangled him, not me. I'm even not saying I was there."

Luna visibly sank. It wouldn't be that easy after all.

Sandrina kept going. "Hobbs liked it rough. He knew Jen was so scared of him that she would go up there no matter what! He was the one who called her to go up there. She was too scared to say no.

She was so pathetic. She let guys walk all over her. I guess she finally snapped. I'm telling you what I told the cops. Jen killed him!"

"I don't believe you," Luna said. Just one look at Sandrina, with her high-risk rage, and Luna knew Sandrina was full of shit. Luna thought about Jen in the hospital, and Jen's files in the DV room. Jen was a victim here. Sandrina was clearly covering her own maximum ass.

Sandrina stood up, and everyone in the unit became deathly silent. "I can take everybody down with me—the whole fucking operation, from the big man all the way down to Jen. Because it's all a part of a great big plan. I'll take your ass down, too."

Sandrina stopped. For the first time, she realized she might have gone too far. She looked at Luna's eyes, a burning stare. "You look familiar. It's your eyes. What was your name again?"

"Luna Cruz," she said. Something came to Luna at that moment. "Jen is my half-sister by the way."

Sandrina didn't move for a long moment. "I heard about you!" Sandrina said at last. "Down in Mexico. So you're the one!"

"The one?" Luna thought about Keanu Reeves in the Matrix movies, he was also called "the one." She had no idea why anyone down in Mexico would confuse her with Keanu Reeves. "Who in Mexico was talking about me?"

Sandrina said nothing, and suddenly looked away, as if she, too, wanted to count the number of bricks in the pod walls. Was this giant woman finally nervous?

Apparently Luna's reputation for legal acumen must have preceded her. Sandrina now shrunk before her eyes, and the Amazon turned into a wallflower.

"Get me out of here," Sandrina said, standing up too quickly. "Get me the fuck out of here! Guard!"

Sandrina walked over to the door and waited patiently. She turned her back on them, and did not glance back.

• • • • •

Sandrina kept standing with her back to them as if she was somehow afraid of Luna. They all stayed in the same place. It was a shift change of the correctional staff and there would be no movement in the jail until the new shift of beefy female guards had taken over. The inmates were higher priority than the lawyers, so the toughest guard on shift took Sandrina away first. Sandrina had come in like a lion, but she walked away like a lamb.

Luna still couldn't understand Sandrina's sudden change in demeanor. Luna was good, but she wasn't that good. Luna had prosecuted Mayhem Moreno back in Crater. He had seen Luna at Jen's arraignment in Albuquerque. Maybe Mayhem had said something and word got around the MDC.

"It's still going to be a few minutes," one of the guards called over to them. "There's a lockdown in D-6, so they lock down the entire joint. That only makes the natives more restless. Make yourselves comfortable."

Comfortable? She had to be kidding. Luna was already getting light-headed from the stale air. She didn't know how much more of this she could take.

Thuc Doan Le had listlessly resumed sweeping the same spot of floor. It didn't take too much imagination for Luna to visualize Jen standing there, broom in hand, in that same daze. But Jen would not sweep the same spot; she would sweep different spots at random and never finish the floor during her life sentence.

Either Sandrina was lying, or Jen was. It was that simple. It all came down to faith. Whom did she believe? Sandrina or her sister? Sandrina's sudden freak-out also meant something, but what? If it came down to a matter of faith, all right, Luna would have to make a choice. Sandrina was a convicted liar and a convicted whore. Jen was no virgin, but Jen was her blood, or half of it.

"Excuse me," Thuc Doan Le said in a very quiet, heavily accented voice, moving the broom in Luna's general direction.

Luna stared at Thuc Doan Le's tattoos for a moment; she stared right at the dragon's mouth. If the dragon could talk to her, what would it say? Luna tried to imagine the swirling dragon jumping off Thuc Doan Le's little, shriveled arm.

"Your sister is innocent," the dragon would say.

Was that her father's voice?

"Adam Marin is an asshole," the dragon would continue. "Sandrina is lying. Don't let them fuck with your sister. Get a restraining order against his ass! Put him in jail. Hell, kill him yourself. Think of Denise and Denny. They are your blood!"

Luna kept staring at the dragon on Thuc Doan Le. It hadn't moved at all. She turned to Thuc Doan Le and forgot herself; she actually thought she was talking to Jen. "I'm going to save you!" she said. "So help me God, I will save you."

Thuc Doan Le said nothing, and kept sweeping as if the action would magically dissolve the floor and whisk her back to her homeland on her broomstick.

"You can go now," the guard said and pressed a button. Just then the electronic doors to the Maximum Bitch Unit clicked open. Shift change was over.

Luna felt as if she had dragon wings as she raced her car downhill to the courthouse and ran up to the second floor just before closing. She handed the restraining order back to Synthia, the clerk.

"I'm glad you're back," said Synthia. "She's lucky to have someone like you."

Luna smiled. Luck had nothing to do with it.

Chapter Twenty-Six
Stipulations

LUNA WENT BACK TO Jen's dingy hospital room. Jen was alone; her roommate had either died or gone home. Luna told Jen about filing the order. Jen's big eyes were puffy, it was apparent she had been crying most of the night.

"How could you do that when I told you not to?" Jen demanded, as Luna sat down next to her.

"Because I'm your lawyer. And, I'm your sister."

Jen pouted. "I don't know. . . ."

"I checked your files," Luna said. "I found that you had a restraining order against Hobbs, but you didn't go to court."

"I never go to court to fight for myself," Jen said at last.

"Why don't you go to court?"

"I don't know. It would only make things worse." Jen shrugged. "I was afraid of him. He was all about being a lawyer and liked controlling people."

"So if he attacked you, why did you go all the way to the volcano to see him?"

Jen stared at her. "Luna, you've got to believe me. He said he needed to see me—really needed to see me. I panicked and went up there, just so he wouldn't come after me. I do things sometimes like totally without thinking. Dr. Romero told me I had poor impulse control. And no self-esteem, I mean low self-esteem."

"Sandrina still says you killed him."

"I said I hated him. I didn't say he deserved to die. But I could never kill someone. Never! Never! Never!"

There was no "like," no "totally." When Jen said "never" just now, she meant it. This time.

A male nurse came by. "Visiting hours are over."

Luna looked at the nurse. "Dr. Pang said I could stay."

"Well, Dr. Pang doesn't make the rules here."

Luna looked at the blank hospital wall. Thuc Doan Le's dragon suddenly returned and stared at her from the wall.

"Believe her," the dragon whispered, opening its mouth widely to blow a smoke ring that surrounded the bed.

Luna looked at Jen again. "I believe you," Luna said at last, and got up to go. "I've got to get some dinner."

"Luna?" Jen called as Luna got to the door. "Thanks for filing the restraining order. No one has ever stuck up for me before. I love you. Really. . . ."

Jen looked at Luna as if expecting her to say something. But Luna still wasn't sure what she was supposed to say, so she stayed silent.

"Are you coming back?" Jen asked.

"Tomorrow."

As she left, Luna carried with her a strange feeling in her stomach.

Luna came back the next night, then the night after that. She learned to sing the Korean lullaby almost as well as Nurse Song herself, and sang Jen to sleep with it one night. Finally, Jen was cleared to leave on Thursday. Nurse Song even ditched work to be there and she and Luna walked Jen to the hospital exit.

Nurse Song whispered in Luna's ear. "Thank you so much for being there for her. I've been so busy, I couldn't visit her as much as I liked."

"It was a pleasure," Luna said. She thought for a second. It really was.

Jen gave Luna a big hug. "Thank you for being my sister." Luna and Jen said at the same time.

"Jinx," Jen shouted. They both laughed.

It was then that a thunderbolt of emotion hit Luna. She realized what the strange feeling was that she'd felt in the pit of her stomach. "By the way, I love you, too, Jen."

Chapter Twenty-Seven
Emergency Hearing

"Do I REALLY HAVE to do this?" Jen asked, as Luna dragged her up the steep curving stairs of the District Courthouse. Jen wore Luna's University of Colorado sweatshirt and loose jeans. All her other clothes still chafed against her bruises.

"Yes," Luna said, pulling Jen up the final stair of the curved staircase to the second floor. They stopped at the Domestic Violence reception room and checked in. A sign said THIS ROOM IS MONITORED BY CAMERAS. There were no visible guards, so Luna felt uneasy. A camera couldn't stop Adam Marin's fist.

The respondents (the abusers) sat in the inner lobby. A few tattooed men actually wore the kind of tank top nicknamed "wife-beaters," but one man wore a suit and tie. A woman sat nervously in the alleged abusers section, but in her pink flowered t-shirt Luna wondered if she could really abuse anybody.

Synthia directed Luna and Jen to the petitioner's (the victims) waiting room on the other side of a divider. It was crowded with women, some with black eyes, and others who had less visible wounds. Some men, a few surprisingly big, also sat on the petitioner's side.

Jen now looked more frantic than usual, even worse than when she was in the U.S. Attorney's office. "Can you get me a cup of coffee?" she asked.

"No!" Luna said sharply.

"Maybe he's not coming," Jen said, almost wistfully. "Could I go to the bathroom?"

"You will stay here until he gets here," Luna said. "He could lose his job if he doesn't show." She didn't know if that was true, but she hoped it was.

Marin arrived at the last possible moment. His attorney was a nice matronly woman with a cane named Dale Keeton. Keeton came across as a friendly, but firm—a schoolteacher from a small town.

Luna met with Keeton in one of the cramped conference rooms in the hallway. "I'm going to make sure your client does serious time for this," Luna said. "He tried to kill her!"

Keeton laughed, as if one of her students had just said that the moon was made of green cheese. "This is just a restraining order hearing. To make a criminal case against my client, your client will have to testify. Trust me, you really don't want to do that. Have you seen her record?"

"She didn't kill Hobbs," Luna said firmly. "I sat with her in the hospital. Do you want to see the medical evidence?"

Keeton frowned. "I'll stipulate that domestic violence occurred," she said. "You won't be able to use that against Adam Marin in court. This just gets this part of the case over with. I'm not doing this as a bitch. I'm doing this as a friend."

Luna had been the only female attorney in Crater County at the end, and she now found she enjoyed this new sisterhood in Albuquerque. Luna agreed to the stipulation, and Keeton wrote it out on one of the forms. Keeton had perfect penmanship.

When the case finally was called it wasn't even in a courtroom, just a small hearing room. The hearing officer was a professional looking woman who wore a business suit rather than a robe.

Luna remembered an old joke she'd heard at a bar convention. "What's the difference between a judge and a hearing officer?" The answer was twenty thousand dollars a year and a dental plan, but this hearing officer looked every inch the professional.

Luna took control of the hearing before it even began. "There will be a stipulation," she said to the hearing officer.

The hearing officer went through a few specifics. This was not discount justice; she covered everything in exacting detail. As they got up to leave, Luna faced Adam. "You stay away from her."

Marin smiled. "You can't do shit to me," he said. "I bet they don't even prosecute me for this shit."

"I'll get you someday," a voice said to him. It was Jen.

Good for her.

Marin smiled. "I'm going to talk." He now sounded exactly like Sandrina had before she suddenly lost her nerve. "And when I do," he added, "I'm going to take everyone down with me."

Chapter Twenty-Eight
Impaired to the Slightest Degree

JEN ASKED LUNA TO spend the night in the Mexican Mekong. Jen wanted protection, as she was terrified of Marin. Restraining order or not, a piece of paper wouldn't stop him. Luna wondered if she'd have to use the midget Samurai sword like O-Ren Ishii in *Kill Bill.*

When Luna watched TV with Jen that night, a local station ran an investigative piece about drug dealing in the police force. One blacked-out subject listed as "Officer X" talked about "rampant drug dealing with ties to organized crime and prominent local individuals" in one of those electronically altered voices.

Luna noticed the Lobo Louie poster in the background. Who was afraid of the big bad wolf, indeed? Officer X must have been Marin. Had he already gone to the authorities?

Luna pondered the situation as she tried to fall asleep on the uncomfortable living room couch. Still awake, she heard noises close to three in the morning. Luna noticed the midget ceremonial sword on the wall. Well, at least she was armed.

There was a knock on the door. Luna went to the wall, grabbed the sword, put it behind her back, and answered. "Adam Marin, there's a restraining order against you," she shouted.

"It's not Adam," a soft voice said on the other side. "It's me."

She opened the door to reveal Dellagio, one of those "prominent local individuals" mentioned in the report. He wore a shiny gray suit and white shirt with no tie. He was entirely disheveled, sweaty and blood-stained, and looked like he had partied all night at a Hollywood party from hell. Even his face looked rumpled, and he held a briefcase that had a bullet-hole in it.

Dellagio looked shorter and older, as if all his magic was gone. He had made a deal with the devil to look so good this late in the game, but the devil had just taken his first payment out of Dellagio's ass, along with a late fee.

"What the hell are *you* doing here?" he asked anxiously.

"I'm playing body guard," she said, still holding the sword like a real Laser Geisha. "What are you doing here this time of night?"

"I had to go to Mexico, now that Adam Marin is fucking everything up. I need Jen's help. I can pay her. I can pay you. A lot."

"I told you I'm not interested. We're not interested."

"Let me talk to Jen," he said, slurring his words. "You have an ethical obligation to pass all reasonable offers along to your client. You also have an ethical obligation not to use your sword on an attorney during settlement negotiations."

Ethical obligation? He's telling her about ethical obligations? Luna almost laughed. But maybe she did have a duty to pass on what he had to say to Jen. She reluctantly put down the sword. Dellagio then hurried inside, as if he was afraid his magic wand finger did not work outside the haunted mansion. Inside, he rubbed his finger anxiously. It looked swollen. Had someone broken it?

"So what do you have to say to us?" Luna asked.

"Sandrina wants to bring everyone down," Dellagio said. "And now Adam Marin is talking, too. All the shit is coming down on me. They almost killed me down there, but instead they made me come back to clean up the mess."

None of it made any sense. "Who's 'they?' Who made you come back?"

Fatigue had gotten to Dellagio. He started to say something, then stopped himself abruptly. When he continued, he asked, "What the hell did you do, Luna?"

"I don't know. Zealously represent my client, I guess."

"Well, your zeal is fucking everything up." He looked like a cornered animal. His eyes darted everywhere.

"Are you on something?" Luna asked.

He laughed wildly. "Just a little something to take the edge off. Just a lot of something, actually. But as I was saying. . . ."

He opened the briefcase with the bullet hole in it. It was filled with money. "This is just a taste. Maybe the both of you might like to take a nice vacation out of the country. I know a place you can stay in Brazil. Sandrina won't be needing it."

"And what do you want in return?"

"Just have Jen sign an affidavit saying she never saw me do anything wrong. That way she can't testify without incriminating herself."

"Why would she want to do that?"

"Because I'll sign an affidavit saying Hobbs was a twisted fuck who liked auto-erotic asphyxiation and Sandrina killed him."

Luna frowned. "That sounds too good to be true."

Before Dellagio could say more, Jen emerged from her room. She wore a pink bathrobe.

"Go away," she said to Dellagio "You didn't call me once in the hospital and you heard what happened to me. I don't need your charity right now. Go away. Just go away."

"I only want the best for you," he said. "For both of you. You've both got to get out of here. I told Luna here that I'd sign an affidavit saying Sandrina did it. I can make your whole case go away."

Jen turned toward Luna. "Should I believe him?"

Luna took a good long look at Dellagio. In this condition he looked like someone who'd say anything to save his own ass. "Think about it, Jen," Luna said at last. "His affidavit isn't worth anything. He's not an eyewitness and his alibi for you isn't airtight. The Feds want *him*, not you, and if you don't testify against him, they'll come after you even harder."

Dellagio said nothing. He rubbed his swollen finger again. It definitely had been broken. "Jen, don't listen to her. She doesn't know what she's talking about. She can't help you, but I can."

Jen walked up to him and got in his face. "Luna is the only person fighting for me right now. None of the rest of you give a shit about me. Luna's my friend. Luna's my sister."

That really upset Dellagio, who shook his head incredulously. What the hell had he swallowed down in Mexico? "Are you sure? Do you have any idea what you're doing? She can't save you, I can."

There were those words again. She can't save you, I can. Jen said nothing for a long while, as if making a choice between the two of them. "Luna's my lawyer and she says we should fight."

Dellagio's tone suddenly changed, as if the chemicals within him had just had another strange reaction. He now looked like a five-year-old who didn't get his way, and was now trying to be friendly. He pointed at Luna, lowered his voice. "You realize that your lawyer here, your sister, your supposed friend, was voted out unanimously by her district?"

That hurt. Luna said nothing.

Dellagio continued. "Everyone in this town thinks she's a joke. Now she's totally fucked up your case. You should listen to me, not her!" He pointed to the money again. "You should fire her and let me protect you."

Jen wavered for a moment. She looked at Dellagio and his money and then at Luna. The money sure looked tempting.

Luna knew she should say something, but couldn't think what. How could she argue with all that money? Jen might fire her after all.

"I'm not taking your money," Jen said at last. "I'm staying here with Luna."

He stared at them for one more moment. Jen and Luna then locked hands. Nothing could break that lock. For one brief moment they really had the power of the Laser Geishas, both Blue and Pink. Luna picked up the sword with her free hand. She knew she could use it now.

"It's your funeral," he said at last. "Both of yours." He opened the door, and headed back into the darkness.

After he left, Jen let go of Luna's hand. She began shivering; mustering her superpowers had taken too much out of her. "What the hell am I doing?" she asked. "What the hell am I doing? Maybe I should call him back? What do you think?"

"I think you're doing the right thing," said Luna. She hugged Jen. "Thanks for the vote of confidence."

Jen pushed her away, as if she wanted to take her vote of confidence back. "Did everyone really vote you out? Why does everyone hate you?"

Luna looked away. "Not everyone," she said. "I think I got one vote."

"I'm putting my life in your hands, here. I love you as a sister, but. . . ."

Jen didn't finish her sentence. Luna had gotten her a restraining order, but outside of that, what had Luna done for her lately?

"I'm doing the best I can with what I've got," Luna said.

Jen frowned and didn't say another word as she went back to her bedroom.

Luna couldn't go back to sleep after that. Maybe she wasn't good enough and they should have taken the money. No, she wasn't for sale for "just money." She was proud of that. What would it take to buy her? She knew even she had her price. There had to be something. No, there couldn't be. She loved her sister too much, right?

Still agitated, Luna opened her mail the next day at her apartment at Sky Village. Over the roar of the interstates, Luna realized she had several things to worry about. There was Jen's own case of course, Adam's assault on Jen, and now Dellagio's attempt to bribe Jen. Luna knew that Jen was wavering. If she didn't get results soon, Jen would dump her and go back to Dellagio. Dellagio would sell her out in a heartbeat.

For some reason, the possibility of Jen's leaving got to her the most. Jen would be the final vote against her. The election would truly be unanimous.

Luna hurriedly went to a pay phone and called Vader. He was out. She knew she had to call someone, anyone, before Jen changed her mind. Luna finally got through to the Second Judicial District Attorney's Office to ask about the case, and when they heard her name, the call was routed directly to the district attorney herself, Geraldine D'Amato.

Geraldine—no one called her by her last name—was not even a lawyer. The only requirement in the New Mexico statutes for a district attorney was to be "learned in law." Not even a high school diploma was technically required. Geraldine had ridden an anti-lawyer wave by hosting a cable access show and had frequent appearances at city council meetings.

"Ms. Cruz." Geraldine had a gruff East Coast accent that sounded skeptical of everything and everybody. "In light of all the conflicts and the Federal involvement, the Attorney General's office has taken the Jen Song and Adam Marin cases."

"There's also a potential bribery case against Dellagio," Luna said. "He tried to bribe us."

"We can't touch that one either," Geraldine said. "That's why there's an Attorney General's office to handle the so-called complicated cases. Your tax dollars at work."

"Can you help us at all?" Luna asked.

"Talk to the Attorney General. They're taking over everything these days," she added.

Luna hung up before Geraldine went on a rant about conspiracy theories, with her catch phrase "organized crime, big time."

That meant that until Vader formally took over, everything lay in the hand of Luna's old high school classmate and former boss, Diana Crater. Luna didn't know whether that was a good thing or not, but she finally had an excuse to call Diana after all these months. She had been afraid to call; she was embarrassed after the recall election. But right now she had to move forward. She had to prove something to Jen.

Luna hung up and called the Attorney General's number, which she had memorized when she was an intern. Diana's secretary said she was out.

"It's Luna Cruz," Luna said. "I'm an old friend . . . I guess. I need to see her about one of my cases."

"She's been expecting your call for a while now," the secretary said. "However, she's on a conference call. It could be some time."

"I need to see her personally," Luna said. "It's very important."

"Hold on a minute," the secretary put her on hold. After an eternity, she got back to Luna. "She'll see you at eleven tomorrow."

Luna smiled. Diana could make everything okay. Moments later, she called Jen.

"I know someone who can help us," Luna said. "Diana Crater."

"Diana Crater, like in Crater County?"

"She was my best friend growing up. I worked for her when she was the D.A. in Crater. Now she's the Attorney General."

"That's like a big deal, right?"

"Yeah, Attorney General is like a big deal."

"Can I come?" Jen asked. "I've got to get out of here. I'm dying, here. Totally dying here. If I come with you to see a lawyer, it would be like legal business, right?"

Luna smiled. It would be good for Jen to see that Luna was not completely without friends. "You can come."

Chapter Twenty-Nine
Santa Fe in About an Hour

"ARE YOU SURE THIS is okay?" Jen asked. "I don't want to go to jail for going to Santa Fe. It's not worth it. If I'm going to be locked up, it should be for, like, going all the way to Mexico or something."

"You're going to be fine," Luna said. "This is official court business." At least she hoped it would be.

Jen had actually dressed as if it really was court business, perhaps as a way to compensate for her remaining scars from Marin's assault. She wore nice pants and a preppy pink sweater. She looked like a college student, instead of a nymphet. Luna hoped that she'd actually burned the Gothic Lolita outfits. Maybe Jen was finally growing up.

They headed north up I-25. There was a light dusting of snow once they hit the small town of Bernalillo. The rolling hills dotted with junipers now looked like sleeping Dalmatians. After the Saturn nearly stalled on the steep rise of La Bajada Hill, they descended into Santa Fe's picturesque desert valley, which was nestled against the majestic Sangre de Christo range, the last gasp of the Rockies. The Blood of Christ Mountains, Luna translated to herself. Who was getting crucified, she or Jen?

Right before town, they passed the famous Penitentiary of New Mexico, the Pen. The most notorious section of the original facility closed after riots in 1980, and had been converted into a giant soundstage for filmmaking. How could anyone film something in the same building where twenty people had died horribly? Luna just didn't understand the entertainment industry. Now all the inmates sat in the North facility, a hundred yards up. It made the Metropolitan Detention Center look like a summer camp.

"You'll keep me out of there, right?" Jen asked. Seeing the Pen made her anxious.

"I don't think it's coed."

"Well we're making good time so could we see Santa Fe? As you know, I don't get out much."

"We can do the thirty-minute tour," Luna said.

"How about the three-hour tour?" Jen asked. "Like *Gilligan's Island.*"

"Don't push your luck, or they will make an exception for you and put you in the Pen with the boys after all. We'll do Santa Fe in about an hour."

Luna took the final, most scenic exit, Old Pecos Trail. It was more of a rustic trail than a road, and pointed at the two foothills on the west side of town. She'd learned about Santa Fe geography from a summer internship here. "That hill over there is Song Mountain and the hill over there is Moon Mountain

"Song and Moon?"

"I meant Sun and Moon," Luna said. "Freudian slip."

Luna parked in the lot in the La Fonda hotel in downtown Santa Fe. The hotel looked like a tourist version of the ancient Taos Pueblo that Georgia O'Keeffe had memorialized so beautifully. Luna thought back to the old clinic in Crater, of course. She wondered if they had built anything in its place.

The beauty of Santa Fe quickly made Luna forget the ugliness of Crater. In fact, on a day like today, the adobe, the distant thunderclouds, the white hills, all made Santa Fe look like one big Georgia O'Keeffe painting. In fact the only thing that didn't look like Georgia O'Keeffe was the Georgia O'Keeffe museum, which was showing an avant-garde Navajo photographer, rather than its namesake's work.

Luna had read that the O'Keeffe section was closed due to a robbery.

Luna took Jen to the miracle stairway in the Loretto Chapel instead. The wooden stairway curved around in a dizzying ascent, but unfortunately, tourists weren't allowed to climb it. Jen and Luna were sufficiently impressed anyway. They actually spent a good solid minute in deep in prayer, about all the time they could spare.

They didn't have time for galleries, so they passed through the gauntlet of Native American vendors sitting under the long north porch of the Palace of the Governors, and tried on turquoise jewelry. Jen wanted a silver and turquoise cross, but Luna couldn't afford to buy it for her. To compensate, Luna bought Jen some Green Chile *Pinon* Brittle at Senor Murphy's.

"There you have it," Luna said splitting the candy. "Santa Fe in about an hour."

Luna realized the real reason she wanted Jen with her. She wanted Jen to hear Diana validate her character. Jen's wavering the other night had gotten to her more than she cared to admit.

They walked to the Attorney General's office on the other side of the Santa Fe River. It was a big adobe building that looked more like an old Spanish fort than a government building.

After a brief wait, Diana Crater finally ushered them in. Luna thought of the last time she'd been here, three years ago. Diana had been her boss and they'd asked the last Attorney General for help on the Jeremy Jones case. All through school and life, Diana had been the sophomore while she had been the freshman. Now Diana was on the other side of the desk, the top lawyer in New Mexico at thirty-five. Because of her name recognition, and the fact that a county had been named after her family, she'd be a senator, or even governor, by forty.

Diana, the Log Cabin Lesbian, had grown her hair out, and let some gray in. With her bulk—that she now embraced rather than hid—she looked like a presidential first lady on steroids.

Jen had been in nice law offices before of course. Both Hobbs and Dellagio had offices that reeked of money, and the U.S.

Attorney's Office felt of power, but Diana's office had something else. The artwork—especially the sculptures—were worth more than Diana's supposed yearly salary. Diana's office felt almost royal, like Diana was an Attorney Empress, rather than a mere Attorney General.

Jen touched Luna on the arm. "Your friend is pretty cool."

"Why did you bring her here?" Diana asked instead of saying hello. Luna had gone closer for a hug, but awkwardly sat down when Diana held her hand up like a stop sign.

"I wanted you to meet my client, Jen Song, and see what he did to her, Di," Luna said, pointing at Jen's scars. "You've got to prosecute this asshole."

"Dellagio?"

"No, Adam Marin. We'll get to Dellagio later."

"Do you understand how complicated this is?" Diana asked. "Marin's a cop, your girl's a defendant in a murder case. Marin is already cooperating against Dellagio, who is a suspect in a Federal sting."

" 'My girl' is my sister," Luna said. "My dad had an affair with Nurse Song."

Diana stared at Jen; she looked at her scars then at her eyes. She nodded. "You're very beautiful," she said. "I knew both your mother and your father. They treated me a few times when I was growing up."

For one brief moment, it looked like thirty years of friendship would pay off. Diana had practically been family back in Crater. Diana looked in Jen's eyes and saw Dr. Cruz and Nurse Song, and remembered them treating her at the clinic. She smiled at Jen.

Jen smiled back. "My mom mentioned you," Jen said. "She saved your life. Food poisoning, right?"

Diana nodded, and thought for a minute. She actually softened—she and Luna were playmates again, and Jen the reincarnation of Nurse Song. She smiled at them, not a political smile, a real one. Luna smiled, too; maybe this was a good idea after all.

Then Diana abruptly buried the smile as if Luna stood in the way of her quest for higher office. "I'm sorry, but there's nothing I can do."

Diana avoided eye contact. "Luna my love, my hands are tied." Diana used the nickname she'd stolen from the Cruz family. It did not sound right coming from her anymore. "The Feds are taking over her conspiracy case, and they, not the New Mexico Attorney General's Office, will go after Dellagio,. We have concurrent jurisdiction on the State murder, because Albuquerque is handing it off to us, but the Feds want to take over that one, too. I can't do anything on Marin's attempted murder case until I know what the Feds are going to do."

They sat in silence for a long beat. Luna looked around at the artwork, especially the bronze female nude that looked like Rodin's "Thinker" after six weeks of intense personal training. Everything about Diana was bigger these days.

Diana shrugged. "You knew I would say that, didn't you Luna?"

Luna nodded. "Duh." God, she sounded more and more like Jen everyday.

"So why did you come all the way up here?" She forced a smile. "Luna, my love."

Jen frowned. She looked at Luna as if waiting for something magical to happen.

Luna frowned. With all the doubts she had about herself right now, it was important for Jen to hear this from Diana. Diana was her friend—had always been her friend. Luna had saved Diana's ass with the Jeremy Jones case. Diana would never forget that, right?

"I want to know something," Luna said. "You're still registered to vote in Crater County, aren't you?"

"So?"

"I want to know if you voted me out as district attorney." Luna's eyes pleaded with Diana. Help me out here.

Luna just wanted to hear Diana say the word "no," and this whole trip would be worth it. Diana would then go on about what a great job Luna did in the Jeremy Jones case and Jen would get over her doubts about Luna. Luna would get over her doubts, too. Even the big bronze thinker over in the corner would think highly of her. God, why did this mean so much to her?

Diana frowned. "Are you sure you want your client to hear this?"

"You can talk in front of her," Luna said. She couldn't send Jen out now. It was too late.

Diana stared at the statue, rather than at Luna. "You know that the Attorney General's Office took over felony prosecutions in the smaller counties. It's a better use of legal resources. Closing your office was good for everybody. We're getting very good press these days . . . fighting for the little guy and all that. And it's an open secret that I'd like to be governor some day."

Luna looked at some newspaper clippings framed on the wall. Diana had just convicted a murderer in Mosquero County, as well as two separate trafficking rings in Crater. Good press, indeed.

"You didn't answer my question," Luna said. Luna still hoped Diana would say the words she wanted to hear, say the words "despite" and "great" and "lawyer."

Diana took a deep breath and looked Luna in the eye. Those words weren't coming. "All right, you asked for it. I'm sorry I have to be the one to say this—Luna, your heart was never in it. You did great in the Jeremy Jones case, but since then you've just been going through the motions. You missed a few deadlines, you pled out a few that you should have taken to trial. You were great with the high profile cases in other counties, but you screwed up run-of-the-mill burglaries and restitution agreements that people really care about. You have no idea how many folks in Crater came to me after I got this job. They told me they didn't want you as their D.A.—told me that they absolutely hated you. You just didn't fit in."

"They told *you*?" Luna said. It started to sink in. "*You* were behind the recall? I thought it was about the budget."

"It wasn't about budget. Not really. It was all about you, but it wasn't personal, it was politics."

"Not personal?"

Diana continued. "You went to law school because of parental pressure. You did it for your mom. Hell, I don't know, maybe you just did it to avenge your poor dead dad. Look at you—no office, wrinkled clothes, no phone. You're not really a lawyer. Even when you were the D.A. in Crater, you weren't really a lawyer. You never were a lawyer. I think you're still waiting for the Olympics to call and give you a gold medal. Whatever you're waiting for . . . it's never going to happen. What are you really waiting for anyway?"

Luna said nothing. She didn't know.

Diana continued. "I don't know what you expected me to say, but I'm telling you the truth. You're operating on emotion right now, and you're going to hurt both yourself and your client "

Diana took a sip of bottled water. "Does that answer your question, Luna my love?"

Shocked, Luna said nothing. Diana wasn't done yet. She now turned to Jen. "Ms. Song, technically your coming here could be construed as court business, so I'll let it slide. But if you violate the conditions of your release again, with a lawyer or without, you *will* be locked up for the duration."

Jen said nothing. She kept her eyes out the window, and avoided eye contact with both Luna and Diana.

"By the way," Diana said, "give my best to Nurse Song."

Traffic slowed on I-25 south, right around the Pen. There were black-clad state troopers everywhere. Perhaps there was a jailbreak. One trooper, the spitting image of Adam Marin, directed traffic to one lane. He motioned Luna to let a big truck get ahead of her. Luna followed, but the car in front of the truck stopped suddenly and Luna collided with the truck. Both air bags deployed but Luna's car was nearly totaled.

"Totally totaled," Jen said, trying to cheer Luna up as best she could.

Luna was so angry she banged her fist on the steering wheel so hard she nearly broke a bone. She then hit herself in the head with an open palm.

"Can't you do anything fucking right?" she yelled at herself. "Anything?"

Luna's torrent alerted the trooper. He hurried over and stared at Luna through her open car window with what the courts would call "reasonable articulate suspicion."

"She's my lawyer," Jen said apologetically to the cop. "She's just a little crazy right now."

The cop recognized Jen. "You're that murderer! Are you allowed to be out here?"

"I'm allowed to be with my lawyer," Jen said. "For *her* protection. I have to keep her out of trouble sometimes."

Jen's smile worked wonders. The trooper looked into Jen's eyes and he was hooked. Luna managed to regain her composure and the trooper helped them push the car to the side of the road. They waited for the AAA tow truck.

"What's wrong Luna?" Jen asked, playing the grown-up for the change. "I looked in your eyes and you are like a stranger."

Luna said nothing.

"You look like you could kill somebody," Jen said. "For the first time I was actually afraid of you."

Sandrina had been afraid of her. Dellagio had been afraid of her. Now Jen. Luna realized for the first time that she was capable of violence.

Jen finally forced a smile. "Next time you want to go on a road trip, just leave me at home."

Chapter Thirty
Emotional Distress

THANKFULLY, LUNA STILL HAD insurance for the car and resurrected the vehicle through a mechanic Jen recommended. The mechanic was handsome, and looked vaguely like that tattooed mechanic with his own TV show. He claimed, "Any friend of Jen's is a friend of mine."

Luna didn't want to be "friends," with anyone so greasy, and she politely rebuffed his advances. Where did Jen meet these guys? Luna spent her time with Jen at the house while the mechanic repaired the car. Neither Dellagio nor Adam Marin bothered them. This time, Luna felt like the patient.

"You look more depressed than me," Jen said. "Diana really got under your skin, right?"

Luna said nothing. She didn't have to.

Jen made a special Korean tea for both of them. The ginseng and mysterious spices almost made the pain go away. Boiling water was the extent of Jen's cooking skills, not that Luna was much better. Thankfully, Nurse Song had left them pre-cooked meals for the week. Mr. Song and Nurse Song now spent even more time at work and rarely showed their faces around the house.

Friday night, after picking up Luna's car, they watched a late night movie on TV and fell asleep on the couch. Luna half awoke in the middle of the night when she heard a car screeching outside on Crack Alley. Or was she dreaming? Luna looked around the room.

"Jen?"

No answer.

She almost called again. In her dream (or was she awake?) Jen's bedroom door was open, but Jen didn't seem to be there. Luna almost got up, but the couch grew tentacles. She felt trapped and soon found herself back in a deep, dark sleep.

When she woke the next morning Jen was there, well-rested and relaxed.

"Did you go anywhere last night?" Luna asked.

"Where would I go?"

That Sunday the whole Song family, Luna included, went to a church where everyone was Korean. Luna expected everyone to stare at her, but she found the people to be gracious, both of her and of her poor accused Jen. Most of the service was in Korean, but Luna found it strangely moving. When she prayed, she missed the old silver cross that she used to wear around her neck.

After the service was over Mr. and Mrs. Song went home, while Jen and Luna sat alone for a few moments. Jen had obviously done some serious praying, and neither wanted to break the spell. There was a small gift shop near one end of the church where a Korean woman sold hand-made silver crosses. Jen had some cash and bought two crosses, one for each of them.

"This is for you," she said handing it to Luna. "You need it as much as I do."

They both put on their crosses and gave each other hugs. When they exited the church they were surprised to see a black Escalade waiting for them in the parking lot. The car honked and they both jumped. For a moment Luna thought it was Dellagio, but the dark window of the car rolled down to reveal Victoria.

"I ran into Jen's mom and she said you were here," Victoria said. "I need to talk to you. Get in!"

Both Luna and Jen hurried over.

"Just you, Luna!" Victoria said.

"I can't leave her," Luna said. "If I do, they can arrest her."

"We'll just go over there," Victoria said, pointing across the parking lot. "They don't arrest people at church."

Luna got in the Escalade, and Victoria drove to the side of the lot.

"What's happened?" Luna asked when they stopped.

"I went to his house late last night and found his body," she said, disjointed. Before, Victoria had been Mary Poppins on ecstasy, now she sounded like Mary Poppins on crystal meth.

"Who's body?" Luna asked.

"Dellagio. He's dead. Deceased, terminated, rigor mortis. . . ." Victoria was turning into a wacky Monty Python sketch, she was so agitated.

"I get it," Luna said. "Calm down."

Luna paused and took a second to take it all in. "Did you call the police?"

"Yes . . . of course. I'm supposed to go down there in an hour."

"Why are you telling me?" Luna asked.

"I might be a suspect," she said. "I'm one of two people with access codes to his house."

Luna caught her breath. "Did you kill him?" Luna asked.

"Of course not," she said. "The only other person who knows the codes is Jen."

Luna looked dubious. "She was with me the entire night," although she didn't tell Victoria that she heard the screeching of a vehicle and that Jen didn't answer when she called. Or worse, that Jen had once said that she like totally wanted to kill Dellagio. Luna still found it highly unlikely that a nervous Jen would steal Luna's car, drive all the way to Dellagio's house in the mountains, kill him, and then drive back home.

"She was with me all night," Luna said again.

"Are you sure?"

"Yes," Luna said. She looked at Victoria, who looked like she'd finished a marathon, she so reeked of sweat. If anyone was the murderer right now it was Victoria. Luna made her decision. "Just drop me off back with Jen. I'm sticking with her for the duration."

Luna waited until she and Jen were back at Jen's house. "Where were you last night?"

"I was with you, watching the movie."

"I woke up in the middle of the night and you were gone."

There was a long pause as they got back on the freeway. "I was outside smoking," she said. "I'm not allowed to smoke in the house. I'm only smoking one cigarette a week now."

"Dellagio's dead."

Luna looked at Jen, and tried to read her. Jen looked shocked, too shocked to be faking it.

Jen then cried and threw up out the window at the same time, something Luna had never seen before. No, Jen wasn't faking.

She went on and on about how she wanted a father for her babies. It wasn't so much that Dellagio had died, it was that Dellagio was the daddy, the father of her babies. "They need a daddy," she said between sobs and pukes. "A real daddy."

Luna wiped off her face and eyes.

"I'm going to meet with the U.S. Attorney," Luna said. "You're going to have to say something to him."

Chapter Thirty-One
GSW to the Head

SEVERAL FEDERAL AGENTS STOOD at the gate of Dellagio's massive house in the foothills. He lived only a mile or so from Seek, but the houses here were much bigger, the highest of the high rent district. The property was aggressively xeriscaped, and the cacti looked as if they were about to attack. Dellagio's mansion was unsettling, an adobe interpretation of an old Victorian Lord's country home. The styles were at war with each other, particularly around the windows.

"You don't get to be this rich by being nice," Luna thought. If she had this kind of money, she didn't know what she would do. She tried to imagine the house she'd have if she was an evil drug lord. She'd always liked her mother's home—the Mothership—with its mix of adobe and high tech. Her drug mansion would be the Mothership, but bigger.

Unfortunately, something else ruined the harmony of the desert landscape: FBI, DEA, and FDA agents in their jackets, and a few men in jackets with acronyms she had never heard of.

When she made it to the door a big FBI agent radioed Vader, who came to the front of the house. He motioned her to follow him to the cobblestone driveway, away from prying ears.

"Do you think she did it?" Luna asked.

"Your client, or Victoria?"

"Either one."

"There's a boat load of their fingerprints all over the house."

"They've both been here before, you know that."

Vader shrugged. "They're the only ones with both motive and access. They've both been seen going in and out of the house a few times."

"That doesn't mean anything."

"Maybe not, but the last time your client was with a male lawyer related to this case, he ended up dead."

"She's still presumed innocent of that one."

Vader laughed. Luna waited for a moment, then took a deep breath. "Jen was with me all night. I can vouch for her."

Vader smiled. "Don't vouch yet. Do you want a guided tour?"

He ushered her over the cobblestones and under the crime scene tape. He held her hand as she bent under, and walked her to the living room, more in the manner of a real estate salesman than a crime scene investigator.

There were still corpse chalk marks in the living room, and bloodstains on the carpet marked the head. GSW all right. Luna tried to imagine the sordid scene that must have taken place, but failed to do so. She just couldn't see either Victoria or Jen killing anyone.

Vader kept in real estate salesman mode, talking as if describing the number of bathrooms. "White male dead of a GSW to the head . . . no signs of a struggle," he said pointing to the living room floor.

He then pointed back to the front door. "No sign of forced entry. Assailant punched in the access codes, then got victim's gun, indicating assailant had some knowledge of the house and personally knew the victim. Gun is missing by the way."

Luna frowned. "I ask again, is my client a suspect?"

"One of the neighbors saw a woman go inside. Like I said, Jen's fingerprints are everywhere . . . as are Victoria's."

He paused. He now reluctantly became a cop. "I really should lock Jen up."

Luna stood her ground. "As I said, she was with me all night. She woke up with me this morning."

"You're living with her?"

"Kinda."

"I guess that kinda makes you a material witness," he said, still a cop. "I can lock you up, too."

Luna wasn't sure if he was joking. She looked at Vader, who wasn't smiling. *He* wasn't sure if he was joking either.

They went outside to Dellagio's heated pool. He must have still used it even though it was now mid-November. Sunlight sparkled along the water. Luna didn't know a pool could be so blue. They sat down in the deck chairs like two vacationers.

"You don't have enough to charge her with anything," Luna said, still trying to be friendly.

"I agree," he said. "Luna, I'm not your enemy. But you'd better get me some names quickly, or I'll revoke your client's conditions of release. There's a lot of pressure on me from my bosses."

Luna had almost forgotten that this big man was a cog in the Federal machine, and that machine needed to be oiled. Either Jen or Victoria was the oil well.

Vader and Luna sat in the deck chairs for a few moments, pretending to relax. "Wouldn't you love to live like this?" Vader asked.

"I wouldn't know how."

Chapter Thirty-Two
Death and Dying

THE NEXT MORNING, VADER made Jen go in for paraffin tests, to see if she'd fired a gun. The tests came back negative. Not that that proved anything. As a legal secretary, Jen would have known enough to wash her hands with Ajax or to use gloves. With a rock-solid alibi from Luna, and alternative explanations for the fingerprints, Vader had nothing and let her go.

Jen didn't want to say anything until after the funeral that afternoon. She knew she'd better make an appearance to deflect attention. Since Jen was not allowed to go anywhere except in Luna's presence, Luna had to go as well. Jen borrowed Luna's arraignment skirt to handle her increased size.

"That's scary—when your little sister starts wearing your clothes when she's pregnant," Luna said.

"The Laser Geishas just don't look good flying over my belly," said Jen. "And I'm not Lolita any more."

The cemetery was next to Luna's complex, and TV cameras were waiting in the parking lot when they arrived. Shit.

"Ms. Cruz," the teenaged reporter asked. "Does your client have a comment on Dellagio's murder?"

Jen wanted to say something, but Luna held her tightly. Luna now looked directly at the camera. Time to make a stand.

"No she does not. Jen Song had nothing to do with Mr. Dellagio's death. As her third-party custodian, I can personally vouch that my sister was with me the entire time."

"Your sister?" the teenaged reporter asked. "Don't you mean your client?"

Luna stopped. She looked over at Jen. Did she want to make everything even more complicated? She almost had to. Yes, it was time to take a stand. Laser Geishas United and all. "You heard me," Luna said defiantly.

There was a murmur through the crowd of onlookers, who actually saw the resemblance for the first time. It definitely was the eyes.

The cameras took one last look, then shut off.

"Did I do all right?" Luna asked Jen.

"I think you overdid it," Jen said. "I mean I'm glad that you said what you said, but it could also screw things up."

"You think we should go?"

Jen looked over at the cameras. "If we go now, I'll look like totally guilty."

Luna wanted to be lowered into the ground right there next to Dellagio. Everyone stared at them, then whispered amongst themselves. A dusty wind filled with pieces of tumbleweeds blew through the cemetery, almost as if the dead themselves wanted to evict her from their property. She backed up a few steps, nearly tripping on the woman behind her.

Luna hadn't felt this exposed since the Olympic trials when she had limped the last lap into the stadium, and forty thousand people booed her. The crowd had actually been chanting another athlete's name, which sounded like a boo, but Luna had been too devastated to notice.

The muttering almost drowned out the priest as he said a few words. For a second she thought she saw Mr. Baca, the prospective landlord who had denied her because of her bad credit, but it was too hard to see from this far away.

Luna thought back to the funerals in her life. She'd been to her old boyfriend Nico's back in Crater. That was the last one. Her mother's funeral, of course. She sang at that one, but couldn't finish the song. As Dellagio's body descended into the ground, she tried to remember her father's funeral. She was eight years old. It was a closed casket, since his body had been burnt in the crash; her mother had tried to cheer her up.

"Your father's in heaven now," she had said, pointing. "That's up there."

Her mother had pointed to the full moon, which was shining in all its silver glory in the daylight.

"I might as well be on the moon with my dad," eight-year-old Luna had said back then. Thirty-three-year-old Luna would now agree. Things had not gone right for her since her father died. Shit, in twenty-five years, she still had not recovered.

Jen moved back next to her, and leaned against her shoulder. "I know you miss him," she said, reading Luna's mind. "I know how much you miss your father."

By now, Luna was crying. Jen patted her head with comfort, and wiped the hair out of her eyes.

"I'm the one who's supposed to be sad," Jen said. "I lost someone here today. Denny and Denise lost someone today."

Jen didn't shed a single tear. Somehow, she cowboyed up. Luna did the crying for both of them. As the mourners dispersed from the funeral, everyone gave the two women a wide berth.

"It's you and me against the world, Jen." She held Jen tightly, as if she could stop the world from taking her sister away from her.

"Loosen up," Jen said. "You're hurting me."

"It's going to be all right," Luna said, reluctantly loosening her grip. They said nothing for a while as they stared at the rows of the dead.

"You and me against the world," Luna said.

"Isn't that a song?" Jen asked.

Chapter Thirty-Three
Addendum to the Witness List

THEY WENT BACK TO Luna's nearby apartment for a cup of Korean ginseng tea that Luna had swiped from the Songs. Luna had been here for months now, yet Jen was her first guest. Lately, Luna felt more at home in the Mekong than at her own apartment.

The apartment had just a dash of *feng,* and a smidgen of *shui.* It was cramped for the two of them. But Luna did have four chairs crammed around her table.

"Are you expecting company?" Jen asked, as she sat down and rubbed her belly. "I guess you already have Denise and Denny as your first guests."

Luna smiled. "Hopefully I'll be out of here by the time they come along." Actually, Luna kept the chairs in case her parents came by from the great beyond. One was for her dad, the other for her mom. Jen put her feet on the other chair. That angered Luna just a tad.

"I want a name right now," Luna said. She got up and stood over Jen. She had been able to intimidate Sandrina, so Jen should be even easier. "Your ass is on the line. My ass is on the line. I need a name. *The* name."

Jen thought for a moment. "A name?" She frowned. "The name?"

"Just give me something, Jen. If you think I could have slapped you hard the last time, I will knock you into next week, if you don't tell me something."

Jen closed her eyes as if in deep pain. Thoughts raced across her forehead like an MTV video festival running through an electric blender—snippets of lies, truth, memories and nightmares swirled around.

She opened her eyes for a moment, looked like she desperately wanted to say something, then closed them again as if something had dragged her back into the theater of her mind.

She so didn't want to hurt Luna, but she had to tell, had to tell, had to tell. . . . No she couldn't . . . just couldn't. . . .it would kill Luna. . . .

The thought of being in jail forever, of someone like Sandrina as her roommate, the things Sandrina would do to her, terrified her. She had to say something . . . anything . . . the truth . . . a name . . . *the* name?

Jen finally opened her eyes. "Jonah Ruiz," she said at last. "The guy who worked for our dad a long time ago. The guy who tried to molest you."

Luna felt the memory come back and nearly vomited. She remembered being seven years old in the bathroom with Ruiz opening the door and moving toward her. For some reason, she couldn't picture her dad just now, but she sure could picture that evil bastard Jonah Ruiz with his sweaty forehead and tattooed arms reaching for her pink dress.

She took a few breaths and returned to the present. "Are you sure?"

"I looked up his record when I worked for Hobbs and saw the name 'Luna, C.' as a victim. He was a client of Hobbs, and of Dellagio. I delivered an envelope to him once. He works in a hospital in Las Cruces. I think he's the main dealer for southern New Mexico. He must know where the drugs are coming from."

Luna forced all bad memories out of her mind. She wasn't a seven-year-old; she was a lawyer now. "Can he hurt you at all?"

"He's not going to get me," Jen said. "I can fight him off."

Luna had to spell things out for the girl. "Did you know what was in the envelope you delivered? Did he see you do or say anything that implied you knew what you were doing was illegal?"

Jen thought for a moment. Luna didn't like it when Jen thought so much.

"No," Jen finally said. "I just gave him an envelope that one time. It was marked Attorney-Client privileged. That's it."

Luna looked at Jen again. That part may be true, but there was an entire iceberg of truth beneath that.

"He's our link," Luna said as she began drafting a subpoena on the computer.

Jen stared at her. "You really think if you subpoena a guy like that he's going to show?"

"Maybe I'll serve it personally," she said. "I can also stop at the border patrol checkpoint, the one that is one hundred miles inland on I-25, the one that snared Hobbs. Something doesn't seem quite right with that. I'll kill two birds with one stone."

"Ruiz is not a bird. He's like totally creepy and you really don't want to face him by yourself." Jen said.

"I don't know," said Luna. "This is something I've got to do for both of us."

"You can't go alone to meet a child molester."

"I'll take Seek with me."

"There's got to be another way."

"This is the only way," Luna said. "I'm going to save you even if you don't want to be saved."

Luna tried calling Seek from Jen's phone. They finally connected, and found a date where he would be in Las Cruces doing a trial. He reluctantly agreed to meet her after his trial and accompany her to the meeting with Ruiz.

"You really don't mind?" she asked.

"I know how important this is to Jen."

"To Jen? Don't you mean to me?"

"Luna, I talked to Jen," he said at last.

"You talked to Jen without me present? You can't do that, she's my client."

"It wasn't about the case. It was about her. It was about you. She's a friend of mine now, but that's not important. Jen thinks you're in way over your head."

"I'm doing it for her," Luna said.

"Are you sure this really isn't about you?" Seek asked.

Luna didn't have an answer.

Chapter Thirty-Four
Change of Venue

LUNA SPENT THANKSGIVING WITH the Songs Nurse Song did a nice twist on the traditional turkey, replacing the stuffing with *kim chee*. *Kim chee* is a condiment made by pickling vegetables such as radishes, cabbage, and cucumbers in salt, mixing in seasonings, and allowing the mixture to mature. It follows a basic code of five colors (green, red, white, black, and yellow) and flavors (salty, spicy, sour, sweet, and bitter), which all have traditional meaning in the Korean culture. Somehow it worked. Luna and the Songs tried to pretend they were one big, happy family, but failed utterly and sat silently watching an old movie on television.

The day for the trip to Las Cruces finally arrived in early December. Luna had PMS, which made a bad day even worse. She had originally intended to go with a nice blue pinstriped suit and a blue top, but just as she was about to leave, she noticed the blue t-shirt was one she must have taken from Jen. It said HIGHLAND HIGH JUNIOR VARSITY CHEERLEADER in yellow letters. What the hell. No one could read it under the four-button blazer, and the color matched, so she kept it on.

Luna looked for half an hour for her car keys. Then, getting on the freeway was an ordeal, with accident after accident on I-25. She almost turned around, but forced herself to become Sacagawea. Her Sacagawea was no one's fool and didn't need Lewis, didn't need

Clark, and most certainly didn't need some illiterate French trapper to guide the way.

Just south of town, Luna passed the gigantic Isleta Casino off to her left. She almost turned toward the casino, except she wasn't feeling very lucky. A few miles further, she passed the exit for the rural suburb of Los Lunas. The "Village of the Lunas," Luna said to herself. She almost wanted to move there, just for the name. She knew one of the judges in the town had the last name of Luna. She could marry into the family and change her name to Luna Luna. Luna Luna from Los Lunas.

After her namesake village, and past the small town called Belen—"where the trains meet the plains"—the road was a straight shot south until Socorro, desert on the west and the somewhat lush Rio Grande Bosque to the east. She'd once applied for an entry level Assistant D.A. job in Socorro, but didn't get it.

"Life sucks when you're too stupid for Socorro," she said out loud.

Then, after Socorro, both the landscape and the road were utterly empty. Even the tumbleweeds had abandoned this stretch. Luna felt loneliness, worse than ever before. The *conquistadors* called this stretch the *Jornada del Muerto*, the Journey of the Dead, and the desert plains sure felt *muerto* all right. Further down the road, Luna spied Elephant Butte Reservoir off to the east. The series of gray hills on the other side of the lake really did look like an elephant lying down. Unfortunately, the elephant had drunk all the water in the lake; it was a reservoir of quicksand.

Finally, she spied the border patrol checkpoint where Hobbs had been stopped on the other side of the freeway, just north of the T or C exit. She might as well check it out.

Luna slowed as she passed the station. It wasn't that ridiculous to have a border crossing almost a hundred miles into America; this was the last gasp to get the careless smugglers who had thought they were home free. The "Oxycontin Expressway" was the only road up from Juarez, and if someone managed to sneak past the checkpoint in El Paso, they would still have to pass through here. I-25 was the only road between El Paso and Albuquerque; all other roads heading north were a hundred miles away on either side.

A big border patrolman walked past the line of cars with a vicious Doberman. As a runner, she hated dogs, especially big black ones. The dog alerted on a car filled with college kids. Luna felt for the kids; she could almost feel the dog's hot breath on her thighs.

Then something hit her like a ton of bricks. Prescription drugs don't smell. A U-turn in the middle of the freeway was out of the question so she kept going and got off at the T or C exit and hurried to a gas station to call Vader.

She got to the point quickly. "Why did the dog alert on Hobbs when he drove up? Why did they stop Hobbs?"

Vader laughed. "Nice to hear from you, too, Luna," he said, walking that fine line between friendly and menacing. "They stopped Hobbs because I told them to."

Luna was a little pissed. "You haven't told me everything."

Vader laughed, a deep baritone laugh that she couldn't help but like. "Quite frankly, I know a lot of things I haven't told you. The problem is I can't prove them in a court of law beyond a reasonable doubt. That's why I need you. That's why your country needs you."

Luna couldn't tell if he was kidding with the last bit or not. She wasn't sure if she liked being needed by her country. She hung up and got back on the road.

After T or C, all her suspicions about the Feds in general—and Vader in particular—intensified on the barren stretch of highway. Maybe the Feds were selling illegal Mexican drugs to finance some nefarious plot somewhere else. She didn't know Vader that well, and how much could a U.S. Attorney make, anyhow? She felt tempted, seeing Dellagio's mansion, and had noticed that Vader felt the temptation even more so. His office was filled with trophies, but how about his bank account? What was it filled with?

She tried to put the various conspiracies out of her mind when she reached Caballo Reservoir. Caballo was smaller than Elephant Butte, and the drought had hit it even harder. Caballo reservoir looked more like a salty slush than a source of drinking water. A speedboat was stuck in the muck a half-mile out in the dried quick-sand. It had been stuck there for a long time.

Luna took the stalled speedboat as a bad omen, and drove even faster. After another hour of desert she finally arrived in Las Cruces. Was the city named after the Cruz family? She knew it wasn't, but said "Luna Cruz in Las Cruzes" out loud, just for fun. But try as she might, she didn't feel as if she belonged here.

Luna met Seek downtown in the Third Judicial District Courthouse. The modern adobe building was impressively wide, but much smaller than Albuquerque's.

Seek looked defeated. "You can't win 'em all," he said, trying to force a smile. He did not look that happy to see her. "Let's get this over with."

He didn't give her a hug. They got into his car and she had to push files off the seat and put them in the back. He shook his head. No you can't really win 'em all.

Chapter Thirty-Five
Enema Zoo

THE HOSPITAL WAS AT Exit 1, off University Boulevard. Luna glanced at the campus of New Mexico State University a.k.a. the "Enema Zoo." The Enema Zoo was smaller than UNM, yet its modern adobe buildings were spaced much further apart.

Albuquerque was hardly a big city, but it did have its urban stresses for a small town Crater girl like herself. There was something restful about Las Cruces, the jagged Organ Mountain much more beautiful than Albuquerque's Sandia Crest. The Organs really did look like pipes of a massive stone organ fit for the gods.

Luna's pulse had slowed the moment she took a breath of the fresh Las Cruces air—pecans from the south, and the slight farm fresh smell of cattle and cotton. It was a nice combination for a shitty day like today.

The hospital nestled against the Organs east of town. There was a big mountain with a white "A" on it. It must have stood for the Enema Zoo "Aggies," but Luna couldn't help but think of Hester Prinne and her scarlet "A" for adultery. Nurse Song should have worn a scarlet letter, and she supposed her dad should have, too.

Seek parked and they went in to the front desk. Luna's pulse increased the minute she got out of the car. The hospital had just started to hang up Christmas decorations, which seemed out of place here in the desert.

"I need to see Jonah Ruiz," she said to an attractive African American woman with dreadlocks who, according to her nametag, was named Cherry. Despite some African political posters on the wall, indicating a liberal background, Cherry watched a black and white episode of *Gunsmoke* on her TV. *Gunsmoke* was as reactionary a show as you could get. She even had an autographed picture of the star, James Arness, on one corner of her desk.

Cherry frowned. She certainly didn't enjoy looking up from the guns and the smoke. "You're a lawyer, I can smell one a mile away. We don't have to talk to you without a court order."

Luna knew she'd have to go back to Albuquerque—to Judge Kurtz—to get the court order, but with the border only a few miles away, Ruiz could vanish into the night.

Luna still had her old ID from the Crater County District Attorney's Office and flashed it. "This is an official investigation out of the Crater County D.A.'s Office."

"I guess that's okay then," Cherry said as she watched Marshall Dillon gun down another bad guy. "Just sign in."

Seek smiled a guilty smile, but didn't say anything.

They did get Albuquerque TV in Las Cruces, so there was a chance that Cherry would know about her recent past and realize there was absolutely no reason in hell—no justification whatsoever—to let Luna talk to a hospital employee without a court order.

Cherry pushed the dreadlocks from her eyes, and stared at Luna for a moment as if she recognized her from somewhere, but she quickly turned her attention back to *Gunsmoke.* "He's in the basement."

Luna scribbled her name badly, deliberately obscuring her letters. Cherry's eyes focused on the next shoot-out and didn't notice.

They hurried down to the basement of the hospital and wandered the hallways. Luckily, they didn't have to actually go into the morgue before they found Ruiz mopping the hallway outside. Luna now felt very conscious of the junior varsity cheerleader t-shirt hidden under her blazer.

Ruiz had become a wizened little figure. Someone had once remarked about the "banality of evil." Ruiz had too many tattoos to be strictly banal, but he blended into the gray background.

"Mr. Ruiz," she said, touching him on the shoulder with a very firm hand. Luna remembered when she was a waitress in college and had to put her hand into the grease trap to grab a ring that had fallen in. She felt the same way now.

Ruiz flinched. He turned around and stared at her, and knew he knew her from somewhere. He hurried down the hall, as fast as his wobbly legs would carry him.

How do I play this? Luna thought to herself. What would Sacagawea do? "Mr. Ruiz," she shouted. "I'm an attorney and I need to ask you a few questions."

He kept walking away, muttering to himself. Seek hurried over and grabbed him by the arm.

"It's about Jen Song." Luna said, catching up.

Ruiz looked down at his feet. "The Chinese girl?"

"She's Korean," Luna said. "There is a difference, you know." Time to play hardball. "Mr. Ruiz, my name is Luna Cruz. You worked for my father. I was the one who sent you to prison and I can do it again."

Ruiz nearly fainted when he recognized her. Luna grabbed his other arm and held him up. She felt the brittleness of his bones. Considering all that he had done in his life, she'd be more than justified tearing him in two.

Luna felt physically ill, just breathing the atmosphere around him. He had an odor that all the disinfectant in the hospital could not wipe out. Ruiz squirmed for a second, then froze, more afraid of her than she was of him.

"Let's talk in here," he said nervously. The three of them entered a big broom closet, the size of a one-car garage. It was filled to the brim with chemicals. Luna took a whiff of Ruiz. The man actually smelled like death from cleaning blood and guts off the floor. He held his broom as if it was a scythe.

"You're a big girl now," he said strangely. "I remember you when you were little. . . ."

That certainly didn't make her more comfortable. Luna had a small tape recorder in her pocket. She clicked it on secretly. "I want to ask you a few questions."

"What do you want to know?" he replied. "They'll be looking for me soon. They're always looking for me."

He was afraid of these people, whoever they were. Luna wondered if he was talking about the hospital staff or someone else.

"Did you ever meet Paul Dellagio or Ed Hobbs?" she asked.

Ruiz shook his head again. "I don't know either of those guys, except for what I hear on TV."

"Dellagio was your lawyer on a car crash," she said.

"I didn't meet him," he said again. "I talked with a paralegal over the phone."

"Did she have an English accent?"

He smiled. "I don't remember. All you *gringos* sound alike to me."

"I'm not a *gringo*," she said.

"Well, you're a *coyote*," he said using a derogatory expression for her mixed race status. "The other guy, Hobbs. He did the criminal case I had here, but he did it by phone from Albuquerque. Don't know nothing about him, either. I talked to the Feds already. Told them every thing I knew."

"I'm not the Feds. You've got to give me something," she said. She was pissed. She hadn't been called *coyote* in years. "Look, you worked for my father, Dr. Cruz. He kept you on in spite of your record, probably helped you out a few times before you attacked me. You owe him . . . you owe me."

That got to him. He smiled, remembering all the old man had done for him. "Dr. Cruz? I haven't heard that name in a long time."

"The pills come from Mexico," she said, boring a hole in him with her eyes. "From where?"

"A *farmacia*," he said.

"Duh," Luna said. "Which *farmacia*?"

Ruiz paused, as if he was about to tell the world's dirtiest joke. Luna cringed. A joke from such a man would be really, really dirty. He closed his eyes. What was he thinking of?

"Which pharmacy?" she asked again. "God damn. I wish my father had killed you when he had the chance!"

Ruiz wilted from her breath, then motioned her to lean forward. She hesitated, but it was clear he would say nothing unless her ear was right next to his lips. She felt his hot breath on her face, just like when she was seven. She nearly gagged.

"Go to *Del Norte Farmacia* in Juarez," Ruiz said at last. He giggled at the thought of something. "The main one with the clinic. It's a few blocks over. Take the Stanton Street bridge."

"I know where that is," Seek said, proving he wasn't just a potted plant.

Ruiz giggled again. Was it dementia or just evilness? "Since I told you what you need to know," he said, "could you make an old man happy?" He reached for her as if he didn't care one way or another.

Luna flashed back to childhood. It would be different this time. She surprised herself by pushing Ruiz—a good shot to the chest—and he buckled under the force, crumpling into a heap on the floor.

He didn't breathe.

"You killed him!" Seek cried.

"I don't care," Luna said. She really didn't.

Finally Ruiz gasped for breath, as if surfacing from the deepest depths of the ocean. He was still in shock. He looked as if he wanted to say something, but another glance from Luna shut him up. He closed his eyes.

Seek stared at her. "Remind me not to get you mad."

Luna and Seek did not help Ruiz up, but left him on the floor. They could still smell his stench, even out in the hallway.

Chapter Thirty-Six
The New Donkey Show

THEY REGROUPED IN SEEK'S car; he had moved it across the street from the hospital. Seek was actually afraid Ruiz might call security, but Luna seemed willing to take on all comers. She was very, very tired, and she certainly was not in the mood to drive all the way home, not this late in the afternoon. The prospect of spending the night in a fleabag motel in Las Cruces, dreaming of Ruiz's wicked laugh, was not a welcome prospect either.

Seek hadn't recovered from his trial and didn't look all that excited about spending any more time with her.

Luna called Vader with Seek's phone. She had still not gotten around to replacing hers since she smashed it. "I talked to Jonah Ruiz," she said. "Is that name enough for you?"

"We talked to him a couple of months ago. He gave up your client, Jen, you know, as a courier. I don't see him as a drug kingpin on account of his dementia. I certainly don't see him as a member of the Mensa Mafia."

Luna was about to give him the name of the *farmacia,* but realized it was the only piece of information she had, and it wasn't much.

"Shit," she said, not realizing she'd said it out loud.

"You'll need more than shit," Vader said, hanging up.

She might as well go into Mexico. It was only an hour's drive.

She reluctantly convinced Seek with her rapidly diminishing sex appeal.

"In and out," he said at last. "I'm serious. Fifteen minutes max."

She nodded. "In and out. Mexico in a minute."

Maybe she just had to prove she was not the *coyote,* or worse, the *gringo,* that Ruiz had deemed her. She didn't have much of a plan. She would use the camera on Seek's phone to take a picture of the most likely evil drug lord. Hopefully, Jen would recognize said drug lord from a meeting in Hobbs's office. She'd then give the picture to Vader and let him sort things out from there. Maybe that would be enough to save Jen.

She called Jen from Seek's phone, which he was very reluctant to give her for the second call in two minutes. "Jen, I'm going to Mexico with Seek. If you don't hear from us, send a search party."

"I don't know if that's a good idea," Jen said.

"I'm doing this for you, Jen."

That shut her up. Luna tried to imagine what a real, live, evil drug lord would look like. She tried to be politically correct and envision a group of clean-cut FBI corporate criminals. Yet for some reason she thought of Manuel Noriega, and Al Pacino in *Scarface.* She then shuddered at her own racism. Maybe Ruiz was right and she really was a *gringo.* No, she would keep her mind open.

"Before we go, I need a massive caffeine injection," Seek said. "You do too. You look dead."

Luna and Seek stopped at a big chain bookstore off I-25. In addition to books, the store also had a coffee bar that was as sophisticated as life got in Las Cruces. Luna pounded down a frappuccino, hoping the coffee and sugar would revive her. Seek bought a book, a legal thriller, from an author doing a signing. The author dressed in an expensive black jacket with a dark shirt. He tried to portray Hollywood hipness, but looked weary from addressing all the people in Las Cruces who only used the bookstore for the cappuccino in the cafe. It was Christmas, and many people were buying the book as a gift for the lawyer or the criminal in their lives.

A man with a shaved head was in the author's face. "You should write a book about *me*, ese."

Luna wondered if her life would ever be a novel. No, never. No one would ever give a damn about a nobody lawyer in New Mexico.

"Luna, you look so much better in real life," the author said in a strange voice, breaking her reverie.

Luna realized the man was talking to her. She vaguely recognized him as the hapless lawyer from the courtroom during arraignment. He must have been a lawyer and an author, the guy whose personal ad she'd seen on the Internet and rejected.

She ignored him. Authors in bookstores were right up there with clowns as people who creeped her out.

"You'll be sorry, Luna," he said with a laugh, as if he knew something he wasn't telling. She was out the door and in the car before he could say more.

Off in the distance, to the west, they saw the remains of an electrical storm that was now framed by an intense double rainbow. She looked back inside; the author had disappeared.

Seek sipped his frozen coffee drink as he drove south down I-25, which eventually ran into the I-10. They soon passed La Tuna Penitentiary just over the Texas border, next to Wet-n-Wild Waterworld, which was closed for the winter. If Jen did Federal time, would she end up at La Tuna? Luna wasn't sure. As she saw the United States flag fly over La Tuna, Luna couldn't help but think of Vader. He obviously knew a lot more than he was letting on. What was his agent named? Griego?

She didn't know why crossing into Texas made her nervous. Then it hit her. She was a lawyer in New Mexico. She was a nobody in Texas. What the hell would she be in Mexico? El Paso had identical stores to those in Albuquerque, and similar architecture as well. Yet the two cities were different, the landscape was more rugged, the Rio less lush, and the arroyos deeper—sort of

Albuquerque with erosion. Twenty miles of exurban El Paso later, they took the downtown exit on El Paso's Santa Fe Avenue, then headed south. There was a lot of construction, so they had to turn a few times before they found Stanton Street, the road to the bridge. Seek certainly didn't want to drive his nice car across the border into Mexico, so they found a cheap lot on the American side, the "Last Lot in America."

"Maybe we should do this some other time," Seek said. "And just hang out in El Paso tonight. You know, this parking lot creeps me out. It's like the parking lot of the damned."

Luna looked around. The lot was firmly under American jurisdiction, but it seemed part of Mexico as well. Transients, terrorists, prostitutes and runaways all lurked in the lot, waiting to hitch a ride or drop off their car for the duration. This would be the perfect lot for a terrorist to store a bomb—or a body—in the trunk. Several of the cars were totaled. The lot apparently doubled as a junkyard for parts as well as people.

Luna saw an ambulance hurry to a corner of the lot. A girl lay on the ground, surrounded by onlookers, some helpful, some not. Was she giving birth? Hard to tell from here.

The EMT loaded the girl into the back. A cop car arrived and followed the ambulance.

"They're arresting her?" Luna asked.

"They're not letting them give birth over here any more," Seek said. "It's usually a dodge to get citizenship for the kid and benefits for the mom. If she's illegal, they'll arrest the mom after the baby comes, then send her and the kid back."

Luna shivered with anxiety. She didn't want to stay here one minute longer than she had to. But if she didn't cross over, Vader would lock up Jen for sure. Still, she felt a growing apprehension, and it wasn't just the caffeine from the frappuccino. A few years ago, many young Mexican women had gone missing, then turned up dismembered in mass graves. With her dark skin, Luna could easily fit the profile of the missing women.

"I'm fine," she said. "Let's go."

It was hot. Luna took off her blazer, and was slightly embarrassed to display the Highland High Junior Varsity cheerleader shirt. She didn't care anymore; it was too hot. "Go Hornets," she said out loud.

A cab driver came over to them, soliciting business. "No donkey show," Seek said, gesturing the man away.

"No, not donkey show," the driver said. "*Farmacia.* Cheap. No prescription."

Donkey or no donkey, Luna didn't like the look of the driver. "Let's just walk."

Luna and Seek crossed over the Rio on the Stanton Street Bridge. The bridge crossed the Rio like a rainbow. As they ascended, she looked down at the water. It was hard to believe that this was the same Rio that flowed through Albuquerque. Here it looked like a drainage ditch from a chemical plant, the water an industrial gray, and just a few feet deep. As she crossed, she saw a little plaque that officially announced the border. As she began her descent down the other side, she developed horrible cramps. Some rainbow.

They each gave a quarter to an un-smiling woman at the turnstile on the Mexican side. "Remember, this is a one-way bridge," the woman said, sensing that Luna was a Mexican virgin—someone who had never been to Mexico before.

Luna was about to ask the way back, but she was already through the turnstile.

"Welcome home," Seek said as they emerged into Mexico. A big sign said "Feliz Navidad."

"This ain't my home," Luna said. The Cruz family hadn't lived in Mexico for over four hundred years and back then it was part of Spain. She took out a scrap of paper with a scribbled address. Unfor-tunately, a hot gust of desert wind blew it back through the turnstiles and over the bridge. She tried to chase after it, but was refused entrance to the bridge. Oh well, she'd find the *farmacia* somehow.

Luna had expected the architecture on the Mexican side to be adobe, but it was a weird mix of everything, and all of it bad—big, concrete government buildings mixed with one-story brick bodegas. Each bodega was painted a different shade from a drunken rainbow, but much of the paint was faded. Most of the bodegas had been converted to *farmacias.* More cab drivers came up to them, saying they'd take them to the *farmacia* with the lowest prices in town.

"I guess all the donkeys died," Seek said with a smile. "They're soliciting for the pharmacies now. I don't know if that's a good thing."

Luna leaned a little closer to him. Damn, he looked good. "Fear and poverty are an aphrodisiac."

They followed the throngs of Americans, and eventually ended up on the main drag, *Avenida Juarez.* They walked to the next major intersection, a wide street called *Avenida 16 de Septembre,* where everyone headed right, so they followed the crowd toward the twin spires of a church, *La Mision de Nuestra Senora Guadalupe.* The church looked like a Mexican Notre Dame, and it had a small plaza that felt like something out of the middle ages. They were less than a mile from the border, and they were officially lost.

La Mision plaza, with its kiosks of vendors, bustled with activity even though it was a late weekday afternoon. The crowd was now primarily Mexican, the few Americans were mainly drunken college kids, servicemen from Fort Bliss, and elderly people looking for prescriptions. She also saw a few body builders in tank tops looking for their daily doses.

Luna walked up to an old Anglo lady buying the world's ugliest plaster statue of Jesus for five dollars (American) from a vendor. She really did have blue hair that matched her blouse, just like a redneck Marge Simpson. The rest of the woman's clothing was a powdery blue as well, so was the tunic of the Jesus for that matter.

"Do you know where *Del Norte Farmacia* is?" Seek asked. So much for his sense of direction.

"Could you please help a fellow American?" Luna asked. That

was what a destitute Humphrey Bogart had said in *The Treasure of Sierra Madre.*

The Blue Lady looked at her, judging her. Her statue of Jesus most definitely judged them, too. Evidently they passed the test. The Blue Lady pointed at a bunch of *Del Norte Farmacias*, all small, all round the plaza. It was almost as ubiquitous as Starbucks, with lithium instead of lattes. "Which one?"

Luna thought for a moment. "Is there a main one?"

"You mean the big one, the one with the clinic?"

Luna nodded. That's what Ruiz had said. "Yes."

"Follow me," the Blue Lady said. She only had so much faith in her plaster Jesus, and wanted to back it up with modern medicine. "I'm going there anyway. You can find everything there."

That sounded promising. The Blue Lady made a few quick turns and they soon arrived at the termination of a dead-end alley near the Stanton Street bridge—the bridge you couldn't cross back over. They had missed the building on their way in. Luna was missing a lot of things these days.

The woman didn't say anything as she went inside a door under a small sign. The building looked more like a warehouse than a pharmacy, and like its University of New Mexico counterpart, it also was made of cinder blocks painted to look adobe. But here, the brown and turquoise paint was fresh. The *farmacia* did well for itself, as did its neighbors. It was right next to a clinic and a dentist's office. There was even an upscale bar and liquor store on the same block. She didn't ask about a donkey.

"Voila," the Blue Lady said as she followed a horde of other elderly Americans, as well as a few skanky men and women who were obviously pill poppers. A white man with an intricate Maori tattoo covering his face mentioned something about "needing help after his operation," but Seek pushed him away. The Maori quickly found another victim, who gave him a dollar. The Maori hurried inside.

"From here on, you're on your own." the Blue Lady said.

There was an American and a Mexican flag painted on the adobe facade of the building. Luna stared at the American flag and thought about Vader again. Did he know about this place?

Just then, a Mexican ambulance crew picked up a man from an alley near the pharmacy. The man was hurt, GSW to the chest. He clung to life, clung to his Raiders cap as if it was his greatest treasure. Luna gasped. It was Cruz from the mental health unit. That guy did get around.

Luna didn't want to ask what happened, or whether it had anything to do with the *farmacia*. From the looks of the injury, Cruz wouldn't be getting around anymore.

Inside, the place was as packed as a mall at Christmas. This late in the day the elderly were leaving and the pill poppers were coming in. It resembled the university pharmacy, but was nearly twice as big and painted an antiseptic pink, like a delivery room. Armed guards in clinical white uniforms stood everywhere. The Blue Lady was obviously a regular as the guards smiled at her. She cut in line and wandered in ahead of several people. Some older Americans protested, but she gave them a dirty look and they soon relented.

Luna looked around. "This place is a gold mine," she said. The few remaining elderly people had the dazed look of casino patrons signing up for their player's club cards. The pill poppers, including the Maori with his fresh dollar bill, sat on one side of the room.

A drunken soldier from Fort Bliss looked as if he needed a magic pill to cure his hangover, or perhaps he'd contracted something nasty from a local prostitute, or worse, a local donkey.

"Think about the money they're making when they ship these drugs to Albuquerque," Seek said.

"Albuquerque?" Luna said. "Think about Denver, or Dallas or even L.A. or New York. . . ."

"So who are we looking for?" Seek asked. "If I was an evil drug lord, who would I be?"

Luna took Seek's phone out of his pocket as if she was playing with his privates. She smiled at him seductively. He gave her a dirty look, then relented. "You just love me for my phone," he said.

"I'll just take a few pictures and then cross-reference it with Jen. She probably knows one of these guys and we take that to the Feds."

That almost sounded like a real plan. Now who was the evil drug lord? For a second, she thought she saw Agent Griego sitting with the pill poppers. That went with her wild Federal fantasies of a vast conspiracy, but it wasn't him. Shit.

She walked over to look at the pictures of the pharmacists and doctors on the pink wall. The pictures were blurry—they certainly wouldn't show up well on Seek's little camera.

Luna was surprised for a moment at one photo—the head of the pharmacy and clinic, a Dr. Mondragon. Where had Luna seen that guy before? There was something about the eyes. He was a handsome Hispanic man of about seventy, and was in incredible shape. Didn't that asshole Mayhem Moreno talk about a Mondragon cartel? This Mondragon guy might be head of that cartel.

For a second, she almost pulled the frame off the wall, but a guard eyed her. She quickly remembered why the photograph was so familiar. The man in the photo was a dead ringer for Mr. Baca, the potential landlord who had turned her down for bad credit, the man who looked like what her father would have looked like.

"You know that guy?" Seek asked, noticing her stare at the picture.

What was Mr. Baca doing all the way down here? And why had he changed his name to Mondragon?

She looked at the picture on the wall again. This guy was balder than Baca and he had a goatee, rather than a beard. His eyes were much bigger. Maybe it wasn't Baca, but she wasn't sure either way.

"I don't know."

The Blue Lady now yelled at the clerk, who was standing behind a bulletproof glass wall. "I want to see the manager," she shouted. "I want to see Mondragon! I'll call the *Federales,* my son-in-law is a Mexican and he works for the mayor of Juarez!"

The whole place suddenly became silent. A guard gave her a look that indicated he would shoot her right there—and if he had enough ammunition, all the witnesses, too. The clerk nervously pressed a button and whispered something in Spanish.

There was absolute silence for another moment, then the clicking of an electronic door. Another lady said something, but the others quickly shushed her. Apparently summoning Mondragon was like summoning the Loch Ness Monster.

A figure walked in from a black doorway. Unlike Dellagio, who drew people in, all the techs and clerks rushed away from the figure as if terrified of him. He looked at them as if wondering if he should grind them up into capsules and stuff them into pill bottles. From the attention Mondragon got, he was definitely the biggest of the big enchiladas down here.

As he came to the window, he really did look like Mr. Baca. Luna inched closer, until she was about twenty feet away. As she got a clear look at him, she realized that Mondragon wasn't Mr. Baca at all. No, not at all.

It only took a moment for it all to sink in. He was a little smaller than she remembered, of course. The goatee was new. There'd been some plastic surgery and his head had been shaved. But she knew those eyes. Even from here, she knew those eyes. She had looked at those eyes every day for the first eight years of her life. Hell, she still looked at those eyes in the mirror every single day. She already had his picture on her wall. Mondragon was her father, alive after all these years.

Her father was the bad man, and Luna shuddered as she realized her entire life had been a lie.

ACT III: LASER GEISHA GREEN

Chapter Thirty-Seven
Withdrawal

LUNA HAD AN OUT of body experience, except instead of heaven, she'd ended up in Juarez by mistake. She didn't talk to Mondragon; she didn't bother to take his picture with Seek's camera phone. But she did take another long look at him, just to be sure. . . .

Shit! It *was* him. He had aged very, very well, but you never forget your father's eyes, her eyes, Jen's eyes. She could never forget, never, ever!

Should she call out to him? "Dr. Cruz?" Or, "Daddy?"

"Is something wrong?" Seek asked.

"Everything is wrong!" Luna said. "My whole life is wrong."

"You know that guy?"

Luna said nothing. She took another glance. Luna desperately wanted to say something to him, but what could she say?

"You ruined my mother's life," was one thing. "You ruined my life," was another. He had also ruined Jen's life as well.

You motherfucker! She said to herself, as the words didn't come out of her mouth. Technically it was a true statement.

She had dreamed of this moment all of her life. Hell, every night when she looked at the temperature picture she pretended she was three years old again and everything would be all right. That photo had always cheered her up. Be careful what you dream of. Dreams can come true, and that's not always a good thing.

Luna didn't have the heart to face him, didn't know what she would say if she did. The Blue Lady was deep in an argument with the man, and Luna saw her chance.

"Let's get out of here," she said. "Now!"

"Aren't you going to take a picture?" Seek asked.

Luna didn't know. She still wanted to grab the photo off the wall, but some instinct of self-preservation kicked in. This Mondragon looked like the kind of guy who didn't like his picture taken. Look what had happened to the guy who had gotten dragged out on a stretcher. The guards had already noticed them, and were headed in their direction.

"Let's get the fuck out of here," Luna said forcefully.

Seek was surprised at her tone and they quickly headed outside. She then hurried over to an alley and kneeled down. She threw up for several minutes, maybe to stop herself from thinking. Some got on Luna's shirt. Seek held her hair out of her face. Thank God for small favors.

"Are you alright?" he asked.

"No. I'm not," she said. "That was my father."

"You told me your father was dead. . . ."

"That's what I always thought."

Luna wanted to go back inside, but now was not the time. She felt the Mexican winds blow her far away from the pharmacy. They didn't want her to go back inside either. She thought about the stages people went though in losing a loved one—anger, denial, depression, bargaining, acceptance. What were the stages when the dead come back to life?

Seek, supposedly the Ivy League athlete, barely kept up with her as she hurried back to America. It was as if she was reliving that fateful race in the Olympic trial, going into the stadium in Colorado, the time she had literally walked into the stadium, dead last. This time she ran fast enough for time to bend backward on itself like something out of a Superman comic. She wanted to run so fast that the earth would spin in the other direction. Or maybe it already had.

Seek shouted at her several times to wait, but she ignored him as she pushed through the time warp all the way back to the *Rio*. They ended up at the Stanton Street bridge.

"You can't get out this way!" a Mexican guard shouted as he pointed them toward the *Avenida Juarez* bridge, a few blocks west. Seek had to physically stop her from trying to make a run for it over the bridge. He grabbed her arm and escorted her the two blocks, staying as close as possible to the barbed wire fence blocking them from the border. Luna sure didn't want to get any deeper into Mexico than she already was.

Neither of them had a quarter to get back over the Avenida Juarez Bridge, which became the Santa Fe Street Bridge over in El Paso. Luna paid a twenty-dollar bill for both of them. The Mexican woman inside the booth did not give them change. To Luna, it was just another pound of flesh.

They pushed through the people on the bridge, easily going faster than the automobile traffic going into America. Her demeanor quickly aroused suspicion at the border crossing on the American side at the Port of Entry.

The American border guard, a tough Latina, shouted something at her in Spanish, then switched to Texan English when he saw her limited comprehension.

"What country are you from?"

"I'm American, damn it!" she said. She showed an ID.

"Do you have any liquor or medication to declare?"

She was about to say something smart, but Seek came up from behind. "No, she doesn't."

The guard eyed them. Had she done her quota of full cavity searches for the day? She thought better of searching them. The line was already too long as it was. The Maori was a few places behind them, and to the guard, that search looked like a lot more fun.

• • • • •

Luna and Seek hurried back to his car. His side mirror had been swiped. The attendant just shrugged. "It's the border, *ese.*"

He swore softly, then drove back on the I-10. She held her breath until they crossed back into New Mexico at Exit 0. She recalled Sacagawea finding her long-lost brother after ten years. People really do come back from the dead. But for Sacagawea, it had been a happy occasion.

Luna didn't say a word to Seek the entire time he drove. It seemed just moments later when they exited the freeway into Las Cruces. She had thought Las Cruces was the city of the Cruz family—who knew that the real city of the Cruz family would be Juarez?

They stopped at the courthouse. Her car was still there, but had a parking ticket. She had stayed too long. It wasn't like she would pay the ticket. Let there be a warrant for her in Las Cruces. Everyone else in her family had already broken the law.

Seek walked her to her car, and held the door open. He didn't smile, instead, he looked relieved to finally be rid of her. He'd been a gentleman for the last few hours, but that gentleness had worn off, and the manliness had somehow increased, but not in a good way.

"You need to know that I'm not your chauffeur," he said, nearly slamming the door behind her. "I'm not your bodyguard either."

She wanted to protest, but it was too difficult. She and Seek were never meant to be, she supposed. It didn't matter. Breaking up with her boyfriend was about as important to her as the ticket. She ripped up the ticket and threw it on the ground. More than anything, she wished Jen were here. They could cry together—a good long cry.

Luna didn't say another word; she just turned the ignition and flipped on the radio. She blinked, and suddenly the car was seventy-six miles north, near Truth or Consequences. Truth or Consequences, indeed. Her car was now almost out of gas, just like she was.

She took the T or C exit and her brain kick started, now that she had to pay attention to the road. For her father to become Mondragon would involve faking a death and staying hidden for several decades. She wondered who the body that was supposed to have been her father really was? Probably a prisoner, a sex offender that even the other convicts didn't want to spend their eternities with. Back in the day, guards just threw bodies out in the mesa and let the rattlesnakes eat them.

Her dad had put Ruiz away for what he had almost done to her. Had he kept in contact with that motherfucker while he was in jail? Worse, had he hired that creep to do his dirty work after all that had happened?

She headed up the main street of T or C. If that really was her father, he would have called them at least once during all those years. It wasn't like they were hard to find. Either she or her mother had lived in the Mothership the entire time. The phone number had never changed. He had never dropped her mother, or her, a note. He just let them sit there suffering the slings and arrows of outrageous fortune.

Her real father could never do that. Never! Never! Never!

Then why hadn't he called them? Why? Why? Why?

She nearly ran over a pedestrian, another blue lady scurrying across the main street of the funky wild-west downtown. Luna knew she had to stop, take a break, and bring her head back to the current time line. Maybe she had gone to an alternative universe, but she knew that this T or C still had hot springs where you could drown away your troubles.

She went to one of the spa resorts near downtown. The word "resort" was a misnomer—just some fences, a few mobile homes, and several rickety wooden structures lying over sulfur smelling tubs. Still open at this time of night, the set-up looked even more rickety in the moonlight.

The hot springs overlooked a placid section of the Rio. Luna rented a private bath in one of the smaller, more solid structures and watched the flow of the water in the moonlight. She wasn't exactly sociable right now.

When she entered the bath, the spring water smelled strongly of sulfur. It literally smelled like hell, but right now that was a good thing. She undressed, scanned her body again to make sure there was no residual slime from the afternoon. She almost expected her youthful muscles to have sagged as if they'd aged a hundred years. No, she was still young, still clean.

She said the word "clean" out loud. It sounded funny coming from her lips. She hardly felt clean right now.

Luna descended slowly into the sulfuric waters. They burned for a second, but they scalded away any germs she might have caught from Mondragon. She wiped her body with a house towel, then sat still for a few moments and let the sulfur seep into her skin and into her veins.

Luna looked out at the moonlit outline of the barren hills of the outside world. She felt she wasn't of this earth any more. She wondered if she could even breathe the atmosphere out there. No, she most definitely couldn't go back out into the world.

Maybe saving the Cruz bloodline wasn't a good thing after all. First, her dad had been a total lying bastard. Second, her dad had committed the felonies of faking his death, desecrating someone else's corpse, and trafficking illegal prescriptions in Mexico and in the United States. Third, he was no doubt a drug dealer who worked with child molesters. Fourth—and worst of all—he had abandoned his own flesh and blood, his own wife and child, in Crater County, New Mexico, the worst place on Earth.

Luna knew one thing. Men don't hide out in Mexico and ruin their eight-year-old daughter's life because they had good intentions. Jesus Christ, he could have told her mother something, but he let her mother suffer for the rest of her life. Earlier today she had not cared if she'd killed Ruiz—what about Mondragon?

Luna felt like drowning, dissolving herself in the hot sulfur. It would save her the time of becoming acclimated to the smell down there in hell. She soaked in the water and felt the sulfur go all the way up to her brain. Luna lowered herself underwater for a moment, just to feel the total immersion of steaming water all around. She got some water in her nose and mouth, and coughed for air. She still had some self-preservation instincts after all. After a few more moments, the water began to feel great, despite the smell. Her muscles relaxed, even though her brain was battered.

She finally got out of the hot tub before her muscles totally dissolved. But instead of getting dressed, she lay down on a bench right there in the structure, curled into a fetal position, and cried.

It took some wheeling and dealing with the resort operator, but after she emerged, she used the house phone to make a collect call. At least Jen accepted the charges immediately.

"Jen," she said. "I think our father has been involved in this from the very beginning."

There was static for minute. "Jen?" Luna asked.

"I can hear you," she said. "Barely."

"He's still alive!" Luna shouted into the phone. "He's the drug lord."

The static got worse. Luna could tell that Jen had said something but couldn't make it out.

"What did you say?" Luna asked.

"I said 'Duh.'" Jen replied. "Who do you think posted my bond?"

Chapter Thirty-Eight
Dormancy

AFTER SHE GOT HOME that night, Luna didn't sleep. God, she wished she had taken the pills back when she was in the old clinic and had never taken that damned picture off the wall. Why couldn't it have been demolished along with the building? In the middle of the night she tried to take the picture down, but she had put in too many nails. She didn't want to risk ruining the walls of her rented apartment.

When she woke up, Luna knew she needed a place to confront Jen. Her apartment was too cramped, and Jen's house held too many distractions. After the debacle at the Flying Star, restaurants were even worse.

Luna knew they'd have to make an outing of it. Jen hated her confinement more and more every day. As they talked over the phone that morning, Jen wanted to go back the Bosque. But when Luna looked out her window, past the cemetery to the volcanoes beyond, the answer was obvious—a return to the scene of the crime.

When she arrived at the Song house, Jen was ready, waiting outside. "That U.S. Attorney called," she said. "He wants to know what happened."

"I don't know what happened until you and I have talked."

• • • • •

Although its crest was barely a hundred feet off the mesa below, the volcano really did feel like a moonscape. The scramble over the black rocks was just steep enough to be intimidating. There was a slight fall wind to make it a little brisk, but otherwise the weather was perfect for this late in the year.

Jen kept glancing at the stray lizards darting under the black rocks, as if she wanted to follow them into the earth below.

Luna spread out a picnic lunch, and handed Jen a bottle of Mountain Dew that she hoped would serve as truth serum for the day. "So you knew the entire time that my father, I mean *our* father, was alive?" Luna asked after Jen had her first sip.

"Pretty much," said Jen, taking another green gulp. "I mean, no one told me, but I put the pieces together. Especially after my mom got all that money."

"So your mom knew too?" Luna asked.

"Duh."

"Why didn't you tell me?" Luna demanded. "I'm not just your lawyer. I'm your sister. This is *my* father we're talking about."

"*Our* father!" Jen shouted. "He's my father too."

"I've thought he was dead for nearly thirty years. Do you know what I've gone through?"

"Yeah, I do," Jen said, the green liquid now racing through her veins, hopefully preventing her from falsehood. "Luna, you've got to believe me. I understand what you're going through. Look how fucked up I am."

"Look how fucked up we both are," Luna said. "Are you two close?"

Jen shook her head. She was in pain too, and not just for deceiving Luna. "I've never actually met him," Jen said. "Not once. I've never even talked to him on the phone. You've got to believe me. I think my mom's maybe seen him twice the entire time since he left. I got suspicious when she went to Mexico a couple of times and came back with money. I think Dellagio called him the night of the murder, but I never knew for sure."

"But don't you. . . ." Luna was so angry, she couldn't think what she wanted to say next. She tried again. "Why didn't you tell me?"

Jen looked her in the eye. "Would you really want to know your father faked his own death and is probably the kingpin of a major drug smuggling operation?"

Luna looked out at the vast emptiness of the desert. A gust of wind suddenly made her shiver. "Yes, I would have wanted to know!"

"I was wrong, then," Jen said. "I should have told you. I didn't think you could handle it. I'm sorry."

"How can I trust you anymore?" Luna asked. "Too bad you're not a virgin. I'd do a human sacrifice right now."

"Are you going to hit me again?" Jen asked, afraid of Luna. She looked for a rock to hide behind.

"I should. I really, really should!"

"I don't know anything," Jen said. "I'm figuring this out for myself. Luna you've got to believe me." She kept repeating, "Believe me, believe me," like a new mantra.

The jury was out on the issue of belief, but Luna kept pressing. "So the real reason your mom hired me is that if I figured it all out, I probably wouldn't go against my own father?"

"I guess so," Jen said, still leaning back. "Maybe they really do think you're good. You've got to understand one thing: I don't know anything. I called Dellagio on the night of Hobbs's death, and he must have told my father. Dellagio then told me everything would be taken care of."

"Has it been?"

"I'm out of jail," she said. "And I've got you. That's something, at least. I'm glad you're my lawyer. I'm really, really glad. You've got to believe me."

When she said those words, "You've got to believe me," this time Luna could tell that Jen meant it. To Luna, it seemed that Jen's entire core depended on whether Luna believed her or not.

Jen started crying. "How do you think I feel? I have a father I've never met. The father of my babies is dead. I finally get a job as a legal secretary, a real job, something that I'm good at it, and it turns out that I only got the job so I can help out a drug dealer. My mom hates me, my step dad hates me . . . my real dad hates me. All I've got is you, and you hate me, too."

Luna looked at Jen. She wanted to say that she didn't hate Jen, but at that moment she wasn't sure. They were all alone there on the surface of the moon. In the silence, they felt a rumbling. Maybe the volcano would indeed erupt every forty thousand years, like clockwork, but the sound came from above.

It was a supersonic jet headed out from Kirtland Air Force Base, probably to bomb someone somewhere. Jen touched Luna on the wrist, as if Luna could protect her from anything nuclear.

"I want you to know one thing, Luna," Jen said. "When I said I love you, I meant it. You are the only person in my life who has loved me for me, not because I'm a pawn, or a piece of ass, or . . . or whatever. . . ."

Luna wiped some dust off her face. "Jen, I'm not your sister any more. I'm your lawyer."

"You're always my sister."

"Half-sister," Luna said. "Or is that 'like totally' bullshit too, like the rest of my life?"

"That isn't bullshit," Jen said. "That's never been bullshit. I mean look at us, once you get past the Korean part, we even look the same, like the Laser Geishas."

Luna took a good look at Jen, perhaps the first one in awhile. Jen was certainly more voluptuous than she, but yes, one could certainly see the resemblance. They had the same chin for example, and definitely the same elbows, the same knees. The eyes of course. But did they have the same heart? They sat for another ten minutes in absolute silence. More jets flew off in the distance as Luna puzzled it together.

Jen valiantly tried to hold still, but she shivered as the wind picked up. She got up and walked around for a few minutes and did a lap around the edge, as if it was some kind of ritual.

Luna walked over to Jen at the edge of the volcano. "You understand you could be innocent of murder, but still convicted of conspiracy."

"You're talking like my lawyer again." Jen sounded as if she was disappointed.

"You understand that the only chance I have to save your miserable little life is that you bring in our father?"

"I don't know if I can do that," Jen said.

"I don't know if I can either," Luna said.

Chapter Thirty-Nine
Obligatory Exposition

Luna had dinner with the Song family that night at the house in the Mekong.

"I saw Dr. Mondragon down in Juarez," Luna said over the soup.

Nurse Song looked at her. "So you know?"

"I know," Luna said.

No one said anything after that. They ate some delicious Korean *bulgogi* in total silence—Luna didn't bother to ask what the meat was, it could be rhinoceros butt for all she cared. She even let the *kim chee* torture her mouth without complaint. After dinner, Mr. Song politely excused himself and went to work. No one was unhappy to see him go.

Luna faced Nurse Song. "You told me the money was clean."

"It is clean," Nurse Song said. "I got the cash from the *Del Norte Farmacia,* a legitimate Mexican business. I really don't want to go into more detail than that."

Luna agreed. She didn't want to know too much, because she might have to answer questions about the money to the ethics board. Luna thought for a second. She would probably never see the hundred thousand sitting in her trust account. She would never be rich after all. But this had never been about the money.

"So could you tell me about my father's apparent death?" Luna asked. "Off the record."

"Let me put the dishes away first," Nurse Song said. "Does Jen have to hear this?"

Luna looked over at Jen. "She's my client. She's my sister too, so she has a right." Luna paused and looked at the dirty sink. "She can hear . . . but only if she helps with the dishes."

Jen did help with the dishes, and did a good job for once in her life. Finally, when the kitchen and the dining room met Nurse Song's standard for absolutely, positively spotless, they went into the cramped living room.

"I'm just telling you what I know," she said. "Your father and Dellagio met in Chicago, and originally they began dealing amphetamines to medical and law students. Your father convinced Dellagio to come to New Mexico, and they set up their first drug ring. I met him that way . . . as a client."

Both Luna and Jen looked shocked. "I had a drug problem," Nurse Song said. "Amphetamines mainly. I got hooked while in nursing school here."

"You had a drug problem?" Jen asked. She may not have loved her mother, but she never saw a fault in her before.

"We have addictive personalities in our family," Nurse Song explained. "I think you got some of your personality traits from me."

"So you were involved in the dealing," Luna said. "You dealt with human scum like Jonah Ruiz."

"Yes, I did," she said sheepishly. "I kept him from you except that one time, when Ruiz tried to get you in the bathroom and then I called your dad. Your father stopped him and pressed charges. He told him he'd go have to go to jail or he would kill him."

"Then why is Ruiz working with my dad since he got out?"

"I don't know," she said. "You'll have to ask him."

Luna shook her head. "So why did my father fake his death?"

"People were talking. About us. About the drugs. Crater is a small town, and it was only a matter of time before somebody turned on him. If he had been caught, they'd have killed him, and me too. They probably would have taken you out as well."

"Who's they?"

"The other people involved in the cartel. Bad people."

"So what happened?"

"Off the record, right?"

Luna nodded.

"I helped him set up the death, and identified the body. It was a corpse from the prison that Ruiz got for us—someone no one would miss. Your father said he would tell the medical board about my drug use if I didn't help."

"Did you use while you were pregnant?" Jen asked, interrupting.

"I'm so sorry, Jen," Nurse Song said. "At first we thought you were retarded, and I felt so terrible."

"She's not retarded," Luna said defiantly. "She just has trouble paying attention. It's a pretty common issue. But she's getting over it."

Luna knew she'd have to turn the conversation back to the topic at hand or she'd be stuck in the middle of twenty-five years of angst between the Songs.

"Why didn't my father tell me?" Luna asked. "Why didn't he tell my mom?"

"He figured she'd be happier knowing him as a great doctor, and not as a drug dealer. As to why he never told you, I suppose you'll have to ask him that."

Luna frowned. She didn't know if she ever wanted to see the man. "So after he fakes his death, my father goes to Mexico. . . ."

"Not at first," Nurse Song said. "He started in Colombia. Then Peru and Venezuela—all over South America until he knew it was safe to come back. He made connections there and switched from medicine to pharmacy, which wasn't that hard for a man with his brains. He's in Mensa, you know. He sent me some money . . . then he married someone else."

Nurse Song was on the verge of tears now. "He has a whole new family. He moved to Juarez a few years ago. That's as close as he'll come."

So Luna did have another family somewhere. She didn't know how to feel. So far, her family had been nothing but trouble.

There was silence, a moment of tension between Nurse Song and her daughter. They had never talked about this before. Luna didn't know which was worse, not knowing you had a father, or knowing that you did and not knowing him at all.

Luna knew she had to change the subject. "So why was Hobbs killed?"

"That was Sandrina," Jen piped in.

"I don't ask too many questions," Nurse Song said. "They sent me money to bond Jen out and hire a lawyer. Jen said Dellagio suggested you. I was surprised, but I've always liked you Luna, you know that."

Luna didn't know whether to take that as a compliment or not. She changed the subject. "What about Dellagio's death?"

"I don't know anything about that," Nurse Song said.

"That was Victoria," Jen piped in, again.

Luna gave Jen a dirty look. "Do you still talk to him?" Luna asked. "My father?"

"No. Well, maybe once every two years or so. I send him newspaper clippings about the two of you, but he never responds. I just talk with his secretary. He broke my heart just like yours."

The women sat in silence for a few moments. They all had a common enemy.

"So what am I supposed to do?" Luna asked no one in particular. Luna looked at both of them. "You are my clients and we have a very difficult decision to make. Our only hope of saving Jen is to somehow bring my father, I mean Mondragon, to justice here in America. I can't do that without your permission."

"Let me think about it," said Nurse Song at last. "He gave me a lot, but then again, he did ruin my life." She glanced over at Jen.

"Are you talking about me?" Jen asked. "Did I ruin your life?"

"No," Nurse Song said apologetically. "You know what I mean."

"We've got to talk," Jen said. "Just you and me."

"I've got to work tonight," Nurse Song said.

"Call in sick," Jen said. "We've really, really got to talk."

Nurse Song looked into Jen's eyes. "You're right. I'll call in sick. I guess we do have a lot to talk about."

"I'll check in with you both tomorrow," Luna said.

That night Luna went for coffee at the Flying Star with Seek to see if their relationship, or whatever it was, could be salvaged. The Flying Star did have a wine license, so coffee soon turned into an exotic Croatian wine, and Luna had the late Hunter S. Thompson buzz of alcohol and caffeine. The two substances fought a battle in her blood stream and Seek took her back to his home in the hills afterwards. She was pretty drunk; half of her was in the mood, and half of her wasn't. Seek, however, was a gentleman and set up a bed for her in his guest room.

He looked at her. "I'd like your permission to ask Jen out."

"I don't get it," Luna said. "What do you see in her? Jesus Christ, she's pregnant with a dead man's baby."

"She's just got this quality—when you see her you just want to take her in your arms and protect her from evil . . . and she has really big tits."

Luna didn't know what to say to that one. "Let me think about it."

The guest room had an amazing view of the lights of the city below. Luna thought of Sacagawea again—how this poor Indian girl had been kidnapped by another tribe when she was a little girl and never knew her parents. She never had to deal with them again.

Sacagawea had it easy.

Chapter Forty
Counteroffer

HUNG OVER THE NEXT morning, Luna met with the Song women at their house in the Mekong. The living room was now messy. There had been a coup overnight. Jen had apparently forced a regime change over household cleanliness. What else had changed?

"We've been thinking," Jen said. She paused. This was a big step for her, as her mother was letting her be the grown-up for a change. "Dr. Cruz or Mondragon or whatever his name is, never did shit for me and he treated my mother like dirt. I say you go to the Feds and do whatever we can to plant his ass in jail. Money or no money. Are you with us?"

"I'm with you," Luna said.

Luna was early for her appointment with Vader, it's not like she had anywhere else to go these days. She sat in the lobby with a few Native Americans who were dressed in casual western clothing. The New Mexico U.S. Attorney's office handled all the major crimes on the reservations. An adorable little Navajo girl, whose turquoise jewelry was two sizes too big for her, smiled at Luna. It was the world's saddest smile.

The girl looked so innocent, yet so incredibly sad. Luna instinctively knew what she was here for. Luna had been a victim once too, so she felt a connection to the girl. Luna had to wait nearly an hour for some of the Navajo contingent to leave before Vader was finally able to usher her inside past the mysterious OCDTEF sign. "So why are we meeting?" he asked. "Do you have a name for me?"

Luna fidgeted nervously. "I went to Mexico a few days ago," she said.

"I heard," he said. "Border patrol in El Paso flashed your picture up here as you came back. You looked like shit."

"Did you follow me in Mexico?" Luna asked. Suddenly, she was nervous. Maybe the Feds might not need her help after all.

"Not exactly," Vader said, shaking his head. "Our jurisdiction ends at the border, and quite frankly, now is one of those times when our relations with our Mexican counterparts are particularly sticky. Then again, all times are particularly sticky. . . ."

Luna smiled, then frowned. Stickiness was not necessarily a good thing. "I have reason to believe that the main *Del Norte Farmacia* is a prime supplying point for the prescription drug trade."

"Tell me something I don't know," Vader said. "I tried to get an agent in there."

Luna had a brainstorm "There was a man who I kept seeing, a tough kid with a baseball cap. I think his name was Cruz. Is he one of your agents?"

"*Was* one of our agents," Vader said. "He's dead. They killed him."

Luna didn't mourn the man, but abruptly shivered. She took a deep breath before continuing.

"I also think that Dr. Mondragon, the head of the pharmacy, is really a Dr. Cruz, late of Crater County, who was presumed dead almost thirty years ago."

Mondragon chewed on that for a moment. "Any relation?" he asked, trying to joke.

"He was my father," Luna said. She paused for a long time. "He is my father."

For the first time in his life, Vader was at a loss for words. This was news to him. Vader stared out the window as if the answer lay on top of the Sandia Crest.

"I gave you a name," Luna said slowly and distinctly. "So will you drop the charges against Jen?"

He still wasn't convinced. "And I assume you have some kind of documentation."

"No. I don't have anything."

"Do you have any idea what the U.S government, or even the Mexican government, requires before they can extradite someone?"

"No. But they got Noriega from Panama. It can happen."

"Mondragon, or Cruz, or whoever, is a bad guy, but he's not in the same league as a guy like Noriega."

Luna wanted to say that as far as she was concerned, both her father and Noriega were in the same damn ballpark.

Vader closed his eyes for a second. "Would you or Jen be willing to infiltrate his cartel, gain his trust, so we can extradite?"

Luna said nothing for a long while. She was hardly a spy. Jen was definitely not a spy. This wasn't a repeat episode of *Alias*.

"Would I have to wear a wire?"

"If you wear a wire, you'll be killed."

Luna sighed.

"Well?" Vader asked.

"I guess so," she said. She suddenly wasn't as convinced as she was before. "I don't think Jen would, but I could. I guess. . . ."

"Hold that thought," Vader said. "Would you excuse me for a moment?"

Luna went back to the waiting room. The little Navajo girl was still out there, still shell shocked. "It's going to be all right," Luna said to the girl. "They can help us here."

The girl smiled at her. "I hope so."

The receptionist took a call, then signaled to Luna. "You might as well go. He says for you to call him back at the end of the day.
"

• • • • •

To get her mind off life, Luna ran up the La Luz trail on the west side of the Sandia Mountains. Near the summit the trail switchbacked between a sunny side that was desert, to a shadowy side that was lush with vegetation. Luna felt she was crossing between good and evil, over and over again. After the final of eighteen such switchbacks, Luna finally made it to the Summit House. Luckily they had a vending machine with Sheep Springs Mineral Water. She kept some dollars in her pocket just for this very occasion. She drank her fill, then called Vader from a pay phone. Even if she had a cell phone, she doubted it would work all the way up here.

"Well, my superiors are actually excited about your info," he said. "But not *that* excited, considering all the wars going on in the world. We're on our own here. Quite frankly, do you have any idea how much of a bitch this will be to set up?"

"What does that mean?"

"That nothing's going to happen for a while."

Luna looked out at the city below. She wondered if she could see all the way to Mexico from here. She thought briefly about running back down, but decided to take the Sandia Peak Aerial Tramway. She was tired.

Chapter Forty-One
Continuance

VADER WAS RIGHT. IT was a bitch to set up. Albuquerque actually had a winter for a change, and a white Christmas. The Mekong had several days of slush—just enough to ice up the roads and annoy the crap out of people. The wind reminded Luna of Crater.

For Christmas at the Songs, Luna bought Jen baby clothes, Jen bought Luna that author's book, the legal thriller that she'd seen down in Las Cruces. "Don't tell me how it ends," she said.

Luna didn't know where January and February went. She ran even harder. "Life" was what happened between workouts. Luna got in better and better shape, as Jen's belly got bigger and bigger. Despite Luna's best efforts, neither Vader nor Diana dropped the charges against Jen. Vader did lock up Victoria, just to lock up somebody for Dellagio's murder. Luna kept pestering Vader about Mondragon, but he repeated that he had to talk to his mysterious "superiors" and "get everyone on the same page."

"Who's everyone?" she asked. "And what's the same page?"

"You don't want to know," he said. "To either question."

"We don't have forever here," Luna said. "Jen's about to blow."

"What do you mean?" Vader asked. "She's about to go into labor?"

"Labor is the least of her problems right now," Luna said. "She's just getting more restless every day."

• • • • •

There was a story on the Most Enchanting Newscast, wondering whether Jen Song would ever be brought to justice. Channel 8 then re-ran the rather un-enchanting file footage of Luna pushing Jen back the first time they met.

"God, so much has happened since then," Luna said out loud.

When Luna and Jen went out they received dirty looks from the public, so they confined their meetings to Jen's house. The only place they felt comfortable together was at the Korean church. God hadn't turned his back on the two of them, even if everyone else had.

Money was still tight for all of them that winter of their discontent. The bank wouldn't release the money in Luna's trust account until the case settled. They let her have another few thousand dollars or so, but that was it. Luna had lived off credit cards for a while, but now the cards were nearly maxed out and her monthly payments were killing her. Her meager savings from her job as Crater County D.A. had also come to an end.

At least the phone situation was settled . . . sort of. Luna still had such bad credit that no phone company in town, or on the Internet, would give her service. But the message on Jen's phone now announced, "This is the law office of Luna Cruz."

Just when Luna thought things couldn't get worse, she bounced a rent check and was summarily evicted from Sky Village. With her bad credit and limited funds, Luna had no choice but to move in with the Songs. They moved Luna's bed into Jen's bedroom and the two sisters became roommates. That had to violate attorney-client canons somewhere, but Luna had no choice.

It was an awkward situation, but they all made the best of it. Nurse Song and Mr. Song (Luna never learned his first name) finally separated. He moved out, possibly even back to Korea. Luna got along with Jen just fine, but Nurse Song soon treated Luna as the "Number One Daughter," the daughter who was supposed to be the good one. That created a hint of jealousy between the two sisters.

Luna joked to Jen one night. "We're co-dependents now."

"Don't you mean co-defendants?"

"That too."

Luna's law practice finally picked up, sort of. Initially she felt like a streetwalker in sensible shoes, hanging out in the courthouses hustling twenty-dollar arraignment hearings, but soon acquaintances started passing on one hundred dollar sentencing hearings to her. She handled "time waivers" in juvenile court and "aggravated DWI firsts" in Metro. That soon led to youthful offenders and aggravated drunk drivers, second. Luna didn't particularly like routine defense work, but it paid her bills . . . well, some of them.

Jen became her legal secretary by default. Jen's mind worked in funny ways, but it did work rather well once you grew used to it. Soon, Luna couldn't survive without her. Although her grammar was terrible, and her spelling was worse, Jen could think like a criminal and come up with defenses that Luna had never imagined. With Luna's help, Jen passed her Internet classes with flying colors. She even considered law school.

Luna thought Jen would make a damn fine lawyer. The girl could be very persuasive when she put her mind to it. Maybe it was those Cruz eyes.

Life was very stressful for the extended Song family, even though the family was just Luna and Jen most of the time. Nurse Song now took every shift she could muster to make ends meet without her husband. Jen still couldn't go out alone because of the house arrest, and she grew more and more antsy. She talked about taking the babies somewhere—like the big island of Hawaii. Jen admitted that she did feel something for volcanoes. Jen was about to explode in all senses of the word.

Luna met with Vader a few times for casual coffee, on the pretext of discussing the case, but since there wasn't much to discuss they moved to personal discussions. The casual coffees soon turned into casual dinners. He was even her date on Valentine's Day. She loved the sound of his voice.

Despite their break-up, Luna also hung with Seek on the "down low," as they said. They met a few times at places where lawyers wouldn't know them: lunch with the tourists in Old Town, gambling penny slots at Sandia casino, even drinks and dancing with the criminals over at a local dive. It was hard to classify their meetings as friendship or a relationship, especially since he seemed to be biding his time before Jen delivered. That wasn't to say things didn't get heated between them. After a few too many drinks downtown on St. Patrick's Day, they had another encounter.

Luna's thirty-fourth birthday approached on April twentieth, and as she tried to think of the highlights of the last year, she realized there weren't any. One morning in April, she finished a long run and found Jen waiting anxiously outside on the dirt lawn. Jen had pajamas on, as if she had just jumped out of bed.

"I just heard from that U.S. Attorney guy," she said, even more breathless than Luna. "He called on my phone. He told me to tell you, it's on."

"It's on?" Luna said. "What's on?"

"Go meet him at the shooting range," Jen said. "He'll give you the details."

The shooting range was way out on the west mesa in the shadow of the volcanoes. Vader had his earphones on. He fired his Tek-9 at a distant target, trying to adjust for the vicious spring wind. He failed and totally missed the target. He was no Annie Oakley, and most certainly the force was not with him.

He took off his earphones and turned to Luna. "You willing to terminate with extreme prejudice?"

"Terminate with extreme prejudice? Isn't that what the CIA told Martin Sheen to do to Marlin Brando in *Apocalypse Now*? What exactly do you mean?"

"Just that our choices of official actions have dried up. But there are still some unofficial things we can do."

"Unofficial?"

"I've got contacts on the Mexican side," he said. "We've got a window next week. I'm taking some personal time. You get in and get something to the Mexicans; maybe they can act. Or maybe you can somehow convince Mondragon to cross the border and we can handle it over here."

He didn't spell out what "handle it" meant, so Luna wasn't sure exactly what he was implying, or whether she wanted to know.

Luna was confused. She asked again about a wire.

"If you wear a wire, he will kill you—daughter or no daughter. These guys *are* smart enough to frisk you. It's the Mensa Mafia after all."

"Do I get a Delta team?"

"You're looking at it," he said. "I'll accompany you to Mexico. Unofficially of course. I've got some friends on the Mexican side. Unofficially as well. But most of the time you're on your own."

Vader put his ear plugs back in and fired another shot. He missed again.

Luna went back and had tea with the Songs. Jen chugged down the hot liquid. She was definitely drinking for three.

"I'm doing it," Luna said. "I'm meeting Mondragon."

They both stared at her. "Are you crazy?" Jen asked. "Remember you told us what happened to that last agent, the guy in the Raiders cap?"

"I'm doing it for you," she said.

Luna turned to Nurse Song, "Could you call him and set something up? Call Mondragon?"

Nurse Song frowned. She didn't want to do this, but she looked at her daughter. She knew she had no choice. "What do you want me to tell him?"

"Tell him that his daughter needs help, needs money."

"Which daughter?" Nurse Song asked. "You or Jen?"

"Both of us." Luna looked around at their meager surroundings. "You know what? That's actually the truth."

Luna and Jen sat with Nurse Song as she made the call to the main pharmacy. "It's the only number I've got," she explained.

Nurse Song left a message, saying it was an emergency with her daughter's case and she needed to talk to someone. Whoever was on the other line didn't sound very cooperative.

Luna took the phone away from Nurse Song. "Tell Dr. Mondragon that Luna Cruz, his *daughter*, desperately needs to speak with him. I have information that would be very useful to him, and I'd like to meet him in person at the pharmacy."

There was a click on the phone. "I will talk to him and then get back to you," a female voice said in heavily accented Spanish. The voice had a nervousness to it, almost as if she was afraid of what she would find out.

The three of them sat by the phone for the next twenty-four hours. Luna wasn't sure if she even went to the bathroom. Finally, someone called. Nurse Song picked up, and put the call on speaker. Luna and Jen hovered by the phone.

"Tell her to come tomorrow," the female voice said. "Dr. Mondragon is eager to meet with Senorita Cruz. It has been a long time."

Eager? Luna was positive that something was lost in translation.

Chapter Forty-Two
Jornada del Muerto Express

THE DAY OF THE journey had finally come. After all these years, she would actually talk to her father. Maybe something interesting would happen before her birthday after all. Vader drove. They crossed the Rio Grande for the first time just south of Albuquerque. I-25 crossed it one more time near Caballo. A hundred miles south of that, the Rio became the border between the United States and Mexico.

The Rio looked even muddier than usual. Luna hated to think about all the trash that had been dumped into it upstream.

"Deeper and deeper into the heart of an impenetrable darkness," Luna said out loud, quoting Joseph Conrad.

Luna went through the phases of death as she went to see her father in life. She was in anger mode all the way to Los Lunas. Maybe it was just caffeine, but she kept thinking of ways to kill Mondragon. She liked the sound of rocket-propelled grenades, or perhaps she'd hit him with a bullet at the top of a balcony and he would fall into a bloody fountain below.

Denial kicked in around Belen, at mile marker two hundred. She didn't have to do this. She could just go back and plead Jen guilty. She would never have to see her father. He wouldn't bother her; she wouldn't bother him. She nearly asked Vader to turn around near Socorro, at mile marker 150.

Depression hit around a steep dip in the highway, a gigantic arroyo known as *La Canada Alamosa,* just north of T or C. Her soul sunk with every mile, and with every foot they descended in elevation. Seeing the dry lake and the dead elephant hills of the butte made it even worse. A few miles later they crossed the Rio for the second time.

Luna looked over at Vader. This is my Delta team? He was a nice guy, in a fatherly sort of way, and that deep voice sure was sexy. She appreciated all he was doing for her, but he was more of a lawyer than a Delta. That made her even more depressed. What the hell was she doing?

She hit bargaining mode by the green chile fields near the village of Hatch, forty miles north of Las Cruces. Maybe Mondragon could give them enough information to lead to the capture of some even bigger criminal. That would save his sorry life, she thought as they reached the first exit for Las Cruces.

Luna kept running through various scenarios in her mind as they crossed into Texas, Exit 0. She had to go to the bathroom and didn't want to go into Mexico on a full bladder, so they pulled off. Actually, she hoped if she went now, she wouldn't have to go once she crossed the border.

They took one of the first exits to El Paso. Luna quickly ran into the nice Sunland Park Mall off I-10. She saw a Barnes and Noble across the street and wondered if that same writer was in there. Just to be safe, she went to the mall instead. With its typical American stores, Luna could still pretend that she was in the middle of America and nothing was about to change.

Luna hurried into the mall bathroom and changed in the stall. She got out and looked in the mirror. She wanted to look nice. No t-shirts, but she didn't really know how to dress for an event like this. She was in her best black suit. Her dad should be proud of her even if he was about to die . . . or whatever was about to happen.

• • • • •

Vader parked in the big lot on the American side of the border. Seek had called it the Parking Lot of the Damned; it was literally the last lot in America. She had been here before and had felt uneasy. Now the lot looked even worse than it had just a few months ago. Some cars were extremely dusty, as if the owners didn't plan on coming back. Luna spotted several shady characters, and she had a feeling she was being watched.

"We can still back out," Vader said. "But make up your mind. I really don't like hanging out here with a nice car."

Luna stared at the Stanton Street Bridge rising out of the earth a few blocks away. She didn't say anything. Vader made a call, talked to someone in Spanish, then hung up. "It'll be a few minutes. Let's wait here before we cross over."

A sudden rain came out of nowhere. They called them monsoons down here, as if El Paso had been plopped down in a rain forest as opposed to the desert. Fifteen minutes later the monsoon stopped abruptly, then a rainbow came, one of the brightest rainbows she'd ever seen. Vader checked his watch again. "Last chance. You can't back out after this."

Luna said nothing. She had to call Jen first. She stared again at the rainbow that rose over Juarez. She could kill Mondragon and flee south. She'd been willing to kill Ruiz; she could go to Brazil and hang with Sandrina's buddies in Rio and live on the beach for the rest of her life.

Kill her own father? Was she serious? She wasn't sure. Like Sacagawea, she would go with the flow until she hit the end of dry land and ran out of options. She wouldn't worry about coming back.

"Well?" asked Vader.

"Let me borrow your phone." She called Jen on Vader's cell phone. It was weird hearing "Law Office of Luna Cruz" on the other end.

"Should I do this?" she asked Jen.

Jen didn't say anything.

"Jen?" Luna asked again.

"I don't know what to say," Jen said, crying. "Do what you have to do. I just hope I see you again. Call me when you get back. The minute you're back in America! I'm so worried about you!"

Jen sobbed some more, then hung up.

After counting to a hundred, then counting back to zero Luna was ready. The rainbow had faded.

"Let's roll," she said.

She and Vader crossed through the Last Lot in America, then up the Stanton Street Bridge, and over the Rio into Mexico. It was the same guard as last time, who again reminded her that this was a one-way bridge. "You can't come back this way," she said again.

"I know," Luna replied.

The sun now set over the desert hills to the west. Luna could see smoke coming from some of the hills on the Mexican side. At first she thought it was lava from volcanoes, but then realized it was probably just campfires. The full moon had already risen over the modest Juarez skyline.

As they got closer to the turnstiles of Mexico, Luna wondered whether she was going home or running from it. She felt carried along with the tide of Mexican workers returning after their workday in America. She'd reached the final stage, after anger, denial, depression and bargaining. That final phase was acceptance, right?

What came after the acceptance phase? Oh yeah—death itself.

Luna looked down at the brackish waters of the Rio. She imagined what it would be like to swim across. She smiled. As a triathlete, this stretch of water was the final leg of her personal triathlon.

On the Mexican side, Vader took her to a side street a few blocks from the *farmacia* where a rusted Ford pick-up pulled up to them. Out came a skinny man dressed in a t-shirt. He looked like an addict asking for money, but he hugged Vader profusely. Vader hugged him back. There was something hinky about the guy, but Vader treated him as an old friend. The two spoke rapidly in Spanish.

"This is Guillermo," Vader finally said to Luna in English. "He's my counterpart over here. He'll help you as much as he can."

Some counterpart. Some help. Guillermo looked like he was so deep undercover that he couldn't uncover himself anymore.

"I've heard a lot of things," Guillermo said in perfect English, another Mexican with a Texan accent, more Waco than Juarez. At least his voice was friendly. "I think you should initiate contact alone. We can follow you from a safe distance; then you can call if you need us. Mondragon has several houses, some of which we don't know about. He'll probably take you to one of them."

He gave Luna a number. "Call me from a pay phone if you have to reach me."

Luna memorized the number and ripped it up. She took another look at Vader and Guillermo. They looked like Laurel and Hardy. No, she didn't have a Delta team.

Guillermo knew a shortcut to the *farmacia,* and they arrived more quickly than she expected. I'm not ready for this. Luna thought.

Vader and Guillermo shook her hands, then waited outside, nodding at her.

"Good luck, Luna," Vader said.

"What do they say on Broadway?" Guillermo said. "Break a leg."

This isn't Broadway, Luna thought as she entered the *farmacia.* Or is it?

Chapter Forty-Three
Over the Mexican Rainbow

INSIDE, HER OLD FRIEND the Blue Lady, was first in line. The woman must be addicted to something if she came back here after what happened. Maybe that was why she was here as well, Luna thought. She was jonesing for a father fix.

Luna took a deep breath, then went to the counter and told the clerk in English that Luna Cruz had arrived to see Dr. Mondragon. Should she add, "I'm his daughter?" She decided not to.

The clerk was a tall busty Latina with bleached blond hair who looked like a Mexican Marilyn Monroe. She smiled a Hollywood smile. Juarez was a Mecca for cheap dentistry as well.

"He's been expecting you," Marilyn said in English. She'd been the one Luna had talked to over the phone. "It will be a minute, however. Make yourself comfortable. He was expecting you a little earlier, and something came up while he was waiting."

"I'm sorry," said Luna. She couldn't think what to say after twenty-five years so she winged it. "Traffic was a bitch."

Marilyn forced a smile. Luna felt as if she'd been flagged at airport security. She waited in the soft chairs with the other offenders, mostly crotchety old American people.

"Are you okay?" asked a woman in pink polyester. Her pink outfit matched her pink hair. "You're shaking like a leaf. You can get ahead of me if you want."

Luna said nothing. If this was Broadway, she had a severe case of stage fright.

"He's a good doctor," the pink polyester woman said after a few moments. "Don't worry."

Marilyn kept forcing smiles at Luna as the time passed. "He hasn't forgotten about you," she said.

Oh yeah? After an eternity and a half, Dr. Mondragon came out to see her. She couldn't bear to call him Dr. Cruz, and couldn't bear to call him father, much less Dad or Daddy. He was shorter than she remembered, at least an inch shorter than she.

He didn't hug her; he just shook her hand briefly, as if greeting a patient with a possible communicable disease. She felt tears well up, and did her best to hold them back. She didn't know whether to hug him or not.

A big bodyguard frisked her. The bodyguard wore black, and looked vaguely like Antonio Banderas in the movie *Desperado*. He was a man who could be either a mariachi or a murderer depending on the gig—so big he was the size of a full band of men. He ran his fingers over her body as if touching a guitar. Luna still felt violated, as if he was invading her all the way to her core. The desperado finished the frisk, then nodded at Mondragon.

Mondragon took the first step and hugged her. The hugologist in her officially declared this a real hug. He had a tear in his eye. She tried to push him away, but somehow she found herself hugging him back. A consulting hugologist would term her side of the hug to be real, as well. She couldn't hold back tears either. After holding the hug for way too long, they released each other. They wiped away the tears, and pretended to be two business partners.

Luna didn't know what she wanted to do anymore. Any semblance of a plan was long gone. In her mind, she paraphrased words Mike Tyson had said in his prime—everybody has a plan until they get hit. Everybody has a plan until they get hugged, she thought.

She looked at Mondragon for a long moment. The clock quickly turned back. He was indeed her father again.

"Luna, *mi amor,*" he said. "I hope you haven't eaten. My wife, Rosa, has cooked up something special. Obviously, I expect you to be our guest tonight."

Luna knew that she now had to make a decision. Once she left with him, any pretense of personal safety was gone. She knew she couldn't count on the wiry Guillermo. She hadn't counted on going to dinner with her quarry.

Mondragon had just hugged her; he wasn't going to kill her now, was he?

"I am hungry," she said, the only answer she could think of. She wasn't sure what she was hungry for.

"Follow me," he said as he walked down a corridor into the back.

Mondragon ushered her into a black limousine waiting outside. The desperado joined her in the back seat. "We'll have plenty of time to talk later," he said.

Luna looked out the rear window. Guillermo's beat-up Ford followed them. The driver also glanced back, then rapidly whispered something to Mondragon in a Spanish dialect that Luna could not make out. Mondragon whispered something back and the driver spoke into a walkie-talkie. Luna froze. What were they doing?

The driver made a few sharp turns until they hit a long dark alley. The beat-up Ford was still a few cars behind them. The limo stopped suddenly, and the desperado pulled her out, and took her by the hand through a crowded, covered *mercado*. The mercado reminded her of an old world Arab market, except here a glass skylight covered a narrow alley between two decaying buildings. Being indoors, it smelled worse, like urine and leather. Somebody prodded her on one side, then stole her purse on the other and disappeared into the crowd. She wanted to turn, but the desperado's grip on her was firm. Suddenly the desperado made a sharp right turn down another alley of vendors. Mondragon followed closely behind.

After a few more twists and turns Luna was completely lost. They exited from another alley, and the desperado put her in a different waiting limousine, this one white. The desperado slammed the door behind her. Belatedly, Luna realized that this limo was actually a hearse.

The hearse headed out into the crowded streets of Juarez. It was hard to believe that America was less than a mile away, because everything felt so foreign. Guillermo's car still waited on the other side of the plaza, stuck in traffic. Guillermo probably had no idea that she had switched cars. She was now completely on her own. Well, technically she wasn't. She was with family, right?

They crossed through a barren park in the hills, outside the city. Then they slowed and came to a stop. It was totally dark now and they were completely alone. Luna shivered. Mondragon said nothing. Then he touched his forehead as if trying to read his own mind, and looked at her again, as if judging a peasant family's goat to see if it was ready for slaughter.

For a moment, Luna feared the desperado would kill her right there, then dump her body into the park. She thought about the undercover agent who had been shot—was this desperado the shooter? Luna stopped breathing.

Mondragon whispered in that strange Spanish dialect to the driver. Outside, a stray dog passed the car. Once the dog had safely passed, the car started again.

Luna finally took a breath, as they drove through a fashionable section of Juarez, with big adobe homes.

"It's nice," Luna said. She had no idea how much homes like this would be worth in Mexico. "I'm surprised."

"Juarez constantly surprises you," he said.

The white hearse finally arrived at a big ranch way out in the desert foothills. The house looked exactly like her old place back in Crater—the Mothership—but it was bigger, much bigger. So what should she call this place—the Fathership? If money bought a lot of house in Crater, it bought even more in Mexico. The Fathership was built into a jagged hillside.

Now she knew exactly what kind of a house she'd have if she were an evil drug lord. The home in its adobe blended so well into the hillside, it wasn't ostentatious. It even looked energy efficient, like it belonged to an environmentally conscious evil drug lord. One thing was different from her mother's place, though. A giant adobe fence topped with razor wire ran around the entire compound. The driver rolled down a window and punched a few keys on a security panel. The gate opened up, and Luna noticed that a camera on top of the fence followed their entry.

Guillermo was long gone. Vader was probably back over the border by now. No she wasn't in Crater anymore. She was somewhere over the Mexican rainbow.

Chapter Forty-Four
Sacagawea for Dinner

INSIDE, THE FATHERSHIP WAS done up immaculately: the perfect combination of *feng* and *shui*. Luna thought of the Mothership back in Crater. The art and artifacts here were similar, just bigger and more expensive. A pretty maid in a uniform, a *telenovela* starlet, asked if she needed a drink.

Luna refused. She didn't want to drink in front of her father. She remembered he had let her drink a gin and tonic once just to watch her face scrunch up from the taste of alcohol. That was the first time she remembered throwing up. It had scared her away from drinking until she went to college. No, she couldn't drink in front of him.

"We will talk more later," he said. He put his firm hand on Luna's wrist. "Obviously, I trust you not to make a scene about the whole situation."

The whole situation? "I haven't made scenes since I was eight years old," she said in a voice a little brattier than she intended. "I've grown up, you know."

Mondragon smiled, "Are you sure?" She remembered all the times he had said that. She wasn't sure about anything right now.

Luna noticed that some of the artifacts looked like ancient tribal weapons. She wanted to grab one of the Mayan obsidian daggers, just to have an option. Luna looked at a signed original RC Gorman painting on the wall. Gorman was the famous Navajo artist who was known for his paintings of barefoot Indian women in bright clothes. This particular woman was in her fifties—well fed and looking utterly content as she gazed into the grayish middle distance. Luna smiled. This was Sacagawea—home at last.

In the expansive living room, Luna met Dr. Mondragon's wife, Rosa. Rosa could almost pass for her own mother, Ruth, although she was a few years younger, and, Luna hated to say it, much prettier. Luna took a closer look at Rosa. Her face was almost too perfect. Rosa looked as if she'd had some plastic surgery, but it was tasteful, like environmentally-conscious plastic surgery.

Rosa gave her a polite hug and kissed her on both cheeks. She looked reluctant to see Luna, but was ever the gracious hostess. "It's good to meet you at last," she said. She spoke in English with an unfamiliar Spanish accent. Not Mexican, but another Latin county.

At last? How long had they been expecting her?

Rosa then called her two daughters on an intercom. Instant family, Luna thought. She heard the quick shuffling of feet, as if Luna was a Christmas present they couldn't wait to open. The older one carried the younger. Selena was seventeen, and dressed in a school-girl uniform of white button-down shirt, and blue plaid skirt. Selena put the younger one down, and kissed Luna on both cheeks.

Anna, at three, was the spitting image of Luna in the picture that had been on the old clinic wall. Anna hugged Luna's knees like a puppy dog.

"*Madre de Dios*," said Rosa. "You all look alike."

The starlet maid came back with appetizers—egg rolls with salsa—and whispered something in Spanish to Dr. Mondragon.

"I have to take this call," he said.

How many times had he said that at dinner when she was eight? Luna thought that someone was having a baby, as in the old days, but she quickly remembered those days were long gone. The desperado stayed very close to her and she could see a holstered handgun on his left side. He moved his hand closer to the trigger.

"There have been a lot of kidnappings. You get used to it. He's kinda cute, at least. I like them big and dumb," Selena said, pointing at the desperado. Selena's accent was charming, like the voice on the CD *How to Learn Spanish in Seven Days*. Luna had actually ordered the CD while she was the district attorney, a way of reaching out to her Spanish-speaking constituency who had always regarded her as an Anglo. Unfortunately, Luna had lost the CD after only a day and a half, but that was another story.

Both of them reached for the same egg roll at the same time. Selena let her have it. "You look hungry," she said. "You have to try the egg roll with the salsa. It's mama's specialty."

Egg rolls and salsa? It was a bizarre combination, but it was delicious. She quickly grabbed another egg roll and made another dip.

Rosa did what her own mother would have done, and made the best of a bad situation. Rosa explained that she was from Venezuela, from one of the prominent Jewish families there. Selena was the second half-Jewish/half-Hispanic girl Luna had ever met. The first was herself.

Luna didn't know what to say. She looked at Selena, who looked back. The resemblance between Selena and herself was frightening. They both had the Cruz eyes, of course. But Selena could be her younger, prettier, clone.

"What did Dr. Mondragon say about me?" Luna asked. That seemed safe enough. The desperado turned toward her, but made no motion toward his gun.

Selena looked at Rosa, and Rosa smiled. "That you're family," Selena said. Selena smiled as if she had already decided to like Luna.

Luna didn't want to pretend that she was a distant cousin. She paused for a moment. Would the desperado kill her for what she had to say next?

"You know that Dr. Mondragon is my father," she said. The desperado stiffened. Luna looked at Selena and tried to maintain composure. "That makes you my half-sister."

"Of course," Selena said. "He's talked of you often." Selena gestured to the desperado that everything was okay. The desperado didn't change his expression. He hadn't made up his mind about Luna. Yet.

Rosa thought for a moment, as if deciding whether to accept Luna or not. She was the real power here.

"It's okay," Rosa said at last. "We know everything."

Selena smiled. "How do you say? Papa said he had sowed a few wild oats."

They know everything? Luna was a little angry that her father wrote off her mother so casually. Selena came closer to Luna, gave her a hug. A real hug. A long-lost, half-sister hug.

"I've always wanted an older sister," Selena said. Luna looked at Selena, and saw the girl she had wanted to be at seventeen. The girl stood up straighter than she did, as if she still felt she could take on the world. Luna could tell by Selena's firm grip and taut musculature that the girl was an athlete. Selena had confidence; she would not choke on the last lap of Olympic trials as Luna had.

"Do you do any sports?" Luna asked, checking out her legs. "You look like an athlete."

"I play football, what you Americans call soccer," she said. "I'm trying to get a scholarship to Stanford next year, although my father wants me to go to Northwestern where he went."

Luna didn't know what to say. "Good schools."

Selena looked at Luna with appreciation. She really did want an older sister. "Do you want to read my entrance essay?" Selena asked. "I'm always a little worried when I write in English."

"Selena, *mi amor*," Rosa said, much as Luna's mom had said, "Luna, my love." Rosa shook her head at her daughter. "Luna's our guest. She doesn't want to read your essay. Let's eat first."

Luna laughed. Dinner looked as if it would be an ordeal, especially with the desperado looking over her shoulder. She needed something, anything, to break the ice, and besides, the egg rolls had turned the tide on the war on hunger.

"No, I can honestly say there's nothing I'd rather do right now than read her essay." Luna actually meant it.

"I'll check on your father," Rosa said. It was unclear whether she was talking to Luna or Selena. "We'll have dinner in fifteen minutes."

"I'll get the essay," Selena said, and hurried out.

The desperado stayed put keeping his eyes firmly on Luna. Selena had accepted her, but he sure hadn't.

Little Anna sat on Luna's lap. Damn, she was cute. Jen was probably this cute too, once. Luna tried to imagine herself or Jen growing up in such surroundings, but failed utterly. Luckily, Selena hurried back with the essay.

Luna read all twenty pages. Jen had barely written ten pages on smoking bans. Selena had thrown together twenty pages on the intricacies of international politics, and was filled with a young girl's optimism about helping her fellow man. She covered a lot of ground; if there was such a thing as good ADHD, Selena had it.

"Your essay is amazing," Luna said. "I'm sure you'll get into whatever school you want." Luna looked at Selena again. Does this little girl know where the money came from that would pay her school tuition?

Selena smiled at Luna. She was only a little spoiled. Her skin was flawless. Everything about her was perfect. Luna had always been self-conscious about her nose, but Selena looked as if she'd had a nose job.

Luna then looked down at little Anna sitting on her lap. She definitely had no clue about any of this. Anna said "I love you" to Luna in Spanish.

Luna faked a response in Spanish back to her. Both girls giggled at Luna's awful grammar and accent. Luna giggled too, then stopped abruptly.

Do I want to ruin these girls' world?

Before she could answer, Rosa returned. "Your father has an errand to run. Again. We'll have dinner without him." She muttered something else in Spanish along the lines of "So what else is new?"

• • • • •

The desperado stood guard with them in the dining room while they ate. He made a motion toward his gun once during the soup course, when Luna talked about her law practice. She abruptly changed the subject, so he stayed his hand and stood like a statue straight through dessert and coffee. The dining room had a view to the rugged brown Franklin Mountains in El Paso, but the view was blurry through the bulletproof glass.

Rosa's food was beyond delicious. Luna's mother had a secret recipe called "Sixteen Dollar Burritos." Rosa's seafood burritos must have cost the equivalent of a hundred dollars in pesos.

Selena sat next to her, asking questions about her life. Luna was vague. She'd been an athlete, now she was a lawyer. She quickly changed the subject to life in Mexico.

Anna was incredibly well behaved for her age, and constantly reached over to Luna to touch her skin, as if Luna herself was a human teddy bear.

Luna wondered if she had ever been that cute.

They had a long conversation about the differences between Mexico and the United States. Big Macs were called *Los Big Macs* over here.

"*Viva los little differences,*" Selena said at last.

"*Viva los little differences,*" Luna agreed. Rosa kept filling her plate with bottomless portions and little Anna kept holding her hand.

The starlet maid stood expectantly, but Rosa shooed her away. Selena reluctantly got up and did the dishes.

"I don't want to spoil her too badly," Rosa said.

Luna started to get up.

"Luna sit down!" Rosa cried. "You're a guest!"

Selena smiled and touched Luna on the shoulder. "She's family. She can help if she wants."

Luna took Selena's side, and as she took her own plate in she felt another strange feeling in the pit of her stomach. She'd been accepted, right?

"Please stay the night," Rosa said giving her a hug. "We've got the guest room made up for you."

"Where else would I go?" Luna asked.

The desperado took her to the guest room without a word, and locked the door behind her. Luna knew she had already conquered the women of the house, but the men would be much tougher.

The room was beautiful and featured an original Frida Kahlo self-portrait. Unfortunately, there were no windows. "Are we trapped here, Frida?" Luna asked to the picture. Frida didn't say anything.

But it wasn't a terrible prison. The room did have its own luxurious bathroom. Luna undressed, plopped into the bathtub and was delighted to find a Jacuzzi. The water jets in the bathtub were even adjustable.

"This is almost as good as a massage from Victoria," she thought as the water surged over her aching body. It was very close to being erotic.

After she got out she looked for a phone. Nothing. She went to the door and tried to open it, but it was still locked.

"*Welcome to the Hotel Mondragon,*" she sang to Frida's picture. "*You can check out any time you want, but you can never, ever, ever leave.*"

Chapter Forty-Five
Discount Skulls

A KNOCK ON HER door jump-started Luna's morning. Luna quickly awakened from her uneasy sleep. If they wanted to kill me they would have done so already, Luna reminded herself.

"Come in," she said.

Selena opened the door and stood there in workout gear. "I always do a morning workout," Selena said in her charming accent. Her teacher must have been a diplomat. "Do you want to join me? I brought you some clothes. You're my size."

"I used to be your size," Luna said. She patted her rear end. "This is all muscle."

"If you say so," said Selena.

"Where's your father?"

"He's already out," she said with a frown. "It's just you and me."

"Are we going to run?"

"In this polluted air?" Selena laughed. "I want a real, how you say, mellow workout because I have a football game tonight. We have our own gym here, one of the benefits of being a rich bitch."

"You are rich," Luna said, "but I don't know you well enough to know whether you're a bitch or not."

Selena just laughed.

• • • • •

The Mondragon family gym was the size of a good-sized health club, but not many clubs had landscape paintings on the wall—including another RC Gorman Indian woman and a Georgia O'Keeffe painting of a New Mexico landscape with a cow skull and a flower floating in the stormy gray sky.

"Reminds me of home," Luna said, happy she had managed to fit in Selena's clothes after all. "Except for the skull, of course. Oh, my god, those are originals."

Selena shrugged. "No big deal," she said. "I can get you a cow skull if you want. This is Mexico, after all. I can get you all the skulls you need dirt cheap on the black market."

They both laughed. Rosa, already dressed immaculately, checked in on them, and gave them both hugs. "Don't wear her out *mi hila*, Luna," she said with a smile. "I hear you're an Olympian."

"Almost," Luna said. She couldn't help but like Rosa. If Rosa had been in her corner instead of her own mother, who constantly asked her to study instead of train, who knows what she could have accomplished?

Luna and Selena got on the latest models of Lifecycles. These models hadn't even made it to Luna's gym in Albuquerque yet. They looked at each other, and both set their bikes to the highest level.

Sure enough, the desperado stood by the door. He wasn't there to work out, but Luna could tell he enjoyed watching the two women sweat. Luna felt a little uncomfortable.

Selena looked at Luna with admiration. "Did you get a scholarship to go to college?"

"Yeah. University of Colorado," Luna said. "I applied early admission to Stanford, but didn't get in. My essay wasn't as good as yours and English is my first language."

Selena giggled. "I applied to Stanford early admission, but did not get in either. Some of the other schools are giving me an extension to apply since I'm a foreign student.

"You will get in somewhere," said Luna. "You seem really smart."

"I don't know. I have trouble paying attention sometimes."

"So do I," said Luna. She was about to say, so does Jen, but why make things more complicated?

They talked for the next forty minutes. Luna was careful not to say anything that would upset the girl. She couldn't help but like Selena.

They talked about boys. Selena was a Catholic schoolgirl and still a virgin, but she sure could go on about cute boys. Luna laughed. She had one sister who was pure, and one who was not. She supposed she was in the middle.

The desperado kept staring at them, and Selena squirmed under his glare. Luna thought of Ruiz. She sensed that perhaps the life of the rich girl wasn't all it was cracked up to be.

"My dad says if he ever touches me, he'll kill him," Selena then answered a question that hadn't been asked. "One of the guards, once. . . ."

She didn't finish the statement. She didn't have to. There was a tear in her eye, and as Luna hugged her, she could sense loneliness in the girl, a feeling of confinement. Selena wasn't that different from Jen in some ways, or from Luna.

"My dad had him killed," she said. "He just disappeared."

Luna didn't know whether Selena was exaggerating or not. "Something like that happened to me, in a way."

They said nothing for a minute, did some squats, went really low. Luna knew she had to bring up Jen. Selena deserved to know that she had one more family member.

"There's another sister, too," Luna said. "Up in Albuquerque. Her name is Jen. She's part Korean."

Selena frowned. One long-lost sister was enough, for now. "Are you two friends?" Selena asked.

"We're very close. You're about to become an aunt, or a half-aunt, I suppose."

"A half-aunt," Selena giggled. "I like that word. I've always wanted a bigger family. Or half-family. How do you say, I see things as half-full rather than half-empty."

Selena by this time was lifting heavy free weights, as if she was trying to impress Luna. At one point the girl strained, and Luna grabbed the bar. For one brief moment, Luna thought about dropping the weight on the girl's neck.

I'm going to destroy your world, little sister, she couldn't help but think. She grabbed the bar and helped Selena lift. "You can do it, Selena, *vamanos.*"

After they finished, Rosa came in with fresh strawberry-banana smoothies for both of them. It was the best she had ever tasted. Luna remembered that her own mother had never made a fresh strawberry-banana smoothie for her after a workout. Is that all it took to bribe her, a fruit smoothie? This whole situation was a lot more complicated than she had expected. Juarez constantly surprised you, all right.

After another almost erotic bath in her Jacuzzi with the great jets, Luna met Selena for a delicious breakfast of "hundred-dollar *huevos rancheros.*" The green chile tasted just like the famous "Crater Green" she had grown up with, but somehow it tasted even better in Mexico.

Ironically, Rosa was in the same international women's group as Luna's late mother. The two might even have talked by e-mail about a petition for peace in the Middle East or something, but had never made the strange personal connection.

Luna wanted to probe further, but the desperado closed his eyes as if that would make his other senses more acute. Luna noticed a receiver in his ear. He was Mondragon's eyes and ears all the time.

"Senorita, Senor Mondragon wants to see you," he said to Luna. He talked in English as if he hated the language and anyone who spoke it.

He frisked Luna before she went into the office. Luna felt violated again, but took a deep breath and then followed him inside. Mondragon's office was filled with diplomas from various South

American institutions. His American diplomas were nowhere to be found. There were family pictures on the wall, but of the new family only. There was even a picture of him taking Anna's temperature, just as he had taken hers. Luna nearly gagged, but tried to bury her feelings. She saw a "humanitarian" award that looked like a globe. She could take it and smash him over the head with it, ending this whole thing right now.

"Why are you here, Luna, my love?" he asked, all business. He wore a gray suit with a nice red and blue striped tie. He looked more like a doctor about to give a lecture at a pediatric convention than an evil drug lord. "Obviously, I'm aware that someone followed us for awhile on the way over here. Do you know anything about that?"

Luna stiffened. She had always been a terrible liar.

"I'm pretty sure I was followed on the way down."

He frowned again. "So I ask again, why are you here?"

Luna paused. She might as well go with part of the truth. "I just want to know why you left us, why you never gave us any word? I just want to know."

"Are you sure?" he asked in that same fatherly voice. "That feels like another life." He took a deep breath, then another. Mondragon knew the desperado had frisked her, but he still seemed wary, suspicious that Luna had a secreted tape recorder somewhere on her person. He made a few false starts, just like he had way back when.

"This was all about helping people in the beginning. A lot of people couldn't get the drugs they needed at prices they could afford. Mainly elderly people. Sick people. That's how this all began. Your government was the one that said it was illegal."

Luna couldn't help but notice that he said "your government." He didn't consider himself American anymore. Luna didn't condone her father's actions, but she couldn't help but sympathize with customers like the Blue Lady, despite her taste in clothes and art.

"Everything was unraveling in Crater," he continued. "Some very bad people wanted to kill me—the cost of doing business in this world, I suppose. I heard people wanted to blow up my house, or take you or your mother hostage because of my business operation. I couldn't subject you to that kind of danger."

"Why didn't you tell us?"

"I couldn't drag you down with me if it all fell apart. I couldn't put you at risk if someone came after me. Trust me, it would have been worse for everyone if I had stayed. It might even have been fatal for you and your mom."

Luna didn't know what to say. "But why would you get involved in something like . . . something like this?"

He laughed for a long time. "As I said, we began to help people. We still help people! You saw the lines. I feel so good when I can make their lives better."

Luna nodded. There were some rough spots around the edges, but maybe this wasn't so bad. Maybe he wasn't so bad. "So why did you have Jen call me?"

"To help you get back on your feet," he said. "I heard what happened to you in Crater. I knew that you would do a good job for Jen, and so far you have."

How could she hate him for saying that? She felt so happy to see him again, to hear his voice. That was undeniable. To sit in this chair and talk with her father after all these years . . . she had prayed for it every night of her life. And now here she was. Be careful what you pray for. . . .

There was another awkward pause. He finally took control; he was her father after all. "Do you have any questions?" he asked at last. Then he smiled and added, "Luna, my love."

She felt a shiver when he said that. She was eight years old all over again. She forced herself to put that behind her. "Why did Hobbs get busted?" she asked, all business.

"Hobbs was greedy. He wanted to transport the drugs himself, didn't want to wait a few more weeks."

"Did you set him up?"

Mondragon didn't answer.

"Why did he get killed?" Luna asked.

He looked at her, then out the window. He still acted as if he didn't totally trust her. "I had nothing to do with that," he said. "Kinky sex gone bad."

"And why was Jen hooked into it?"

"Jen?"

"Your other daughter."

"She was there. I had no control over that. Once Sandrina started talking, there was no way to keep Jen out." He smiled. "No, I did not sleep with Sandrina. Enrique out there did, however."

She felt relief, but knew she had to press on. "And Dellagio?"

"I think you overestimate my role," he smiled. "I had nothing to do with that. But let's just say I am not sad to see Dellagio gone. Originally, I had hoped Jen would testify against him. He was getting dangerous."

"But weren't you worried that he would try to take you down?"

"I'm a simple Mexican pharmacist," he said. "Dellagio is a big time lawyer. To the Feds he was a far better target. He would gain nothing by taking me down."

A simple Mexican pharmacist. He was anything but that. "One last question," Luna said. "How can you work with a man like Ruiz?"

He frowned. "You have to make compromises in life, Luna. I'm sorry that it upsets you so much. I heard you nearly killed him."

He walked around behind her, and placed a hand on her shoulder. His hand pressed just a little harder than she expected.

"So why are you here Luna, my love?" he asked again.

Luna didn't know what do say. To kill you . . . to have you love me . . . both . . . neither. . . .

"I don't know," she said at last. That was the truth. "I just wanted to see you. To find out. . . ."

She didn't finish her sentence. She didn't know what she wanted to find out.

He looked at her again and laughed. He was about to say, "Are you sure?" but he realized she hadn't answered the question at all. "You really don't know why you're here, do you?"

She shook her head. Might as well be honest. "I really don't."

"After I heard what happened to Ruiz, I was worried that you were angry with me and I felt I might be in danger."

Luna said nothing for a long beat. "I'm cool," she said at last.

"I want to show you something." He moved another RC Gorman picture, this one of a Navajo woman, another sitting Sacagawea, to reveal a safe.

Is this his secret stash of drugs, she wondered as he opened the safe? Does he want me to do coke with him or something?

Instead of cocaine, he pulled out an ancient scrapbook brimming with pictures. "Chan Wol Song sent me these over the years."

Luna saw thirty years of pictures of herself in carefully organized news clippings. Mixed in with clippings, she saw one picture of Jen from the Highland High yearbook—the picture of her with the junior varsity cheerleader team. That was it for the twenty-five years of Jen's life. He probably didn't even know her name. She was just the wildest oat.

Luna was about to say something when she turned the page to see the stories of her college running successes, then her triumphs as D.A. of Crater County. Thankfully, there was nothing about the election.

"I've always been proud of you, Luna," he said. He gave her another hug.

She hugged him back.

Mondragon thought for a long time and finally smiled. He pointed at a picture of Selena with her soccer team.

"You might as well see Selena's football game tonight. She's really quite good. It'll be just like old times."

Luna smiled. She still had a warm feeling from the hug. It already was like old times.

Chapter Forty-Six
Memoirs of a Mexican Laser Geisha

SELENA'S HIGH SCHOOL COULD be any Catholic girls' school in the south-western part of America. It was built in the mission style, and had nice grounds that looked more Southern Californian than Mexican. The playing field was brand new and the green grass was in sharp contrast to the dirty streets outside. The school must also have the only healthy palm trees in Juarez.

"I bought the stadium for them," Mondragon said. "Obviously, it was the least I could do."

Luna wondered what he meant by that. He had never bought her a stadium. And all he had ever bought Jen was a lawyer.

They sat in the stands with the other parents and a few boyfriends. Little Anna sat on her lap, her new favorite resting place. The ever-present desperado sat with them, glaring like he would take out the other team's goalie, if she gave Selena so much as a dirty look.

Luna spied Guillermo looking thinner than ever, standing near the edge of the stands. He played it just like another beggar on the street and that did little to assuage Luna's fears. The desperado spied him, but ignored him. The desperado could easily grind Guillermo into a burrito and dip him in *salsa verde,* if he wanted.

A few of the boys shouted "Selena! Selena!" when she took the field in her blue uniform, as if she was her namesake, the famed

Tejano singing sensation. Selena blushed and gave a big wave to the crowd.

Selena's team played a public school from El Paso. Selena was amazing; she didn't need the desperado's help to run circles around the other players. Selena scored three goals and was hoisted on the her teammate's shoulders after they won 3-0. Luna was strangely pleased that she rooted against the Americans for a change.

Selena came over to Luna and hugged her. Hugged her real tight. "I'm so glad you came."

Luna smiled. "I am too." Shit . . . she meant it.

Luna spent the next few days with the Mondragons. After the second night, they stopped locking her door. No matter how early Luna awakened, Rosa was already up and immaculately dressed in the colors of a Diego Rivera mural. She always had a delicious, healthy breakfast prepared. Selena would always rise ready for a workout. Luna knew she was supposed to call the number for Guillermo, but she didn't get around to it.

The next day she thought the desperado watched her too closely all morning. There was no way she could call Guillermo, or any one else. By eleven, she didn't want to do it on an empty stomach, and later, not until she had done her afternoon workout. By night, it was too late, she reasoned.

The next day, she wasn't sure if she had the digits reversed or not. She had forgotten Guillermo's number. She figured Guillermo would get to her when the time was right, and besides, she didn't know what she would say to him. She didn't know enough to bring down the house of Mondragon. She didn't really know anything, other than Selena was a good football, how you say, soccer, player.

Luna had to stay awhile longer. Just a little longer. What did they call this? Deep cover? But deep cover never had food this good. If it weren't for the sadistic workouts with Selena, she'd be obese by now.

As for Selena, she had senioritis, and decided to use all her sick days at school and spend them with Luna in the few nice nooks and fashionable crannies of Juarez. When she was with Selena, Luna felt as if she was in a magic bubble. The merchants didn't bother them, and when they gave Selena a special price "just for her," they actually meant it. Selena bought her a cow skull from the *Mercado* by *La Mision* and they put a flower in it and put it on Luna's bureau, just like the Georgia O'Keeffe picture.

"It's you," Selena said.

"No one ever told me I was a dead cow before," Luna said, smiling.

That afternoon, Selena took her to a place at the Juarez City Market that sold rattlesnake cowboy boots, at less than a third of what they'd cost in Albuquerque. "You can be the rattlesnake lawyer."

"I think that's been done," Luna said.

Selena smiled, and paid for the boots before Luna could protest.

When they worked out or shopped, they talked about Selena's various boyfriends. Luna did her best to give the girl advice as she sat each night in Selena's bedroom. The walls had pictures of *telenovela* stars and soccer players that Luna had never heard of. But Selena also had an ancient poster of the Laser Geishas vanquishing an evil robot.

"*Laser Geisha Azul,*" Luna said in a robot voice.

"*Laser Geisha Verde,*" Selena replied on cue. "She's my favorite, the new one they brought in when the ratings started to slip. Everyone likes *Laser Geisha Rosa,* the pink one, but she's like totally messed up."

Luna hadn't thought about *Laser Geisha Rosa* in a while, but the words "like" and "totally" brought her back for a moment. Jen would survive without her, right?

Instead, Luna looked around Selena's room. This would be my room, Luna thought, if I were a seventeen-year-old Mexican virgin. There wasn't a single decapitated doll in the room.

After exhausting boys as a topic, they turned to colleges. Luna even convinced her to apply to UNM in Albuquerque as a safety school. Selena's SATs were not quite Ivy League, and the language barrier was bigger than she had admitted. Selena reluctantly revealed that she had also failed biology.

"I did too," Luna said. "I think our father kept all the knowledge about biology to himself."

"How about accounting?" Selena asked.

"A 'D' "

"Me too," said Selena.

Luna quickly felt as if she had known her new sister all her life. By the third day, Luna felt they must have bonded in a past life as well. Selena was a demon with a credit card, and Juarez had some amazing boutiques. Selena had slightly more adventurous taste in shopping than Luna—she was younger, after all. Selena bought outfits, jewelry, shoes, even more cow skulls for Luna, as if she was trying to win her love. It worked.

On the fourth morning, Mondragon asked them to help out at the *farmacia*. Some of the techs had gotten sick; something bad was going around. Luna thought it was ironic that workers at a *farmacia* got sick, but she didn't say anything.

The desperado stuck with her the entire time. She was never out of his point blank range. Part of her wanted to sneak out to the gigantic warehouse in the back, the site of any potential wrongdoing, but she knew she wouldn't get the chance. Not with this behemoth literally on her ass. She must have caught her father on a bad day when she first met him. Since then, he had been the ultimate host.

At the *farmacia,* she stood at the counter next to her father as he helped patients. She still saw the same man she had seen at age eight, taking orders, listening to people, and telling jokes. Her dad was a funny man in both languages. He would laugh at the customer's jokes, no matter how bad they were. She had loved that laugh when she had told her own bad jokes way back when.

Maybe he was doing it for her benefit, but no one in line looked especially suspicious. The crowd looked far more upscale than the crowd at the UNM pharmacy. The crazy Maori tried to get in, but a guard politely turned him away. Everyone had an American prescription. Mondragon went out of his way to explain the side effects of each of the drugs, far better than any American pharmacist ever did.

Mondragon had a gift for instant diagnosis. He would look at someone and know their condition, sometimes even before they did themselves. All the patients smiled; he was always right. They smiled even more when they saw the bill.

"Gout," he said to one old lady, a clone of the Blue Lady except for her fondness in pink for both her outfit and her hair.

When he got her diagnosis right, and got her prescription at a fraction of the cost, she had tears in her eye.

"You've saved my life," she said in a thick West Texas accent. "*Gracias. Gracias!*"

"*Da nada,*" he said.

Apparently, as long as the phone didn't ring, he was the nicest man in the world. He did excuse himself for a few phone calls, and he always locked the door behind him. At those moments, his demeanor changed instantly. He wasn't her father. He was someone else—someone she didn't know.

There was one brief meeting with three men, one who looked like a government official, one man in a military or police uniform, and a white man in cowboy boots and hat who just had to be American. The three men left with smiles on their faces and bulges in their pockets. Mondragon must have given them more than just Viagra. Luna tried to calculate the amount of the bribe, if that's what it was, but had no real idea how much money it would take to keep a place like this humming. Mondragon had mentioned the compromises he had to make in life.

After the men were safely down the street, Mondragon emerged. He looked pale, as if he'd just given a pound of flesh and a pound or two of blood to the men. Yet once he saw the line of people waiting at the counter, he hurried back over and became his cheerful self. He knew most of the regulars by first name. He even got some people their pills before they asked.

Luna couldn't help but laugh. It seemed like half the men were there for "erectile dysfunction." She was sure Guillermo waited outside, but he did not come in the entire day. In a way, she was glad.

One tech, who was borderline retarded, spilled some pills on the floor. Luna thought of the last time she'd seen so many pills, back at her dad's old clinic when she had broken in. God, that was a long time ago. Mondragon made her and Selena clean up the mess.

"I don't want to spoil my daughters," he joked to the other workers in Spanish. They all laughed. They loved him, just as the staff at his old clinic had loved him, too.

At four in the afternoon, Mondragon said that they had done such a good job, they could go home early.

"I don't want to go home," Selena said.

"Me either," Luna said, echoing her sister.

"Are you sure?" he asked with a smile.

Then Luna noticed a big black car had pulled up. Something big was going down. He walked them to a side door and gave them both hugs. Luna, the hugologist, noticed that her hug was exactly the same duration and intensity as Selena's hug. He then hurried down the alley to talk to the visitor.

Luna knew she should stay behind and check out the visitor, try to eavesdrop on their conversation, but the after-effects of the hug lingered. The desperado politely grabbed her wrist and escorted her and Selena back to the waiting limo.

She wanted to ask again about the warehouse that they drove by, but she didn't.

That night, Luna and Selena relaxed together on the roof of the Fathership, as if they'd been together since Eden. Luna had borrowed one of Selena's bikinis, and though it was tight, she could fit into it. She pretended she was in a different part of Mexico. Acapulco.

Selena talked about the family's beach house on the Pacific, and Luna closed her eyes. She hadn't seen the ocean in years.

"But sunsets are better over here," Selena said. "It's all the pollution."

Juarez was polluted all right, but somehow the chemicals combined with the sun to make a truly magical pinkish light.

"I never thought I'd like pollution so much," Luna said.

When Mondragon got home, he came up to see them. He had changed into casual clothes—Bermuda shorts and a polo shirt over a discreet gold chain—as if he'd just come from a barbecue with the greater Juarez drug and/or medical community. Luna wondered if she was now part of that community.

"It's good to see both of you together," Mondragon said. "I love my daughters."

"We like being together," Selena said. "*Gracias, papa.*"

"*Gracias, papa,*" Luna echoed. When did she start talking Spanish?

"*Da nada.*"

Mondragon smiled. "Selena could you excuse us for a moment? I need to talk some business with your sister."

After Selena left, Luna and Mondragon watched the lights and fires come up over Juarez, and all the way to the hotels and office towers of the El Paso skyline. Above, the moon had a strange light to it in the carbon monoxide of the Mexican air. Even the moon looked different from here.

Mondragon broke the silence at last. "I just wanted to say that I'm sorry I died."

"What?"

"You know what I mean," he said. "I didn't think it would affect you as much as it did. Obviously, I did leave you insurance and an inheritance. I didn't expect you both to run through it so quickly."

"Mom liked to travel. She hated to be stuck in Crater. As for me, I couldn't work while I was training for the Olympics," Luna said. "Besides, insurance and an inheritance aren't the same as a father."

"But you accomplished so much without me," he said. "I lived for the moments when I saw the clippings Chan Wol sent me."

"I accomplished so much? I didn't get into the best law school. I didn't make the Olympics. I got voted out of the one good job I've ever had. I'm a starving lawyer now on the edge of default and disbarment."

He came over to her. "Luna, I've followed your life since middle school. I've always been so proud of you."

"Are you sure?"

"I've got something for you that you will really like." He laughed and pulled something out of his wallet. "Actually I am still on the voting rolls in Crater." Sure enough, he showed her an official Crater County absentee ballot. "They don't clear the voting rolls on the computer. I used my real name, even used this as my forwarding address and had them send me an absentee ballot. I voted for you."

That did it. They both started to cry. They sat there for the next few minutes, saying nothing. There was total silence except for the tears. Even the polluted breezes felt good right now, Luna thought. She had never felt more at home in her life.

Then Mondragon got beeped. He looked down at the beeper and frowned. He hurried away without a word.

Selena came back out and handed Luna a towel and some bottled water. She noticed the tears, and wiped them with the towel. "Are you okay?"

"I don't know."

On the seventh night, Luna found herself locked in her room right before dinner. She pounded on the door for almost an hour before the desperado finally opened it and gestured to her to follow him. The hallway was dark.

"You didn't pay the power bill, huh?"

The desperado said nothing.

"You don't like me, do you?" she asked.

He didn't respond. He didn't have to.

It was pitch black in the house, and totally silent. For a moment, Luna had a vision of a mobster getting whacked by the people he thought were his family. After a few more steps in darkness, the desperado took her into the kitchen. All of a sudden the lights came on. Selena, Rosa, and little Anna were there. Mondragon held up a cake.

"Happy birthday, Luna," they all yelled. They sang to her in Spanish.

Luna cried. She had achieved acceptance all right. She drank too much tequila that night with her family, and they toasted everything they could think of. Even the tequila worms tasted good that night when she dipped them in Rosa's salsa.

At the end of the night, it was just Luna and Mondragon. Even the desperado had gone off to sleep. The obsidian dagger was just inches away, but it might have been in another country.

"Luna, my love," he said at last. "I have a business proposition for you."

Luna could read her father's mind. "You want me to join you?"

He said nothing for a moment, then nodded. "You could be a real lawyer. Have a real office. Have a real client. Me." He pointed to the living room as if it was an extension of himself. "And obviously make real money so you can have a house like this. Art like that."

"I don't know," she said, playing devil's advocate. "Look what happened to Dellagio and Hobbs."

"That's because they were weak. Obviously, you're not perverts like they were. I'm tired of dealing with criminals."

"Like Ruiz?"

"I hate having people like Ruiz working for me," he said. "I want people like you."

"To do what?"

"I'm not asking you to do anything illegal. You're a criminal lawyer now, an advocate for those with no voice. I'm just asking you to be my advocate, my voice."

Luna expected herself to say "No." She expected herself to say, "Not even!" or maybe she would just grab the obsidian knife. But she said nothing for a long while, and she didn't even think about the knife. Her devil's advocate had died for the moment. She remembered sitting in Dellagio's office, wondering what it would take to buy her. Now she knew.

"Let me think about it," she said at last.

"I want you to be sure," he said. "I want you to be sure."

Luna knew there was something more she should ask, but the tequila had fogged her mind. She knew she had forgotten something, forgotten someone, but couldn't remember what it was.

As she stumbled to her room, her father propped her up as she walked. He was surprisingly strong. Luna imagined he could have carried her on her back if really wanted to. He then tucked her in. "Good night, Luna, my love."

She closed her eyes and fell fast asleep.

Chapter Forty-Seven
Plea Deadline

THE NEXT AFTERNOON A buzz came from the front gate of the Fathership. Moments later, the desperado came over to Luna as she was having coffee with Selena and Rosa. Rosa showed her the label. It had been her dad's favorite even when she was a kid, a tangy Afghan blend. The desperado almost acted like he trusted her, almost acted like she was indeed part of the family. Almost.

There was a ring at the door. He checked it out and then returned. "Senorita Luna, it's for you," he said.

As she went to the video monitor by the foyer, Luna didn't know what to think. She didn't know if she wanted Vader and his Delta team to rescue her. She didn't know if she was happy or sad when she looked on the video monitor. It was a very pregnant Jen.

What could she say? For a moment she thought about sending Jen on her way. Jen had broken the law by crossing the border, even into Texas. Coming into Mexico made it a felony. She would be an accessory. Jen would only complicate things, Luna thought. The last thing she needed was complication. Her life finally made sense.

Jen looked at the surveillance camera. Even in the grainy black and white, Luna saw the tear in Jen's eye. There was a green button on the wall, was that for the laser mode of the camera? For a brief moment, Luna wanted to press the green button, and end it all right now. But then she looked again at the tear in Jen's eye.

"Send her in," Luna said.

The desperado went out and frisked Jen too roughly considering her condition, then reluctantly let her in. Jen wobbled on her feet as if Denise and Denny were in the first round of a twelve-round fight with each other.

Luna met her in the living room, right by the RC Gorman painting, and ushered her to the couch. They didn't hug. If she didn't need Luna for balance, Jen would have pushed her away.

The desperado sat with them, and looked as if he wanted to evict both Jen and Luna from his domain. He had tolerated Luna for the past few days, but wouldn't hesitate to throw her out on her allegedly muscular ass if he had the slightest excuse. Jen was certainly that excuse.

"What the hell are you doing here?" Luna asked. "You know that by coming to Mexico you're officially a fugitive and they can send you away for years. Mexico will deport a nobody like you in a heartbeat. Shit, just going to Texas, just leaving Albuquerque, sends you to prison."

Jen tried to laugh. "You told me once that if I was going to see you, it was okay. Remember?"

Luna frowned. "That doesn't apply in Texas, and definitely doesn't apply in Mexico."

Jen ignored her statement. "Why didn't you call me?" Jen asked. "There are phones in Mexico. I've been so totally worried about you. I thought you were dead. I was going to send a search party for you."

Luna didn't know what to say. She had indeed forgotten about Jen in the past few days.

Jen practically shook her. "What the hell are you doing here?"

Luna didn't know what to say anymore. She started to say five different things then finally shook her head in defeat. Might as well tell the truth. "I don't know."

Jen was still angry. "I heard from your old friend, Washington, the guy you call Vader, the U.S. Attorney. Sandrina's pleading tomorrow to some drug bullshit. She's definitely testifying against me, and saying that both she and I were in on the murder. She's signing an affidavit and everything. I'm in like deep, deep shit."

Luna let that all sink in. Jen was definitely going down, but she didn't want to dwell on that now. "How did you get here?"

"I took a bus to El Paso, then got a cab and asked to see Mondragon, the drug lord. They took me right here."

Jen wasn't kidding. She had seen the cab go quickly down the hill, as if trying to make a run for it. Jen tilted to the side for a second. Were Denny and Denise going to do a jailbreak of their own?

"Are you feeling okay?" Luna asked.

"No, I'm not." Jen was crying now.

Selena came in from the kitchen, "Luna, who's here?"

She stopped when she saw Jen crying. Selena froze. Her impeccable manners finally failed her. Luna almost felt as if she was caught in bed with a lover. Jen looked up, and stared at Selena.

Luna grimaced. "Jen, this is my sister . . . this is our sister, Selena. Selena, this is Jen."

There was definitely tension in the air. Jen did not get up. Selena did not come toward her.

Selena turned toward the door. "I've got to go to practice."

Luna and Jen sat in silence. Mondragon came by moments later; he must have hurried over from the clinic. He did not look happy to see Jen. He could love Luna, but Jen was one wild oat too many.

"Obviously, you can't stay here," he said. "You're an American citizen, a fugitive and subject to extradition." He did not use Jen's name. Did he even remember it? "I've heard people are looking for you. I'm a Mexican citizen now, but you are not. I can't protect you from the *Federales,* or whomever is looking for you. I'm in a delicate enough situation as it is with my own government—and with yours."

Luna thought for a minute about the men who had come by. Life was not perfect in paradise.

"So that's it," Jen said. "After like twenty-five years, it's 'You can't stay here. People are looking for you.' That's it?"

Mondragon said nothing.

"That's bullshit," Jen said. "That's like totally fucking bullshit!"

Jen had difficulty getting up, but did so and walked toward Mondragon, as if she wanted to take him out with Denise and Denny's help. She noticed the obsidian knife.

"Jen, calm down," Luna said. Luna grabbed her before Jen picked up the knife and the desperado shot her in the back.

"Which side are you on?" Jen shouted.

Luna didn't know. There was a long beat. Jen pushed her away and headed for the door.

"I can have my driver take her back to the bus station in El Paso," Mondragon said, talking as if Jen wasn't even in the room.

Luna looked at Jen, who had stopped by the painting. Jen looked at her with big tropical eyes, the Cruz eyes. One glance and you had to love Jen.

Mondragon looked away, as if Jen was a fly in the car that would eventually make it to the open window if you ignored it long enough.

Jen touched her arm. "Luna, I need your help right now. Like I totally need your help, right fucking now!"

Luna froze. The way the sun hit the living room, it was the most beautiful room she'd ever seen. If she played her cards right, this could all be hers. Luna knew if she went out the door with Jen, she would never be able to come back here.

One look at Mondragon confirmed this. He was a man who did not like complication, and never had. Jen had always been a complication. He had finally come around to tolerating Luna, and was slowly starting to go the next step, to actually love her after all these years apart. Jen was way too much for him right now . . . a reminder of a moment of weakness. He hated his own weakness.

Jen tightened her grip on Luna's arm, more for balance than anything else. Without Luna's help, she might end up giving birth in a Juarez gutter.

Luna tried to play it both ways. "I can ride with her by bus back to Albuquerque, to make sure she's all right. Then if she's caught, I can say it's court business. Then I can come back tomorrow."

She looked over at a disappointed Mondragon. He was hurt. He had finally accepted Luna, and her choice of Jen over him hurt more than he let on.

"As I said," Luna continued. "I can come back tomorrow and we can talk about your offer."

"You'll come back?" he asked. "Are you sure?"

Luna looked at Jen and then at him. She wasn't sure of anything anymore, but she didn't say anything.

He smiled warmly. The compromise worked for him. "I'd like that." He glanced at his watch. "I have to go back to the *farmacia*."

Luna got in the back seat of the black limo with Jen. The desperado looked at them. "Is she okay?" he asked in English, still hating the sound of the language. He didn't care about Jen at all; he just didn't want Jen to mess up his nice leather seat.

"She'll be fine," Luna lied.

He took the car over one of the bridges on the east side of town. The driver knew of a special lane, and pulled behind a Mexican government vehicle.

The American border patrolman stopped them for a second. Jen moaned. The border patrolman looked at Jen in the back seat. "Is she all right?"

The desperado gave a knowing glance at the border patrol and mentioned Mondragon's name. The patrolman waved them through. The desperado drove them to a parking lot in El Paso just a block from the station for a small bus line whose green buses ran between El Paso, Albuquerque and Los Angeles. Luna recognized where they were—the Last Lot in America, the Parking Lot of the Damned.

Vader would be long gone by now, right?

Luna stayed in the car. There were a few cop cars in the street and she didn't want to attract any attention with the wobbly Jen. What should she do? She thought about calling Vader, but he'd be obligated to bust Jen for crossing state lines. No, she'd have to take the bus with Jen, and make it to Cruces at least. Being in New Mexico would keep Jen's little stunt merely a "violation of conditions of release" and out of felony status, right? One more pregnant woman rushing up to Cruces wouldn't attract attention, would it?

It was ironic. They were within walking distance of the main *Del Norte Farmacia,* yet she felt she had crossed more than just a border. She was in a different world, a different life. They had made it out of Mexico, now they just had to make it out of Texas. But Luna took look at Jen and knew that the bus to safety had come and gone.

"My water just burst," Jen cried. "I have to get to a hospital!"

"Jen, we can't do that," Luna said. She thought of the ambulance and the police car that had busted a poor woman the last time she'd been here. "You'll go to prison if I take you to a hospital here."

"Earth to Luna," Jen shouted. "I'm fucking dying here."

Luna stared into space. The desperado looked at her, his patience was at an end.

"Do something Luna," Jen moaned. "You're the smart one."

Jen felt herself losing consciousness. Luna's face was the last thing she could make out. Those eyes, they were her eyes, her father's eyes. Everything grew fuzzy. She couldn't breathe any more. She was slipping away. She didn't think she would ever come back.

Déjà vu slammed into her brain like the splinters from the door when Adam Marin slammed her into the wall. For some reason she thought of the volcano, of the night with the dead body. Only this time Luna had taken her role. Jen felt like she was Sandrina. No, now she was the dead body. Her mind wasn't working right anymore. It had never worked right.

Luna, Luna, Luna . . . Luna was the one who would know what to do. Luna would save her. She felt something trying to force its way out of her. But it wouldn't go. It was trapped. Then Jen completely blacked out from the pain.

Chapter Forty-Eight
Seizures

AFTER GLANCING AT THE unconscious Jen, Luna looked at the desperado. He wanted to throw them both in the Rio and let them float out to the Gulf for the sharks to eat. Jen moaned again, and gasped for breath. Maybe there was another way. . . .

"Let me talk to Mondragon," Luna said to the desperado.

The desperado pretended he didn't know English.

"Give me your fucking phone!" Luna shouted. "I have to talk to my goddamn father!"

The desperado didn't like English much, but did know the English word "father." He reached down for his gun as if he wanted to shoot her right there, but Luna kept staring at him. She was his boss's daughter, and he'd listen to her until the big boss told him differently.

Humbled, he dialed a number and handed the phone to her.

"Jen's in labor!" she shouted into the phone, not even waiting for Mondragon to say hello. "Jen! Your daughter! She's unconscious! She looks like she's going to die."

"Eclampsia," Mondragon said immediately. Luna didn't know if he had correctly diagnosed her, but it sure sounded right.

"You've got to come help her or she will die. I don't know what else to do."

"I can't do that," Mondragon said. "You know that."

Jen wasn't moving. Whatever eclampsia was, it couldn't be a good thing. Luna now knew that she would have to make her closing argument, the most important closing argument of her career.

"She's having twins!" Luna yelled. "They're your grandchildren, damn it! You took an oath to help people and yet you've spent your entire career ruining lives. You left me when I was eight. You left Jen before she was born. You ruined both of our lives. Every day of my life I thought about how much I missed you. Every day of her life she thinks the same thing. You have no idea what has happened to her because of you! And now she might die, or her babies might die unless you come over here right now. Is that the kind of a father you really are?

"You ask me which would have been worse, seeing you in jail or thinking you were dead. I would have had a real father if you were in jail. What the fuck will you tell Selena and Anna? That you let their sister go to prison rather than help her? That you let your daughter and grandchildren die?"

Silence on the other end. Jen moaned again. It was loud enough to hear in Acapulco. The desperado wanted to leave them there to rot. He'd kill them both in a heartbeat if Mondragon gave the word. But would Mondragon give the word?

"I'm not sure," Mondragon said at last.

Not sure. When had her father ever not been sure?

Jen's contractions came closer together. Luna held Jen's hand, and did what she could, which wasn't much. She couldn't tell if Jen was still conscious, but she held her hand tightly anyway. Luna didn't know what else to do. She had failed biology, just like Selena—and just like Jen. She was just about to damn the consequences and call 911 when she heard footsteps in the darkness. Mondragon appeared out of nowhere, a black bag in his hand.

"I'm sure," he said, answering her question from a few minutes before. "I'll take it from here." he said.

He immediately attended to Jen. He looked a little rusty; he'd been a pharmacist rather than a doctor for the last few years. Had he lost his touch? In a few moments, the first baby was delivered. Luna turned her head away. She couldn't look at the blood.

"The first baby is stillborn," Mondragon said. "It would have been a boy . . . my grandson . . . I'm sorry. . . ."

He put the dead body down in a blanket. Luna looked down at Denny; he looked like a bloody doll. She nearly threw up.

"Jen are you alright?" Luna asked.

Jen didn't say anything . . . she wasn't moving. Her face was beat red, and her eyes were open but no one was home.

Suddenly, helicopters flew over the Last Lot in America. A spotlight shone directly on top of them. There was darkness all around, then police cars got closer and closer. Luna could not see in all the glare.

"This was a trap," Mondragon said. "You set me up."

He got up and faced away from her. Jen moaned in pain. Mondragon looked at the waiting limo. The desperado had already started the engine and pointed his gun straight at Luna. In mere moments, the desperado could have Mondragon racing down a few side streets and back into the safety of Mexico.

The desperado shouted some words in Spanish, but Mondragon held still. He was thinking.

Luna knew that Jen's life, her life, hell . . . Mondragon's life, came down to this single moment. She ran to Mondragon and grabbed his arm. The desperado kept his gun pointed firmly at Luna's forehead. One shot and she was dead.

The desperado shouted something at her in Spanish. Luna did not look at him; she didn't care what he had to say. Jen was all that mattered.

"If you leave her, I will kill you myself," Luna said to Mondragon. This was a closing argument, all right. This was the whole case right here. She grabbed a sharp instrument from his medical bag and pointed it at his throat. She knew she could get in a good swipe at

292 Volcano Verdict   Jonathan Miller

the jugular before the desperado took her out. She would have killed Ruiz; she knew she could kill Mondragon.

"Jen needs you right now," she said. "Do you even care what I think of you?" she asked. "Did you ever? Saying you're proud of me isn't enough. Giving me money isn't enough. Hell, even voting for me wasn't enough. Now is your chance to make it up to me. This is your last chance!"

The sirens grew closer. She relaxed her grip slightly; Mondragon could still make it to the car. One nod to the desperado, one shot at her, and this would all be over.

The desperado smiled. Shooting Luna would definitely make his night. Taking out Jen would be a bonus.

Mondragon said nothing for what seemed a long, long time.

"You win, Luna, my love," he said at last. Mondragon went back to the car, took a deep breath and became a doctor again—a good doctor, just as she had always imagined him to be.

The headlights now surrounded them; it was too late to leave. Was it too late for Jen? A shadow emerged from the headlights. For a moment, it looked like a demon.

"Luna?" the figure yelled. It was Vader. "We've got this place surrounded. You're safe."

Safe from whom? Luna thought. "Don't shoot," Luna yelled. "He's helping Jen deliver her baby!"

The desperado wasn't real fond of American law enforcement. He started the car, but gunshots took out the tires. He tried to duck out of the car, as if he could crawl the few hundred feet to the Rio. For a moment the lights from the helicopter lost him. Then he was caught in the spotlight. He kept moving.

Mondragon would have to deliver the baby amidst all this commotion. Luna felt as if she was at a drive-in movie and Jen was the feature presentation.

There were a few more anxious moments as the desperado let off a few more rounds, but he took a GSW to the body. He went down hard.

Just then Denise entered the world. Mondragon held up the crying baby and handed her to Jen.

Jen didn't reach for the baby. Was she still unconscious?

Another long beat . . . Jen didn't move . . . Luna nearly fainted. My God, was Jen gone for good?

A million sirens seemed to converge on the parking lot. But louder than all of that was Denise's crying. Jen didn't move for what seemed like forever. Finally, Denise's crying roused her.

"What happened?" she asked.

"It's a girl," Mondragon said.

"Duh," said Jen.

"She has her mother's eyes," Luna said. "And her grandfather's."

"Thank you," Jen said, tears in her eyes. "I love you . . . papa."

"I love you, Jenita, my love." Mondragon hugged her briefly, then got up. He faced the officers. "I'm unarmed." He put down his bag, kicked it away just in case they thought it was a bomb or something.

Vader then slapped cuffs on him.

"You've got nothing on me," Mondragon said.

"You're an enemy combatant," Vader said.

"What?"

"It's going to have to do for now."

As Vader read Mondragon his rights, Luna didn't know whether to be happy or sad.

More cops came over to arrest Jen. Luna stood next to her. "I'm her attorney. She was here on official government business, which is allowed under the conditions of her release."

Luna shrugged. She realized that she had just lied to the United States government on behalf of a fugitive. That was a felony.

Vader looked at her. He could bust Luna now, and probably save himself a bunch of paperwork.

"It's okay," Vader said, ushering the cops away. "They're with me. Both of them. I mean all three of them."

Chapter Forty-Nine
Suspended Sentence

JEN'S MURDER CASE GOT *nolle prosequed,* which meant the State was dropping the case. Still, neither Attorney General Diana Crater, nor District Attorney Geraldine D'amato, ever prosecuted Adam Marin. Prosecuting cops was not good politics. He did lose his cop job, then later worked as a bouncer in one of the downtown strip clubs. Marin knew half the girls already from his days as a vice cop. Luna swore he'd gotten off too easy for nearly killing Jen, but a civil suit was out of the question in light of Jen's reputation.

Sandrina died in jail before she could testify to anything. She probably had been better off when in segregation from the other inmates. Ironically, according to the papers, it was Thuc Doan Le who had killed her with a broom handle.

Victoria bonded out eventually, and then disappeared. There was a rumor that she later ran for an Eastern European Olympic team, but that was never proved.

Months later, Luna got an e-mail from someone named "VicOnTheRun" asking her to race along the Rio. She waited patiently at the Bosque that afternoon, but no one ever showed. "She's afraid of me," Luna thought. "Just as well."

Mondragon had no doubt been involved in some bad things, but he really didn't have a provable connection to the death of either Hobbs or Dellagio. He didn't even have a connection to the death of the undercover agent down in Juarez, or at least not one that could be proved. In light of the lack of evidence, and the reluctance of witnesses to testify against him, the government decided not to go for the death penalty after all. Mondragon was moved to Albuquerque for trial in Federal court on drug and conspiracy charges. His bond was ten million dollars, cash only, which even he couldn't afford.

Mondragon spilled his guts, and turned on the others in his cartel. He was right. He was only a cog in the wheel and the government was very interested in what he had to say about all the bigger cogs. Some of those cogs could even be extradited, which made things even better.

He served his time in the new Federal jail in downtown Albuquerque. Luna rented part of Dellagio's haunted mansion for office space with fellow female attorneys Assed and Keeton so she could see him every day over lunch. Ironically, even though they had to meet through plated windows, Luna felt closer to her father than ever.

There was some talk about him going into the witness protection program, but he decided to take his medicine, so to speak. He ended up taking a plea in exchange for a ten-year sentence, out in five with good time. He lost his medical and pharmacy licenses, but was allowed to learn massage therapy on the inside, and he had a job waiting at the Sacred Yucca when he got out.

Mondragon also formed a relationship with Jen, and she took her course work up for him to review. He did draw the line at doing one of her papers for her. She did it herself with some minor corrections and got an "A." He actually posted the paper with the grade in his cell, as if he was proud of her at last.

Nurse Song kept her nursing license, even after her role in Mondragon's disappearance was uncovered. The statute of limitations had long since expired, and she had an exemplary record. She decided to become the staff nurse at a home for juveniles with substance abuse problems. She soon moved in there and became a kind of den mother.

"They're all my children now," she said. It was as if she was trying to undo all the mistakes she had made with Jen. She actually had Jen come in and give the girls a parenting class. "This is my daughter, Jen," Nurse Song said. "She's already a better mother than I ever was."

Nurse Song told how she had failed her daughter, talked about her addiction problems, and asked Jen if she would ever forgive her. When Jen and Nurse Song hugged each other, there wasn't a dry eye in the room.

Selena moved into the tiny Song home in the Mexican Mekong right after Nurse Song moved out. Selena did not do as well on the SATs as everyone had thought she would. She had some residual learning disabilities, just like the rest of the Cruz daughters. Luckily, Selena earned a scholarship to UNM to play on the women's soccer team. She also wanted to be near her dad. Seeing her dad in jail was tough, but she got used to it.

"It's not so bad," she said to him one day. "Just don't pretend to die on me, okay?"

Jen and Selena finally became friends, although there was always a little sibling rivalry between them, especially when they started taking some of the same classes at UNM. Jen even helped Selena with several papers.

As for Luna, she finally felt like a grown-up, especially after the bank released the escrow funds to her and the disciplinary board declined to investigate her further. She was worth more than a six-pack of domestic beer after all. She was a "real lawyer" in Albuquerque at last. Finally, she felt like she fit in. Her credit actually became good enough for her own phone, her own office in the haunted mansion, and a part-time paralegal, in addition to Jen.

Socially, she was almost too popular. After her final fling with Seek, she also hung out with Vader and hooked up with a few men from her past.

"I'm becoming a slut like Jen," she said over dinner with her sisters.

A short time later, Luna called her sisters together. "I want you to come with me," she said. "I have a doctor's appointment and I need my family."

"What's going on?" Jen and Selena asked at the same time.

Luna smiled. "I just want to be sure of something and I want you to come with me."

The urgent care facility for the Mexican Mekong was right next to a Wal-Mart Super Center near San Mateo Boulevard and Crack Alley. The clinic had a dome on the top and could almost pass for an observatory, rather than a clinic. Luna remembered the time she broke into her dad's old clinic in Crater. Shit, that was another lifetime ago.

Luna cased the joint. There was a window on the second floor. She could climb in if she had to, but she was happy that she didn't have to break in . . . this time. She looked at the pictures of the doctors on the walls. She didn't recognize any of them.

Inside, the staff made her wait forever. She almost wished she had broken in and done the tests herself. Finally they told her the news.

"Are you sure?"

They showed her the results again. And again.

She smiled and hurried out to meet her family.

Selena, Jen and Denise sat in the waiting room. Jen was demonstrating her mastery of puzzles to Selena, when Luna emerged. They rose to greet her, but from Luna's smile, they already knew.

"I'm pregnant," Luna said, hugging them.

"Duh," said Jen.

"I really screwed up," said Luna with mixed feelings. "I failed biology, you know. I didn't think this would happen to me."

Jen nearly slapped her, coming microns away from her. "You stupid little bitch," she shouted. "That's what you said to me."

"I meant it," Luna said. "Still do."

"I meant it too," Jen responded. Then a pause. "Don't you know when I'm kidding?"

"Not yet." Both Jen and Luna said at the exact same time.

"Jinx," both said.

They smiled at each other and gave each other another hug. Luna then smiled, a tear in her eye. God, she loved her sister.

"What the hell do I do now?" Luna asked.

Chapter Fifty
Reversible Error

JEN SAT ON TOP of the volcano and watched the sunset. It had been two years since she had spent that night up here with Hobbs and Sandrina. It was almost time for the Fourth of July fireworks again.

She loved her extended family dearly, but she needed time alone and Selena had grudgingly volunteered to baby-sit Denise. Luna was about to give birth and acting like she was the first woman to ever give birth without a father for the baby. Jen felt strangely relaxed. She had finally found the right dosage of her meds. Her mind was at peace; she was at one with the earth, the sun, and the moon.

Jen didn't regret killing Hobbs anymore, nor killing Dellagio. Her mind had finally cleared up now that she wasn't so stressed. It was like fifty fogs had lifted. She shouldn't have driven so fast when Sandrina called that night, but Hobbs wanted the double bang and she had some morals, at least about sex. Sandrina could sleep with him, so she didn't have to. He had obviously expected Jen to do something else with her body, other than strangle him while Sandrina was on top of him. But he had thought that the strangling was all part of the game, and didn't resist until it was too late.

Dellagio hadn't been too hard to take care of either. Men were suckers for her Lolita look. When she went over to his house, she said she'd take the money. She knew where he hid his gun, swiped it when he went to the bathroom, then shot him after he popped open the safe. Anyway, she was glad that Seek had become the baby's father figure, as opposed to Dellagio.

Now that Mondragon was in prison for the duration, the whole territory was hers. Not only the desert around her, but everything from Juarez all the way to Wyoming. On top of the volcano, she was truly the queen of the world. Perhaps the best thing about knowing Luna was that her sister had finally helped her gain the confidence to seize the brass ring. It was one big brass ring.

She wasn't sure of the exact spot where Hobbs had died, but she felt his spirit, a cool breeze on an otherwise hot afternoon. She didn't want to think about it anymore. That part of her life was way over.

It was a beautiful sunset. She was about to ask herself what the hell she should do now, but she already knew. She had some unfinished business to attend to in Adam Marin. She called Adam. Luckily, he'd kept his same number.

"Yeah, baby," she said in the same sexy voice she had used on Hobbs that night, the same voice she had used on Dellagio to get into his house. Like she said, men were such suckers.

"Let's put it all behind us," she said. "That was all Luna pushing the restraining order, not me. I love you. I still love *you*, baby."

It didn't take too much convincing. Apparently he still loved her, too. There was a thin line between love and hate, after all.

"I know a great place where we can watch the fireworks tomorrow," she said. "Let's make fireworks of our own . . . Bang . . . Bang . . . Bang. . . ."

As she set a time for the date, and baited the trap with a few more "I love yous," she played with a baggie of pills she had with her from her last trip to Mexico. Like Hobbs, Marin was a big guy. She tried to calculate dosages in advance, but she was still lousy in math . . . too much would just be enough.

Beneath her, the volcano rumbled again. . . .

THE END

Author's Note

Albuquerque really does have dormant volcanoes on its west side. They remain an excellent place to watch fireworks on the Fourth of July and engage in various and sundry activities. The Maximum Bitch Unit, Crack Alley, the War Zone, Sun and Moon Mountain, the Balloon Glow, Enema Zoo and the Zoo Docket are all real places or activities. Counties in New Mexico can vote to dissolve, district attorneys can be recalled and you really cannot wear open-toed shoes to the Metropolitan Detention Center.

There really is a Border Patrol checkpoint one hundred miles inland at Truth or Consequences, New Mexico and it has indeed snared several lawyers who thought they were above the law. At least one did die under mysterious circumstances.

Crater County is not a real place, but it remains a state of mind. The Laser Geishas are fictional, as far as I know.

Luna Cruz is entirely fictional, although there are more starving lawyers than you might expect. I've been one of them. As for Jen Song: three words. Attorney, client, and privileged.

About the Author

Jonathan Miller is an author and attorney practicing criminal law in Albuquerque. He is a graduate of the Albuquerque Academy, Cornell University, the University of Colorado Law School, and the American Film Institute; and has taken writing courses at the University of New Mexico and UCLA-Extension. He hopes to use the proceeds of this book to pay off his student loans before he dies.